STOLEN KISS

Strongheart seized Dara's waist and dragged her from the saddle. As he trapped her wrists at her sides, ignoring her gasp of outrage, she squirmed against his massive chest.

"Damn you. Let me go."

His voice hardened mercilessly. "We will settle this dislike you have for me, Princess."

"I hate you."

She struggled harder.

He held her firm.

Tilting back her head, she looked up at him and realized antagonizing him had been a terrible mistake. One glance at his furious face and fear gnarled her stomach. Sweet Jesu! Her father had told her to beguile the man. Whatever had possessed her to antagonize him?

She kicked his shin as hard as she could. He flinched, but instead of releasing her, his hands tightened on her wrists.

"If you do that again, I will not be the only one riding back to Ferns with a sore bottom, Princess."

"You cannot—"

One cocky eyebrow raised. "I could."

She drew herself to her full height. "You cannot come to my land and order me about. If I were a man—"

One finger, strong and gentle, pressed against her lips, silencing her. "If you were a man, I'd knock some sense into you with my fist. But if you were a man, I would not have kissed you. Your problem is not the fact that I stole a kiss. The problem is that you liked it."

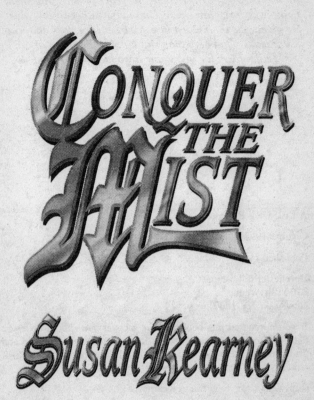

CONQUER THE MIST

Susan Kearney

LEISURE BOOKS   NEW YORK CITY

*To my mother-in-law, Joanne, for years of encouragement
and positive reinforcement. And to my father-in-law, Wes,
for giving me an interest in wild, Irish ancestors and who
would make good hero material himself. But most of all, to
both of you for giving me a wonderful husband.*

A LEISURE BOOK®

October 1998

Published by

Dorchester Publishing Co., Inc.
276 Fifth Avenue
New York, NY 10001

ISBN 0-8439-4437-4

Printed in the United States of America.

Chapter One

"Have the fairies stolen your wits, Da?" Princess Dara O'Dwyre paced the upper hall, berating her father beside her and glaring at the Norman knight who stood below the dais. At her chilly words, the Norman Roland de Clare saluted her with his goblet and a scoundrel's grin, nettling her even more.

Dara met the devilment in the Norman's dark eyes squarely while she continued the argument with her father. "This stranger just rode into Leinster. We know nothing about him, yet you wish to put him in charge of our castle defense. To be sure, Da, there could not be a worse time to trust a stranger, especially a Norman." Without a shred of remorse, she spat out the last word as she would a curse. "Do we not have enough border troubles without inviting problems inside County Wexford?"

At her harsh words, the Norman's bronze face remained implacable, his stance casual, although a muscle clenched in his jaw. Dara thought it significant that while she insulted his honor he maintained such iron control. Perhaps he wanted more than the position of chief marshal. Only a warrior with an ulterior purpose would endure her harangue without protest.

Conor O'Dwyre, King of Leinster, ran his hand through his curly gray hair and sighed. He sat for a few moments in silence, considering her argument. Unlike Dara, who'd inherited a sharp tongue from her mother, her father always thought long and carefully before speaking. But sometimes of late, he drifted, needing a bit of prodding.

"Da?"

"We need his expertise. A Norman warrior can teach us English strategy. He won't upset things."

She spun on her heel and set a hand on her hip in frustration. "The devil take him! He has already upset things. I should be setting a trap for the raiders instead of arguing with you."

At her words, the Norman warrior's eyes widened slightly. His lips twitched, whether in anger or laughter she couldn't tell. With a rising sense of desperation, she refused to allow his muscled arms and superior weaponry to impress her as they had her father and his men. She had no doubt that on the battlefield, Strongheart was aptly named. However, one bold man, no matter how fine a warrior, could not save them from the constant border raids. If Strongheart thought he could ride in, display his fancy armor, shield, and spear, and convince them to trust him, he'd overestimated his powers of persuasion.

She raised her hand to the four-leafed shamrock she wore at her neck, the O'Dwyre symbol of their right to rule. The tips of her fingers traced the gold edges of the rare emerald enamel leaves outlined in gold, inlaid with tiny pearls, and encircling a sparkling diamond. The treasure had been handed down from one generation to the next—her family had ruled Leinster since the mists of time.

O'Dwyres had built Castle Ferns on O'Dwyre land. O'Dwyres had defended Leinster and died for the right to rule from Kilcowan to Cloncurry. She and her father continued the tradition. This was her home, her people, her family, and they had no need of any bloody Norman to teach them to defend what was theirs.

When her father opened his mouth to speak, she held up her hand, struggling to maintain an even tone. "I know the plan. You will keep him so busy training the men-at-arms and archers, I'll barely know he's here. That is what you always say whenever you make a decision I do not like."

As she stole his argument, Conor rubbed his gray beard sheepishly. "He'll cause no trouble."

She rolled her eyes and gave him a wry look. Furious that she couldn't prevail upon her father to change his mind, she ground her teeth together to overcome the urge to argue further. Above all else, he had to appear Leinster's leader. But in truth, more and more of late, he refused to see reason. Still, she could only say so much in the

11

public hall, and by the prowling, predatory intelligence glimmering in Strongheart's dark eyes, he had knowingly taken advantage of her predicament.

She tossed her hair over her shoulder in a gesture of defiance. "Men always cause trouble."

"Impertinent chit." Her father's affectionate grin softened his words. "The Norman is different."

"Just like the last marshal you hired was different?" she asked caustically. First she'd had to fend off his unwanted attentions. Then, the traitor had near gotten away with their gold. "Have you already forgotten the wee bit o' trouble he caused us?"

Her father had the grace to look somewhat abashed. "Lass, how could I know the man spied for O'Rourke?"

Dara bit back a sharp retort, suspecting there would never be peace between the clans. The O'Dwyres would always have to fight to hold their land. She had been born in Castle Ferns and to her this was more than just a home. After her mother left them, the solid castle walls of the O'Dwyre estate represented safety and strength to her. The dark gray, ivy-covered stones stood rooted on O'Dwyre land, linking the past with the future. Castle Ferns protected her, as it would her children and her grandchildren. It was a comforting thought that though O'Dwyres would come and go, Castle Ferns would always shelter them.

Strongheart's presence threatened their home more severely than losing a bit of gold or cows to their old enemy, O'Rourke. Wherever the hated

Normans ventured, they conquered the native people of the land, looting, raping, pillaging. Normans had taken over Wales, and now their relentlessly greedy eyes looked westward to the uninhabited riches of Eire. If only her father's mind was clear, he would see the Norman was the first of a conquering race, the vanguard of an army of invading warriors. But age could make a fool of any man, even the King of Leinster.

She shook off the disconcerting thought that her father was not the wise leader he once was. Ignoring the giant Norman who watched every sway of her hips with unseemly interest, she stepped beside the king's great chair, placed a hand on his forearm, and spoke softly. "You could not know of O'Rourke's treachery, but we must suspect all strangers, especially a Norman."

Her father lowered his voice, and Dara leaned forward to catch the words meant for her ears alone. "You are wise, my dear. Stay close to him. Beguile him with your winning ways and learn his secrets." Then Leinster's king spoke loudly, so the Norman could hear. "I shall keep close watch."

Dara bit off a curse. Her failure to convince her father could prove disastrous. At the triumph sparkling in Strongheart's black eyes, she swallowed the bitter taste of defeat, stifling the urge to punch the arrogant Norman's nose. "Da, have you heard nothing I've said?"

"Enough! I will hear Roland de Clare's opinion of Castle Ferns's defenses. Above all things, I would keep you safe."

While she paced restlessly with anger she couldn't restrain, Strongheart stood by the large

13

hearth, solitary as a rock island, rooted as a rowan, self-contained as a force of nature. They glanced at each other like wolfhounds taking measure of a menacing new rival. Sweet Jesu, the Norman knight was big! Although her father was tall, very masculine, and a man of great size and strength, the foreign knight towered over him.

Strongheart's dark hair reached to his fine linen tunic embroidered with gold thread. His glimmering, arrogant eyes dominated his face, giving him the appearance of always leaning aggressively forward and making him seem all the more dangerous. His nose was bold and straight, and his cheekbones angled sharply, the hollows almost gaunt above a sensual mouth.

His broad shoulders left no doubt of his profession. Not even the mail that covered his torso could hide the enormous power of his broad chest. But it was his arrogant confidence that proclaimed him the best of warriors.

Unlike the men of her land, he covered his muscular legs with cloth, filling his leather boots until he strained the top lacing. As he advanced, taking huge strides, the great bulge of his thigh muscles shifted.

Although he'd left his lance and helmet with his mount, he carried an axe with a fan-shaped blade, and a broad-bladed sword in a scabbard of wood was belted to his waist.

She swallowed hard in awe of his unusual weapons, and fear chilled her spine. Irish men, without mail or battle-axes, could not fight an army of Normans wearing chain hauberks like his. Irish short bows, spears, and slings could not penetrate his mail. And his longbow, carried across his broad back, was the largest she'd ever seen.

But it was the challenging look in his eyes that had her bracing for an attack. The intensity of his stare made her weigh her words with care.

Suddenly nervous, Dara ran a hand through her hair, trying to ignore Strongheart's keen scrutiny. Let him watch. She would not give up as long as she drew breath. "The Normans' greed for our land cannot be underestimated. They come seeking our rich green pastures just like the Gaels and the Danes before him."

The knight approached with repressed energy, his emotions under iron-clad control, his chain hauberk reflecting the candlelight with each long stride. "Princess, let me remind you, I am only one man."

But quite a man at that. A hard man seeking glory. At her first sight of him, when he'd set down his shield upon entering the hall, her breath had caught at the width of his shoulders and the powerful muscles of his bare forearms. When he entered a room, all were immediately aware of his presence. He projected a virile intensity, and within minutes of his arrival, every maid knew his name and of whence he came.

Strongheart wore the scars of battle on his arm and neck like marks of honor, seemingly uncaring of his isolation among enemies, undisturbed by her mistrust. His strength could be their undoing. All the more reason not to trust him and his piercing eyes that reminded her of glistening black stones on a cloudless day. Although he'd ridden onto their lands alone, he could have hidden

15

knights and foot soldiers in the forest beyond.

She struggled with the almost overpowering need to take a step back. Instead, she lifted her chin, prepared to argue as long as it took to keep Castle Ferns and its inhabitants safe. These days her father's perpetual optimism could be more than irritating—it could be dangerous. "If you allow him to stay, more Normans will follow, enough Normans that the land will no longer be ours."

"Strongheart is a soldier, not inclined to settling in one place, I think. I'd wager he's never herded, milked, or butchered cows," her father protested mildly.

She gathered her courage to leave her father's side, and locked her gaze with the brooding stare of the Norman as she approached him. "Tell me you do not covet the fertile lands of County Kildare. Tell me you do not longingly eye the abundant wealth of Carlow, Kilkenny, and Wexford, and I will say you lie."

Strongheart's coal-black eyes lit up like a banked fire, and he measured her with a hard intensity before he answered. Dara hoped that in the end, his words would do him no good. Her father usually indulged her behests. When she called the Norman a liar, she thought he would shout, pound his great fist on the table, or demand she leave the great hall.

Instead he laughed, the deep sound rumbling in his chest, and he bowed, mockingly. "I applaud your fine hospitality, Princess O'Dwyre. If you accuse all your guests of dishonor, the bards must sing the truth of it from Cork to Derry. Is your shrewish tongue and lack of manners the reason you are not wed?"

"Sweet lamb of divine Jesu!" Rage boiled in her stomach. She was all the more furious because he had every right to fault her lack of hospitality, but she'd never admit it to him. Nor would she admit she found him interesting—all the more reason to send him on his way.

At his remark about her lack of a husband, her cheeks flushed hot. How like a man to get the situation backward. Battles had been fought for the right to claim her. The kings of Connacht and Munster had offered for her. And he, arrogant man, thought no one wanted her?

How dare Strongheart stand and insult her in their castle? But worse, he'd turned the table on her. She'd called him a liar for which he had no defense. And like any good warrior without a defense, he'd attacked, insulting her and changing the subject. The man was clever. But so was she.

She swallowed the anger and allowed her father to hear her real fears. "Is it not bad enough that traitors surround us? Must we bring one into our midst?" She spun, clenched her fist at the Norman, and let loose her building rage. "We do not offer food and drink to our enemies. Get out, I say!"

The Norman's expression did not change. He didn't acknowledge her attack by so much as a flicker of an eyelash. He simply turned his broad back to her.

He might not have been so arrogant if he'd known her skill with a dirk. Even if he had no craving for their rich lands, no good could come of his presence here. Why didn't her father see that the

17

Norman represented a threat more dangerous than Munster, Meath, Connaught, and Ulster combined?

For now, the *Ard-ri*, the Irish high king, remained in Connaught, settling the constant border disputes between the lesser kings from afar. Instead of lessening, the old enmity between the *Ard-ri* and her father had only intensified during the last eighteen years. The Norman's presence here would give Leinster's enemies reason to unite, and they could not afford to take that chance. The longstanding feuds had already taken too many innocent lives.

From the southeast, the ambitious Borrack MacLugh, King of Munster, coveted the rich lands and vast cattle herds of Leinster. Only an old agreement kept him at bay. And one-eyed Tiernan O'Rourke, King of Meath, was forever a thorn in the side of the O'Dwyres, staging quick raids across the border, leaving only flaming villages, hungry old men, and motherless children behind.

A Norman in Castle Ferns would escalate the confrontations. One look at the Norman's superior armor and their enemies would fear Leinster's advantage. And what men feared, men attacked. Leinster, with her moist skies feeding lush fields, would become a bloody battleground. Great numbers of men would swarm over their land. Dara's throat tightened with thoughts of never again riding free through the open country. The armies would set fire to the crops, ransack the villages, and ruin Leinster's open green pastures.

Dara prayed the *Ard-ri*'s army would remain in Connaught. While her family had troubles in Leinster, they'd solve them without the high king's interference. She saw no reason to invite Strongheart onto their land. That her father had even considered such a decision distressed her deeply.

More and more she had to cover up her father's mistakes. Although Conor O'Dwyre had the strength of three men, his forgetful spells came more frequently now. But since Leinster's men still followed Conor into battle without hesitation, the O'Dwyres had no need of a Norman gaining the men's allegiance, usurping her father's authority.

Strongheart set down his silver goblet of wine on the great yew table, then strode toward her father. Her heartbeat quickened in alarm, and Dara's hand closed on the handle of the dirk at her waist. But the Norman's hands stayed clear of his magnificent diamond-and-amber encrusted sword.

His tone resonated lethal confidence. "Your men lack training. Purchasing mail for the men-at-arms and armor for the horses is vital. And the triple rings of stone on the southern wall need major reinforcement."

Dara's stomach lurched in growing resentment and horror. His sharp eyes had assessed their every weakness.

Stiffening her spine, she wrapped pride around her like a cowl. "Ferns is the finest castle in all Eire."

Strongheart raised a dark brow. The set of his mouth bordered on mockery and his tone remained dangerously even. "Pillars of bronze, roofs of tile, and gongs of silver will not halt an army. And neither will your spiked tongue."

"Och. The great Norman knight has come to safeguard Leinster. If I believed that, I'd have the sense of a flea."

"Stop snarling. I cannot afford a fight between you." Her father leaned back in his chair, rubbed his beard, and stared hard at Strongheart. By his long silence, Dara knew he still considered the man's suggestions.

"I want to see what he can do. You may stay—"

"No!" Acid burned Dara's stomach as she rushed to her father's side, blinking back tears of defeat. Conor could not force the Norman on their people. Castle Ferns would not harbor a traitor.

"You will not gainsay me, daughter."

Fully aware that tears wouldn't change her father's mind, she forced herself to speak with strength. "I say what I please. We cannot afford another mistake."

"Strongheart can stay the night. I will decide by—"

"Raiders," bellowed a guard from the lower bailey, interrupting their argument.

At the first sign of trouble, the Norman's hand moved so quickly to his sword, his hand was a blur. He spun, sword half-drawn from his scabbard before she could shout, "Where?"

"Sletty," came the reply from below.

Conor pounded the arm of his chair with his fist. "The thieves grow bolder; they steal our cattle during the day."

With a sudden rush of panic, Dara's blood

drained from her face. Her maid, Sorcha, had gone that morn to visit her brother in Sletty, less than a half-day's ride away. At this hour, perhaps Sorcha was already on her way back, but Dara could not shake off the dark premonition smothering her like a cloak. Sorcha was like a mother to her; she couldn't bear to see her harmed.

At the news, her father leapt from his chair with a hoarse battle cry on his lips and sprinted down the stairs, with Strongheart close behind. Perhaps this time they'd catch the thieves and end these constant border raids.

In the bailey, women hugged their men good-bye and offered bread and cheese for the journey and children raced about the men. Below, horses whinnied at the call-to-arms. Men cursed. Dogs barked at honking geese.

Dara ran lightly down the steps, seized her bow, and slung it over her shoulder. She grabbed her traveling pouch packed with clean cloths for bandages and needle and thread for stitching. After seizing a few bundles of herbs and filling a waterskin, she stuffed the supplies into her pouch.

She slipped a dirk into her boot, then hurried outside to see the men already mounted and galloping across the scrub land. But she couldn't stay behind without going mad with worry. Not with Sorcha's life at risk. Dara sprinted to the stables and bridled her red stallion, Fionn. Hiking up her tunic, she vaulted onto his back.

"Go, Fionn." She goaded him with her heels, and he bolted after the warriors.

Her great steed's powerful hooves devoured the distance between Dara and the men, sending the

21

occasional hare zigzagging for cover. Overhead, a kestrel hovered, steadily holding its position in the air with no more than a tremor of its wings. If only finding Sorcha would prove so effortless.

Although her father would not be pleased by Dara's actions, he would not stop her. Often her tracking skills brought them victory, especially when the raiders hid cattle in a marsh. Besides, he knew how much Sorcha meant to her.

The sky grayed to a weighty, depressing gloom, but no impending storm would stop Dara. Drawing in great draughts of air, she followed the dust blowing in the eternal west wind. Beneath Fionn's hooves, the verdant green pastures whirled away, becoming hilly crag. She topped a heady rise and the wind keened, blowing her hair back from her face and giving Dara her first clear view of Sletty in the distance.

From the peak, the village looked deserted. Not a whiff of smoke emerged from the wattled huts. Only chickens clucked in the empty mud lane through the village's center.

After sending for her father's help, the villagers must have hidden the swine, sheep, and milk cows in the nooks of these hills. At least the raiders had not burned the thatch roofs. No bodies lay in the street. Perhaps Sorcha was safe.

She rode down to join her father and his men, who had stopped to confer with the smithy. When she advanced, the warriors drew their mounts aside, leaving her a clear path to her father, then closed ranks protectively behind her.

* * *

By the rood! What is Princess Dara doing on a raid? So great was Strongheart's incredulity, he almost shouted the words aloud. He glanced from her straight back, high chin, and squared shoulders to the faces of the Irish men. Not one warrior looked surprised.

From their casual acceptance of her presence, he gathered Irish princesses rode on daily raids, or at least Dara O'Dwyre did. Apparently riding into danger was an everyday occurrence for the red-haired woman who rode as if she were part of her stallion, indifferent to her tunic hiked well above her knees, revealing delicate ankles.

If the king risked his daughter's life by allowing such pagan behavior, it was no concern of Strongheart's. Yet pretending nonchalance was proving more difficult than he'd imagined. Neither the long hair that reached her thighs, nor her hose hid the shapely muscles with which she straddled the bare back of her huge roan stallion.

When he caught her fierce glance darkened with the merest hint of worry, her eyes sparkled like the sun glinting through Leinster's emerald forests. Her straight, short nose seemed to turn up at him, and her full lips clamped together in disapproval. The air crackled with tension, sizzling his flesh from his scalp to his toes. For one brief moment, he forgot to suck in air. Then she moved on, breaking the eerie spell she'd cast over him.

Strongheart took a deep breath and exhaled slowly. He would have coveted the King of Leinster's daughter even if she'd been as gnarled as a crone. To find such an enchantress only increased his determination to have her and her rich lands.

Her ruby lips were made for kissing, her provocative eyes flashed with clear emerald sparkles, and her fair skin had a golden glow that made him yearn to possess her. If he ever owned such a treasure, he vowed to guard her well. Had these Irishmen no pride to allow a woman to ride with men into battle?

When Conor spied his daughter, he interrupted his conversation and held out his hand to her. " 'Tis dangerous to ride alone. Why did you tarry so long?"

She squeezed his hand and nodded toward the pouch stuffed with remedies tied to her waist. "I came prepared."

"For battle?" Strongheart nudged his horse forward.

With a defiant toss of her glorious hair, she squared her shoulders. "I am always ready to defend Leinster's assets."

"And most beautiful are those assets." He ran his gaze from the tips of her smoky lashes to her booted toes, taking in the proud tilt of her chin, the enticing curves of her breasts, the graceful way she sat her horse.

Her eyes glared at him icily. "I'll slice the throat of any man who tries to take what is mine." Turning her horse, she gave him her stiff back.

Bloodthirsty wench. Strange how she objected to an honest compliment. Odd how she was savvy one minute, guarded and cool the next.

Conor finished his questioning of the smithy and urged his mount southwest. The band of riders rode hard, past ruins engulfed in ivy, through a wood of oaks undergrown with holly, and onto the upland moors.

As they rounded a rocky crag, the path deteriorated into battle-site unevenness, and they startled a flock of white-fronted geese and feral goats. Despite the majestic peregrines, ravens, and sparrowheads flying above the rough terrain, Strongheart's gaze repeatedly returned to Dara. Keeping his destrier abreast with her stallion, he was nearly mesmerized by the rhythmic bounce of her auburn tresses.

With her creamy complexion flushed from the wind and her long hair streaming like a banner behind her, she fired his imagination. Her intelligent sea-green eyes, the boldness of her presence, sent his thoughts whirling. What would it be like to taste her provocative lips? To hold her naked in his arms? To watch her face when she experienced her woman's pleasure for the very first time?

As if sensing his thoughts, she looked over her shoulder. He'd half-expected her to frown or sneer, but she grinned in challenge and dug her heels into her stallion's sides, darting ahead.

Accepting her silent dare, Strongheart dug in his heels, and his horse broke free of the pack. To catch her, he used all his horsemanship to prod his steed faster. Unburdened by saddle or armor, she rode as well as any knight, perhaps better since her diminutive size seemed no match for the powerful stallion. Catching her did not prove easy.

Finally he came abreast. She rode high on the stallion's withers, her face aglow with exhilaration, her eyes sparkling. No matter how much she was enjoying this ride, she shouldn't have left herself unprotected.

"Hold up. Conor's men are far behind," he shouted, his voice muffled by a strong western gust.

She began to rein the stallion in. And then above the wind, a woman's scream pierced the air, followed by several sharp curses.

Dara paled. He expected her to draw her horse to a screeching halt. Instead, she leaned forward, crooned in her stallion's ears and dug her heels into his flanks. Fionn bolted ahead, and he realized he'd caught her only because she'd let him.

In frustration at being left to eat her dust, and worried over her safety, he yelled over the pounding hooves, "Stop! Don't go alone!"

" 'Tis Sorcha!" Dara shouted back, riding on without pause.

Bloody fool woman. Would she risk her life for a maid? As she put herself in danger, Strongheart's gut clenched.

Another scream resounded from the copse of elms directly ahead of them. Through the trees, Strongheart spied a clearing where several men squatted around a campfire. At the northern end of the cleaning, a larger group herded milling cattle.

Dara veered toward the woman struggling on the ground at the far side of camp. Did the princess not realize the danger? While he would take on any man with his sword, he'd estimated ten times that number in camp.

Heedless of her own safety, Princess Dara charged straight into the group of men, scattering bellowing cattle in every direction. With her horse at a full gallop, she flung herself from the stallion's back into a throng of startled men.

Strongheart's heart slammed into his chest. Rarely had he seen such courage in knights wearing full battle armor. The fool girl could die before he reached her. He raked his mount's sides with his spurs. Without taking his gaze off the spot where she'd jumped off her horse, he withdrew his sword and hefted his shield, guiding his animal solely with his knees.

He dared not risk a moment to look back to see how far behind Conor's men lagged. As he neared the throng, the raiders pulled back from the attacking Irish princess, leaving him a clear view.

Sorcha lay with her legs splayed wide, her arms held tight by two men. A huge man, naked from the waist down, kneeled between her thighs.

After leaping from her horse, Dara had landed atop the shoulders of the rapist. Suddenly the man toppled, his neck spurting blood as Dara yanked her knife from his neck. He was no longer a threat to Dara. But another raider advanced upon her from behind.

He urged his mount forward, but his steed would never reach her in time. "Watch your back!"

Men closed in around him. He lost sight of her in the fray. His sword sliced through the men's leather armor like a knife through lard. Still, by sheer overwhelming numbers, they forced him from his saddle and kept him pinned.

He sliced and parried, ducking past one man only to have another in his way. The coppery scent of blood filled the air as he fought in desperation.

But no matter how slick the grass ran with blood, he couldn't reach Dara.

Horses milled, circled, then bolted, all except his battle-trained mount, which held its ground. The panicked horses stampeded the cattle, and in their fright, their hooves knocked embers from the fire's protective stone circle. Flames whipped across the grass. Smoke blocked his vision. The unmistakable stench of burnt flesh permeated the air, filling his nostrils.

And the maid never ceased her screaming.

As Strongheart blocked a knife with his shield, he thrust his sword into another raider's heart. Between parries, he searched for Dara; with each downed opponent, he edged closer to where he'd spied her last. If she lived through this hour, her father should beat her for risking her life so wantonly.

Where in bloody hell was she?

Thick dark smoke prevented him from finding her. Sparks caught one man's clothes on fire, and he ran wildly through the melée, his frantic howls ignored by his fellow raiders. Strongheart stumbled over a corpse. A sword came toward his face. With a war cry, he raised his shield, blocking the blow. A pike stabbed under his raised shield, and he countered with the thrust of his sword. Before the man he'd smitten fell to his back and died, another took his place. Then, at his side, a third appeared.

Surrounded, Strongheart struggled to regain his footing, turning in a slow circle to protect his back. Four men attacked at once, two from the front, two from behind. From a crouch, Strongheart lunged forward, moving his back farther from the enemy, and simultaneously running down a forward opponent. Before he freed his broadsword, the other two attacked from the rear.

He spun, abandoning his sword and pitching his shield at one adversary to delay him, then rending the second with his axe, splattering brains and flesh in a death blow. Shifting to the side, Strongheart readied for another charge, but the third man fled and the fourth's deadly strike never came. Instead, the Irish raider collapsed to his knees with a startled look in his eyes, a knife's hilt protruding from his nape.

Strongheart squinted through the smoke, searching for the fighter who had come to his aid. He spied Dara supporting the half-naked maid with one arm. The Princess must have thrown her dirk with the other!

Finally, her father's men charged, the king roaring his fierce battle cry, his men taunting their enemy with death. Conor's men-at-arms surrounded the wood, trapping the men fleeing with the cattle. Their foes stood no chance of victory since they were afoot. Fire and smoke flushed the raiders straight into Conor's converging men.

Strongheart retrieved his fallen sword, but before he reached Dara's side, a raider grabbed her from behind, tearing her from the maid. Sorcha cried out, stepped toward Dara, and then collapsed to the ground.

With his arm locked around Dara's throat, the raider forced her toward a rearing horse tied to a fir. She struggled, stomping the man's instep, jamming her elbow into his gut. Although her struggles delayed her captor a moment, the leather armor protected the man from her blow.

The man pressed a knife to Dara's skin. Strongheart's heart shot straight to his throat. He dared not close on him, for he could lose her before her next breath.

Her attacker backed away. "Drop your sword, Norman."

Strongheart threw down his weapon. Slowly, he shrugged his shoulder and eased his bow into his hand.

Ever the fighter, Dara raised her knee and slid her hand to her boot.

Her captor jerked her upright, but her struggle to reach the weapon she'd hidden there was just the distraction Strongheart required. In an instant, he drew the bow.

"No." Dara's eyes widened. For the first time since her capture, fear flickered across her horrified face.

A woman had no place in battle. Especially this woman.

Strongheart loosed his arrow.

Chapter Two

With the knife at her neck, Dara faced death from the raider behind her, as well as from the Norman before her. Strongheart's arrow flew straight toward her. Terror squeezed her throat.

The arrow struck, its immense force knocking Dara to her knees and freeing her from the man clutching her throat. Behind her, the raider shrieked his death knell.

Turning, she gasped in pain as her hair caught on the shaft, and she yanked the trapped locks loose. The Norman's great arrow had narrowly missed her, piercing the raider's right eye, killing him instantly.

Ignoring her nausea at the gruesome sight, she rolled free, scrambling for the dirk hidden in her boot, at the same time frantically searching for Sorcha. She spied her, but before she could reach her, another Norman in battle garb galloped into the smoky clearing and abducted the maid.

Tears threatened to spill down Dara's cheeks. She had come so close to rescuing Sorcha only to lose her to another bloody Norman. Strongheart had lied. As she'd suspected, he had not come alone. He may even have conspired with their enemy and set a trap for her father and his men.

Fear rose up to choke her. She fought the urge to aid Sorcha. Against mail, her small dirk would do no good. She had to reach her father's men and bring help before the fire spread. Picking up her skirts, Dara sped through the bushes, desperate to lose herself in the smoke.

"Gaillard," Strongheart commanded to the heavy-set Norman, "take the maid from the woods."

Terrified she'd never see Sorcha again, Dara sprinted from the burning grasses and into the smoking trees to hide. If Strongheart meant to kill her, he would use his bow again. Her shoulders tensed, expecting an arrow between her shoulder blades, but she kept her feet racing.

Trees burst into flames around her and fiery sparks flickered dangerously close to her skirts. Branches crackled overhead. Hot air seared her lungs, and she placed an arm over her mouth to block the hellish smoke. Still she coughed, and feared he'd track her by the uncontrollable hacking breaths. With a sick feeling of failure churning in her gut, she realized the fire had outrun her. A spark almost caught at the hem of her tunic. She wouldn't reach Da in time to warn him. Within moments she would succumb to the smoke.

A horse's hooves thudded on the ground behind her, and she glanced back in confusion. Strongheart galloped toward her, his hand empty of a weapon, his arm outstretched.

If she stayed in the clearing, the flames would engulf her. Clasping Strongheart's large hand, she jumped. With his great strength, he lifted her easily onto his horse.

She scrambled for balance to ride pillion behind Strongheart and caught sight of the other Norman as he encircled Sorcha's plump waist with powerful hands, lifting her onto his massive thighs. Then Strongheart's destrier bolted forward. Dara clutched his mailed sides, scarcely able to wind her arms around his thick chest.

During the short ride out of the wood, Dara tried to breathe in clean air and expel the smoke. But when her father and his men spied them and let out a cheer, she still hadn't drawn a clear breath or put her spinning thoughts in order.

As Strongheart reined in his mount, her father approached, his eyes dark with concern, trailing Fionn behind. Her heart lifted at the sight of her horse, and while she decided what to say, she dismounted to inspect her stallion, running her hands over his flanks and down his legs.

Conor spoke gruffly, but she heard the distress in his tone. "Are you hurt?"

She coughed. "No, Da."

"You should beat her," Strongheart said, seeming to take pleasure in taunting her while she had not the breath to answer, "until she cannot sit that horse for a week."

Conor cast Dara a fond grin. "The lass is wild

33

like her mother. Both of them have a propensity for trouble."

Dara hid her face against Fionn's warm flank. *I'm not like her. I'm not.* What Dara had done was for another. Her mother only pleased herself.

Strongheart scowled at her as if she were a temperamental child. "By the rood! Your daughter could have been killed. Riding straight into the enemy is a fool's scheme."

Hiding the hurt her father had caused by mentioning her mother, she forced a demure smile and mounted Fionn, preferring to argue from the back of her horse, where she was closer to eye level with the Norman. "I had a plan."

"Really. What was your plan?" The Norman's every word reeked with skepticism.

She cocked her chin at a saucy angle and confronted the Norman with a brazenness she was far from feeling. "While you distracted the men, I'd save Sorcha."

His frown vanished, wiped away by astonishment. "You were so sure I would defeat them all?"

She met his arrogant gaze with one of her own and shrugged with casual indifference. To let him know she was shaking inside would be revealing weakness to the enemy. "Either your fighting skills or your death" —she paused for emphasis— "would have created the diversion I needed."

His jaw clenched, his mouth tightening a fraction more. "You little fool! You had no way of knowing how many men waited inside those woods. They could have killed *you.*"

She shook her head, struggling to keep her tone even in front of the others. But she hurled the words at him like stones. "My face is well known. At worst, they would have held *me* hostage. It was you who almost killed me with your arrow."

Dara expected an angry denial. Instead, he stared at her with a slight hesitation in his hawk-like eyes before breaking into a mocking grin. "You will learn not to doubt my skill. My shaft always finds its mark."

While the men around them chuckled at his boast, she stiffened her spine. Despite her best intentions to remain above his stable-yard humor, heat rose to her cheeks. She'd made a grand mistake in the clearing, throwing her dirk into that raider to aid Strongheart.

Twisting on Fionn's back, she faced her father and pointed an accusing finger at Strongheart. "This Norman nearly murdered me."

Her words wiped the smiles off the men's faces, and they rode closer, protectively. Conor looked askance at the proud warrior, awaiting an explanation. Strongheart didn't alter his tone, but projected his voice so all could hear him. "I killed the raider who held a knife to her throat."

Dara tossed her hair over her shoulder, glowering at them all. Rancor sharpened her tongue. "By accident, no doubt. Your arrow missed me so nearly, I lost a lock of hair."

Except for the one muscle pulsing in the side of his neck, Strongheart didn't reveal his fury at her accusation. "If I wanted you dead, you'd be dead. I saved your life. Do not make me regret it."

As he eased his mount closer to hers, the heat of her temper flared hotter. The lively twinkle in

Strongheart's eyes, as if he was enjoying the argument, incensed her more.

Before she could form the ball of spit she meant to spatter across the Norman's face, her father intruded. "Lass, you are skilled at the gab. Does the Norman speak truth? Or does he lie?"

Today her father seemed sharp, his old self, and she must use her wiles to convince him the Norman only meant them harm. Damn this Norman rogue for encroaching on her and her people.

"Da, how can you ask me that?" Instead of arguing against Strongheart's logic, she stirred the doubts any Irishman would have had against a man from Britain. Defiant, she gestured across the field to the other Norman, who'd followed at a slower pace, just now leaving the wood with Sorcha. "The Norman told us he rode alone. Clearly, he lied."

The men murmured among themselves. But no one reached for a weapon, out of fear or respect she couldn't guess.

Brilliant black eyes glowed with the fearsome power of old granite from Strongheart's weather-toughened face. "I rode into Castle Ferns alone. However, no knight travels without a squire. Once I gained your trust, I intended to bring Gaillard to the castle."

She flashed him a look of disdain. "We shall never trust a Norman."

Strongheart turned his horse toward Conor, his back straighter than an arrow. "My skill with a bow is unparalleled. 'Tis no brag, but truth. I shot the raider without risking your daughter's life. Despite her determination to die a martyr, she was never in danger from me."

"Ha," Dara muttered.

He didn't address her. Didn't bother to raise his voice but spoke with haughty confidence. "Put me to a test. Should I not possess the skill I claim, you may do with me as you will."

Apprehension nipped her, for surely the tall, strong, and absurdly attractive Norman would win Conor over with his warrior skills. She had no more time to waste trying to enlighten her father. Sorcha needed her.

Before Conor replied, Dara flicked her reins and dug her heels into Fionn. The horse lunged toward the deep wood. Let her father administer the test of Strongheart's skill. From the Norman's immense self-possession, she knew he would succeed. Proving his skill with the bow would only be his first trial of many. Later, she would devise other challenges to reveal his treacherous nature.

It wasn't just his skill with a bow that threatened them. He might be able to hide his lust from the others, but she knew he wanted her. She recognized the look in his probing gaze. Strongheart was not the first man to try to use her to gain control of Ireland's richest county. She'd read the determination in his eyes, the suggestive curve of his smile, noted how he hadn't let her from his sight, always positioning himself nearby.

Holding tightly to the reins, she forced her thoughts away from the Norman knight. Dara raced toward Sorcha, the woman more her mother than the one who had birthed and abandoned her. *Please God, let Sorcha not be hurt too badly, in mind or spirit.*

Fionn's long strides covered the field, and soon Dara drew alongside her maid. Gaillard had ridden free of the burning wood and stopped by a stream running through the heather and gorse. Her friend rested on Gaillard's saddle, leaning weakly against his barrel chest. The squire had removed his helm, revealing a shock of white hair, a flaring mustache, and a kindly countenance.

Dara's gaze dropped to her friend. Never would she forget the sight of the raider pulling his turgid flesh from between the maid's bloody thighs. At the blood soaking Sorcha's skirts, she forced back a cry of dismay. Was the life blood Sorcha's or from the rapist Dara had killed?

Her stomach churned at the memory of Sorcha's screams, and the spurting blood of the man she'd killed. She'd plunged her dirk into his neck like a Viking berserker gone mad with battle lust. Ruthlessly, she squashed down her nausea.

Although her heart lurched at the memory, she steadied herself. Sorcha needed her. Now was not the time to fall apart. She had to be strong for Sorcha's sake.

Gaillard's hefty shoulder supported Sorcha's head, her chestnut hair dirty and matted. "What should we do?" he asked.

"I must stop the bleeding." Dara untied her traveling pouch and dismounted, then helped Gaillard ease Sorcha to the ground. Placing her friend on the grass, she squeezed the moaning woman's hand. "I'm here, Sorcha. You will be fine."

"Thirsty."

Dara tipped a wineskin to her friend's full mouth, her best feature after her warm brown eyes. As she sipped weakly, Gaillard knelt beside her. The maid opened her eyes, looked at him, and screamed.

The knight flinched and twisted the end of his mustache. "Lady, I mean you no harm."

"You are safe, Sorcha. Sir, please. We need privacy."

Gaillard nodded and led his horse away. Across the meadow, her father cantered into the wood with most of his men-at-arms, leaving six men to escort them home. She easily picked out Strongheart among the escorts since he towered over the Irishmen. He headed toward her, sitting straight and proud in the saddle, obviously pleased he'd proven his skill.

His warrior abilities caused a shiver to skitter over her shoulders. As long as he remained in Leinster, her home was endangered. Not until he left would she be satisfied. Only Castle Ferns made her feel safe. It gave Dara the security she'd never received from her mother. Whenever she was troubled she climbed the tower and stared out at Leinster's rich herds of cattle, and the walls wrapped around her, providing solid comfort and protection. But the Norman imperiled all she held dear.

Enough. Sorcha needed her help. Turning her attention from the men and thoughts of war, Dara unpacked her supplies. By the time he neared, Dara was lifting Sorcha's skirts.

"Stop," Strongheart ordered. "That is no job for an untried maid."

"Do you see a healer nearby?" she snapped. Pushing her annoyance with him aside to concentrate on the woman who'd taken the place of her mother, she set about easing her pain.

Dara peeled the bloodied skirt from Sorcha's legs. "Leave until I am through," she ordered, her voice as frosty as a mountain stream.

To her surprise and further annoyance, the Norman didn't argue, but then he never did the expected. He dismounted and, from pouches tied to his saddle, he removed strips of clean cloth as she lifted Sorcha's skirts and inspected the damage. Dara didn't want his help, but with Sorcha bleeding, there was no time for obstinacy. Efficiently she cleaned the wound while Strongheart held the woman's head in his lap.

"This woman, she is dear to you?"

Dara bit her lower lip. "Sorcha has been both friend and mother to me. Without her . . ." As the woman moaned, Dara choked on unshed tears.

"When men are without honor, my lady, then they are little better than animals." Big hands stroked Sorcha's forehead, and Strongheart's voice softened. "Take a tunic from my bag and place it under her hips. Raising the wound may stop the bleeding. And there is salve. Apply it generously to the wound."

While she worked, she thought upon his gentleness and generosity, so different from the warriors she knew. He offered the maid a sip of wine and hummed a lullaby. Dara cared not why a knight stooped to helping a servant woman, but was thankful he distracted Sorcha from her pain.

When Dara finished her ministrations, her

hands were shaking. Why could they not live in peace? Men fought the battles but it was the women and children that suffered most. Long ago Dara learned that tormenting herself over the way of the world served no useful purpose.

She had done all she could there and knew she should be thankful Sorcha slept. "She must not be moved."

"We cannot stay in the open until she heals. Tomorrow, we will carry her to Ferns."

Thankful he didn't ask whether Sorcha would live, Dara used a waterskin to rinse the bloodstains from her hands, wishing she could wash the memories from her heart. The raiding beasts had held Sorcha down, uncaring of her protests, laughing at her screams.

The brutality of the rape had brought out a matching savagery in Dara, one she'd long suspected lurked inside her, waiting for the right moment to erupt. Her blood had boiled so hot, her passions had soared so fierce, she feared she'd never tame them.

She took in a deep breath and stared off into the mist, vowing never again to lose her self-control. Her hands and feet felt icy, her entire body numb, but she couldn't suppress the mad terror of her thoughts.

During battle, she'd turned into a wild animal, surging with primitive impulses she recognized all too well. She'd believed she'd conquered the wild temperament inherited from her mother. Finding it unvanquished twisted her stomach with revulsion.

She had to conquer the passion that overwhelmed her, if not for herself, then for the good of her people. From her experience, blood lust always led to trouble. Eire would need all the cool heads available to keep the minor skirmishes from breaking into all-out war. Strongheart's presence could only cause the balance of power to tip out of kilter. Fear of the Norman might cause all Leinster's enemies, MacLugh, O'Rourke, and the *Ardri*, to unite and invade her home.

Why was the Norman here? Did he spy for his British king? Although her father did not yet believe her, the Norman would bring change to Eire's shores. She wanted him gone to avoid war. If he stayed, she sensed another peril, one of a more personal nature. His combination of strength and gentleness appealed to her on a level she didn't want to admit—not even to herself.

She stood alone for a long time while the villagers brought food and supplies and the men pitched camp. Sorcha lay under a mantle, sleeping. The wind keened, bringing chilly air, but Dara barely noticed the dropping temperature or the dark clouds scudding in from the west.

Several men approached, but when she didn't answer their queries concerning her comfort, they left her alone. Strongheart soon joined her, and then she shivered. Without a word, he removed the cloak from his hauberk and placed it over her shoulders, wrapping her in warmth, his male scent mixing with leather and engulfing her in a cocoon of heat. He stood close, peering at her intently. For a moment she ached to rest her head on his chest and take comfort in his strength, but she resisted the temptation. She would always resist.

He spoke softly. "Rape is not an act a lady should witness."

"I'm told men cannot control their passions." *And neither can I*. She did not regret avenging Sorcha's pain. When her dirk plunged into the raider's neck, fierce satisfaction had surged through her. What kind of woman was she to allow a killing rage to overwhelm her usual good reasoning?

" 'Tis no wonder you are cold." Strongheart took her elbow and led her gently to the campfire. He found her a place on the far side of the fire, across from the men roasting a haunch of beef.

Since she had no desire to discuss her failing self-control with him, Dara let the Norman believe witnessing the rape was the only thing upsetting her. If he thought his kindness would warm her to him, he'd learn differently. Other men had been kind and she'd sent them on their way.

His sudden thoughtfulness only heightened her suspicions, since after she'd accused him of attempting to kill her when he loosed his arrow, he had no reason to treat her gently. But after all she'd been through this day, she didn't have the energy to fight him now.

Pulling herself from the comfort of the fire, she examined Sorcha. The maid slept lightly and the bleeding had stopped, so Dara returned to her place by the fire with a lighter step. When Strongheart offered her a cup of ale, she drank deeply, and the cool draught quenched her parched throat.

Strongheart handed her a trencher piled high

with bread, meat, and cheese. "How is she?"

"Better, I think." The meat smelled so tempting, Dara picked up a piece and dropped the morsel onto her tongue. She fanned her mouth to cool the hot meat, and the Norman smiled at her.

At her first glimpse of his beautiful white teeth gleaming in the firelight, she stopped fanning her burning tongue and stared. His entire countenance changed with his smile, the harsh planes of his smoke-darkened cheekbones softened, and the fine lines at the corners of his black eyes made him appear younger. If before she'd thought him attractive, now she found his smile devastating.

He removed his mail and hauberk, revealing a jagged wound on his muscular arm, and her gaze lingered on his broad chest tapering to a flat stomach and long, powerful legs. She'd assumed he'd come through the skirmish unscathed and wondered why he'd risked his life for her. His actions bespoke a courage and determination which she found intimidating and ominous.

Seemingly oblivious to her suspicions, he set aside the most tender pieces of meat for her without commenting on her prodigious hunger. She needed no further reminders of her unusual sensual appetites. They shared the trencher in silence until the last morsel of food disappeared.

She finished her ale, staring into the fire. "Your arm needs stitching."

At the husky turn of her voice, his eyes glittered with smoky intensity. "Are you offering to sew my wound?"

She nodded, surprised she'd agreed, knowing it would have been churlish to refuse.

He rose to his feet with the grace of a wolf awakening after a nap. "I would bathe before you tend my wound."

Bathe? Her mouth dropped open. He might as well have said he would fly. Strange men, these Normans.

It was common knowledge that dirt protected against all manners of illness and evil spirits, so he could not know of her penchant for soaking in a tub. She, at least, had the sense not to flaunt the teachings of the church by bathing openly.

While he disappeared into the darkness, she again visited Sorcha. Her friend continued to sleep, and Dara didn't disturb her. Returning to the fire, she made her preparations, laying out needle and thread, healing herbs, and her wineskin.

One of her father's men approached and spoke softly so no one else could hear. "Lady, your father commanded us to give you privacy with the Norman. We will remain within shouting distance should you have need of us."

As he stepped back into the shadows, Dara wrapped her arms across her chest. At least her father had listened to her words and was testing the Norman. She wondered if Strongheart suspected, wondered if most kings used their daughters as bait. But then, Conor was not a typical father—her mother had made that impossible.

"Beguile him," Conor had told her and then arranged the privacy for her to do so. Just how far did he expect a maid to go? Somehow she didn't think a beguiling smile and a handful of soft words would charm Strongheart into revealing his plans.

45

With darkness, the men settled onto their blankets around the fire. One man played a lyre and another sang a love ballad. A few soon snored.

In the chill air, Dara held her hands to the fire. The Norman must be freezing in the stream. Perhaps he'd drown of a cramp. She sighed. She'd never be rid of him that easily.

When he finally appeared, she jumped at his looming nearness. He'd crept upon her with the stealth of a red fox stalking a hare, and her heart thudded against her ribs.

At the sight of his bare chest burnished by the light of the campfire, her eyes widened, and she swallowed hard. He moved with an unruffled grace and a commanding confidence, towering over her, devilishly attractive, and his sun-darkened chest and muscular shoulders made her acutely conscious of his masculinity.

The shadow of a beard strengthened the lines of his square jaw. Drops of moisture clung to his damp forehead, and when she took in a deep breath to regain her calm, her senses careened from his musky male scent.

Get hold of yourself. She'd seen a bare chest before. He was skin and muscle the same as any man.

Pretending a nonchalance she was far from feeling, Dara fought to keep her voice casual. "Sit near the fire, and I'll look at your arm."

He did as she asked, flexing the muscles of his shoulders as he seated himself, then turned his injured arm toward the fire's light. Bathing had reopened the wound and fresh blood oozed from the gash.

Ignoring the nearness of him, she concentrated on the wound. "The slash is long and deep, but the muscle appears uninjured."

His silence unnerved her. As she touched his flesh, he didn't flinch, but no matter how gentle her touch, she knew she must be hurting him. She frowned. Beneath her fingertips, his skin was firm and hot. Had bad humors set in?

Her hand went to his forehead, checking for spreading putridness. He raised a brow, his pulse quickening at his temple, but he let her touch him as she wished.

She spoke in a cool, efficient manner, belying her urge to smooth back a dark lock that fell over his forehead. "Are you always so warm?"

He grinned lazily. "Warrior princesses have a way of heating my blood."

"Let this cool you off." His unnervingly personal smile reminded her she must work on building her resistance to the man. She poured wine over his wound to make the blood run freely. "That should wash away the bad humors."

He didn't move, except for his lips that split into an even wider grin. "We'll have to work on that temper of yours, Princess."

"Is that so?" She stiffened, waiting to be condemned for her unladylike behavior.

"Aye. I find your spirited nature . . . exhilarating."

She raised her brows at his surprising gallantry. "Did you suffer a knock on the head? You make no sense, Norman. If you find me exhilarating, then why do I need to work on my temper?"

"Passion needs saving for the proper moments."

"Get on with you." She ignored his teasing, suspecting he wanted another reaction from her. Well, he would not get one. She couldn't sew him up and argue at the same time. After patting the wound dry, she threaded her needle. "Can you sit still or should I call a few men to hold you down?"

"You'd enjoy that, wouldn't you?" he accused, his tone mild, his eyes hard, but his mouth twitched with humor.

Could six men hold him? She knotted the thread, then held the needle up for him to see. "Perhaps you should not trust me with such a mighty weapon."

"If you are as accurate with your needle as you are with your dirk, I have nothing to worry about."

She pinched the wound closed with the fingers of one hand while she sewed with the other. His muscles tensed beneath her fingers, but he remained as still as a cairn.

"When I was a child, I pestered Da for a fortnight until he taught me to throw a dirk." She spoke as she sewed, attempting to distract him from the pain, distract herself from flesh the color of fine ale, golden and intoxicating.

His tone was more curious than condemning. " 'Tis unusual for a woman to have such skill."

"My guards are not always there when I need them."

He shot her a look that said her guards were inadequate, but he did not insult her people aloud. "Your mother didn't object?"

She squeezed his skin tighter between her fingers. "I never speak of her."

Thinking he would ask more questions, she prepared to rebuff him. Instead he revealed a little of himself. "My mother died when I was still a boy."

Recognizing the longing in his tone, she sympathized. "Have you memories of your mother?"

"I remember crying when I was about three years old. She swept into my room and held me close, disregarding the stain of my tears on her blue silk dress. She always smelled wonderful, of rose perfume and rice powder. I can't remember her face, but sometimes when I close my eyes, I recall her special scent and her melodic voice."

Was he attempting to gain her sympathy? The circle of firelight amid the darkness seemed conducive to sharing confidences, but not many men would lie about a childhood story and their mothers. Despite her wish to feel otherwise, his tender story touched her and deep down she warned herself to beware.

"You are fortunate. I have no memories of my mother," she admitted, and then immediately was sorry for sharing something so personal with him.

"She died at your birth?"

Only because she heard commiseration in his tone did Dara resist the urge to stab him with the needle. He couldn't know the nature of her loss and couldn't realize her discomfort with the topic.

Dara let his question hang unanswered in the air between them. After knotting her last stitch, she turned his arm and admired her sewing. The flesh remained closed, and though he would scar, it would be a minor one.

Turning his shoulder to inspect her handiwork, his brows lifted at her neat stitches. "Thank you."

She allowed herself a satisfied smile. "I'm good

with embroidery. Did you doubt my skill?"

"I'm just amazed you did such a painless job. Perhaps now, we can call a truce." He reached for a clean tunic and slipped it on.

She backed away from his intense gaze and packed away her supplies to avoid meeting his stare. "This conversation changes nothing between us."

Faint amusement persisted in his tone. "Just like a woman. So we are back to being enemies, are we?"

She answered quickly, fiercely, over the pounding of her beating heart. "We shall always be enemies."

"I saved your life, Princess."

"And I saved yours. It changes nothing." She crossed her arms stubbornly over her chest, wary of him. The Norman's presence could inflame Leinster's enemies into consolidating their forces against her clan. If his presence escalated the constant border clashes into a war, she could lose her home. And all her life she'd longed for peace. "You are Norman. You will try and steal the land that is our legacy."

His eyes had a burning, faraway look in them, and then they focused on her, full of half promises. "Once I convince your father of my loyalty, you will welcome my help. If your enemies unite, Leinster cannot stand alone."

She shivered at words that rang like a prophecy. "If you think us doomed," she asked in a broken whisper, "why did you come here?"

"Opportunity." He winked, his expression hungry. "I've come to sample Leinster's assets."

Chapter Three

Fire sparked in Dara's emerald eyes, and Strongheart glimpsed the passion she did her best to hide, along with her daring and her capable intelligence. He barely resisted the urge to draw her close and taste her full lips.

She shook her finger in his face. "Finally. You admit the truth. You came to Eire—"

"To make a new home."

Her mouth twisted in contempt. "There is nothing for you here, Norman. Go back to Britain while you still can."

"Are you concerned for my safety?" He stepped forward, stopping in front of her, looking down at her in confusion. She was complex, this Irish princess—one moment bold and sassy, the next sad, with a perceptiveness beyond her years. He had the feeling she carried a heavy burden on her slim shoulders, and when she squared them, he liked the way she refused to retreat.

She tilted her chin higher. "Do you not know a threat when you hear one? Even your skill cannot save you from all of Leinster's men-at-arms."

She didn't understand there was more to battles than sheer numbers and strength, but he saw no reason to enlighten her. "Leinster's army is no threat to me. I am not your enemy."

"Prove it."

Her words were an invitation to thrust his hands in her long mane and tilt her head back. They stood so close, he could see flecks of bronze in her deep green eyes. As he pulled her to him, her full lips parted in surprise and her breasts crushed against his chest. His head dipped and their lips touched. He groaned at the sweet taste of wine combined with her heady feminine taste. For an instant she stood, sweet and pliable.

The instant she realized what he was about, her hand flew toward her weapon. Anticipating her attack, he trapped her hand and pulled her from the revealing light of the fire. The men around them didn't stir. No one remained awake to watch, with Conor's guards protecting the perimeter.

Hooking his foot behind her ankles, he toppled her to a blanket, his lips all the while keeping contact with her mouth. Her fists pounded his shoulders. Her feet kicked his shins. But he ignored her futile fury and easily captured both her wrists in one of his, drew her hands above her head, and threw a leg over hers to prevent her kicking.

She tried to bite him, but he was ready, jerking back, then covering her mouth with his free hand.

She wriggled furiously, helpless against his strength. Finally she tired of her struggle, but her every muscle remained tense.

"Kiss me. Then I shall let you go," he whispered.

She shook her head, quivering, but refused to look away as if doing so would signal some kind of defeat. At her silent defiance, his blood ran hot.

He nibbled her ear. "I am in no rush." Tracing a path down her neck with his lips, he nuzzled the hollow of her throat, breathed in the scent of sweet heather. Her body arched, wrenching her off the ground.

"Just one kiss, and I will set you free," he promised softly, pleased he'd found a reason to hold her in his arms. She was so soft, silky, sensual.

Her stillness told him she was considering his offer and her trembling revealed her lack of trust. But soon, she'd realize she had no choice. She'd yield to him, and she'd learn he was a man of his word. This time, he had every intention of letting her go—but not until he'd tasted the full softness of her lips.

She nodded once, agreeing to a kiss, her eyes fierce.

"If I remove my hand and you scream, I will take more than a kiss." He would not take more than she would freely give, but it was not yet time for her to know that or she'd refuse to cooperate. "Do you understand?"

Again she nodded. Slowly he removed his hand from her mouth.

"Let me go," she demanded, her voice a whisper with a thread of silken desire woven through her demand.

"After our kiss."

"Why are you doing this?" she hissed. Unwittingly she put on quite a show, her breasts rising and falling from her exertions and perhaps a bit of excitement.

"To prove I will do as I say. To prove you can trust me."

Her supple curves quivered beneath him. "Then be done with it."

He shook his head and bit back a triumphant grin. "You must kiss me."

She stiffened in outrage. "Beast! I cannot even move."

"Careful, your tender words of love might incite my lust," he teased.

She groaned in obvious frustration and bit her lush lip. "What is it you would have me do?"

"Everything."

She eyed him uncertainly. "Everything?"

"Aye. I am ready to do your bidding." He tightened his hands on her delicate wrists, just enough to prevent her from hurting herself by struggling.

"Sweet Jesu! You are insane." At his offer her heart fluttered madly against his chest. A flush rose up her neck to her cheeks. She cocked her head to the side, sheer astonishment in her tone. "Let me see if I understand you. You intend to follow my instructions?"

"Aye."

She licked her lips. "And if I kiss you, you'll let me go."

"Aye."

Her brows arched with astonishment. "I'm supposed to direct you?"

"That's right, Princess. You must tell me what you want and how you want it done." He peered at her intently, seeing interest war with the anger in her tantalizing eyes. If she found him pleasing, he might have a chance with her. With her squirming beneath him, he'd responded like any man. Yet he must show her he would not act like a rutting beast but a man of his word. Holding still while her soft curves enticed him was more difficult than any training exercise his father had ever put him through. But he'd succeeded in replacing her fears with his suggestion.

Her panting eased as she turned over his offer in her mind. "You are serious?"

"I would not jest about such an important matter. What would you like me to do, Princess?" he asked invitingly.

A spark of excitement lit her eyes, and he wondered what naughty thoughts raced through her mind. At the sudden challenge in her expression, she clearly schemed to best him.

"Kiss me," she demanded boldly.

"Where?" His lips teased kisses across her knitted brow, her straight nose, her rosy cheeks.

"Bring your lips closer to my mouth."

He tilted his head to taste her lips, enjoying the mounded softness of her breasts against his chest, the sweet scent of her hair, the reckless glimmer in her eyes.

"Not too close," she ordered.

He obeyed, barely containing a grin. So the Irish princess played this game as well as a Norman knight.

She nibbled his lower lip, then ran the tip of her

tongue there. Thoughts of winning vanished as sheer pleasure shot heat straight to his loins. He groaned.

"Lower your lips to mine," she demanded in a sensual whisper that demanded instant obedience.

He caressed her inviting lips with a whisper-light softness. "Like this?"

"Harder."

She played one hell of a dangerous game if she sought to manipulate him by inflaming his passions. Still, at her request, he increased the pressure, kindling a blaze of fire. Damnation! He'd never expected her to feel so good, taste so good. He wanted the kiss to last for an eternity.

She turned her head to speak, and was bold in her demand. "Open your mouth. Give me your tongue."

Lifting her head, she strained her neck to reach him. He released her wrists, supported her head with one hand and basked in the warm willingness of her kiss and her searching tongue. The intimacy inflamed his desire into a blaze until his head spun. She arched against his chest, and he lost himself in her lush lips, which tasted of sweet-meats and Irish wine.

She wound her hands into his hair, tugging him closer. She had to recognize his need. Had to know what she encouraged. He shuddered, his arms tightening about her. Breathing hard, she drew her head back. "Release me."

Strongheart shook his head to clear the dull roaring in his ears. By the rood! Where had the woman learned to kiss like a seductress? Would she guess how much her demand cost him? Of all the women he'd ever known why must this Irish princess be so hard to resist?

If she had not pulled away, he wasn't sure what would have happened. What had she done to him? Had she cast a spell? Wild and untamed as Leinster's green mountains, impassable as her dark bogs, Dara had draped him in the mystic darkness of ancient Eire.

As he withdrew his arms from her, he longed to see her face clearly. Such passion couldn't be faked, and he wanted her to admit her reaction to him. He yearned for a hint of a smile, a small caress, an acknowledgement of what they'd shared.

She rested on her back, gazing up at the stars, seemingly unaffected by what had just passed between them. If only he could deny the lust she'd incited. Shifting his breeches to accommodate his stirring fullness, he knew he should move away to the fire, where the breeze couldn't carry her feminine scent, where he couldn't see the soft silhouette of her breasts, but he could not leave her.

He'd meant to arouse her with his kiss. Instead, she remained calm, motionless, belying the passionate trembling he'd felt only moments before. He knelt at her side, but she stared into the darkness, fingers laced behind her head, refusing to look at him.

"Are you all right?"

"And why shouldn't I be?" Her flat, toneless voice matched her stillness.

What could be wrong? He had neither hurt her nor frightened her. From the passionate, demanding way she'd responded, his kiss could not possibly have been her first experience. She'd known exactly what to do, so his reaction shouldn't have taken her by surprise. No man alive could have reacted otherwise when kissed like that.

Clearly passion hadn't overwhelmed her. Not when she'd inflamed him with her wild abandon, then demanded like a prim-and-proper maid that he hold to his word. She should be taunting him for his daring, or trying to stab him with her dirk. Her dark and murky stillness unnerved him, and he wondered why she appeared so composed.

His hand cupped her chin and his thumb caressed the soft smoothness of her cheeks. "Did I offend you, Princess?"

She shoved his hand aside with bleak outrage and sat up, drawing her knees to her chest. Clasping her legs, she rocked and mumbled to herself between clenched teeth. "Did you think I would like being tumbled? I will not be like *her*. I won't."

Baffled by her words, he cocked his head to one side. "You won't be like whom, Princess?"

Her hands released her knees and slapped the ground, then she stood. " 'Tis no concern of yours. I wish you cursed dreams."

Dara stomped away from him, her back stiff, unwilling to admit she would not sleep this night. Strange sensations still rippled deep inside her. Somehow she didn't think kissing the Norman was the kind of beguilement her father had in mind.

Her hands trembled at what he'd made her do, at what he'd make her feel. She'd discovered controlling her unruly passions with this man would not be as easy as dismissing other men's advances. A peck on the cheek would never have rid herself of him. So she'd decided to tease him with what he could never have, hoping he'd leave in frustration. Her plan had worked too well. He hadn't been the only one caught in the web of desire she'd spun. She'd been filled with a curious inner excitement, a feminine sense of power at the realization she'd drawn such a response from him.

She'd almost wished the Norman had been unable to keep his word. He would not easily have forgiven her if she'd drawn the dirk from her boot and stabbed him to keep him from taking further liberties. Did he comprehend she'd incited his desire so she could reject him? Or did he think himself such a great kisser that she'd been unable to resist?

She needed a moment alone to calm herself. If the Norman followed her to Sorcha's side, she'd scream the entire camp awake. She had no wish to discuss the incident with him and hoped that if she ignored their kiss and the strange stirring in her blood, by tomorrow she'd forget the way she'd responded to the Norman. A hated Norman.

Even now, as she leaned over her friend's side, she wanted more of his touch. How could a man so skilled in the art of war be so gentle? Even when he'd tripped her, his strong arms had cradled her fall. She'd intended to fuel his desire, then let him suffer with unsated lust, but her plan had reversed itself, and she'd become so lost in sensation that for a moment she'd forgotten he was a stern, unyielding, and relentless Norman intent on conquering Eire.

Her mood had shifted continuously since his arrival, and she was having difficulty reining in her impulsive nature. Each emotion, whether anger, disappointment, embarrassment, or passion, seemed heightened and more intense than ever before. When the Norman had covered her with his taut body, the bunched muscles of his hard thighs had twisted her insides with excitement. Her fingers had clamped in his thick hair and a tight clenching sensation had seized her lower body.

His kiss had been carnally devastating. His raw sensuality had done peculiar and dangerous things to her. With one kiss, he'd aroused her body and scrambled her brain. What had happened to her good sense? Muttering a curse under her breath, she fled to the one person who understood.

Sorcha lifted her head. "I saw . . ."

"What?" Dara offered her friend a drink, wondering what she'd seen, how much she could guess.

Sorcha swallowed some wine and her warm brown eyes stared intently at Dara, her voice sharp. "Too much. You gave him too much."

Dara dropped the wineskin, and her hands clenched into fists at her sides. "God help me. I lost my head." Her voice choked, emotion bleeding from her like spilled wine. She drew a ragged breath and regained her senses. Sorcha needed rest, and she shouldn't be worrying about Dara's weaknesses. Pushing aside her doubts for the moment, Dara stroked a stray lock from the maid's forehead. "Are you in pain?"

Sorcha sighed, softening her tone. "Nothing like

the torment you are feeling now. You only kissed him, lassie. You didn't sully yourself like your cursed mother."

Sorcha's words were meant to ease her pain, and Dara did her best to accept them as fact. Again she tried to turn the conversation away from herself. "Could you eat some meat?"

"I'm not hungry." Sorcha closed her eyes. "You rest and we'll talk tomorrow."

Dismissed, Dara wandered to her blanket. If the Norman thought to claim their land by conquering her, he must be insane. Even if her father allowed a match between them, which he wouldn't, the *Ard-ri* would kill Strongheart before handing over Leinster's wealth to a Norman renegade. Besides, there was the small matter of the marriage agreement already made.

She spent most of the night tossing and turning, her mind replaying her response to the Norman's kiss and what she should have done differently. By morning, she'd admitted her mistake and had come to only one conclusion: He must never touch her again.

The smoke from the glen had lifted during the night, making the air clear and sweet. Now at first light, the mountain mists hung over the moorland, muffling the whistle of a blackbird in the fern and the bark of a dog in the distant village.

Sorcha's bleeding had stopped and she'd regained much of her strength. While her father's men rounded up the cattle, Dara and Sorcha shared the morning meal of goose eggs, oatmeal porridge, and barley bread.

Strongheart gathered the horses and saddled his

mount before joining the women at the fire. Even as she was aware of his every move, Dara was determined to ignore him.

But when he joined them, he spoke not to her but to Sorcha. "You're in no condition to ride. Gaillard can take you up before him again."

"One of our men can carry her," Dara insisted.

"Gaillard has a saddle. With his feet anchored in the stirrups, 'twould be safer if she rode in his arms, and she could sit sideways as a lady should."

Sorcha nodded in calm acceptance and Dara stood, dusting her hands, then rubbing the shamrock locket at her throat. Though his suggestion would give Sorcha comfort, his condescending tone unnerved Dara. The man overflowed with arrogance. Now that they were free of the danger of raiders, he needed a lesson in humility.

"Excuse me." She walked from the fire, leaving Sorcha alone with the Norman.

"Don't go far. Raiders might still be about," Strongheart called after her.

She didn't answer, but waved away his warning. She'd lived here all her life and knew the dangers far better than he.

After tending to her needs in the privacy of the woods, Dara cautiously edged to where the horses stood waiting. Pulling her dirk from her boot, she raised the sharp blade to cut the Norman's cinch strap, but the sturdy knot gave her an idea, and she resheathed her blade.

Her fingers worked quickly and when she'd finished, she laughed under her breath, anticipating his embarrassment. Mounting Fionn, she waited for the others to join her.

Gaillard mounted and reached down for Sorcha. Strongheart lifted the maid into his squire's arms. Gaillard cradled her, and she nodded once to Dara that all was well, then settled against the squire's chest. The squire urged his mount into a walk, leaving Dara and Strongheart to catch up. They would travel slowly, with her father's men herding the cattle back where they belonged.

From a pouch on his saddle, Strongheart withdrew a bouquet of primroses and handed them to Dara with an endearing flourish. As she inhaled the sweet scent, she realized he must have awakened in the early morning and gathered the flowers. His thoughtful gesture made her regret her prank.

She lifted her head from the nosegay and opened her mouth to warn him. Strongheart was already climbing into the saddle.

Before she could utter a sound, the saddle slipped sideways and his horse reared. The Norman's powerful thighs clamped the animal's flanks tight, but the crooked saddle spilled him into the dirt. He landed on his backside with a curse, and nimbly rolled to avoid the bucking stallion's hooves.

Clasping her hand to her mouth to cover her gasp, she chewed on a knuckle. She hadn't thought her prank dangerous. She'd only intended to dump him on the ground as he'd dumped her last night before taking that kiss. How in the name of Jesu had she come up with such a dumb idea? The Norman had so befuddled her, she was committing childish acts she'd outgrown long ago. His magnificent physique, his rakish glances, the seductive curve of his mouth had her profoundly aware of his intense attractiveness. But she'd never give him the satisfaction of knowing he had the least effect on her.

As he scrambled away unhurt, her concern subsided. She would never let him know his tender gesture, his gift of flowers, had softened her toward him—if only for a moment. "So how do *you* like being tossed on the ground like a sack of winter wheat?"

He ignored her taunting words and rose to his feet. Grabbing the reins, he controlled his horse with a few soothing words. Strongheart scowled at her, removed the entire saddle from the horse's back, examined it carefully, then shook out the blanket.

The rough texture of his voice was almost as intimidating as his glower. "Did you put a burr beneath the blanket as well as loosen the cinch?"

"I have no wish to harm your horse," she replied blithely, unwilling to admit she hadn't expected the animal to buck wildly when the saddle slipped.

Dara watched him rub his hands on the seat of his breeches and took satisfaction in knowing he'd have an uncomfortable ride back to Ferns. He deserved it. It was his fault she hadn't slept a wink all night. All the flowers in the world could not make up for his having forced her to kiss him. Or for his making her all too aware of his every mood.

"If you ride on raids with men, you must learn to behave like a warrior—not a reckless child." At the hard ruthlessness in his voice, she stiffened in the saddle.

If her father placed him in charge of Leinster's

defense, Strongheart could forbid her to ride with the men. His words proved the changes she so feared would curtail her freedom. She straightened her back to cover her alarm, refusing to shrink from his cold black eyes. "I'm seventeen years old and Leinster's only heir. I do as I wish."

"Seventeen is old enough to know better than to loosen a cinch."

At the note of censure in his tone, she tossed his flowers to the ground. "And what of your games?"

He placed the blanket over his mount's back, and he looked up, his dark eyes boring into her. As their gazes met, the glint in his eyes sent icy fingers of warning trickling over her shoulders.

"If you had a good man to bed you, you would not be so upset over one insignificant kiss."

She cursed under her breath. How dare he belittle her efforts and call their kiss insignificant? That kiss had been hot enough to brand flesh. Just recalling the incident brought heat to her cheeks.

First he'd demanded what she hadn't wanted to yield, then he'd belittled her effort, and her fury rose with the rising sun. "Norman, if you dare touch me again, I'll stick a knife between your ribs and carve out your heart."

His eyes glittered dangerously. "Your trick could have maimed or killed me, woman. All because of a kiss?"

At his fury, and at her own peculiar urge to apologize, she backed Fionn out of his reach and lied, "You tasted like swine."

His lips twisted in a cynical smile. "I think you liked it."

The ridicule in his tone, his accurate and arrogant guess, and the knowing mockery in his glance sent a shiver spiraling down her spine. "There's a wee devil sitting on your shoulder for sure, Roland de Clare, and I hope he delivers you to hell."

"What you need is discipline." His commanding tone scared her more than if he'd shouted, especially as she realized they were all alone, but she'd never let him know it. His jaw clenched so tightly she heard his molars grind. His hands gripped the saddle tighter until his knuckles whitened, his rage all the more evident in the precise way he replaced the saddle on his horse's back.

She recalled his hands on her, pulling her so close their two bodies had melded in the dark. "I need nothing from you. Stay away from me."

He raised a brow. "Or?"

"Or next time you *will* be maimed."

At her threat, his face darkened, his lips tightened, and his eyes narrowed a fraction more. She swallowed hard, no longer thinking it safe to taunt him. Her heart thundered in her chest. He tugged the cinch strap tight. Before she could dig her heels into Fionn's sides to flee, he grabbed her horse's reins.

"Get down," he ordered.

She turned her head, searching for her father's men, but they'd given her the privacy her father demanded. She shifted uneasily in the saddle. "You have no right to—"

He seized her waist and dragged her from the saddle. As he trapped her wrists at her sides, ignoring her gasp of outrage, she squirmed against his massive chest. Where were her father's men?

She flicked her hair off her face with a jerk of

her head so she could see. "Damn you. Let me go."

His voice hardened mercilessly. "We will settle this dislike you have for me, Princess."

Dislike? The Norman had the sensitivity of a rock. "I hate you."

She struggled harder.

He held her firm.

Tilting back her head, she looked up at him and realized antagonizing him had been a terrible mistake. One glance at his furious face and fear gnarled her stomach. Sweet Jesu! Her father had told her to beguile the man. Whatever had possessed her to antagonize him?

When his nostrils flared, she kicked his shin as hard as she could. He flinched, but instead of releasing her, his hands tightened on her wrists.

"If you do that again, I will not be the only one riding back to Ferns with a sore bottom, Princess."

Alarm, anger, and embarrassment rippled along her back. Her breath quickened, and she flushed crimson with resentment and humiliation.

"You cannot—"

One cocky eyebrow raised. "I could."

She drew herself to her full height. "You cannot come to my land and order me about. If I were a man—"

One finger, strong and gentle, pressed against her lips, silencing her. "If you were a man, I'd knock some sense into you with my fist. But if you were a man, I would not have kissed you. Your problem is not the fact that I stole a kiss. The problem is that you liked it."

His words stabbed her as truly as an arrow piercing her heart. A shudder racked her when old

67

wounds that he'd opened now bled anew. Damn him for seeing what she'd tried so hard to keep hidden. After a kiss like his, she'd have had to be stone not to respond.

When her stomach had tightened and her pulse had raced in enjoyment, he'd all too easily made her feel passion against her will. She hadn't wanted to respond, and still, she hadn't been able to control herself. At the memory of her failure, her head dropped in shame and her shoulders sagged.

With one kiss, he'd wiped away years of her hard work to repress her emotions, but she wouldn't give him the satisfaction of confirming his high opinion of himself. He might try again, and her nerves were too raw to feign disinterest.

Of all the men interested in her, why did she have to respond to this one? She didn't even like him. He was too arrogant, too sure of himself. She thrust away the memory of him cradling Sorcha's head in his lap, ignored the memory of the flowers he'd gathered for her, now trampled by Fionn's hooves.

His presence would bring war. And war brought death.

Blinking back tears of frustration at her failure, she stared at his gleaming leather boots and forced herself to remember she was not a maid free to flirt with a man. She was the Princess of Leinster and her actions would have consequences, not just on her life, but on all her people.

Strongheart's voice softened to a husky whisper. "Dumping a man on the ground is no way to show your feelings. Perhaps we should try another kiss so you can practice proper appreciation, Princess."

Princess. His tongue wrapped around the word more like a caress than a title of respect. Instead of soothing her anger, the reminder of his attempt at seduction increased her rage. She ought to smack him across the face.

Her head jerked up and their gazes locked. At the sight of granite-hard, glittery anger that matched her own, for once she controlled her violent impulse. However, she couldn't rein in her tongue. "The only feeling I have for you is disgust. The only thing I need to practice is ridding my people of a cursed Norman before our enemies invade and do it for us."

Or before he steals your heart.

Now from whence had that traitorous thought come? Long ago she'd vowed to dam the passion that coarsed through her veins with the force of a surging river. Despite the bad seed who had spawned her, she'd worked hard to earn the respect and trust of Leinster's men-at-arms, their women, and their children. For the most part, she'd succeeded. No bold Norman warrior could ride into Leinster with his plans of conquest and cheat her out of the respect she'd worked so hard to gain, or harm her people.

"I did not come here to hurt you, Princess."

He sounded so earnest she almost believed him. Almost. But she was not so naive to believe a warrior like him would not assess Leinster's vulnerabilities and take advantage for personal gain. His great size and his hardened muscles bespoke an accomplished warrior, a victor of many hard-fought battles. The lowing of Leinster's cattle would act like sirens' music upon his ears. The lush verdant fields of green grass and herds of fattened cows were too tempting a prize for such an ambitious man to ignore. And Strongheart was more than ambitious. She sensed a ruthless determination in him even as he'd softened his words to soothe her temper, but though she could not control her physical response to him, his honeyed words would not work on her.

Nor did she owe him explanations, and so she refused to respond to the honesty in his expression. He might believe in his heart what he'd told her, but he didn't know this land, and it was not her place to educate him. He hadn't been born here. He didn't know and love the spume-packed cliffs of the coast with winding promontories and spiked inlets, golden strands of beach, deep, blue lagoons, and clear rocky bays. He'd never appreciate the giant Irish deer and great auks or their forests and bogs, the mountains covered with bracken and shrouded in mist. He'd never come to love the ever-falling rain, the magnificent daytime skies.

He didn't realize how difficult it was to defend the huge herds of cattle that comprised most of Leinster's wealth. By their nature, cattle needed acres of grazing land, and to find enough food the herds roamed the mountain glens and forest passes from Dundonnell to Cabury.

Protecting the herds from raiders was an onerous task that made usurping the land much easier than holding it. O'Rourke, their nearest enemy, was an expert at sneaking across the border to steal sheep and cows from the vast pastures, hiding the animals in the marshes, then later stampeding a herd back into his own lands. It was the nature of men to take from the weak, so she had to be strong.

"Let me go," she demanded in as even a tone as she could muster.

His hands flexed and his mouth opened to speak. The thunder of hoofbeats galloping across the damp dirt and sweet-smelling grass interrupted his words. In one swift movement, Strongheart pushed Dara behind him, sheltering her with his huge body, and drew his great sword.

Dara peeked from behind his broad back, recognized her father's man-at-arms, Seumas, by his awkward seat on his horse, and mounted Fionn. Once astride Fionn and out of Strongheart's reach, she explained, "That's my father's man, and he detests riding a horse. Something is wrong."

From the lather on his mount, Seumas must have ridden all the way from Castle Ferns. As he neared, he shouted across the clearing, his face grim. "MacLugh has come for his betrothed. He says he's waited long enough to claim his bride."

Chapter Four

Betrothed? His bride! Why had no one told Strongheart Princess Dara was betrothed? The news
struck him as hard as a death blow. He turned to
Dara's worried face for answers. As if guessing his
intent, she urged Fionn toward Seumas, racing
across the moor, leaving him to eat her dust.

Strongheart sheathed his sword, then mounted,
swearing softly under his breath, knowing he
wouldn't catch the Princess of Leinster until she
reined in her stallion. The armor, saddle, and
heavier load slowed his powerful war horse down.

Breathing in the soft morning air, he galloped after her. In the magic Irish light, Dara O'Dwyre
looked more a wild hoyden than the titled princess
of Ireland's richest county. As she rode, her slender
body seemingly part of her horse, her magnificent
red hair cascaded behind her, and he imagined

how she would look with that fiery hair splayed on a white silk pillow. Another man's pillow.

Acid burned his stomach at the thought. He would not give up so easily. No matter how many guards had surrounded them last night, what manner of father would have left her alone with one man when she was promised to another? And if her heart belonged to another, why had she kissed him with such passion?

He reminded himself that all was not yet lost. The lass was not yet wed. Perhaps there was still time to change the King of Leinster's mind.

Although Strongheart had said otherwise, with her flashing red hair and snapping green eyes, men from far and wide would have sought her hand if she were a mere peasant. As King O'Dwyre's sole heir, Dara's husband would one day assume leadership of Leinster's vast lands. With her lands and beauty, she'd make any man a fine wife. So why was the princess only betrothed and not already wed?

Dara pulled her horse to a skidding halt in the middle of the clearing and pressed her head close to Seumas's in hushed conversation. When Strongheart arrived, Dara's lips had settled into a hard line, her eyes pinched tight with distress.

"Has Sorcha taken a fever?" Strongheart asked.

Seumas shook his head. "Nay. We were discussing MacLugh's visit at Castle Ferns."

Dara sighed, tugged on the reins, and reeled Fionn around, looking as if she carried the weight of Ireland on her slumped shoulders. Under Strongheart's appraising eyes, she straightened, a look of resignation on her face. "Da needs me, but I must check Sorcha first."

What had Seumas been whispering in her ear? Strongheart didn't like the disadvantage of being taken by surprise. If Castle Ferns's visitors represented a threat, he should have been apprised of the situation.

The castle defenses were poor compared to Norman standards, and he estimated an armored band of knights could easily overrun Dara's home. It was a good thing he and Gaillard were the only Normans in the county.

There was opportunity in this green land for a man with a strong sword and the will to fight. While his people were the foremost race in Christendom, their courage and ruthlessness had made them conspicuous. Dara's acute suspicions extended far beyond her years or experience to recognize the vulnerability of her land.

From his exhibit with his longbow, she must have realized his people had mastered archery with bows that carried death at a distance. Could she foresee the consequences of a battle where Norman calvary, clad in mail armor and armed with long lances and shields, fought the undisciplined Irish who still fought with rocks and slings? His people had conquered every region from the Elbe to the Pyrenees and established internal order. This land would be no different.

Dara was right. What man would not covet this rich country of rolling hills and open air where forests still covered the greater part of the earth? It was not by accident he'd come to County Leinster to win lands to replace those his father had lost. He'd given equal consideration to the other counties of Munster, Connaught, Meath, and Ulster. But Leinster was the most vulnerable, hence his opportunity would be greater.

All his careful plans had not taken into account Conor's daughter. Eyes blazing in the innumerable greens of the pastures challenged him at every turn. Like a mythical creature in a fairy world, she seemed to know his intentions when he'd done naught to create suspicion.

His eyes strained to follow the slender figure on horseback ahead. Dara had almost ridden out of sight when she drew alongside Gaillard and Sorcha. When Strongheart caught up with them, Dara had already checked her charge and seen to reseating her maid across Gaillard's thighs.

"I am fine," Sorcha assured Dara, her hand pressing Gaillard's chest. "He makes a fine pillow."

His squire's face reddened, and he twirled one end of his mustache. "Are ye saying I'm soft, woman?"

"Aye. Soft in the head," the maid huffed.

Dara giggled, her eyes brimming with merriment. "Well I'll leave you in good hands. Da needs me."

"Promise me," Sorcha demanded, "you won't be riding that demon so fast your guards cannot keep up with you. 'Tis not safe."

"I promise," Dara agreed as she remounted.

She'd given in too easily. Apparently her maid didn't believe her any more than Strongheart did.

Sorcha snorted. "I mean it, missy. I'm responsible for you and I don't want anything to happen—"

"If she rides out of sight, when I catch her at the castle, I'll beat her," Strongheart said, hoping he'd sounded convincing since he could never lay a hurtful hand on the lass. Her head jerked to stare at him, and at the challenge he glimpsed in her eyes, he thought perhaps he could win these rich lands without fighting a bloody battle—if Mac-Lugh and a betrothal agreement didn't stand in his way.

Strongheart realized with a sinking feeling she'd never forgive him for fighting MacLugh and bringing war to her land. They'd both seen the effects of war. Sometimes it took years for the villagers to rebuild their homes. With the men off to war, if the crops could not be brought in by the women, many often starved through harsh winters.

And after meeting Dara, he'd rejected his plan to take her home by force. Why fight hundreds of men and risk destruction of the land when he had only to break one betrothal agreement and convince one small lass to wed? Somehow, he would find a way to win her. As he and Seumas rode hard, following the lady, the idea brought him immense satisfaction.

A wife would give a man comforts and heirs. These people would accept his rule more easily with Dara O'Dwyre, the rightful successor, at his side. She would see to his meals and clothing during the day, warm his bed at night. In turn, he would conceal her follies, defend her and her home, offer her security, solace, and serenity—a fair trade for what he'd ask of her.

Now he had to convince Conor and the princess—no small task, but then he wasn't considered one of the most wily and determined knights in Christendom without reason. The fact that his reputation had not preceded him could work to his favor. Perhaps MacLugh would accept a challenge for her hand.

With a small grin of satisfaction, he set about planning his campaign.

With the sun directly overhead, Dara rode through the triple rings of stone, left Fionn in the stable, and gave instruction to a groom to cool him down well before giving him an extra ration of oats. Hurrying across the bailey, she spotted Strongheart.

When he didn't dismount, she hid behind a pillar of bronze. Among Leinster's men, who were clad in black wool tunics, Strongheart, in his burnished mail, shined like the sun among the night stars. He might make a tempting target, but she'd seen his fighting skills and knew he could defeat the best of her father's men.

From her position she watched Strongheart deploy the men-at-arms, checking each for weapons before sending them to guard the stronghold. With the likes of MacLugh about, he'd taken sensible precautions, ones she or Da should have ordered. As she watched the Norman give one man a slap on the back and another a dressing down for drunkenness, she realized the ease with which Strongheart assumed command.

Having the burden of defense lifted from her shoulders should have eased her worries. Da's forgetful spells had made him grow lax, and she'd covered his deficiency as best she could. In addi-

tion to managing the household staff and seeing
everyone clad and fed, she oversaw much of the
estate, keeping the accounts of their lands, listing
the revenues and profits of their clan. She managed the tilling of the fields, decided which crops
to plant to ensure winter fodder for the horses,
pigs, and cows, and sent hunting parties out for
game. One less job would lighten her load. But
leaving the castle defenses in Strongheart's obviously capable hands made her uneasy. She didn't
trust the Norman's motives any more than she
trusted O'Rourke's or MacLugh's.

"There you are."

Dara jumped, then winced at the sound of
Neilli's shrill tone. She'd hoped to steal into the
castle and make her way to her room undetected.
Even though she meant to cancel the betrothal
agreement, she would not have MacLugh see her
looking like a dairy maid. If Sorcha had been
there, she would have helped smuggle her inside,
but Dara would just have to convince the heavyset
cook to help instead.

Neilli planted her fists on her ample hips. "Our
visitors will be needing a meal and that lazy Roisin
left the soup to boil over in the fire. I told her to
put in the salt, and she spilt it over the butter."

Dara contained her sigh at this minor calamity.
Why couldn't her servants solve problems when
they arose? Did she have to do all the thinking
around here? "Melt the butter in a dish over the
fire, and the salt will fall to the bottom of the bowl.
The rest of the butter will be sweet, and the salt
can be put in the soup."

"And how would you be knowing such things?

Last time you baked bread, 'twas hard enough to break a tooth on," Neilli teased.

Dara never had been good at cooking. While she knew by heart every recipe cooked in the castle, for some reason her mind never stayed on what her hands should be doing. "Never mind that. I must reach my room without MacLugh, seeing me like this."

"Och, if your Da catches onto your shenanigans, he will not be pleased."

Dara lifted her tangled hair from her shoulders. "Neither will he be pleased if I come to the dinner table looking like a banshee."

Neilli stuck her head inside the hall, then waddled back, her hips swaying. "If ye be quick up the stairs, I think you can pass without notice."

The strains of the harp hurried her steps, and, safe in her room, Dara shut the door behind her and tugged her tunic over her head. She had planned her meeting with MacLugh for some time. She had her arguments ready. But a trickle of fear wound down her spine. Could she break the betrothal without causing a war? She tossed the tunic to her stuffed mattress and clenched her fists, vowing never to bring war to this land.

Hurriedly, she picked out clean clothes. Instead of the bath she longed for, she would make do with the bowl of boiled rosemary water atop the table beside her bed.

She placed clean clothing over the back of a chair and turned to the water basin. She stopped short with a gasp, her eyes widening in surprise.

Atop her bedside table rested a giant bouquet of primroses in an empty wine bottle. The yellow blooms amid the green leaves perfumed the air with their sweet fragrance. The tension inside her eased. The flowers were a pleasing surprise, but who could have done such a thing?

Suddenly she recalled the handful of flowers Strongheart had given her, the ones she'd arrogantly tossed in the dirt, and knew he'd been responsible. The man was too bold. How had he arranged to place the primroses in her room so quickly? During the return ride to Castle Ferns, Strongheart must have collected the flowers that thrived in the peat bogs. He'd gone to considerable trouble to please her. In her experience when a man sent gifts, he wanted something from the recipient. Aye, she knew what he wanted from her, but it would take more than flowers to cause her to lose her good sense.

This was not the first time he'd taken her by surprise. She still couldn't put from her mind the kiss he'd stolen, but if she allowed herself to dwell on her response, she'd go daft with worry of yielding to her passionate side. Concern replaced her pleasure. The Norman must not interfere. He must not challenge MacLugh, but allow her to settle the matter. Somehow, she must get word to him. With guests waiting below, this was no time to dally.

Quickly she washed her face and hands, replaced her tunic with a fresh one of soft, green wool that brought out the color of her eyes, and braided her hair. Grabbing her embroidery, she sedately descended the narrow stairs, careful to keep the wool from brushing the rough stone walls.

Dark smoke spiraled its way from the hearth

through the hole in the castle roof, and a shiver of apprehension trickled over her. From the stairs, she had a clear view of the scene below. King Borrack MacLugh's men had not removed their weapons, which wasn't all that unusual. But the constant handling of those weapons was.

While a kitchen girl turned a roast on the spit and the dripping fat sizzled in the fire, men gathered round, drinking ale and listening to the blind harper, rumored to have the second sight, pluck his tune.

Morcolle, her father's warhound, padded over to greet Dara, placing his cold nose in her hand, and she ruffled his thick fur. Ignoring the Norman's nod, she took the chair beside her da, pretending an ease she didn't feel, grateful for the warmth of the warhound at her feet.

Putting her embroidery in her lap, she kept her eyes modestly downcast, but not before noting MacLugh's perusal of her. He hadn't changed in the two years since she'd last seen him. In contrast to the richness of his clothes, his beard was still unkempt. He was short and thick, and she'd never liked the way his gaze lingered over her breasts and hips, sizing her up like a brood mare. He smiled at her only with his thin lips, his pale blue eyes hard and chill.

MacLugh slapped his hand on his thigh, his movement sloshing the ale from his goblet. "I will have her."

At the neighboring king's words, Dara's hands shook, and she pricked her finger with the needle. Only years of subduing her emotions allowed her to remain seated while she longed to run out the door and hide in the stable.

"Hush," her father ordered. "Carolan has not finished his song."

A few of MacLugh's men reached for their weapons, but the King of Munster gestured to them, and they resettled in their positions. The confrontation had only been delayed, not averted.

From behind her, Strongheart handed Dara a clean white cloth to dab away the drops of blood on her finger. Oddly grateful for his presence, she pressed the cloth to her finger, the pain there insignificant compared with the pain in her heart. Her fate rested with Da, and though he'd made her promises, she wondered if he'd remember them.

At all costs, she must hold her tongue. To do otherwise would reveal Da's faults and weaknesses to a man that coveted Leinster. While Dara had felt free to speak against the Norman, he was not of their land, did not command an army that lived on their border.

The blind harper ended his song, and the men clapped in appreciation. Before the applause died, Conor rose to his feet, his glass held high. "I would like a prophecy."

Carolan rested his harp on his knee. "No, please, my lord. Ye will not be liking what I see."

Although he kept his opinions to family, Dara knew her father did not believe in prophecy. Her heart pounded with sudden hope that he had not forgotten his promise. But what mischief had he hatched?

"Would you deny me your gift?" Conor demanded. Never had he spoken so harshly to Carolan, a man who depended on his lord's benevolence for his daily bread.

Carolan licked his cracked lips. "This ought be spoken in private, my lord."

Men avoided each other's eyes. Dara's hand went to the shamrock at her neck. The Norman's brow arched. A few men squirmed in their seats. One rubbed a rabbit's foot for luck. Several spit in the clean straw at their feet. When the kitchen maid removed the roast from the fire to a platter on the table, no one moved toward the table.

Conor raised his glass to the crowd of deadly silent men. "We are all friends here. Let the prophecy begin."

The blind man set down his harp, reached for his ale, and took a hearty swallow. Finally he cleared his throat. "She will bring with her destruction and death. She will divide the kingdom and set clan against clan. She will cause the downfall of kings and the deaths of princes."

Silence followed Carolan's prediction. Conor staggered back a step, clutched his chest, and sank into his chair.

Strongheart's gaze went to Dara's face. She stared into the flames, her shoulders stiff, chin high, gnawing hard on her lower lip lest a hint of her thoughts be revealed on her face. Da had pulled quite a few pranks in his lifetime, but Carolan's prediction was so incredible she'd almost believed it herself.

"She is mine by right and I will have her," MacLugh muttered, casting a dark, uneasy scowl at her.

Begorra! Would the stubborn man not back out gracefully?

She risked a glance at the Norman, who looked as if he longed to come to her side. She shook her head slightly, and he kept his distance, yet stood clearly prepared to draw his sword if needed.

Leinster's king did not raise his voice, but the deep boom carried through the great house. "Dara, will you have this man?"

"She has no say in this matter," MacLugh objected before she said a word. "The law—"

"A king makes his own laws," Conor insisted, "changing them when it suits his purpose."

"Liar!" MacLugh jumped from his chair, pointing his finger at Conor. "You are a traitorous, cowardly liar."

Conor ignored the insult and threw his hands wide. "I offer you peace."

King MacLugh laughed, the sound rough and caustic. "You call this peace? O'Rourke steals our cattle daily, and you're too old to protect the border."

From nods of a few of Leinster's men, Dara suspected MacLugh's accusation had a bite of truth to it. That was why her father considered giving the Norman more authority, so Leinster's defenses could be strengthened. Still, finding an Irishman for the position would have made more sense.

"Can we not settle our differences?" Conor asked, interrupting her thoughts.

MacLugh fingered the hilt of his sword. "Our differences will not be settled except by blood. War between Munster and Leinster or virgin's blood on my sheets, the choice is yours."

At MacLugh's crude threat, Dara let a gasp escape her throat. Not that she was shocked, but the insult could not go unheeded. While she was not frightened, many a woman would be in tears, and she must act the part of lady.

Strongheart's hand moved to his sword hilt. It wasn't his place to interfere. Again she caught his eye and silently signaled him to remain still.

"Come, come," Conor admonished. "Let us eat. Let us be friends. If not friends, then let us agree not to be enemies."

MacLugh spat on the floor. His eyes, beady and hungry, stared at Dara with suspicion. "Perhaps the lady is no longer a virgin? Does a babe already grow in her womb?"

Dara held her back so rigid, she feared she'd snap if this conversation did not come to an end. Her fingers itched to draw her dirk and aim it true.

Despite her silent behests, Strongheart stepped forward, placing himself between Dara and MacLugh. "How dare you insult the princess?"

MacLugh took in the Norman's mail and jewel-encrusted sword and sent a confident sneer at Strongheart. Nevertheless, he kept his hand clear of his weapons. "I say what I please. Dara O'Dwyre is my betrothed. And no one denies me what is mine."

Dara looked from Strongheart's calm demeanor and blazing black eyes to the sneer on MacLugh's thin lips. Every MacLugh and O'Dwyre warrior in the hall had risen to his feet. The air prickled with tension sharp as a blade of ice. It was so still she could hear the piping of an oystercatcher. In the space of a breath, the room could turn into a battleground. But Dara would not have blood shed in her home.

"I beg your pardon, my lords." Dara pressed her hand to her brow. "I fear these loud words have my head spinning."

MacLugh's lower jaw dropped in momentary surprise as if he'd forgotten her existence. Her father signalled his permission for her to settle the men. Strongheart didn't move a muscle, but she caught sight of his lips twitching before his face again settled in a harsh mask.

Stepping boldly to MacLugh's side, Dara lightly placed her hand on his sword arm and spoke softly, as if raising her voice would cause her more pain. "Perhaps, my lord, we should become better acquainted."

With MacLugh's frown, his forehead creased. "Why? You have no say in such matters."

Dara signaled the kitchen girls to bring in the rest of the meal. They placed on the broad table tempting platters of roast venison spiced with meadow garlic, coddle, heavily salted pork, and pottage—made of finely chopped meat with vegetable sprouts and flavored with rowan berries. The succulent aromas rose up to tease the men's nostrils and, reminded of their hunger, their tempers cooled.

The cooks had prepared a salad of young dandelions, watercress, and sorrel from their herb garden. As the men's gazes swept over oysters, mussels from the lough, soups, goose eggs, and apple pudding, they edged toward the table. Under the eyes of so many men, the kitchen maids giggled, tripping lightly back and forth to the kitchen and returning with elderberries crystallized in honey, hot wheat breads, and fine Leinster cheese.

"Come." Dara tugged on MacLugh's arm, leading him to the table and indicating the seat to her left. The men seemed happy to forget the arguments for the moment and follow.

Her ploy had worked and the tension in her shoulders eased. But when she spied a sprig of purple violets by her plate, her heartbeat quickened and her gaze flew to Strongheart.

Since he towered over the others, she easily picked him out of the crowd of warriors as he joined her and MacLugh at the table. Not by a flicker of an eyelash did he betray his action, and yet she held the Norman accountable. What other man would dare to offer flowers to a lady in front of her betrothed?

The men didn't need urging to dig into the feast. King O'Dwyre took his chair at the head of his table, with Strongheart at his right hand.

"So, lady," MacLugh asked between bites of roast, "how did it come to pass that the King of Leinster goes back on his word?"

She kept her voice modestly meek. "Da is honoring my wishes."

Grease dribbled down his chin, and he wiped it away with the back of his hand. "Why should a maid's wishes be binding?"

Having led him down this path of conversation like a sheep for slaughter, she delivered the death blow with a gentle smile. "Truly. Our betrothal was an arrangement between our mothers. 'Tis not binding."

MacLugh sputtered. "Your da needs me guarding his border, girl. You had best reconsider."

More likely MacLugh was helping O'Rourke steal their cattle, but she kept her tongue between her teeth until the urge to mutter unladylike words passed. "I admit 'tis hard to make such important decisions," she lied.

Across the table, Strongheart choked on his wine.

"Perhaps you could sway the colleen?" Conor suggested.

MacLugh pounded his fist on the table, sloshing ale onto the fine linen. "I have not the time nor the patience for such—"

Strongheart lifted his goblet. "Courtly love. What maiden would not be swayed by small kindnesses? Flowers. Small gifts. A poem."

Aye, Strongheart well knew the skills to court a woman. His kisses were as masterful as his skill with a bow or a sword. No matter how attractive she found him, she wouldn't let his tactics sway her.

MacLugh stabbed a rasher of bacon with his knife. "Norman, if you know of such things, what do you suggest?"

Strongheart didn't take a moment to consider. "Perhaps the lady would like a handkerchief, a fillet for her hair, a wreath of gold or silver, a girdle, a tassel, a ring. Any little gift which is pleasing to look at or which calls a lover to mind may win a lady's favor."

MacLugh belched, pushed away from the table, and rubbed his stomach. "Well, girl, what gift would sway your mind?"

Stalling, she replied, "I'll have to give it some

thought." Did King MacLugh think her simple? He would not buy the Princess of Leinster as wife for the price of a trinket.

And what of Strongheart? Did he seek to give the Irish lessons in courtly love? Did he think a few flowers would win her undying gratitude and the richest county in Eire? She didn't trust the twinkle in his dark eyes or the way his lip twitched as if he were trying hard to keep his amusement inside.

Strongheart shook a finger at MacLugh. "You cannot ask a woman how she likes to be surprised."

MacLugh's hand clutched the handle of his dagger but Strongheart paid his unspoken threat no mind. "Use your head. A woman needs tenderness, understanding, flowers, in her life."

Conor nodded. Some of the single men guffawed but several married warriors smiled in agreement.

"If ye know so much about women, why are ye not yet wed?" MacLugh asked with a crafty sneer.

"It takes a special woman to tie a man's heart to the land."

It was more likely the other way around. It would take a special land, like Leinster, to tie Strongheart to a woman. Again Dara kept her tongue while she sought to keep peace in her home.

She tossed Morcolle a bone and with a nod, directed the kitchen maids to clear the meal, hoping the men's hearty appetites had mellowed their warlike mood. Before the men could begin their argument anew, she directed the kitchen maids to refill the goblets with hearty Leinster ale. "Carolan, tell us a story."

Carefully, the blind man straightened his legs before the blazing hearth, his joints cracking. He set his ale by his feet and the men's conversation hushed in anticipation of a good tale.

MacLugh belched and stood. "I have no time for children's stories." He grabbed Dara's arm in a move too quick to avoid. " 'Tis time for the lady and I to become acquainted."

MacLugh had cunningly used her own words against her, and were she to object, it would appear unseemly. His grip tightened on her arm and despite the bruises she'd wear later, Dara, weary of the fighting and constant bloodshed, did not object for fear the men would draw their weapons.

"Carolan, please continue," Dara said, acceding to MacLugh's demand.

Accompanied only by Morcolle, they walked through the room. MacLugh did not release her arm until he drew her outside.

A light rain had begun to fall, shrouding the pastures in shades of gray. Despite the people about, Dara had never felt so alone. It was market day and, after coming to the castle to trade, villagers, huddled under blankets to keep dry, drove a stream of carts and wagons back home. Cattle ambled through the crowd, ignoring the screaming children who chased them with sticks. Dogs herded fat sheep, scattering chickens, and the air was heavy with the mingled odors of animal dung and sweat.

King MacLugh had the power to take her away

from her people and the only home she'd ever known. If such a move meant her people would finally live in peace, she'd sacrifice her happiness. But such a powerful alliance with MacLugh would bring the might of O'Rourke and the *Ard-ri* upon the land.

"An alliance between us would bring war," she said to MacLugh with gentle conviction.

"Bah. 'Tis no concern for a woman."

Her hands twisted in her tunic. "And why not? At best we wait home alone while our fathers, brothers, and sons go to war. At worst we lose those we love." She stopped under the protection of an archway, sheltering them from the rain.

"Do not try to beguile me with your lying tongue. I'm not fool enough to believe you will not wed me for fear of losing me."

"Think, MacLugh. The *Ard-ri* will never let Munster and Leinster unite and threaten his power."

"Together we could defeat him," he boasted.

"And at what cost?" Dara squashed her darkest memory, the death of her half-sister, that rankled within her like a festering sore. Although she hadn't suffered from the nightmares in over a year, she hadn't forgotten her loss or the screams of an innocent child.

To avoid the destruction and death that hinged on her decision would require the luck of the little people. If she refused to marry MacLugh, he could raid their borders and cause untold problems. Her acceptance of their alliance would surely bring down the wrath of the other Irish kings. And the glint of suspicion and lust in his eyes didn't leave

91

her much reason for hope. Like all men, MacLugh saw marriage to her as a way to obtain power and increase his wealth. If she accepted him, there would be war—as there would be if she refused.

Chapter Five

Strongheart left his place by the hearth and stepped out of the hall into the drizzle, searching for Dara. His gaze took in the villagers' departure and the guards he'd placed in strategic positions throughout the motte and towers.

Spying the brown warhound against a far wall, he advanced toward the rain-sheltered archway. Walking softly in the wet grass but remaining out of sight, he edged close enough to hear Dara and MacLugh's words.

"To gain all of Eire," MacLugh said, "war is a cost I am more than willing to pay. Your fears are foolish. Why can you not be more like your mother?"

Dara gasped.

MacLugh's voice turned wily. "Would you not like to be high queen?"

Strongheart heard a loud slap, like the sound of a hand striking flesh. Having no idea why Dara felt such insult, he still yearned to protect her. He inched forward to peer around the corner but when MacLugh merely laughed, Strongheart kept his presence secret.

Dara's face burned red with fury, and she twisted her hands as if in pain. "I am nothing like her."

"So true. For you will not have a choice." MacLugh's hand snaked out to seize Dara, but she stepped into the rain and yanked her dirk from a sheath at her side.

Strongheart restrained his immediate reaction to defend her. Well aware of her ability with a blade, he forced himself to remain hidden, prepared to leap to her defense if she required help. Although he'd much rather take on the man for her, he already knew Dara well enough to guess she wouldn't appreciate his interference, so he forced himself to wait.

If MacLugh had one whit of sense he wouldn't dare attack his intended bride. And for the moment the King of Munster was ignoring her weapon, either having no knowledge of her skill or slyly waiting to see if she'd let down her guard.

So far, she'd made the right move, stepping beyond MacLugh's reach where the warrior couldn't immediately overpower her. For now, Strongheart allowed her to fight her own battle. But letting her face the danger had his heart pounding. Just in case, he silently readied his sword, wondering all the while what MacLugh thought of the timorous maid she'd appeared to be during dinner turning

into a dangerous woman, threatening him with a
blade.

"Put that down before you harm yourself,"
MacLugh ordered, obviously more annoyed than
fearful she would do actual damage. The man was
a fool. Strongheart had no doubt that if she so
wished, she could carve out his heart and hand it
to him before he died. But then, she had innumerable weapons at her disposal and one of them
was her sharp tongue.

The warhound growled. Strongheart glanced
around the wall at Dara, standing tall, eyes flashing green fire. Despite her aristocratic cheekbones, the graceful arch of her neck, and the
delicate lines of her chin, she had a strength surprising in a woman. She'd never looked so beautiful, brazen, beguiling.

Her chest heaved but her voice remained firm.
"A woman who can defend herself always has a
choice. And I'll not be choosing a man who resorts
to force."

From the first he'd suspected she didn't want the
Irishman, but it was nice to hear her say the
words. Especially since Conor often let her have
the final say. The Norman's hopes rose as he
sensed her heart did not yet belong to MacLugh
and he still had opportunity to win her.

"So that's the way the wind is blowing," Mac-
Lugh spat. "You prefer the courtly ways of the
Norman."

Did she? Was the Irish king hurling insults?
Mayhap he'd picked up on the connection Strongheart felt whenever he looked at her. Had the

man so easily read that he already looked at Dara as his?

"I prefer to be left alone," she replied coldly.

So the lady still needed convincing. He would not have her feeling any other way, since he looked forward to changing her mind. He might have even believed her harsh words against him if he hadn't recalled her response to his kiss and the warmth in her eyes when she'd spied the sprig of flowers by her plate.

MacLugh leered at her bodice. "You're ripe for the plucking, and I'm just the man to do it."

Morcolle barked a warning. At that moment, Gaillard and Sorcha rode into the bailey and Dara glanced their way. MacLugh lunged, grabbed the wrist that held Dara's knife, and squeezed until she dropped her weapon to the muddy ground.

Strongheart stepped into view, advancing with sword in hand. At his sudden appearance, Mac-Lugh swung Dara in front of him, using her as a shield. Anger, not fright, raged in her eyes. If MacLugh had seen her face he might have anticipated her continued resistance. But when she kicked his shin, she took him by surprise and he let out a muffled curse. Her elbow slammed into his stomach, and his arm loosened around her neck.

Dropping to the mud without hesitation, she rolled, coming to her feet with dirk in hand. MacLugh drew his sword, and Strongheart had seen enough. Even a seasoned warrior wouldn't think a dirk equal to a sword.

Strongheart stepped in front of Dara. Behind him, Dara let out a sigh of protest, but Strongheart kept his gaze on the Irish king, waiting for the man's attack.

From his opponent's stance, Strongheart surmised the other was well versed with a blade. With a surge of anticipation, the Norman looked forward to defeating Dara's enemy and freeing her of any betrothal promises to this man. From the lust in the king's eyes, which was slow to die despite the challenge of combat, the Norman realized this man wouldn't relinquish his passion for Dara until his last breath.

Killing the man would set her free to wed another. Him. Balancing on the balls of his feet, the Norman breathed calmly and cleared his mind for battle.

Dara slipped around him, her eyes flashing fierce with suppressed rage. "The first man to strike a blow shall never sire a child."

Dara threatened a vital part of the combatants' anatomies, and Strongheart liked her threat not one whit. Hoping his countenance didn't appear as astounded and worried as MacLugh's, the Norman kept his blade raised but heeded the warning. Yet he didn't lower his sword.

Before either warrior responded, another horse, its rider wearing the colors of Munster, thundered into the bailey. "Raiders to the north! Thank the saints, I have found you, MacLugh. O'Rourke is raiding the north border."

MacLugh's men, roused by the rider's shouts, poured into the bailey and mounted. With a salute of his sword, MacLugh backed away from Strongheart. "Another day, Norman." Leaping upon his horse, the King of Munster dug his heels into his mount and departed in a great splash of mud.

Annoyed by her interference in the quarrel, Strongheart turned to Dara and sheathed his weapon. When he saw her lower lip tremble and the trickles of rain running over her mud-splattered face, her hair cascading over her shoulders in wet disarray, he tempered his anger.

Stepping closer, he put a protective arm over her shoulder. "Did he hurt you?"

Her gaze followed Sorcha, who was walking unaided into the hall. "Only my pride. I shouldn't have let Sorcha distract me."

"You shouldn't have to defend yourself."

She sighed and replaced her dirk. "Aye. Men shouldn't threaten women, but they always do."

Stubborn woman. Why must she deliberately misunderstand him? "I meant, you should have a husband to look after you."

She glanced straight into his eyes, revealing unshed tears. "Why should I be tied to a man for life because of his lust and greed?"

He didn't bother to conceal his astonishment. "You never wish to wed? Or have children?"

"Bairns would be nice." For a moment she softened, but then, as if remembering she must think of her position and the political situation, she stiffened. "But a husband must be chosen carefully. I would not have a warrior husband who will bring war."

"Without a strong man to hold this rich land, you will lose your home."

She shrugged out from under his arm, straightened defiantly, and placed her fists on her hips, but he wasn't fooled. He'd spied the pain and fear she'd tried to hide despite her cool tone. "I don't need looking after by the likes of a Norman."

She spun away from him, and he would have let her go but for a question preying on his mind. "What did MacLugh mean by comparing your mother to the high queen?"

Her eyes widened with startlement and the beginnings of erupting anger. "You were behind the wall, spying the entire time."

"I didn't like the look in the man's eyes or the danger in your being alone with him," he admitted, watching her features go rigid as she closed her emotions tighter than a clam.

" 'Tis none of your concern," she insisted with a stubbornness so great he wanted to shake her.

Forcing himself to remember the confrontation she'd just endured, he tilted her chin with one finger until their gazes locked. Another woman would have tears in her eyes—in Dara he read bold rebellion. "I'm making it my concern. I'm making *you* my concern, Princess."

"No." Wet and muddy, she stared at him with the composure of royalty that belied the rapid pulse at the delicate curve in her neck. A raindrop drizzled onto her long lashes, and she batted it fiercely away, leaving another smudge of dirt along her cheek. Never had he seen her more bedraggled. Never had he seen her more ravishing.

Only the presence of the men in the courtyard prevented him from taking her into his arms for another kiss. Drawing a ragged breath to steady himself from rashly taking what he wanted, he called to a passing servant and ordered a hot bath for Dara.

However reluctant he was to release her, she needed a hot bath. And she needed time. But with the castle defenses weak and the rising troubles on the border, time was the one thing that wasn't his to give.

On the way to Dara's room, Lir, one of the maids, stopped her. Lir kept her brown eyes downcast and didn't refer to the mud Dara tracked through the hall. "Neilli wants to speak with you, and," her nose wrinkled in disgust, "the Munster men left fleas behind."

"They acted no better than a pack of wild hounds." Dara swept her dripping hair from her cheek. "Spread alder leaves upon the floor. The fleas will stick. Later, we can sweep them out of the hall and burn them."

Before heading toward her room, she stopped in the kitchen to confer with Neilli about which of the food left over from the feast to save without worry of spoiling and which to give to the departing villagers. A groom met her in the hall and told her that one of their prize mares would soon foal. She asked to be kept informed before wearily heading up the stairs.

When she reached her room, Sorcha had a fire blazing in the hearth. While her friend still looked pale, she was once again walking with brisk efficiency.

It was too soon for Sorcha to be waiting on her. "You should be in bed," Dara admonished.

"And the Norman was right. You need a hot bath."

Dara would have given Sorcha a swift hug but

had no wish for Sorcha to suffer a chill from her wet clothes. Instead she settled for squeezing her hand. "Has the bleeding stopped?"

Sorcha nodded, refusing to meet her eyes and see her scowl. "Take off those wet clothes."

Dara grinned at Sorcha's bossiness. She truly must be better. With a wave of her hands, she shooed Sorcha toward the door. "I'll bathe . . . if you nap."

Sorcha left the room and called back over her shoulder. "Fine. I'll just bring you a cup of tea and then take a wee nap."

Nothing had changed. Sorcha always managed the last word. And her friend had also managed to follow the Norman's orders. Who else could be responsible for the scented candles lighting the room—Or the wine goblet resting within easy reach of the tub of steaming water?

Amidst flower petals sprinkled in the bath water, a bottle floated. Curious, Dara drew the bottle to her and found a note inside.

How did Strongheart find time for these diversions? Since he wasn't there to watch, she smiled and unrolled the parchment, reading aloud. " 'After your bath, Princess, I would like to take this cloth and dry you. Slowly.' "

Wanton devil. And yet the idea sent a tingle of excitement across her shoulders and down her back. The thought of him rubbing the thick drying cloth over her bare flesh heated her blood, banishing her chill.

Dreamily she removed her clothes, poured a goblet of wine, and eased into the hot water scented with rose petals. She lay her head back against a rolled cloth and shut her eyes. Images of the Norman assailed her.

Sinking into the tub until the water covered her breasts, she rubbed soap on a cloth, building a good lather. She recalled the fury in Strongheart's eyes when MacLugh had used her for a shield and had no doubts he would have defended her with his life. His big hand had hefted his jeweled sword loosely, ready to mete out death.

Yet she also remembered those same hands gently smoothing hair off her forehead and cupping her chin. Drifting the lathered cloth over her legs, she recalled his marvelous male essence, spicy and clean, and when he'd kissed her, his mouth had been both coaxing and demanding.

After rinsing her legs, she moved the cloth over her arms and shoulders, relaxing in the warmth of the water. The odd sensation he'd caused with his kiss once again fluttered deep in her loins.

She swished the cloth between her breasts, wondering how Strongheart's touch there would feel. She imagined his big hands warming her like the suds trickling over her flesh, his fingers teasing her puckered nipples into peaks of pleasure. The ache in her core deepened to a surge of heat, and this time she put a name to her feeling—desire. Desire to hold him, touch him, kiss him.

Desire for the Norman? Her eyes snapped open. No, it could never happen. Quickly she held her breath and ducked her head beneath the water to clear her thoughts. No matter how appealing, she couldn't allow him to seduce her with flowers, scented bathwater, and inappropriate notes.

After downing the goblet of wine in one gulp,

she set it down with a thump. She roughly lathered her hair, in an effort to stop her thoughts from drifting too easily.

From now on she must not only beware the Norman's bold advances, she'd have to guard her thoughts more closely, for a match between them was impossible and could only lead to war with their neighbors. War with Britain. She'd have to be wary of his determined moves, suppress the part of her that was drawn to him. For the first time, she wondered if she had any more discipline than her mother. She must find the strength to resist. She owed it to her people to keep her good sense. She had to stay wise to the Norman's tricks.

Strongheart tracked the departing MacLugh clan until he was assured they'd truly left. As he turned back to Castle Ferns, the rain had stopped, but his thoughts remained dark. It would have been better for Leinster if he'd killed MacLugh. After Dara's rejection, the insulted king would return with an army since fighting was the only way he knew. And Leinster must be ready.

Leaving his warhorse for the groom to cool down, Strongheart sought out Conor in the stable where a mare had just begun to labor. The warm scent of hay mixed with the faint odor of manure. But the stable was warm and dry, keeping the rain at bay.

Conor scratched between the mare's ears and crooned softly. "Easy girl. Save your strength." When Strongheart entered the stall, Conor looked up, as if expecting Strongheart to seek him out.

Susan Kearney

" 'Twill be her first foal and she refuses to settle down."

Inching his way along her flanks, Strongheart took care not to startle the animal. "MacLugh will be back. How many men can he raise?"

"Not enough to take Leinster," Conor assured him, his voice resonant and impressive.

"MacLugh is ambitious." Remembering Dara's assessment of the political situation, Strongheart asked, "Suppose he and O'Rourke join forces?"

Conor sighed. "In that occurrence, I'd be needing a powerful ally myself. But it won't transpire. The MacLughs and O'Rourkes have been raiding each other's borders for nigh onto five generations."

The situation lent itself to perpetual warfare, with the five kings changing sides and enemies as easily as changing their clothes. Strongheart had to state his suggestion tactfully—unfortunately, convincing a man with words wasn't his forte. "And between feuds, do not your enemies sometimes unite to take on a common foe?"

Conor stroked his beard, his attention diverted from the mare. "It might come to pass."

"Perhaps you could use an ally? Someone to help hold these lands."

Leinster's King spoke not with eagerness but matter-of-factly. "What are ye suggesting, Norman?"

"I can hold Leinster for you."

Conor threw back his head and roared with laughter, unsettling the mare. "You are just one man. If MacLugh wants Leinster, he'll return with the fighting men of Munster at his back."

Strongheart reined in his temper. "I have the funds to hire Norman knights."

Conor gave him a shrewd glance. "And what's to prevent your Normans from stealing my land?"

"Me. I want to marry your daughter." Strongheart was surprised to find his motives came from wanting Dara and defending her home rather than thoughts of conquest. The image of her in his bed was so appealing, he ruthlessly shoved it to the back of his mind.

Now was no time for dreaming. With the men of Leinster's skills inadequate and their numbers too few, too spread out, holding Leinster's vast lands would be difficult. The castle needed fortifying and the men-at-arms needed training in warfare.

"Dara?" The King's eyes lit. "That little filly was meant to run wild. She isn't ready to settle."

Strongheart raised a brow. "She'd tame under the right man."

Conor shook his head, and Strongheart knew Leinster's king had not seriously considered his offer. "If Dara agrees, come back and we'll talk at greater length. In the meantime, see to training my men and the castle defenses."

At least Conor gave him some hope, but he'd done so knowing how set Dara was against him. Winning her was the key. But then he'd known that from the start. And while he wooed the lady, he would defend her home. "We need armor, weapons, and more horses," Strongheart insisted, knowing he could do only so much without proper equipment.

"I'll consider it." Conor turned back to the mare, ending the conversation.

Strongheart decided against pushing the man. Once he earned Conor's respect, it would be easier to convince him that Leinster was in dire need of weapons and armor.

While he now had the position he wanted, he wouldn't be satisfied until he'd strengthened Leinster's defenses with well-trained and well-armed men. But being put in command was a start. Tomorrow he would take charge of the men.

Right now, he intended to speak to Dara. She should still be in her bath. With a grin of anticipation, he left the barn, entered the castle, and climbed the stairs to her room, wondering how receptive she would be to a marriage proposal. Would the bath and wine have relaxed her into a pliant mood?

He'd last seen her with mud splattered on a face tight with worry. Still, he'd noticed her wet tunic fused to maidenly curves. Taking Dara to wife and making Leinster his home brought a surge of determination, and he took the steps three at a time.

For the first time in many years, his head and heart were in full agreement. He would have the land. He would have Dara.

Now all he needed was her agreement. She might be stubborn, but he was prepared to storm her defenses, until her thoughts, her feelings, and her heart revolved around him.

Strongheart knocked on her door.

Chapter Six

At the knock on the door, Dara jerked awake and the soap plunked into the tub. Gauging from the coolness of the bathwater, she'd dozed. The knock must be Sorcha returning with her tea. At the rap of another knock, she stood in the tub and wrapped her hair in a drying cloth. "Just a moment."

If Sorcha knew how long she'd spent in the tub, she'd be in for a scolding. Her friend had never understood Dara's need for bathing and insisted she'd catch her death of cold. Unwilling to listen to a lecture, Dara dried off quickly, pulled her shift over her head and damp shoulders, and wriggled the material past her hips. She was reaching for her tunic when the knock sounded again.

"Come in. Could you comb out—" Dara's eyes widened.

107

Strongheart stepped into the room, devilishly handsome. For a moment she froze, taking in his incredibly broad shoulders, slim hips, and long, sinewy legs. For an instant, his commanding air of self-confidence had her tongue-tied.

Grabbing her tunic, she held it in front of her, but not before he got a good look. She hadn't taken the time to dry thoroughly, and the wet, thin white linen of her shift was almost transparent. His eyes lit with intense interest. Blood rushed to her cheeks. And the sight of Strongheart's twitching lips stoked her fury.

"How dare you come in here!"

He released a devilish chuckle and crossed his arms over his broad chest, a twinkle in his eyes. "Princess, I knocked, and you invited me in."

" 'Twas a mistake. I thought Sorcha was bringing tea. Now leave," she ordered, drawing as much dignity about her as she could under the circumstances.

Her heart was beating too fast, and she had trouble drawing air into her lungs. The drying towel had fallen from her hair. With her locks tangled and dripping over her shoulders and down her back, she looked as disheveled as she felt.

She needed her full concentration to match wits with the wily Norman. But how could she think when all that separated her from his gaze was sheer linen and a tunic?

If only she could control the dryness in her throat or the sudden pounding of her heart. His ruggedly handsome face had an inherent strength she found devastatingly attractive. With the way her traitorous body responded to his closeness, she didn't trust herself to let him near.

"I came only to talk."

His words might have been meant to calm her frazzled nerves, but his size alone alarmed her. The very way he stood there and took pleasure in confronting her when she was most vulnerable had her steeling her backbone and praying for strength. When he remained standing, staring arrogantly, she reached for the wine bottle. "I'll only tell you once more. Get out."

He crossed his thick arms over his chest. "Your father sent me to speak with you."

"Liar!" Da might suffer from spells of forgetfulness but he would never send this man to her room.

She cocked her arm and threw the bottle. Her aim was true. She would have hit his handsome, smiling face, but he sidestepped her throw with nimble grace and caught the bottle, his expression never changing.

"A princess would make me a good wife."

"This one is spoken for." She took a step backward, thinking from the heated look in his gaze that he meant to compromise her virtue and force her into marrying him to preserve her good name. It wasn't fear that caused her retreat but her own raging desire surging up in response to him.

He took two steps into the room. She retreated until her back rested against the wall.

"MacLugh is not the man for you."

She didn't fail to catch the determination in his tone. While she would never marry MacLugh, she had no intention of revealing that to the Norman.

Although he stood across the room, the space between them contracted until she could feel heat radiating off him. His black eyes bored into her and she felt impaled by his iron-hard gaze while anxiety spurted through her.

From their first meeting she'd sensed the danger in him—his strength, his skill, his determination. The cold draft from the door carried his clean scent, and she wished to take another step away to clear her spinning thoughts. She hadn't expected him to come here, looking better than a Norman had a right to look. And she hadn't expected her body to betray her desire. Even now the heat intensified in the pit of her stomach, and she wondered what kind of woman she would become if she couldn't control her body. "I do not wish to discuss my plans."

"You do not want to argue with me, Princess?" He threw his arms wide, then settled his hands on his hips.

He had yet to touch her. But though she might not be experienced, she knew when a man wanted her. His coal-black eyes burned with the same intensity as when he'd forced her to kiss him. There could be no denying his desire. Or her answering response as she fought her longing to let him take her into his arms. If his mere presence almost made her lose control, she could not allow his touch.

She choked out a nervous laugh at her predicament. To scream and alert others to her situation would bring accusations about her reputation she'd fought so hard to avoid. Although she couldn't deny her attraction to the Norman, she feared the passion flaring like heat lightning between them more. How was it possible to feel such attraction while her mind fought the very idea of wanting him?

"I don't want to argue with you," she said. "I don't want to do anything with you."

The moment she challenged him, she realized her mistake. His brows raised and his voice softened to a dangerous, husky murmur. "You enjoyed our kiss, Princess."

" 'Twas an act," she denied.

"A man knows when a woman is playacting and when she feels true desire."

"You are wrong." Swallowing hard, with every muscle in her body strained rigid, she clutched her tunic with fingers numbed by tension. From across the room, he'd stirred her blood, and she cursed her rebellious body for betraying her.

"I may be wrong about many things—but not about us. You will be mine."

His implacable expression unnerved her, yet his softly whispered words sent a fresh wave of longing straight to her heart. She ached to surrender to her desire, rise onto her toes, press against his hard chest, and permit him to take care of her.

"I will never be yours," she insisted, but even to her own ears, her voice lacked conviction.

His face set in a hard line, all harsh angles, like granite in moonlight. The flickering candles reflected the gaunt cheekbones and squared jaw, the determined tilt of his head, the carved muscle of his neck, and the etched power of his bare arms. But it was his expression that unsettled her. His ambition to have her, combined with pure ruthless wanting, shot fear through her. It wasn't a rational fear like that of being struck by lightning, but the fear of something elemental and just as primitive—the simmering, sizzling tension between them that she couldn't escape.

When he finally turned toward the door, she didn't know whether to feel relief or disappointment. And then he turned to face her again.

"Since I'm a reasonable man, I'll give you time to adjust to the idea of our marriage."

No matter how appealing she might find the Norman, she couldn't marry him. Not when every king in Ireland would raise armies to keep a Norman from gaining Leinster's rich lands. However, she refused to argue his suitability and the political ramifications while standing behind a tunic. Sensing he wouldn't go until she replied, she stalled for time. "The final decision shall be mine."

"And Conor's," he agreed. "All I ask for is the chance to convince you."

From his insistent tone, she surmised he would not back down on this point. Still, she pushed to see how much maneuvering room he'd allow. "And if I say no?"

A muscle clenched along his jaw. "You cannot."

She trembled at the intractable sound of his words. "Why is that?"

"Your father has given his permission for me to court you."

She didn't doubt him, and became increasingly uneasy under his scrutiny. Her father would promise the Norman much to gain his aid. With O'Rourke stirring trouble in the north and MacLugh threatening to return, Leinster needed every fighting man it could muster.

She raised a brow, hoping her haughty expression would put him off. "And you need my cooperation?"

"I think courting more pleasant than fighting," he agreed lightly.

"Especially when the rewards are Leinster and Castle Ferns."

When he didn't deny her accusation she let out her pent-up breath in a frustrated rush, tossed her hair over her shoulder, and tried not to show her disappointment. It would be nice to be wanted for her own charms and not her title or wealth, but she should have known this Norman was no different from her many Irish suitors. Except that never before had she had difficulty with her will yanking her one way, her emotions another.

His mouth curved in tenderness. "I would make a good husband, Princess. I could hold this land for you."

Anxiety trickled down her spine. No matter how sincere, his rash promises would not convince her. "You would bring war."

"There is always war. Would it not be best to unite with a powerful ally? I would protect you."

At his sincerity, her insides melted like heated wax. Even if he defeated her enemies, he couldn't protect her from herself or the torrent of confused feelings flooding her. And if his mere words caused her to consider his proposal, how would she resist him if he touched her or kissed her once more?

She'd turn into a replica of the shallow woman she despised—a woman like her mother, who cared only for pleasure and neglected responsibilities. She clenched her fingers tightly on the tunic, telling herself she had no more backbone than a Kerry slug to fall so low. And yet, when he looked into her inflexible eyes, she wasn't sure she had a choice. Why did he have to tempt her with his soft words and affable smile?

If only Da would send him back to England . . . but Leinster needed his skills too badly for that. And if he stayed, she would have to allow him to court her. Silently cursing the hot-blooded nature she'd inherited from her mother, she fought to steady her trembling hands as her blood pounded an erratic rhythm. How long would it take him to wear down her resistance? How long before she yielded to the primitive side of her nature that she'd tried so hard to keep at bay?

"I'll give you two days."

"Thirty."

She shook her head. "Five days and you leave after you train my father's men-at-arms."

He chuckled, shooting her a look of amused admiration. "Twenty days and you agree to ride with me every day."

"A fortnight and you will not try to kiss me."

He grinned, his air of confidence as appealing as the first rays of sun after a harsh winter rain. "Agreed. Are you up for a ride around the motte?"

Desperate to be free of his presence so she could collect her thoughts, she hesitated. But he pressed her with a reminder of her responsibilities. "During our ride I'll decide the best way to shore up Castle Ferns's defenses."

Strongheart left, and she finally drew her tunic over her head with trembling fingers. Where would she find the strength to resist him?

Luckily, the rains started once again, canceling their plans and allowing her time to rebuild her own defenses. The following morning Strongheart began training Leinster's men, and it wasn't until the next afternoon that they took their ride.

Strongheart met her in the stable with a wide smile. "I'm glad you accepted my invitation."

"I keep my word." She tried not to stare at the flowers braided into Fionn's mane or the panniers of food strapped to his destrier's saddle. Nor did she wish to meet Strongheart's eyes. Instead she focused on a spot past his right ear.

He might sorely test her this day, but she'd decided as she lay tossing and turning in bed the previous night that her best defense was indifference. She wouldn't feast on his scrumptious black eyes, admire his broad shoulders or his courtly words. She'd keep her wits about her and maintain her composure at all costs.

But despite her good intentions, that morning she'd secretly watched him with the men and knew her indifference could not be so easily maintained. Even from a distance, she conceded he possessed a camaraderie with their men, instructing without belittling, automatically assuming the burden of command.

As the men stripped their tunics to practice hand-to-hand fighting, she couldn't veer her eyes from the Norman's magnificent chest, where water droplets sparkled on rippling muscles and powerfully bulging arms moved with the grace and speed of a sika deer. His slick-backed hair emphasized strong cheekbones. And his black eyes glittered with a superior confidence as he unwittingly put on a show of skill and mastery the likes of which Leinster had never seen.

He defeated opponent after opponent, but when one of her father's men tossed him, he roared in approval and clapped the man on the back, a broad smile of respect on his roguish face. After watching how well he'd fit in and the respect he'd won from Leinster's men, she knew keeping up her guard while they rode would prove even more difficult.

Strongheart gave her a leg up to Fionn's bare back, barely restraining himself from caressing her slender ankle. She hadn't said a word about the flowers he'd braided into her horse's mane, and yet he'd seen the encouraging flicker of a pleased smile before she'd once more turned impassive. If she thought to ignore him this day, he would not allow it. He meant to take every advantage of the fourteen days she'd given him to wage a campaign the likes of which she'd never seen.

As they rode under a bright, overcast sky—what the locals called a fine day—he remained silent and patient, secure in the knowledge that Dara was not as indifferent to him as she tried to appear. There hadn't been a cloudless day since he'd come to this land; the skies had ranged from a weighty depressing gloom to a lustrous, almost heavenly pearl. When the clouds did shred away from the sun for a few minutes, the pastures rolled away in innumerable greens set off by the warm stones of endless rock fences. The changing landscape reminded him of Dara and the way she shrouded her emotions, allowing only an occasional glimpse of her warm disposition.

Yesterday, in her room, the passion flowing between them had been unmistakable. Another woman would have been frightened when he'd entered and found her undressed. By the rood, she was lovely. It had taken all his self-restraint to keep his gaze from wandering over every delectable curve, every temptingly revealed hollow of her creamy flesh. She had a wild beauty, seductively high-perched breasts and shapely hips framed by hair tumbling carelessly to her slender waist.

Once Dara's anger had subsided at his invasion of her room, her gaze had revealed a yearning that took every measure of his control to resist. Odd how Dara's reactions seemed backward. Fear came after her desire—not the other way round.

He sighed and patted his warhorse's neck. The rape of her maid might prey on her mind, for a lady should never witness such a brutal act. Despite Dara's bravery it was no wonder she felt fear. He reminded himself to go slowly. Earn her trust.

He cast a sideways glance at her sitting her horse with an ease many a warrior might envy. She'd left her long red hair free to cascade down her back, the tendrils bouncing teasingly along the delicate curve of her neck and over her squared shoulders. Although she looked cold and impervious, he knew better. There was something vulnerable deep in her alluring eyes, an ancient pain of which she never spoke. Her face seemed paler than usual, and he wondered what she was thinking.

While he was trying not to stare at her, Dara

caught him perusing the castle walls for weakness. She sat straighter on Fionn, and he realized from her tender glance at the land how much she loved her home. He didn't want to see her lose her home due to vulnerable points in their defenses. Unless the castle was founded wholly on solid rock, the walls could be tunneled under. But there were methods to combat such tactics and he meant to oversee them. He understood Castle Ferns tied her to the land and her people. She'd want her children to grow up on the moors, play in the heather, and appreciate the lush green pastures.

"Our retainers shelter inside the walls in times of danger," she stated proudly. "Surely you do not see weaknesses in those rock walls?"

The castle with its surrounding bawn was a source of military strength. But Ferns lacked the protection of a moat, and the towers looked old. A few places could use structural support, and Strongheart had already ordered the work to begin under Gaillard's supervision. Funds permitting, he'd like to bring in a stone-throwing machine. Estimating it would take months to set the entire defense in order, but unwilling to disagree on such a fine day, Strongheart kept his opinion to himself.

" 'Tis the villagers who must bear the brunt of the attacks, is it not?"

She nodded. "Houses are burned, cottages ransacked. The cattle and plough horses are driven away and innocent people . . . are killed."

He heard the soft catch in her voice. Had she lost someone dear to her in a raid? Was that the mystery surrounding her mother? Yet there was no dishonor in dying in a raid. And the way MacLugh had spoken of her mother was with the utmost disrespect. He thought it strange how the villagers refused to speak of Dara's mother. Even Gaillard's charm had not yet drawn the information from Sorcha.

"There is too much land to patrol the borders." He patted his warhorse on the neck and sent her a sideways glance. "And the vast herds of cattle make your people vulnerable."

"Raiding is our way of life." She released a small sigh, her fingers twisting a flower in Fionn's mane. "We raid Munster. Munster raids Meath, and Meath steals our cattle. The battles never end, but when our crops are burned and the men do not return, 'tis the women and children who suffer most. The endless raids must cease. I want peace."

Had the wars taken a loved one from her? That would explain the occasional sadness lurking in her emerald eyes. Yet he hesitated to ask directly, hoping she would confide in him. "You don't wish for the riches of Meath?"

She steered around a thick patch of marram grass. "I am content with Leinster. 'Tis my home. But what of you? You never speak of yourself."

Startled by her inquiry, he settled deeper in the saddle. Was she curious due to personal interest or did she seek information to use against him? Her innocent expression gave nothing away. "What would you like to know?" he asked.

"Tell me about your family."

"As you already know, my mother died when I was a child. My father joined her several years ago."

"Are you all alone in this world then? Have you no siblings?"

Her voice sounded sympathetic and less aloof than before. As much as he wished to change the subject, he sensed retreat would be a tactical mistake. To win her trust, he'd have to give her part of his past. "I had a twin."

"Older or younger?"

"He was older by two minutes and glad I was of it. The responsibilities of Pembroke should have fallen to John." He tried to keep the sorrow from his voice but must have failed.

"Is this too painful for you to speak of?"

" 'Twas many years ago." Although his thoughts were lost in the past, suddenly a chill stiffened the hairs at his nape. Like the hiss of air before the strike of a sword, he sensed more than saw a gaze upon him. Scanning past the brambles to the woods for movement, he reined his mount closer to Dara, letting his hand rest lightly on his sword. He'd survived too many battles not to trust his instincts.

"My father was determined to make soldiers of his sons. He relentlessly drilled us in the art of war at an early age. We rode before we could walk. Our first toys were wooden swords. Of the two of us, John was the more aggressive."

"You did not care for your father's training?"

How perceptive she was. Rage at his father's treatment simmered beneath his skin during every battle. He never forgot, never let go of the harsh lessons he'd been forced to master. " 'Twas the only life I knew. When our father caught us reading texts instead of practicing war games, he

burned the texts and beat us. We hid in the stables
and hugged our cat."

Dara couldn't decide which was worse, burning
precious texts or beating children. The picture of
two tear-stained faces, clutching a cat to comfort
them, tore at her. Despite all her promises to remain aloof, her heart went out to the boy he'd
been. Needing to know more but almost fearing
the answer would draw more of her sympathy, she
couldn't curtail her curiosity. "What happened to
your brother?"

He hesitated, watching a strikingly spotted emperor moth rise from the bell heather and alight
on a flower braided into Fionn's mane. She wondered if he felt a stranger here among their bog
grasses, rushes, and liverworts. Could the differences in her land seem as strange and fascinating
to him as he did to her? Surely he didn't interest
her because he was different—because he was
Norman.

The moth flew off and he continued his story.
"At the age of thirteen, we rode at father's side during battle." His face hardened and his voice went
flat. His hand tightened on the reins, his thumb
moving back and forth on the leather. "Our cat
followed us. John lost his life trying to save the
animal. In a fit of rage, Father killed our pet before
my dying brother's eyes."

Dara gasped, her heart aching for him. She
knew the horrible loss of losing a sibling. The agony of his twin's death must have been agonizing.
She glanced into the Norman's stoic face and
glimpsed a hint of pain in his bleak eyes. His massive fists clenched, and she imagined those same

hands when they had been small and he'd been a powerless child, suffering the brutalities of an unfeeling parent.

She would never have guessed they had so much in common. Despite the many years gone by, the tormenting loss of her own half-sister never left her. Just as his loss never left him. But she couldn't allow natural sympathy to alter her view of him.

"Then you became Pembroke's heir?"

His shoulders stiffened and he rubbed his wrist over his brow. "Yes. My father trained me to be the foremost knight in England. Does that scare you?"

" 'Tis cause for unease, not fright."

Softening toward him was not an option—she had to keep an emotional distance. Still, she would know the rest of his story. "And what of your father's lands?"

Although the cords in his neck tightened, his voice, soft and calm, held a note of resolve. "He supported the wrong man in England's civil war. Our family lost Pembroke and our lands, but not our wealth."

So she'd been right all along. Strongheart had come to Eire to seek her land, with her as the ultimate prize. Any sympathy that she'd had vanished like the sun burning off the mountain mist.

He drew his horse so close their knees almost touched. His calloused fingers clenched her arm. Lowering his head, he dropped his voice to a whisper. "Someone's spying from the alder wood. Ride like the wind for the castle, my lady."

Without waiting to see if she obeyed, Strongheart drew his sword and charged straight toward the wood. A fox darted from its hidden hole, and a flock of crows took to the skies, their flapping wings and caws signaling a warning.

Dara's heart leapt to her throat at the thought of him confronting an unknown number of men. She would not leave him to face an enemy alone while she fled for safety. Without a moment's hesitation, Dara drew her dirk and urged Fionn into a gallop.

The spy spotted Strongheart long before he could be identified. Breaking from the cover of the alder trees, the man dug his heels into his mount, used his arm like a whip on his horse's flank, and galloped across the moor, scattering pheasant and startling a red deer. Dara wheeled Fionn around to give chase but Strongheart grabbed her reins, drawing her to a stop.

His dark eyes glinted with barely restrained rage, and his icy voice spoke so quietly she knew he was on the verge of exploding. "I told you to return to the castle."

She raised her brows, meeting his furious gaze with dignity. "This is my land. I don't take orders from you."

"While you are under my protection, you will do as I say. Understood?"

She tried to jerk the reins from his hands, but he might as well have anchored her in stone. "While we argue, he's getting away."

Exasperation filled his tone. "I'll not risk an ambush with you tagging along."

"Fine. Help our enemies. Let him escape."

He ignored her taunt. "Who do you suppose he was?"

"He could have been a spy from the *Ard-ri*." *Or a messenger from the monastery seeking to contact her without the Norman's knowledge*. She shrugged, and kept all expression from her face. She must make a trip there soon—if the Norman ever let her out of his sight.

"Why would the *Ard-ri* send a spy to Leinster?" he asked, apparently accepting her story. As he spoke, he led her and Fionn toward a hilltop where they couldn't be taken by surprise.

"Perhaps he's heard rumors of a Norman among our people." At his frown, she added. "Though in truth the *Ard-ri* and my father are not on the best of terms. Perhaps the occurrence has naught to do with you."

"Does not your father have any friends?" he asked angrily.

Pain lanced her as he prodded scars not yet healed. But, he placed blame on the wrong head, and she would not have him think her father so foolish. "Do not blame Da. Our situation is no fault of his."

He shrugged with skepticism. "If a king is not responsible for choosing his allies and enemies, then who is?"

She refused to tell him about her mother, and so remained silent.

When she didn't speak, Strongheart gave her a suspicious look. "He could be MacLugh's man, I suppose."

"Perhaps. 'Tis more likely O'Rourke or the *Ard-ri* searches for . . . another," she said lamely. The minute the words emerged from her mouth she realized her error. The Norman had a deceptive way of causing her tongue to speak before she'd thought. Although she'd no doubt aroused his curiosity, she had no intention of revealing more.

His tone raised a notch. "Another of your suitors?"

"I warned 'twould be no easy task to win me." She forced a smile, pleased she'd repaired the damage her slip had almost caused.

A cloud passed in front of the sun, chilling her, reminding her she was playing a dangerous game. From the hard planes in his face, she judged the Norman was no fool to be toyed with. Why did she have to find him so attractive?

Between the peculiar stirring of her blood and his sharp wits keeping her off balance, she couldn't concentrate. If only she could master her own good sense. When she'd thought him in danger, she'd ridden by his side, betraying her feelings, and once again proving that when it came to men, she'd inherited her mother's curse.

Strongheart's childhood story had broken down her carefully erected barriers. He suffered the harshest of lives, his father teaching him to live by the sword, and where a weaker man might have perished under the strain, he'd succeeded in becoming a mighty warrior. While he might once have read texts and taken comfort in a cat, no doubt the gentle side of him was now considered a childhood weakness.

She wondered what inner dragons drove him. Had his father squashed all tender feelings? From the looks of the hard, determined man before her, he knew no other way of life than taking want he wanted. Right now he wanted Leinster. And the easiest way for him to gain Leinster was through her.

Yet she didn't fear the strength he could so easily use against her. He was a man of honor. Although she sensed his obsessive need to win, he would use his might for conquest. To conquer a woman, he'd use overwhelming charm.

And damn him, his strategy was working. He elicited feelings that made her blood surge and her breath tighten. Even now, as they rode to the hill's peak without a word passing between them, she was too aware of him, noticing the little things, the way his gaze constantly scanned the horizon, the way he kept his sword arm free for use, the way his glance softened when he looked at her.

Ahead two men suddenly stepped out from beyond a rocky crag. Before she uttered a word, Strongheart urged his mount forward with lightning speed, and drew his sword.

Chapter Seven

Two unarmed men afoot would not pose a threat to Strongheart. But they could be friends of the spy who had just fled, and it could be a trap. With Dara to protect he could not be too cautious.

The two men had shaved the fronts of their heads, the rest of their hair parted in the middle and extended from ear to ear. Both wore brown serviceable tunics with cowls, and sandals. Although their appearance suggested the men were monks and belonged to a holy order, Strongheart didn't lower his weapon until Dara voiced a greeting.

She dismounted and sought to reassure him. " 'Tis the Abbot Mata of Ara-mor and Brother Assicus, a skilled bronzesmith." She turned to the men. "Would you care to share our repast?"

Strongheart sheathed his sword, recognizing

the relief in her tone. Was she merely glad to come upon friends instead of the spy they'd chased away? Or was she pleased they were no longer alone?

Odd how the men showed up here, almost as if they'd known Dara would be at this particular spot at this particular time. But she hadn't known which direction he'd picked to ride. He hadn't decided himself until he'd asked Sorcha the best place to take her mistress for a meal. Perhaps the maid had mentioned their destination to Dara. She could have sent word ahead.

He gave himself a mental shake. The woman had him so wound up, he imagined plots where none existed. If there was a monastery about, he hadn't seen it. But the men couldn't have walked far, since they carried no provisions.

From her relaxed stance Dara obviously knew these men well, so he let her approach the strangers and perform introductions. The abbot, Mata, was a short man, whipcord thin, and the calluses on his palms revealed he worked the land. The smithy was huge, his muscles bulging, his skin tanned and leathered.

"Thank you for the offer," the abbot said, smiling at Dara kindly, "but today is Wednesday, fast day, and no food is taken before the ninth hour."

Monks typically weren't allowed contact with women, nor did they engage in idle talk. Of course, every order followed different rules, but Strongheart had to wonder over Dara's seeming familiarity with the two men.

Mata nodded in deference to Strongheart. "I'm sorry to interrupt your plans. If you would excuse

us but a moment." Turning to Dara, he gestured
to a spot farther away. "I need a private word with
Princess O'Dwyre and then we will be on our way."

Dara looked relieved to be so easily rid of
Strongheart, and he didn't like it one bit. There
could be many reasons for them not wanting him
to overhear their conversation—none of them to
his liking. Strongheart dismounted and approached. "I am responsible for the lady's safety."

The abbot turned to face him without fear or
haste. "I mean her no harm."

Strongheart crossed his arms over his chest.
"She stays with me."

Dara and the abbot exchanged a long glance.
Finally she turned to Strongheart. Not quite meeting his gaze, she licked her bottom lip in the
strained silence. "The monastery is nearby, and I
may not come this way again soon."

His brow curved up. "And what business have
you in a monastery?"

"The monks work and pray. But they also read
and write. For many years Da has supported the
order. The monks copy texts and their scribes are
skilled in illustrating books."

"We are working on a biblical encyclopedia," the
abbot added.

Did they expect him to be so foolish as to divert
him from the real reason they were here? Out of
respect for the religious order, he maintained a
civil tone. "You need Dara's help?"

"Her artistry is among the finest in our land."

So his future wife was as skilled with a pen as a
dirk. He would not let the abbot shock him into

yielding to his patient request. "But you are not here for drawing, are you?"

Dara glared at him. "How dare you harass the abbot? The man is a saint."

"But you are not."

Two bright spots of pink flamed her elegant cheekbones at his comment, and her fists clenched at her sides. As he fought to contain a grin, the corners of his mouth twitched. Just as his body instinctively responded to hers, he instinctively knew that in this instance he could not trust her. "You are scheming and I would know why."

She bit her full pink lower lip and twisted her hands. "This is not your affair. It has naught to do with you."

"But it does." He paused and their gazes locked. He was now certain she'd instructed Sorcha to mention they ride this way. "If it concerns you, then it concerns me."

She sighed, placed her fists on her hips, and her voice rose. "Need I remind you we are not wed?"

Strongheart suppressed his impatience. What would it take to convince her they were on the same side? "And need I remind you that we *will* be wed?"

She rolled her eyes and sent him a smile that held more cynicism than warmth. "I never forget a threat."

" 'Tis not a threat, but a promise."

"You are to be wed?" the abbot asked with a furrowed brow, his head cocked to the side.

"Yes," he said.

"No," she insisted.

The holy man looked from one to the other. When it appeared as if neither Strongheart nor Dara intended to back down, he emitted a warm chuckle. Mata turned to Dara and spoke cryptically. "The *Ard-ri* says he'll consider your request."

Disappointment clouded her face. "Damn. Oh, sorry for the bad language, Mata. Was there more?"

"Yes, child. MacLugh and O'Rourke are fighting to the north."

"Good."

"But they've called a truce."

She gasped. "Not good. Do you have word of peace talks?"

"Not yet. The word is the *Ard-ri* himself might come to settle the dispute."

Dara paled and her breath came in short gasps. "I do not like all my father's enemies gathering in one place. Has the *Ard-ri* committed himself to arbitrate?"

"Word is that he's infatuated with his new red-haired mistress and does not wish to leave her."

Strongheart didn't understand all the implications of their conversation, but several things were clear. For a devout man, the abbot kept himself well informed. And Dara was not pleased with his tidings that Munster and Meath might call a truce.

"And I have a message from your—"

"It will have to wait," Dara cut the man off sharply, looked at Strongheart and flushed to the roots of her hair. She grabbed Mata's arm so hard her knuckles turned white.

For the second time that morning the Norman

wondered what she was hiding. Surely a holy man wouldn't bring word from a secret lover? And what message had she sent to the *Ard-ri*? He'd bet his warhorse Conor knew naught of her shenanigans.

Without a mother's guidance, Conor had let his beautiful daughter run wild, but she needed a firm hand to keep her from trouble. She was so full of contradictions, Strongheart had difficulty understanding her. The picture of her leaping from her horse, stabbing Sorcha's attacker with a knife, was so vivid he would never forget it. The image of her bloodthirsty need for revenge conflicted with her spoken desire for peace.

Why would a woman who hated war wield a weapon like a warrior? Why did she send secret messages to the *Ard-ri*, her father's enemy? And why did she fight so hard to deny the passion they both knew was growing between them?

She might seem light and innocent on the surface, but she'd easily deceive all but the most perceptive of men. Through Sorcha's machinations, she'd outsmarted him, manipulating him to this meeting with the monks.

Perhaps he could use the monk's dire messages to his advantage. With their enemies forming an alliance, she would have need of his warrior skills. If he summoned patience, she would eventually come to him for help.

Unfortunately patience wasn't his strong suit. After the monks departed, he had a difficult time refraining from asking questions. But with a determination inherent to his character, he forced himself to lighten her mood and act the gentle-man.

From the ridge, no one could take them una-wares. The broad-leaved forests below thinned to open meadows before the ground rose to this peaceful hillock. Below, low-lying riverside pas-tures spread before them, abundant with pine martens, squirrels, and song thrush.

Dara unpacked a blanket from the pannier and spread it on the grass. While Strongheart tethered the horses, she removed the food and laid out cold chicken, Leinster cheese, fresh wheat bread, and wine.

Dara used the moment alone to set her racing thoughts in order. Had the spy they'd flushed out of the wood somehow known of her intent to meet with Mata? Or had it been sheer coincidence?

And what of Strongheart? He'd used the utmost restraint and had not asked one question since the monks left. If only she trusted the Norman . . . but too much was at stake.

After carefully removing his sword, but placing the weapon within reach, Strongheart settled be-side her on the blanket. "Do you receive surprise visitors often?"

She scooted as far away from him as she could get while remaining on the blanket. "We are known far and wide for our hospitality," she mur-mured vaguely, without answering his question.

"You can't reach the food from over there, can you?" he teased.

Reluctantly she edged a little closer, her shoul-ders stiff. Why couldn't she relax around this man? She no longer thought he might pounce and force her to give him another kiss. But the reminder of the first time he'd held her caused her stomach to knot and her heart to flutter.

She looked out across the land of greens and purples and dramatic shapes and contours under a changing canopy of blue and white blown in from the Atlantic. This was her home. She'd explored the mountains and moorlands, appreciated the lush river valley, lowland bogs, steep cliffs, and broad sandy beaches. She raised her fingers to the shamrock at her neck and promised herself that O'Dwyres would always live here.

She wrenched her thoughts to the conversation at hand, then realized he'd asked a question and she'd lapsed into silence. He was looking at her with a perceptive intensity that made her want to squirm.

Brushing back the hair from her face, she pretended to be calm.

"I'm sorry. What did you say?"

"What caused the enmity between your father and the *Ard-ri*?"

She helped herself to a drumstick, but the thought of eating made her queasy. "I don't want to talk about it."

Strongheart suffered no such malady. The balmy Irish air seemed to have increased his appetite. His straight white teeth tore into a chicken breast. "And how did he make an enemy of O'Rourke?"

With a sigh, she tossed aside the chicken and sipped her wine. "I don't want to speak of that, either."

He bit into the cheese. "Then tell me about your mother."

"No." Did he suspect that all the answers he sought were different pieces of the same giant puzzle? She couldn't meet his eyes, so instead she looked toward the bullfinches and spotted flycatchers that soared and dipped above the thickets near the wood.

"Princess, we are running out of subjects to talk about."

"Don't you have secrets, Norman?"

From the startled look on his face she surmised her question had taken him by surprise. She hadn't given him time to conceal the pain in his eyes, but within the space of a heartbeat the lines of his face settled into a stoic mask.

"Now you know how it feels to have someone prying into your past." She spoke softly, twisting a blade of grass in her hand.

He reached out and covered her hand with his. "I'm sorry, Princess. Forgive me. I meant only to help."

At his touch, warmth flared from her fingertips, raced along her arm, and settled over her shoulders like a warm shawl. She should jerk away, but how could she when he'd just apologized so gently? The pad of his thumb circled repeatedly in her palm, and she shivered at the intimacy.

You can do this. She was overreacting only because she was not accustomed to being touched. Holding hands was such a small affection—if she concentrated, she should be able to slow her racing blood and curb her hammering heart.

With his free hand, he plucked a berry from a

bowl and raised it to her lips. "Try one. You haven't eaten enough to feed a kitten."

Obediently, she opened her mouth, expecting him to place the berry between her parted lips. Instead, staring into her eyes with a power that wrenched her soul, he teased the succulent berry over her waiting lips. Finally, he let her take the fruit. Her tongue captured the sweet juice, and she swallowed, the sweetness trickling down her throat.

He fed her berry after berry, one by one, until her lips became so sensitized to his touch that she ached for another kiss. She gazed into his smoky black eyes and wondered what was wrong with her. He was Norman. A man who had openly declared his intent of wooing her to gain her land. So why did her stomach tighten every time he looked her way?

It mattered not that he was handsome. Surely it had to be more than his looks that sent her every nerve tingling. She pulled away and lay back with her hands clasped behind her head, gazing at the high soaring clouds with their infinite mackerel patterns in the gray sky.

He lay on his side looking down at her, elbow bent, head resting in his palm. "Your lips are as red and juicy as the berries."

"You must leave me alone now."

He grinned teasingly. "That wasn't our agreement, Princess. If I leave you alone, you'll ignore me, and then you'll never learn what a nice man I can be."

"But I don't want you to be nice," she protested petulantly.

He chuckled, the warm rich sound of his laugh melting her insides to warm honey. His finger touched her temple and drew a tantalizing line down her cheek. "You'd rather I threw you over my shoulder, carried you off, and forced a priest to marry us?"

"Of course not."

"Then what do you want?"

She closed her eyes, debated for a moment, and decided to be honest. "I want my husband to love me—not for my beauty, not for my lands, not for my title. I would want my husband to adore me if I were a peasant, if I had no power, if I came without dowry."

"That's not the way of the world." He sat up then and shifted around by her head, his hands gently rubbing her shoulders. "If you insist on believing in fairy tales, your heart will be broken."

"I'm not a child," she protested, refusing to accept that he could so easily trod on her dreams.

She should stop him from touching her, but the caress felt so good. His hands found her tight muscles and eased them, while at the same time, dangerous feelings welled in her heart. For just a few hours she wanted to forget her responsibilities and pretend she was a mere kitchen girl and he a visiting man-at-arms.

"You aren't a child, but you need someone to take care of you."

The heat of his hands rubbing her shoulders flowed over her back in a rhythm that sent tiny trembles down her spine. "I can take care of myself. Besides I have Da and Sorcha."

"They can't keep you warm at night."

She was about to protest that the cozy fire in her room kept away the winter chills, but his touch had kindled heat through her—and not just in the places he touched. From the roots of her hair to the tips of her toes, she felt flushed. Her flesh came alive on its own accord, tightening, rippling with goose bumps as after a refreshing spring rain.

It could not be an accident that he knew just where to touch, exactly how much pressure to apply. "How many women have you kept warm at night?"

At her question, his hands stopped moving, then continued. " 'Tis not a proper question for a lady."

She arched a brow. "That makes the answer all the more interesting, don't you think?"

"I should turn you over and paddle you," he threatened.

Somehow, she couldn't take his threat seriously. Why would he strike a woman when he could so easily charm her? "Would you beat your wife?"

He chuckled again. "There are much better ways to control a woman."

She wasn't surprised that he'd confirmed her suspicion, and the amusement in his voice made her curious. "Like how?"

"Like this." His hands edged under her tunic.

Her heart galloped. His fingers slid slowly, deliciously lower until his hands covered her breasts. Only her thin linen shift separated her flesh from the warmth of his hands. She hadn't known her skin could be so sensitive. When his palms cupped her peaks in a circular movement, it drove her mad, and her back arched instinctively until she pressed toward him. Her nipples budded, and still she couldn't get enough.

She bit her lip to suppress a groan of delight. She hadn't known such bliss existed. A direct line of fire blazed from her breasts to heat her core. She wanted him. She ached to rip off her clothes and press her bare flesh to his. She wanted his lips against hers. His caress was only enough to tease.

She wanted more. More of him—just like her mother.

No.

She wouldn't let desire rule her actions. Though it took every bit of her determination, she must put an end to this sweet torment.

"Stop. Please, you must not."

"Whatever you say, Princess." He withdrew his hands, giving one last flick of pleasure to her nipples, leaving her gasping, her emotions stretched taut.

She dared not open her eyes until she regained a measure of control. *Breathe—in and out.* Slowly, the roaring receded from her ears, and yet the heightened desire didn't abate. He no longer touched her, but like hunger unappeased, her appetite hadn't been satisfied.

His fingers played with a loose tendril of her hair. "Can you deny you want me?"

"Yes." Opening her eyes, she snatched her hair from his grasp, welcoming the pain that should have distracted her from her sensitive flesh, but instead left her wanting his arms around her.

The sun shined down, emphasizing the glimmer of amusement on his lips and the glint of passion in his eyes. "If I've left you unaffected, perhaps I could remedy that with a kiss."

"No. Do not." She rolled off the blanket and onto the grass, afraid that if he touched her again she would yield to the current rushing through her and be carried away on a tide of passion. Her chest heaved, and she stood shakily on trembling limbs.

He remained on the blanket and looked up at her with mocking concern. "Your face is flushed."

She would never admit how hard it was to pull away. "It's hot."

"And you are breathing hard."

"I'm fine."

"Ah, yes. You are very fine. Never have I felt skin so soft, silky, sensual. A man could feel like a king after the privilege of touching you, of feeling such a wondrous response."

The heat rose to her cheeks at his teasing. "I was cold."

He chuckled. "Hot. Or cold? Or confused? Which will it be?"

"You have the manners of a Kerry slug!" Just as he'd trapped her with all-too-appealing sensations, he'd attempted to entangle her with words. No man from Eire would have been so bold. Panic surged through her at his knowing smile, as if he knew how difficult it was to pull away, as if he knew her secret. Unable to face him for another moment, she spun around and raced to Fionn.

He jumped to his feet. "Wait. 'Tis not safe for you to ride alone."

Behind her, she heard the pound of his footsteps and urged her feet faster. She couldn't let him touch her—not ever again. Leaping onto Fionn's bare back, she grabbed the reins and realized he'd tied his warhorse to hers. It would serve him right to have to walk back to Castle Ferns.

With the horse's reins tied together, she urged Fionn to a gallop, but his big warhorse lagged behind. Glancing over her shoulder, she saw Strongheart's horse limp. Could nothing go right this day? While she might leave the Norman to walk, she would not risk his horse in a gallop with a stone lodged in its hoof.

She pulled Fionn to a halt, slid off his back, and patted Strongheart's nervous warhorse on the neck. "Heh, fella. I won't hurt you," she crooned. Running her hand down his strong neck to his broad chest, she eased slowly along his flank to his rear hoof.

Bending, she forced him to stand on three legs while she surveyed the damage. Within a moment Strongheart joined her, leaning over, his chest so close to her back she could feel his heat.

His clean musky scent washed over her, flooding her with the remembrance of why she'd fled. His deep voice, so close to her ear, made the little hairs on her arms and neck stand on end.

"Did he pick up a stone?"

"I think so. Yes. There it is."

She held the warhorse's foot aloft, and Strongheart plucked out the stone. Then with his thumb, he massaged the pad of the horse's hoof. She recalled those gentle hands on her breasts and stood so abruptly, she knocked against the horse. The warhorse snorted, and Strongheart's hand clasped her waist, helping her regain her balance.

"Thank you for stopping."

"I would not want the horse to pull up lame."

"And what of my feet?" He held out one shiny leather boot, a roguish arch to his eyebrow. "These were not made for walking. We'll have to ride double."

The trip back was a mere hour, but she knew it would be the longest hour she'd ever known. She sat on Fionn's back, and Strongheart nimbly pulled himself up behind her. Gritting her teeth, she pretended his hard body tight against her had no effect.

"My warhorse has saved my life many times, but I don't think he's ever arranged anything quite this pleasant."

She wanted to slap him for sounding so smug. If she'd thought he'd deliberately arranged for his horse to pick up a stone, she would have dumped him onto the ground. With her back to him and his hard thighs cradling hers in such an intimate position, she blushed instead. When Fionn walked, Strongheart's chest brushed her back, his hand wound loosely around her waist. She should order him to remove it, but instead she pretended as if his hand on her waist were nothing more than an innocent girdle. She should be good at the deception. Powerful passions had always coursed through her blood—she just hadn't known how hard they could be to control.

A breeze flung a lock of her hair near his face, and he breathed deeply, then let out a long sigh. "Your hair smells like roses."

She snatched her hair down and tried to still the trembling that ran through her like the summer breeze. "Just remember roses have thorns."

His hand caressed her hip. "Prickly flowers have the softest petals, do they not?"

She tried to sit up straighter, knowing there could never be anything between them. The Norman didn't need to know her secrets. She'd keep them bottled up inside her forever.

Chapter Eight

Dara should have known better than to confront
her father in the sweltering heat of the barn. The
rare cloudless day combined with unbearable
summer temperatures and no wind had left everyone sticky and miserable. Even the weeping willow branches outside the stable failed to stir.

Wiping the perspiration off her brow and careful to step around the cat nursing her kittens in
the corner of the barn, she approached the stall
where he knelt beside mare and foal.

Looking up from the foal with a bemused expression on his face, her father smiled in greeting.
"The wee one is fine."

Her heart turned over as he took simple pleasure in the unsteady colt and the protective mare.
"I'm glad. We can always use another good horse.

144

This breed is much superior to our Connemara ponies."

The deep lines around his eyes crinkled. "Must your thoughts always run to such practical matters? Can you not enjoy the beauty of birth and life?"

Her father knew her so well. She advanced, knelt beside him, and gave him a peck on the cheek. "I'm worried about the Norman."

"You leave the worrying to me."

If only she could, but Da had become even more forgetful than usual. This morning he'd ordered a feast for MacLugh's arrival, forgetting the man had already come and gone. She'd had to cancel his plans and smooth out the difficulties in the kitchen. Dara sighed and pulled her tunic from where it stuck to the moisture trickling between her breasts. "Mata sent a message."

"Well, don't keep me waiting. What did the monk say?"

"O'Rourke and MacLugh have formed a truce. The *Ard-ri* may arbitrate the dispute."

Her da waved his hand, and the foal shied away. "And what of *her*?"

Why could her father not forget her mother? Although he hadn't seen her in years, he always asked about her. Still, Dara hated to disappoint him. "There was no message."

Her father frowned and turned back to the foal. "Mata always brings me her messages."

"We could not speak freely in front of the Norman," Dara explained with as much patience as

145

she could muster. "Come, let's find a spot of shade and perhaps a stray breeze."

They walked outside. Not a red grouse ruffled the grass, and the puffins and greenland whites napped in the heat. The sun beat down unmercifully as Dara led him beneath the weeping willow tree. Only the Norman had the energy to move in the heat, and he ruthlessly drilled the men in the far fields, his huge form dominating the other men and drawing her gaze. While other men moved with a sluggish weariness due to the combination of heat and exercise, he attacked and parried with the precision and fluidity that belied hours of practice.

After she and her father settled themselves against the tree, she came to the point. "I will not marry the Norman."

"Of course not." Conor patted her hand. "You are betrothed to Borrack MacLugh."

She tried to be patient. "We sent MacLugh away."

"He'll be back." Conor smirked with satisfaction. "You can beguile a man just like your mother."

She hated these conversations where she had to resort to explaining the facts to her father in the simplest of terms. "MacLugh wants Leinster."

"Of course he does. What man would not?"

She fanned her face with her hand, feeling limp as the weeping branches of the willow. "What MacLugh cannot gain through marriage, he will try to take by force. He and O'Rourke may be plotting, and O'Rourke still has not forgiven you for stealing his wife."

A dreamy smile lit Conor's face. "I did not have to steal her. At my invitation, the colleen herded her cattle, packed her jewels, and left O'Rourke."

Dara had no wish to argue about the past. "If the *Ard-ri*—"

"The *Ard-ri* has no liking for O'Rourke."

Dara lifted the braid off her neck, coiled her hair, and used it as a pillow against the tree. "The *Ard-ri* may dislike Normans more." Her gaze shot to the field as Strongheart defeated yet another opponent. "You must send the Norman away."

"We need him." Her father's eyes cleared, and he measured her with his old shrewdness. "I am not as strong as I once was. Discipline is lax. The Norman will train our men."

Why couldn't she convince her father that Strongheart's presence could unite their enemies? And all the training of Leinster's men would not put off the armies of O'Rourke, MacLugh, and the *Ard-ri*.

Conor rubbed his chin. "We should buy English armor."

Did men think of nothing but war? She bit back her frustration. "If you buy armor, the men will want to test their advantage in battle. With superior armaments we'll defeat the other clans." She shifted her position and slapped her thigh for emphasis. "Then our enemies will purchase armor and come seeking revenge. Why can we not have peace?"

Her father's chest puffed out. "In my day, I increased the size of Leinster twofold."

Without thinking, the words slipped from her mouth. "Was it worth your daughter's life?" Her hand jerked to her mouth, her throat tight with the old memories. "I'm sorry, I should never have said that."

" 'Tis your temper that you got from your mother."

Her temper was not the only similarity between mother and daughter. Just thinking of the Norman caused her face to flush hot. Whenever he was nearby, her eyes involuntarily sought him out. She couldn't help admiring his strength, nor could she ignore her body, which seemed so tingly and alive.

Controlling her raging feelings proved almost impossible, and the cursed Norman refused to allow her to avoid him. He went out of his way to share a glance, a smile, a caress. And each time her heart jogged a little faster.

Even when he wasn't there, he constantly left reminders. She found flowers by her plate, on her pillow, under her blankets. Last night, beneath her window, Carolan had serenaded her with a love song—leaving no doubt about whom he sang. This morning she'd found a bottle of scent on her bureau and potted yellow gorse in a corner. A grin twitched her lips. Who but the Norman would think to bring a plant inside a room? The way he was distributing flowers, every servant in the castle must be in on his plans.

Keeping up her guard while he constantly wore down her defenses tested her convictions. If only she didn't have such an inner weakness. His touch could rob her of all reason, and she'd become lost in swirling sensation.

She couldn't let those feelings surface, for once

they did, she would succumb, and the balance of power within Eire was too fragile for her to act without reason. The Norman was a threat to peace, and she would not be responsible for starting a war that would engulf all Eire.

Once again she turned to her father and gripped his gnarled hand, hoping to make him see the situation clearly. "Promise me that you will send the Norman away after he finishes training your men-at-arms."

Conor stared through watery eyes gone blank again. "Do as you like, my dear. Do as you like."

Dusting off her hands, she climbed to her feet, intending to do just that. Strongheart had just dismissed the men, who walked back complaining about his difficult training. But even she could see, despite the sweat running in rivulets down their faces, the men bore proud expressions. Gaillard was scooping up lances, spears, and axes, and straightening a target of hay. When he finished, he waved to Strongheart, then headed to the river with the rest of the men. Bathing might be frowned upon, but a swim would be heavenly in this squelching heat.

Strongheart looked up as she approached. "The men need armor, but they are learning the rudiments of discipline."

Leinster's men knew more than the rudiments, but it was simply too hot to argue over minutia. She did her best to ignore the hard, sculpted muscles of his chest that tapered to a flat, albeit scarred, stomach. "How long before the men are fully trained?"

With tunic in hand, he wiped his dusty face. As

if unaware of her perusal of his strong jaw and his brooding stare, he tossed the garment over her shoulder and stood cleaning his sword with a rag, wiping off the bits of grime and dust until it gleamed. "Until they have mail and helms, the men cannot be properly trained."

"Our foes do not wear mail."

He cocked a brow. "Is that what you came here to discuss, training the men?"

Sometimes she thought he had the ability to see right through her. Her stomach fluttered at the heat in his eyes, and savagely she tamped down the emotion. She would not let her thoughts gallop out of control down the path he steered. She would not let him touch her again.

She shrugged casually. "I merely wondered how long it would be till you left."

"That anxious to be rid of me, are you?"

"Yes."

He sheathed his sword and cleaned his dirk. "Do I have that great an impact on you, then?"

She swatted a fly buzzing around her head, wishing she could shoo Strongheart away as easily. "Of course you have an impact on me. I ride with you daily when I should be working on our accounts, seeing to the harvest of cabbages, and cutting hyssop and parsley."

She shut her mouth. Her wits must be scrambled. Here she was muttering about parsley like an addlepated ninny, so she couldn't blame him for shaking his head and grinning.

She fisted her hands on her hips. "The sooner you leave, the better."

This time he chuckled outright. "Better for whom?"

"You'll get us killed."

He shook his head. "I'm here to protect you. Come, 'tis too hot to argue. Where shall we ride today?"

" 'Tis too hot to ride," she muttered crossly, knowing he patronized her. How dare he not take her seriously? Before he'd come, she could reason with her father, but now Conor seemed content to leave Leinster's defense in a stranger's care.

"You're right. Where should we go instead?"

She'd been longing to visit the glade, but she would not take him to her isolated, private spot. Perhaps she could send him to the river with the other men, and she could sneak off by herself. "Can you swim, Norman?"

"Do you think to drown me?" he asked.

She gasped at the surge of memories his question provoked. Not now, she thought, as she struggled against a rising tide of panic. She couldn't let herself remember.

Strongheart watched in alarm as Dara's face paled and she started to sway. He stepped forward to catch her, and though she feebly pushed him away, she was no match for his strength.

Strongheart swept her into his arms, and carried her toward the hall and shade, calling to a passing servant to fetch a goblet of water. Had the heat caused her to almost faint? Or was it something he'd said?

She'd turned white as a goat's tail when he mentioned drowning. His gentle teasing had been innocent. Obviously there was something else she

151

hadn't told him and he wondered how long it would take to learn all her secrets. As he carried her into the hall and placed her on a straw bed covered with hide, she stirred. The maid brought water, and she sipped it greedily. Green eyes flecked with gold raised to his but couldn't hold his gaze. "The heat must have—"

He was beginning to know her well enough to guess when she lied. " 'Twas not the heat."

She lay back and closed her eyes. "I need rest."

He stood over her, watching her chest rise and fall, much too rapidly for someone who pretended such weakness. Was this a ruse to be left alone? If it was, she had no idea how determined he'd become. Yes, he still wanted the land. But he wanted her, too—not just for what she brought with her, but for herself. The thought startled him, but then, why should wanting her be so surprising? He couldn't keep his gaze from following her about the hall, and her gaze surreptitiously watched him, flicking away when he caught her eye.

If he were a holy man he would say they shared a spiritual connection. But his interest was much more worldly. Ever since he'd kissed her, he'd ached to take her into his arms and show her how he felt. He could make her happy. He could protect her. What more could she want? It wasn't as if she didn't respond to him. By the rood, he'd never known such passionate response from a woman. Yet she was determined to fight him, and he could not understand why.

Her lids fluttered, and he caught her peeking at him. Just as he suspected, the brat was faking her discomfort. Well, two could play this game. He'd just see how long she could lie still under his ministrations.

After ordering a maid to bring a bucket of water, soap, and a few cloths, he pulled a stool near Dara's feet and removed her slippers, glad she'd the good sense not to wear hose in this heat.

With the necessary supplies at his fingertips, Strongheart dipped the cloth into the cool well water, wrung the cloth out, then brushed it along her feet. She groaned, her lips trembled, but she didn't open her eyes.

At this hour, the hall was silent. Many of the help had gone off to the coolest spot they could find for an afternoon nap. Strongheart slipped the cloth over each slender foot, taking care between her pink toes. Next he laved soap onto the drenched cloth and lathered her feet, trailing his fingers over her soles and delicate ankles.

He dragged the cloth slowly over her skin, unwilling to miss an inch of flesh. His fingers massaged a tight spot in the arch of her foot and, unable to maintain her pretense, her eyes flew open with a giggle. "That tickles."

"Feeling better?"

"Much."

He dipped the soapy cloth into the bucket, then with a fresh cloth rinsed the soap off her feet, his fingers slowly and sensuously sliding over her trembling flesh. With a drying cloth, he again slowly wiped heel, arch, and toes, thinking how much he'd enjoy washing her entire body. Compared to his leathered, sun-bronzed skin, hers was incredibly alluring, white and soft as the finest down.

He longed to lift her skirts and explore her lean and sleekly muscled legs, but reminded himself to go slowly. He didn't like the fear that narrowed her eyes whenever she felt passion. And it seemed odd that a woman who rode and played games as fiercely as this one could be afraid of her natural feelings.

At first he'd thought Dara's witnessing the rape of Sorcha caused her anxiety, but her fears went much deeper and he sensed they were old. Had some man forced himself upon her? Or was it simply that she hadn't a mother to explain that the act between men and women could be pleasurable for all concerned?

Despite his intention to go slowly, while his thoughts roamed, his hands had wandered seemingly of their own accord, kneading her calves, teasing the delicate flesh behind her knees. She sat up and yanked her feet back, drawing them under her, her face flushed, though whether from the heat or newly found desire, he wasn't sure.

Her long lashes framed eyes as green and sparkling as the pastures after a summer rain. The nostrils of her dainty nose flared with every breath, but her lips parted as if she couldn't draw enough air through her nose. At her gasp, her cheeks hollowed, emphasizing the fine lines of her aristocratic cheekbones. She stood, sliding her feet into her slippers. "I feel better, thank you. I think I'll go to my room and lie down."

Although she hadn't stuttered, her speech was stilted with just the slightest pause between words. Was she lying? Although the castle was shaded from the sun, not a breath of air stirred

Conquer the Mist

within its walls. Forcing his brow not to crease into a frown, he replied blandly. "A nap might do you good."

She practically raced up the steps, not exactly the action of an ailing woman. So the minx wished to be rid of him. He swallowed a grin. What scheme was she up to now?

Dara, heart pounding, sneaked down the stairs, unwilling to endure the stifling heat another moment. Strongheart should have left long ago to seek a cool spot, perhaps join his men in the river.

Dressed in the plain gray tunic of a kitchen maid and with her hair tucked under a cap, she scurried to the stable, head and eyes downcast. The bailey was empty, and she slipped into the stable without drawing notice.

The kittens had scattered to the shadiest and coolest areas of the stable. Fionn greeted her with a snort, as eager to escape the stifling barn as she.

"How about a swim, fella?" she murmured as she slipped on his bridle. "You'd like that, wouldn't you?"

A few minutes later, she galloped across the moor, urging Fionn with her knees, appreciating the breeze. Once they reached the wood, she slowed the animal, unwilling to force speed on such a hot day. Even among the shade of the trees, sweat trickled down her neck, soaking her tunic. She guided Fionn to a private glade, upriver from the spot where the men swam, where the river forked and formed a wondrous waterfall emptying into a crystalline pool of cold blue mountain water. Overhead, green-leaved oaks and ash shaded the well-worn path, and the sunlight left dimpled patterns of light and dark on the ferns and mosses.

Picking up the scent of water, Fionn increased his pace. The gurgle of water descending over rocks greeted them, and finally, they broke through the last of the woods. A jay soared upward at their disturbance, and a doe, startled by their intrusion, fled into the forest.

Fionn no longer needed urging. Instead of stopping at the rocky bank for a drink, the animal whinnied and plunged chest deep into the water. In the clear pool, fish leapt from their path. With a laugh of delight, Dara slipped off Fionn's back and swam farther into the pool.

Her strokes caused lazy ripples upon the water, that spread and flattened in ever-widening circles until they lapped the rocky banks. Tiny crabs scuttled through the shallows, and larger, darting creatures were trapped in the rock-locked pool. The colors of the scene seemed bright and defined without shadow, the pool a blinding mirror of welcoming light.

As a child, she'd come here often to swim and play in the falls and the secret cave. With long, sure strokes, she swam to the waterfall, pleased she'd outwitted the Norman and ridded herself of his overpowering presence. While the pool was not truly warm, the sun had heated the more tranquil waters by a few degrees. But where the diverted river water tumbled into the pool, the water was coldest, and she longed for the icy shivers to sluice over her heated flesh.

A dark head suddenly popped from the depths of the pool beside her. Every muscle froze, preventing her from issuing a terrified scream. Instead she treaded water. And gaped. As he tossed dark hair from his face, she recognized the Norman's glinting eyes, and her fright fueled her anger. "You followed me!"

He spit a mouthful of water in a graceful arch toward his warhorse, from this angle no longer hidden behind a pile of rocks. "Guilty."

"How dare you scare me? What in begorra are you doing here?"

He chuckled. "What do you think?"

Before she answered, he ducked underwater, and she glimpsed his breeches-covered backside and long legs before he dived deep under the surface. He stayed under for a long while, but she refused to let his antics concern her. His sudden appearance had accelerated her pulse and ruined her swim. How dare he follow her, spy on her, act as if he had every right to be here. She could no longer play uninhibitedly below the icy fall and disappointed, swam instead to a smooth rock by the pool's edge.

From below, a hand grabbed her ankle, yanking her under. Furious at his playful mood, she decided he in turn could use a good scare. She shook off his grip and without coming up for air, she swam deeper underwater, searching for the cave. Her hands gripped the hidden entrance, and she pulled herself inside, her head bursting the surface as she greedily gasped for air.

The gloomy interior hadn't changed since the last time she'd been inside. Only part of the cave was underwater. The rest of the rocks piled above the surface, appearing as a solid structure from the glade. Several holes in the rocks let in air and ribbons of light. Peaking through one, she watched Strongheart repeatedly dive in search of her, his actions growing more frantic by the moment. When he surfaced, he'd call her name, but she remained silent, staring at his face drawn in fear. Would he miss her if she'd truly drowned? Or would he curse the opportunity he'd let slip through his fingers?

Deciding he'd suffered long enough, she swam back through the rocky opening and popped to the surface beside him. Since she'd left, dark lines crinkled deeper around his eyes and a muscle in his jaw that had been smooth now pulsed.

"Did you miss me?" she asked lightly, tilting back her hair into the water to smooth it off her face.

"If you ever again scare me so, I'll throttle you within an inch of your life," he said, so quietly, she knew he'd truly been worried.

A bit ashamed of her trick, yet unwilling to admit it and knowing his threat to be pure bluster, she shrugged blithely. "Spare me your theatrics. I suggest you refrain from following me and forego leaping out of the water like some dark monster from the deep, and then I won't have a need to take revenge."

Confusion narrowed his eyes to slits. " 'Tis not the same thing. I thought you were dead."

"I thought I was about to be eaten alive," she countered.

His hand lifted to caress her cheek, his dark eyes reflecting regret. "I am sorry. 'Twill not happen again."

If she'd been standing on Eire's rich earth her knees would have buckled. As it was, she barely managed to keep her chin above water. Men didn't apologize for their actions. Or if they did, they used it as a means to obtain concessions in return.

But the pain in Strongheart's eyes revealed that his apology was sincerely offered. That such a strong man was capable of gentleness set her stomach trembling anew.

The least she could do was match his magnificent gesture. "I, too, acted without thinking and am sorry for the worry I caused."

Although her limbs felt numbed by the icy cold of the water, the intense focus of his gaze on her face heated her to the core. She pointed to the flat rock in the sun, her original destination before he'd so suddenly appeared. "I'll race you."

Without waiting for his answer, she lunged forward, her legs kicking, her arms turning over swiftly. She watched him draw ahead in three strokes, then wait for her as if afraid to let her too far from sight. They may have finished the race together, but it was clearly due to his holding back, making sure she had the stamina to finish safely.

He pulled himself onto the rock, not even breathing heavily. Then he turned and squatted, offered his hand, and hauled her to him. His hands around hers were gentle and warm. His broad chest glistened with water droplets in the bright sunlight, sculpting the corded muscles of his torso. For a moment she thought he intended to draw her into his arms and enfold her in his heat. And despite all her promises to resist, she would have yielded, but he determinedly set her on her feet and let his hands drop to his sides.

She dropped to the flat rock and lay on the sun-warmed stone, her thoughts whirring in gossamer. He lay beside her on his back, hands clasped behind his head, staring into the forest greens.

"What are you thinking?" she asked, her curiosity as natural as the water trickling endlessly over the rocks.

He turned on his side and rested his head in his palm. "I wondered why you almost fainted when earlier I asked if you would drown me." He gazed at her warily, as if expecting her to fall prey to another spot of dizziness.

While the memories still haunted her, she carried them so close to her heart that speaking of them was difficult. Yet Strongheart had spoken of losing his brother, so perhaps he would understand.

"When I was ten, I had a half-sister, Eva. While my father spent time with her mother, I often took Eva for long walks. She became very dear to me."

As if guessing of the disaster that she would impart, Strongheart squeezed her hand, lending her strength. "You were too young to be the sole charge of a child."

His understanding lent her more courage, and she closed her eyes, the memories of that day replaying like a vision. A tightness gripped her chest and she swallowed a lump in her throat. "A group of raiders slipped past our border patrols. Eva and I were playing a game of conceal and seek. I'd hidden myself deep in a hay bale. When I heard Eva's shrieks, I clawed my way out."

Strongheart drew her against his side but even his body heat did not still her trembling. Gently he ran his fingers through her hair and the soothing sensation calmed her breathing.

His husky voice resounded in her ears. "A ten-year-old girl could not have fought off a raiding party."

"I should have run for help," she said the words aloud that she'd carried with her for years. "But I didn't. I watched them drown my sister from the safety of the hay. Later, the villagers thought I had drowned Eva in a fit of jealous rage."

His tone was tender. "When I teased you about wanting to drown me, I had no idea."

"I know." She squeezed his hand and then continued, now anxious to finish the tale. "Within the hour, the raiders burned a village. Everyone exonerated me of guilt."

"But the memory haunts you?"

The pain of losing her sister still clawed at her like a fresh wound. A shudder racked her body and twisted her stomach. " 'Tis the reason I learned to use a dirk. I never again wanted to stand helpless and watch someone I loved die." Her fingers gripped his so tightly, the knuckles turned pale. "I hate the fighting. Why can we not live in peace?"

As if to punctuate her words, a flock of Wexford-coast terns dipped and circled the pond, but sensing their presence, they soared aloft with loud caws of protest.

His eyes bored into hers as if sensing she had yet to tell him the entire story. "You still feel responsible for Eva's death?"

161

She choked over her words. "How could you know?"

He flinched but held her gaze. "Remember the cat that caused my brother's death?"

"Yes."

"It was my fault the tabby was there."

Confused, she let out her pent-up breath with a hiss. "But you said she followed you."

He paused and clenched his jaw. "I lied."

Chapter Nine

Strongheart rubbed his squared jaw, a subdued look of deep pain and maybe anger on his face. "Oh, in the beginning the tabby followed us, but I fed her scraps, and when she tired, I secretly carried her in my pack."

Dara absorbed the warmth of the rock beneath her, yet a shiver trembled through her. "Did your brother know?"

"Yes, but I was the one who enjoyed her furry warmth next to me during the cold, lonely nights of the long campaign."

She reached out and skimmed her fingers over his shoulder, taking in his damp skin, warmed by the sun. "Your brother's death was no more your fault than Eva's was mine."

Strongheart shook his head, showering water droplets about them, his shoulders rigid. "There was nothing you could have done to save Eva. Hiding probably saved your life. But I . . . I directly contributed to my brother's death."

"You were just a lad," she protested, the anguish in the depths of his gaze causing her stomach to contract. That cat must have given the little boy he'd once been the love and warmth he'd missed after his mother died.

His palm splayed across the water drops on the rock, smearing the dampness thin. He lifted his head to look at her, raising lashes spiked with droplets of water that dripped onto the hard line of his jaw. "I was old enough to know better."

Suddenly she understood what drove him to become so proficient with his sword, imagined the sacrifices he'd made, all because of guilt. "And after your brother's death, did you turn yourself into the warrior your father always wanted?"

His head came up sharply, his eyes piercing. "How did you guess?"

She sighed, remembering the aching, hollow emptiness, the obdurate need to demonstrate her worthiness to herself and others. "After Eva's death, I thought our people doubted my loyalty, so I proved my worth by taking on the responsibilities of the lady of the castle. As penance, I'd guess you took your brother's place in your father's eyes, forcing yourself to become the son, the warrior, your father demanded."

As he became lost in memories, his gaze softened, seemingly losing focus, and the sharp edges around his eyes eased. "I was more interested in stories and music than my brother. I remember sneaking into a gypsy encampment to listen to their strange, haunting music. When my father caught me, he beat me for the adventure, but I never regretted my escapade."

She pushed a lock of wet hair behind her ear and sighed at the harsh way he'd been forced to grow up. "Have you ever wondered how different you'd be if you'd had other parents?"

"No." He cocked his head to one side with a questioning look on his face.

She twisted her fingers in the hem of her damp tunic, almost afraid to look at him. "If anyone but Conor, King of Leinster, was my father, I could choose a husband without thought to politics."

"If anyone but Conor was your father, you might not have been given a choice," he countered.

"My choices are few. My people will not accept a common villager as their laird. And 'twould change the balance of power in Eire for me to wed another king. Most likely I'll marry a minor prince."

"You're wrong, Princess. You'll marry me."

His eyes turned smoky and her heart paused before resuming a frenetic pace. The day was sultry, yet gooseflesh tingled over her. His gaze focused on her once more and suddenly she was conscious of the wet tunic molding her every curve, the rock pressing her hip, the sunlight beating down on her skin. As she breathed in the clean scent of the woods, her chest expanded and her breasts had never seemed so sensitive.

Drawing her hand from his, she tucked her fingers beneath the material at the shoulder of her tunic, unsuccessfully attempting to tug the damp cloth from her flesh. Strongheart's gaze followed her movement, and as the corner of his mouth turned in a small smile, she sucked in her breath.

She told herself she responded to him only because his story had touched her, yet deep in her heart she wondered if they were kindred spirits. The bards spoke of soul mates, but she'd never put much credence to their fantastical tales of love. But she couldn't deny that, without a word or a touch, the air around them was charged, like the stillness before a storm.

Slowly, he leaned toward her. So slowly she could easily have avoided his kiss, but her languid limbs refused to follow the orders she gave them to shove him away. His head came within inches of hers, his handsome face blocking the sun, his swarthy features searing her with an intensity that sent a wracking shudder through her. His eyes became mysterious pools, his cheekbones knife-sharp. And yet for all his intensity, she sensed a vulnerability inside him that drew her like goldenrod to the sun.

She yearned to place her arms around his neck and yank him closer but could not bring herself to welcome him. Responding to him was a terrible risk. To lie placidly and wait was not the same as encouraging this madness.

As she took in his musky scent and their breaths mingled, she wondered what about him she found so appealing. He didn't give her time to consider the answer before nuzzling the tender skin in the hollow of her neck, and she exhaled a soft whoosh of air in pure pleasure. His fingers dug into her hair, lifting her head, and his lips nibbled a path over the pulse throbbing crazily in her neck, to another tender place behind her ear. Her back arched and she writhed, her hands guiding his lips to hers.

"Tell me you want me to kiss you," he demanded.

She bit her lower lip and refrained from answering. His lips nipped her brow, her cheeks, her chin, driving her wild.

"Please," she whispered.

"Please what? Please go away? Please continue?"

She tugged on his hair, but he ignored her attempt to draw him closer.

"Tell me, Princess."

She groaned. "Kiss me."

His hand cupped her chin and he stared deep into her eyes, letting her see his banked fire. "I want to please you."

She tossed her head from side to side, filled with wanting. One kiss, his body held close, and then she'd have to let him go.

"Then please me. Kiss me, Norman."

He turned on his side and cradled her head in the crook of his elbow, like a parent holding a babe. But there was nothing fatherly about the tension cording the muscles in his chest or the desire simmering in his eyes.

His lips came down upon hers, kindling the heat inside her into flame. His free hand dipped from her face to the hollow between her breasts, dancing in tune to the beat of her reeling pulse. The hunger of his kiss shattered her control into a thousand shards. Her back arched and she turned toward him, grinding her hips against him, throwing her leg over his, hooking her knee on his thigh to draw him closer.

Her whole body shook, and yet she'd never been so aware. A trickle of water plopped from his hair to his chest to her breast, and gently he massaged the droplet, arousing a raging torrent of desire that tingled from her nipple to her nape, down her spine, and over the backs of her thighs, settling in her core.

With little urging from him, her mouth parted, and her thoughts whirled in a maelstrom. He tasted of fresh bread and wine and pure male need. She wrapped her arms around him, needing to be closer.

When he pulled back, she bit back disappointment and held in a soft sob. He drew in a ragged breath and raked a hand through his hair, staring down at her with a power that crashed her spinning senses to a halt.

"What?" she asked softly.

"I'm checking to see if your fear has returned."

What was he talking about? "What fear?"

"Each time, after you experience desire, you push me away. Are you afraid I'll hurt you?"

Damnation! Why was he doing this to her? She didn't want to think or explain. She just wanted him to hold her in his arms and kiss her some more. But as her whirring thoughts slowly settled into a semblance of order, she considered what she could possibly say. While Strongheart might deserve the truth, he could use her fears against her to break down her determination. Without understanding her dilemma, he'd already done more to undermine her resistance than any man of Eire.

Although, to her chagrin, he was the one who'd pulled back—not she. He'd breached her self-imposed control with barely a murmured objection from her. Despite her years of discipline, of learning to fight, of running a household, despite years of running the day-to-day activities at Castle Ferns, she had learned everything except how to suppress her hot-blooded nature.

Would her worst fears come to pass? Would she respond to any man that offered a gentle touch or tender kiss, losing her self-respect and her virtue along the way? She shuddered at the thought of her secret nightmare turning to actuality.

Instead of weakening, the pull to let him take her grew stronger each time he held her. Even now, she wished to dispose of her flimsy tunic, untie his leather breeches, and make love with the sun kissing their bare flesh.

The thought of exploring his magnificent body and finding the places he would enjoy made her squash a burning curiosity that would lead to the darker, uncontrollable side of her nature. Shocked by her overwhelming need for his kiss and the erotic nature of her thoughts, she squeezed her eyes shut. But she didn't have to see him to recall every detail of his face—the pupils that dilated with desire, the haunting smile, the cocky angle he tilted his head.

She was not afraid he would hurt her, but of how her unfettered feelings could hurt her people. Resisting this male had to be her priority. Her carnal feelings must be disregarded.

Just because he was a virile male animal that pulled at her feminine core, she couldn't forget her responsibilities. Passion could not sway her into believing she could have this Norman—not unless she wanted every king in Eire to invade Leinster. As a man of war, the Norman thought he could hold this land, but even if he somehow succeeded, what would be the cost?

She'd already lost Eva to border raiders. Losing a child, a son or daughter, to more violence was more than she could bear.

"Are you afraid I'll hurt you?" Strongheart repeated his question, drawing her from her thoughts.

"No." Not physically. But on another level he could rip her to shreds.

"Are you afraid I will not stop if you ask that of me?"

"No." She might be the one who couldn't stop.

"Must I guess for all eternity? What is it?"

" 'Tis not you, but me." At his impatience, she opened her eyes. Why did men always believe they were the root of the universe? If only women ruled the world, she was sure there would be fewer wars. Although her heart pounded at the heretical thought, she couldn't help feeling convinced that few women, by choice, would send their fathers, husbands, and sons to war.

Strongheart shifted his weight, his tone husky. " 'Tis understandable you doubt our feelings. Give us time."

Knowing him better had naught to do with her problems. She let the sarcasm she couldn't hold back enter her voice. "You think if I know you better, then O'Rourke and MacLugh will dance a jig at our wedding?"

"Will you let your enemies decide your fate?" he argued.

His words stunned her. Is that what she was doing? Sacrificing herself to make up for . . . No, he was twisting and manipulating her thoughts, making her forget duty and honor. Her insides, like her options, tightened like a fist, squeezing her, pressuring her, and her anger exploded into angry words.

Rolling away from him, she stood. "Did not your enemies decide your fate? You lost your lands. I do not wish to do the same. Leinster is O'Dwyre land. My grandfather was king and his father before him. My son shall grow up here, and he, too, shall be king."

At her fury, his face clouded, his lips tightened. A muscle throbbing in the taut tendons of his neck indicated his rage, but she truly knew the extent of his anger by the deadly soft precision of his words. "I don't live my life cowering in fear at what others think. I seize what I want."

If there were only herself, she might risk all, even Leinster, for the right love. But she dared not gamble her people's security for her own happiness. Taking a chance on him was exactly what she could not afford—too many lives depended on her making the correct decision.

"That is where you and I differ." She dived into the water, letting the cool wetness calm her stormy heart. Without waiting to see if Strongheart followed, she climbed out of the pool, gathered Fionn's reins, and leapt onto his back, heading to Ferns.

* * *

Strongheart let her go, once again confused by her words, but pleased with his progress. She could deny her feelings all she wanted, but when they'd kissed, he'd felt her tremble, sensed her passionate nature.

Although she sought to push him away with her sharp tongue, he would not let that happen, for he recognized her words for what they were—an attempt to send him away. Despite her words, she feared him, but she feared her own passion more.

Slipping into the water to cool his lust, he swam lazily to his warhorse. Knowing that her anger was another side of her feelings for him gave him hope. But he also recognized her stubbornness. A military campaign to conquer this land would have been far easier than courting a princess, but it wouldn't have given him the same satisfaction or pleasure.

Besides, now that he'd come to know her, he didn't relish the thought of making war on her people. Even if she ever forgave him, which would be doubtful, Norman swords cutting through the poorly armed men of Leinster would be more massacre than battle. He had no stomach for such a debacle.

He no longer wanted to spend the rest of his life fighting. Dara had tapped all his suppressed tendencies toward a peaceful, gentle life, qualities his father had tried to squelch in him. But how many times had his father told him that only the weak wished for peace? And only the strongest warriors held the land?

He caught up with Dara in the stable, where she stood by her father, caressing the foal. After

Strongheart rubbed down his warhorse, he joined the two of them, admiring the fine lines of the newest addition. The foal's legs rarely shook when it walked, and its shiny coat glistened in the rays of sun beaming through the doorway.

"She's a beauty," Strongheart said to Conor, his eyes on the king's daughter.

Dara's head jerked up and Strongheart grinned. By her startled expression, he could tell she knew he referred to her—not the foal. Seemingly unaware of the undercurrents, Conor continued stroking the foal. "A fine filly with good bloodlines can give one many years of pleasure."

Strongheart agreed. "Especially once she's properly trained to a man's bidding."

As Conor looked from Dara's flushed face to Strongheart's grin, the king chuckled with a sharpness in his green gaze that revealed his awareness of the subject at hand. "Are foreign ways different from ours? How would you tame a spirited filly, Norman?"

Wondering why the question had come now and not when he'd asked for Dara's hand in marriage, Strongheart moved out of the shadows. Settling in the straw, Strongheart more than rose to her father's challenge. "I'd tame her with kind words, gentle caresses, and a refusal to retreat in large things."

"And on the smaller things?" Conor asked.

Clearly unhappy and uncomfortable with the turn in conversation, Dara's face flamed. Even now, the tension between them stretched thicker than Eire's mist on a dewy morn. Obviously uneasy, she gazed longingly at the door, but she didn't dare leave.

Strongheart nodded. "The minor points are negotiable."

"Depending on?" Conor pressed.

He sighed, choosing his words with care before he spoke. He would have both Dara and Conor understand that if he wed the princess, his word would be the final one—and yet he did not wish his to be a harsh rule. "My actions would depend upon the filly. Does she have good sense? Does she work with me or against me?"

Dara lifted her chin, a defiant gleam in her eyes. "And would you bring Norman knights to defend our land?"

Strongheart did not rise to take the bait. "That decision is your father's."

"Da will never permit you to bring an army of Normans to Leinster. The Irish clans will band together to oust outsiders—starting a war of unprecedented magnitude."

Conor gave the foal a final pat and turned as if to leave the two of them alone. But he paused in the stall, piercing Strongheart with a stare that hinted at the kind of leader he must have been before his forgetful spells weakened him. "I've given you privacy with my daughter because she can defend herself. I think it's time you saw her skill."

"No, Da."

Strongheart's eyes narrowed. So the old man sensed the unresolved tension between them, but why did Dara protest, her sparkling eyes dulled to despair? Was Conor trying to frighten him with his daughter's prowess? Surely he realized that once a skilled warrior recognized her skill, it should not be difficult to overpower her.

The flush on Dara's face receded, leaving her wan, and a slight tremor shook her body. With hands twisted in her tunic, she obediently walked out of the stable to the target area, her head down. What was wrong?

Conor's face was set in an implacable line, his shoulders straight like a man not to be denied. But his green eyes, normally so much like Dara's, had narrowed to icy flotsam, colder and more bitter than a dying man betrayed by his best friend.

"I have already seen her skill with a dirk," Strongheart said in an attempt to avoid unpleasantness and a demonstration of skill that she obviously didn't wish to give. "She killed an attacker during the raid to save Sorcha."

Neither father nor daughter answered. Outside, the sultry heat cooked them, but it was the unspoken words between Conor and Dara that beat upon him. There was much more going on here than a show of skill.

Having no liking for mysteries, Strongheart vowed to spear the heart of the matter. But how could he solve the puzzle when he didn't know the right questions to ask? Looking from the stubborn jaw of the father to the matching jut of the daughter's chin, he doubted either would answer his questions.

As they approached the practice area, a level field of straw and wood targets, several men-at-arms roused themselves to watch the exhibition. Strongheart noticed Gaillard ambling from the direction of the stone rings about the castle, Sorcha by his side.

As if by magic, maids walked down from the castle to watch. Wagering started, the men betting how many targets, if any, Dara would miss. Strongheart glanced again in her direction and noticed that although her face remained pale, her spine had stiffened, and she held her chin high but avoided his gaze.

Yet he sensed there were pressures battering at her that he could not guess. Was she embarrassed her skill with a dirk might exceed his? That didn't seem like the woman he'd come to know. He recalled the proud flash of her eyes when she'd spoken of using the dirk to defend herself or those she loved.

Was she afraid of failing in front of an audience? Strongheart's fists clenched and unclenched, wishing he could help her, but that was impossible since he had no understanding of what was wrong. He knew only that he wanted to comfort her, kiss away her distress and tell her he would take care of her.

The exhibition had a feeling of ritual. After the men set the targets between trees, each progressively smaller and farther away, an assortment of dirks were placed by Dara's hand. She picked up each one, hefted its weight in her hand, then moved on to the next until she held a fistful of weapons.

She worried her lip in total concentration, her focus so total, she appeared to have banished the audience from her mind. Planting her feet shoulder-width apart, she stood with her knees

flexed, elbows tucked close to her tunic, and relaxed, her expression reminding Strongheart of an
experienced warrior preparing for battle.

Around them, the betting ceased. The crowd's
murmurs decreased to silence. Not a leaf stirred.
At least she would not have to contend with the
wind throwing off her aim.

With her left hand, Dara casually flicked a blade
end over end at the closest straw target. About the
size of a man and twenty paces away, the target
would test an adequate warrior's skill. The gleaming weapon reflected a rainbow of sunlight before
arcing into the straw's center.

Several heads in the crowd nodded approval,
the faces clearly expecting no less than perfection.
Without hesitation, Dara hefted the second knife
and threw it straight into a thick tree trunk
marked with a ribbon. Quickly she demolished
two more straw targets before pausing.

When she hefted the knife with her right hand,
Strongheart's eyes widened. He hadn't realized
until now that she'd taken the easier targets with
her weaker left side. But those *easy* targets were
the size of large kettles and over forty paces away.

Strongheart spied only four more targets, but
Dara had seven dirks left. Were they extras in case
she missed? He dared not ask the question aloud
and risk distracting her.

The next three dirks found their targets. From
the corner of his eye, Strongheart saw the betting
reach a fever pitch, but he couldn't take his gaze
from Dara. Never had she looked so provocative,
the sun shimmering upon her red hair, sweat glis-

tening on her skin, and he found it strange to find her unusual skill so appealing.

The last target seemed impossibly tiny, but due to her earlier precision, she still possessed four dirks. Dara rolled her shoulders, let her hands slacken at her side, and jiggled her wrist to loosen tense muscles. Unlike the previous throws, this time, she took careful aim at an impossibly difficult-to-hit target. The silent crowd held its collective breath in the sultry heat of late afternoon.

Dara changed her stance, placing one leg forward, the other behind, twisting her upper torso toward the target. Perspiration beaded her brow, but her hands appeared steady. With an elegant flick of her wrist, a powerful throw of her arm, and an added force from her hip, she grunted and let loose her dirk.

The blade flew through the air and plunked solidly into the tree trunk no wider than the breadth of Strongheart's hand. The crowd sighed and murmured as one. Still there was no applause, no congratulations. The villagers crowded to one side, leaving Dara to face the trees. She lifted another knife, waiting on the balls of her feet, eyes alert.

Suddenly the air whistled, and a log attached by a rope swung out of the branches of a large oak. Dara's wrist flicked. Before the dirk thudded into its mark, another log tied to another tree swung, then another.

Each time, Dara pivoted, took aim and threw with the precision of a master. Never, not even by the finest English knights, had Strongheart seen such an exhibit of skill.

The crowd finally erupted into shouts and

cheers. The men who'd hidden in the trees leapt from the branches. A few dogs barked and children broke away from their mothers to run in circles, sing, and shout. Gaillard helped settle the bets. And Sorcha ordered the kitchen girls back to the castle to begin the evening meal.

But it was Dara who drew his attention. He'd expected smiles of happiness—not a blankness in her gaze, a slump in her shoulders.

Leaving the side of her proudly grinning father, she collected the dirks. Several had wormed their way so deep into the tree trunks she had to brace one foot to the tree and lean back with all her weight to tug the blade free.

Since she didn't ask for help, he didn't offer it. Still, he would have his curiosity satisfied. "I have never seen such skill."

"That was the point, Norman."

Her sharp words would not deter him. "But I saw you defend Sorcha. I already knew—"

Sighing, she yanked a dirk from one of the swinging logs. "The exhibition was not for you, Norman. But for me."

She wasn't making sense, but then he'd known all along that something beneath the surface had upset her. Although she spoke to him now, it was as if he were one of her father's men-at-arms, not a man whose kiss she'd enjoyed a few hours before.

His brow creased. "Does your father wish you to think of yourself as a warrior instead of a woman?"

Her eyes were bleak. "When I was a girl, I begged Da to teach me to use the dirk. I wanted a good teacher. Da was the best. Once he had the eyes of a hawk, and he could hit targets much farther away than I can now."

"Lady, no Norman knight could best your skill."

"Legends of Da's prowess will be told by the bards for generations." She paused, her eyes focused on the point of a dirk. "He enjoyed teaching me all he knew. Of course, I've never equaled his distance since I lack his strength."

"What you lack in strength you more than make up for in skill, Princess."

She didn't respond to his compliment. She didn't say more, which left him just as puzzled as before. Why did she need a reminder of her own skill? The question burned in him, but as others approached he refrained from asking.

The winners offered her a share of the prizes, but she graciously refused. Waving a bandy-legged old man on his way, she teased, "Buy your wife a trinket, 'twill make up for your coming home drunk last market day."

Her words drew a laugh, and the crowd dispersed, the winners no doubt eager to spread tales of their good fortune. With the last dirk collected and placed in a sack, Dara and Strongheart strolled to the castle.

Sunset descended, leaving the two of them in a tense, eerie silence. His pulse raced as if he were about to enter battle. He sensed she would not like his question because a truthful answer would shred away the toughened outer layers she wrapped herself in to protect her vulnerability. But still, he had to know, even if she hated him for broaching her solitude.

"Tell me, Princess, why must you be reminded of your own skill?"

Chapter Ten

Although Strongheart asked his question in a voice soft as melted honey, a reply stuck tight in Dara's throat. As they reached the entrance to the hall, the sun dropped below the horizon, leaving them in the fading light of the last rays of day.

Weary from the tension that had held her rigid through a trying afternoon, Dara flung her hair over her shoulder, raised her head, and gazed into his face. She was prepared to lie to him until she saw concern mixed with curiosity written across his features. Knowing the Norman would pester her until he received an answer, her thoughts raced. What could she tell him that would sound convincing?

Part of the truth might be best. Bracing her back against a warm stone wall, she fought for composure and just the right tone of indignation. "Da probably thought I needed to be reminded of my skill because of you."

He placed one boot on a log, and leaned forward, resting his forearm across his knee. "I don't understand."

"He taught me to fight to protect myself against men—and that was what he wanted me to remember. That the Princess of Leinster can never let herself be . . ."

"Be taken? Be forced?"

"Something like that," she agreed, hoping he'd let the matter drop.

She should have known better. He held so still he reminded her of a cat tensed to spring on a mouse.

"Has a man forced you?" he asked, distaste evident in his tone.

"No," she spoke plainly, attempting to keep her voice steady, hoping he couldn't see the heat in her cheeks at discussing such a private topic in such a public place where any passerby could overhear their words. Yet no one neared the door into the hall, leaving them in a cocoon of privacy. Obviously he had not been taken in by her partial truth. But better that she satisfied his curiosity than to have him or Gaillard start questioning the villagers.

She was already having enough trouble resisting him. If he discovered her secret, she might succumb. "But many of Leinster's enemies would try and take advantage if they caught me alone in the woods."

He suddenly knelt on one knee and raised her hand to his lips. "I make you a promise, Princess.

You need merely say the word 'cease,' and I will heed your command."

Knowing he possessed such control should have reassured her. Having him at her feet should have made her feel triumph. But it did not. She felt torn, empty, drained. In the end, the final say would be hers, and she did not trust herself to summon the strength to fight him and her own passions, too.

Just outside the castle walls, a cat issued a plaintive meow, echoing Dara's wish to cry out in despair. Why did it have to be the Norman that stretched her taut?

His lips touched her hand, and she forgot the warning in the cat's cry. The tenderness of his gesture shot shivers of anticipation along her spine, setting her blood roaring in her ears. She swayed on her feet. The day's lingering traumatic tension had left her feeling fragile and delicate. As if he sensed the weakness flowing through her, Strongheart gathered her into his arms, enfolding her protectively.

"I'm here," he murmured into her ear. "I'll always be here."

She breathed in his male scent, snuggled against the hard planes of his chest, trying to believe he spoke the truth, already fighting the pain of knowing that when he didn't get what he wanted, he'd move on. That was the way with warriors—they moved on to new conquests.

But for now she reveled in the strength of his arms and the heady touch of long, powerful arms locking her in a tender embrace. Her head rested under his chin and against his chest, her ear so close to his heart she could hear its steady, reassuring thump. Her hands went round his back, her fingers digging into firm flesh and holding tight. He smoothed her hair with his fingers, and as he murmured soothing sounds in the back of his throat, he calmed her as if she were an untamed filly.

Although she doubted she could ever stand within the circle of his embrace without feeling passion kindling between them, she knew his touch was meant not to arouse but comfort. She'd never imagined any man could offer her such serenity. Before she'd met the Norman she would have hooted in derision to think she'd found peace in the arms of an English knight and a man of war.

But peace with a Norman would never last. The cat meowed again and, as if the sound broke the spell, she reluctantly pulled away. He let her go without a word, and she was about to flee into the hall and up the steep stairs to her room when she heard another plaintive cry, weaker, yet somehow more insistent.

"The cat in the stable has kittens almost ready to be weaned." She turned in the darkness and walked with him past Ferns's strong walls, her eyes seeking the telltale glitter of slanted cat eyes in the deep grasses of the field. "Do you suppose one of her kittens climbed a tree?"

"And doesn't know how to get down?"

Dara called softly. "Here, kitty, kitty." Then she stood still and listened for an answering cry. Chickens clucked and in the distance cattle bawled. A horse whinnied. They caught the occasional loud word from the hall but no sound of a cat.

Strongheart walked toward a weeping willow, his huge silhouette a darker black against the backdrop of the dusky sky. Reaching overhead, he swung himself into the tree.

Dara ran to the spot where he disappeared, tilted her head back, and searched for him among the swinging branches. She heard a loud meow. "Can you see it?"

"Yes," he muttered. "But it's so far out on the limb I'm not sure the branch will hold my weight."

"Try calling her," Dara suggested.

From above she heard a strange purring sound coming from Strongheart's throat.

Her brows knitted in puzzlement. "What are you—"

"Hush."

The humming sound commenced again, sounding more like a lioness calling her young than a cat. Dara shifted her weight from foot to foot. She rubbed the crick forming in the back of her neck but didn't take her gaze from the tree.

The branches groaned, the humming continued, and she almost felt as if she were in a trance. Then after several long minutes the humming ceased. She jumped back as she heard several branches crack.

"Got her." Strongheart half fell, half leapt from the tree, landing lightly on his feet as if he were part feline himself.

She stepped closer to see. "Is she all right?"

Strongheart had the animal cuddled next to his heart and, as if in thanks, the kitten licked his chin. He let out a low, hearty chuckle. "I'm not your mama, little one."

But the kitten didn't seem to know that. She circled his hand, curled into a tight little fluff of fur, tucked her head into her body and purred. The Norman gently scratched her back with his free hand, drawing even deeper purrs from the animal.

Dara couldn't help wishing she could take the kitten's place. The thought of the Norman running his long fingers and strong hands delicately down her back was all too pleasant to contemplate. To banish her thoughts, she petted the soft fur.

"Oh, you bold thing," she scolded. "How did you get up that tree?"

"Perhaps the warhound chased her. Or idle curiosity caused her to explore further than she should have."

His voice was so soft when he spoke, even if Dara hadn't remembered his childhood pet, she would have recognized his affinity for cats. An odd choice for a man. Cats tended to be temperamental, demanding their own way, and men usually required catering to, not the other way around—still, the Norman was no ordinary man.

She suddenly wanted to replace the cat he'd lost so long ago. "Would you like to keep her?"

"What are you thinking?" His tone changed, grating harshly, and she was glad for the darkness that hid his face. Standing up to him was easier when she didn't have to confront his hard, indomitable scowl.

"I was thinking that most men prefer dogs."

His voice rose as if he was suddenly wary. "Why is that, do you suppose?"

"Because dogs can be trained to do a man's bidding."

"I've always been partial to cats. I like their fiery independence, their fey spirit."

His voice had become so husky she wondered if he spoke of cats or something else. Was he telling her he liked a woman who followed her own mind? But didn't that contradict what he'd said to her father about fillies? Or perhaps he really was just speaking of animals. He had her thoughts spinning in such confusion she didn't know if she was putting meaning he didn't intend into his statements.

"So keep her," she insisted.

The kitten didn't stir. Their hands met over the little furball's back. Their fingers intertwined. His voice turned hard but remained quiet. "I cannot."

The mixture of wanting and vulnerability she heard made her press him. "You haven't kept a cat since . . . you were a boy?"

"Cats do not belong in the middle of battle. They should be in a warm bed where 'tis safe."

Dara yanked her hand back as if scorched, all sympathy for him forgotten. She felt as if he'd thrust a battering ram into her chest, bruising her heart. "What battles are you planning, Norman?"

"Can you not at least call me by my name?"

"A Norman is what you are, and that is what I'll call you," she spat out, knowing she needed the constant reminder to keep her heart free of him.

Snatching the kitten from his palm, she ignored the animal's hiss of protest and marched toward the barn to return the kitten to its mother. Hot tears washed down her cheeks, and angrily Dara

187

Susan Kearney

brushed them away with the back of her hand.

Damn her for a fool. She'd known the Norman came to do battle. What else could she expect from a warrior except talk of war, war, and more war?

Strongheart watched her go with regret. In his attempt to win her, he'd made progress. In spite of her distrust, he felt she was beginning to like him. But she demanded much, his Irish princess. By opening himself to her to win her heart, he'd forgotten the most basic of strategies: *Let your enemy see only what you want them to see.*

He'd begun his campaign to win her by deciding what she liked and giving that to her, the flowers, the perfumed bath water, the afternoon rides. But by exhibiting tenderness he'd revealed compassion and sympathy, and this he could not allow. A soldier had no time for feelings. The softer emotions could have no room in a warrior's life, for they would ultimately lead to his death. No matter how appealing he might find living a peaceful fairy-tale existence with Dara, it would never happen—the land here was too lush, the fields too green, for others not to try to take it. Only a strong man could hold Leinster.

Living in peace pretending all would go well was a dream for naive women and children—not a war-hardened knight. He'd had that dream smashed early in life—when his brother had been taken from him.

After his mother died, there was no softness or warmth in his world. His father's hard-driving ambition had molded Strongheart into the foremost knight in England.

188

And what advantage had that brought? They'd lost Pembroke, then his father had died, and only by Strongheart's wiles had he hung on to the family's wealth of gold and silver. Those riches would stand him in good stead. Although Dara did not seem interested in wealth beyond the richness of her land, perhaps the answer was to convince the father—not the daughter.

Vowing to guard the softer side of his nature, Strongheart entered the hall, his burden heavier than it had been in some time.

Throughout the evening repast, Dara didn't look his way once, and when she found the silver necklace he'd earlier arranged to be placed by her trencher, she gave it away to the first passing kitchen maid.

After the meal, while the men moved outside the hall—for it was still much too warm to remain comfortable inside by the hearth—Dara retired to her room. Gaillard and Sorcha skipped off together, his arm wrapped around her waist, his hand splayed over her backside. Carolan strummed his harp; the men drank goblets of ale. As the sky darkened, one-by-one the others wandered to their beds, leaving Conor and Strongheart alone.

Strongheart's gaze turned from the night sky to Leinster's king. "If I could be sure of marrying Dara, I could assure Leinster's prosperity for many years," Strongheart told Conor, hoping the man had come out of the short spell of forgetfulness he'd exhibited during the evening meal.

Conor walked alongside him, tipped back his head, quaffed the last of his ale, and snorted. "You may be the best warrior in Eire, in Britain, in all the civilized world, but again I say, you are only one man. And one man cannot stop the armies that gather on Leinster's borders."

"There are more men like me," Strongheart insisted. "Men who would follow my orders."

Conor sighed, which led to a coughing fit. Finally he spoke with regal composure. "To bring Norman men to Leinster would cause war."

"At least it would be a war you could win."

Conor fell silent and gazed across the dark pastures of Leinster. Finally he spoke, coming at Strongheart with a new line of attack. "Dara turned you down, did she?"

"She will come round to my way of thinking. But winning a woman takes time—time that Leinster may not have."

Conor shrewdly switched the subject. "What would induce Norman soldiers to fight for Leinster?"

"The usual mercenary compensation. Gold and silver."

Conor spat, his stream of spittle finding its mark, hitting a fly and silencing its persistent buzzing. "Leinster's riches are in her land and her cattle."

Strongheart recognized the king's words for what they were: an admission that gold and silver were rare in Eire. Even if Conor wished to hire Normans, the king did not have such riches.

For the first time since his argument with Dara, Strongheart's hopes rose. Conor needed him, and the need could be worked to his advantage. "Although my family lost our lands, we didn't lose all our wealth. I will pay the knights. In return I would marry Dara and be named your heir."

His optimism increased when Conor didn't reject his idea out of hand. "Holding this land is no easy task. You'd never live in peace."

Strongheart grinned, confident he'd eventually sway the older man. "That would depend on how badly we defeated your enemies, would it not?"

"Dara will not like your plan. She does not see the necessity of bringing Normans to this land when Leinster's men stand ready to defend their homes."

Strongheart practiced his best diplomacy. "The brave men of Leinster cannot fight the overwhelming odds of your many enemies. I only hope there is still time for me to go to Wales, raise the needed men, and return before an attack."

Abruptly Conor stood, signaling the end of the discussion. "I will not be pushed into a decision. I shall think on it."

"Do not think too long," Strongheart urged, to which he received no reply.

He walked the outer wall alone, thinking how close he was to his dream. His heart thudded with excitement. He would have Dara, and he would have this fine land. Perhaps he should have pushed Conor harder, forcing the king to agree. Despite his elation at the way the conversation had gone, tomorrow Conor might talk to Dara, and she might sway him back the other way.

Time was Conor's enemy. Surely word of the king's infirmity, his forgetful spells, must have spread to his longtime enemies. The villagers might be loyal, but for the price of a flagon of ale, someone could always be induced to gossip.

After Strongheart completed his circuit, nodding to the guards posted on watch, he entered the hall, hoping Conor wouldn't forget their conversation by morning. As the Norman lay on his straw-stuffed mattress covered with hide, he tossed and turned, his memories returning to Dara.

He finally fell asleep amidst the snores and grunts of Leinster's men, images of Dara racing through his mind.

Dara lept fearlessly from Fionn, her long red hair curling down her back, a fierce grin on her face. There was a dirk in her hand. Suddenly she threw the dirk at the helpless kitten.

Strongheart tossed the kitten away to safety, but the blade caught him instead, the dirk piercing his heart. He felt no pain, but watched his body shatter into a thousand bloodless pieces. The pieces swirled and blew away like dust.

Strongheart awakened from the nightmare, sitting up with a start, heart pounding and sweat dropping from his hair into his eyes.

By the rood! Never before had a woman haunted his dreams. It was bad enough Dara tormented him by day, must she also haunt him by night?

Knowing he wouldn't fall back asleep easily, Strongheart strolled to the river and took a swim. He returned to the castle with a sense of peace, but the moment he lay down and closed his eyes, Dara's accusing emerald stare prowled in the depths of his mind.

Again he fell asleep.

*   *   *

She came to him like a mermaid out of spindrift, her smile taunting, her body wrapped in gold-spun gossamer, a perfect jewel in the rock pool. She wore a gold tiara that shone so brightly it hurt his eyes. Her laughter tinkled as merrily as the gently cascading water.

"You can have me," she taunted, beckoning him with delicate gestures, hips undulating in unmistakable invitation.

"What of your betrothed?"

She snapped her fingers. "He did not please me, and I turned him into a Kerry slug."

"I will please you, Princess."

She threw back her head and laughed, the long delicate tendons in her neck vibrating with amusement. "First you must catch me, Norman."

Diving into the pool, she swam toward the waterfall. He only took the time to remove shirt and boots before plunging into the warm water. Holding his breath, he swam deeper. With his lungs about to burst, he surfaced to find her waiting for him under the falls. Her tiara had disappeared, and she stood beneath the raining waters. Her flawless skin was dotted with sparkling droplets, her eyes brighter than emeralds. A golden tunic clung to every lush curve.

Once again she beckoned, summoning him with a siren song so sweet he'd go mad if he didn't touch her glorious, glistening skin. Splashing through the shallows, he thought he'd explode with the tightness in his chest. He had to touch, steal a kiss.

He could feel the tightness gathering in his breeches, the material pulling unbearably taut. His *heart caught, but he knew better than to give in to these tender emotions. The impulse was insane. Lust had caught him, and he reached out to her, half expecting her to vanish in a wisp of fairy dust.*

"Do you want me?" she whispered.

He shot his most seductive smile. "What mortal man would not?"

"Do not hold back," she murmured.

He smiled at her eagerness. "Greedy wench."

Sweeping her into his arms, he carried her from the waters to a bed of fragrant grasses covered with the finest silk cloth and strewn with rose petals. He stood gazing down at her water-kissed skin, at her high cheekbones flushed with desire, and thought he'd never seen a sight so fetching.

"I want you, Norman."

"You shall have me," he promised with a wicked grin, "but not yet."

She writhed beneath him. "When? When shall I have you?"

"When I've licked you dry, Princess." He chuckled then, loving the feel of her squirming bare flesh against him.

She pounded his shoulder. "Beast. I must have you forever. You must give me your heart."

His jaw dropped in surprise that she was unaware of his feelings. "My heart is already yours, Princess. I gave it to you long ago."

Dara disappeared as if she were one of the little people. He stood searching for her in the glade, and the trickling water seemed to deride him. One moment she'd been beneath him, soft and fragile to his touch, but now he was alone.

No, not alone.

Thrill to the most sensual, adventure-filled Historical Romances on the market today...

FROM 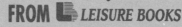 LEISURE BOOKS

As a home subscriber to Leisure Romance Book Club, you'll enjoy the best in today's BRAND-NEW Historical Romance fiction. For over twenty-five years, Leisure Books has brought you the award-winning, high-quality authors you know and love to read. Each Leisure Historical Romance will sweep you away to a world of high adventure...and intimate romance. Discover for yourself all the passion and excitement millions of readers thrill to each and every month.

Save $5.00 Each Time You Buy!

Each month, the Leisure Romance Book Club brings you four brand-new titles from Leisure Books, America's foremost publisher of Historical Romances. EACH PACKAGE WILL SAVE YOU $5.00 FROM THE BOOKSTORE PRICE! And you'll never miss a new title with our convenient home delivery service.

Here's how we do it. Each package will carry a FREE 10-DAY EXAMINATION privilege. At the end of that time, if you decide to keep your books, simply pay the low invoice price of $16.96, no shipping or handling charges added. HOME DELIVERY IS ALWAYS FREE. With today's top Historical Romance novels selling for $5.99 and higher, our price SAVES YOU $5.00 with each shipment.

AND YOUR FIRST FOUR-BOOK SHIPMENT IS TOTALLY FREE!
IT'S A BARGAIN YOU CAN'T BEAT! A Super $21.96 Value!

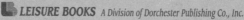

LEISURE BOOKS *A Division of Dorchester Publishing Co., Inc.*

GET YOUR 4 FREE BOOKS NOW—A $21.96 Value!

Mail the Free Book Certificate Today!

Get Four Books Totally FREE – A $21.96 Value!

▼ Tear Here and Mail Your FREE Book Card Today! ▼

PLEASE RUSH
MY FOUR FREE
BOOKS TO ME
RIGHT AWAY!

Leisure Romance Book Club
P.O. Box 6613
Edison, NJ 08818-6613

AFFIX
STAMP
HERE

His twin brother, still in the cloudlike body of a thirteen-year-old boy but with the face of an angel, floated in the air above him. "What have you done?"

Guilt stabbed Strongheart, and he fought against sinking to his knees. "I've fallen in love."

His brother folded his arms across his thin chest, his sad, familiar face achingly dear. "How could you give your heart to a woman?"

"I had no choice. Do you not wish for me to be happy?"

Huge puppy-dog eyes sent waves of sympathy. "To love is to open your heart and permit weakness to seep in."

" 'Tis not fair. I want her."

"Brother, I speak the truth. You can have her without giving your heart."

"She will not like this."

The vision of his brother rose overhead, his halo burning bright. In contrast, his deep-set eyes appeared bleak and lifeless. "Do not give her a choice."

"But 'tis not what I want," he protested.

"Do you not wish to see your sons grow to manhood? Or do you wish to become like me? Dead?"

Sorrow filled Strongheart. "Bring her back to me, please. I will do as you say."

His brother nodded. "Your decision is a wise one. She's calling you. Can you not hear her?"

The breeze whistled in the trees and his brother left him. Once again Strongheart was alone in the glade. Closing his eyes, he summoned his princess. He heard her calling, her voice crying with the wind.

"Strongheart. Strongheart."

*   *   *

"Strongheart, wake up." Dara shook his shoulder roughly. "Wake up."

He grabbed her and yanked her down on his pallet, his arms iron bands of muscle she couldn't escape. She struggled frantically. "This is no time for games. Mata has brought word of an attack."

Chapter Eleven

"Attack?" As Dara stood in the main hall and watched the sleep clear from Strongheart's eyes, he reached for his sword and stood, throwing off his blanket and rising to his feet in one graceful motion.

More frightened than she'd ever been in her life, she twisted her hands in her tunic, determined that he wouldn't see the trembling evidence of her fear. She spoke quickly, past the tightness in her throat. "Mata sent word that Borrack MacLugh and Tiernan O'Rourke have formed an alliance." Strongheart reached for his armor, and she forced her fingers to help him don his mail for battle. "Their armies are gathered on the western border."

"The *Ard-ri*?"

"His official position is one of neutrality, but

197

Mata has heard rumors that he lent MacLugh and O'Rourke men to attack Leinster." Knowing the severity of their situation, Dara forced herself to remain strong and hand him his shield, but she barely contained her tears.

Never before had she been so thankful the Norman had come to their land to help defend her home. Although the armies of MacLugh and O'Rourke would outnumber the men of Leinster, she prayed the Norman and his squire, fighting on their side, would win the day.

Struggling to keep her voice calm, she explained their normal precautions. "As we speak, the herders drive the cattle within the stone rings. Villagers are arriving with provisions of food. Those who cannot reach here in time will take cover in the woods and retreat into the marshlands if necessary."

Around them, women gathered children by the hearth. Others heated huge caldrons of boiling water to cast down if the enemy attempted to breach the castle walls. Sorcha was laying out herbs and clean linens for bandages while she ordered the kitchen girls to sweep the hall free of rushes so they needn't worry about fire. Beds were set aside in one corner for the wounded. Outside, the frantic whinny of horses combined with the clucks of geese and the braying of cattle.

"What of the men-at-arms?" Strongheart placed his helm on his head, suddenly looking more ominous. With his shiny mail, longbow, and sword, he could not have appeared more formidable. Dark, snapping eyes burned with intensity from within the helm, and for a moment she pitied his enemies, the knot in her stomach loosening.

"My father waits in the high tower where he directs our men. I am to bring you there."

"I will find my own way." His hands grasped her shoulders. "Pack a small bundle of clothes, a warm cloak, and your sleeping furs. Don't take more than I can tie to my warhorse's saddle."

Her heart sank like a lead ball in water. "I do not understand." But she did. The Norman thought they might lose. How could she endure losing her home? She couldn't imagine living anywhere but Castle Ferns. Not even losing her life frightened her as much as going through the years homeless.

The Norman's quick and urgent command cut through her panic. "For once, do as I ask."

Her father needed the Norman to plan strategy, yet, when Strongheart turned to leave, she grasped his forearm, keeping her voice low so others wouldn't hear her terror. "Do you think we will lose?"

She shuddered at what would happen to her if MacLugh or O'Rourke got their hands on her. There were worse things than dying.

His gaze gentled. "I would not give you false hope. Losing, 'tis a possibility, and we should always be prepared."

His head dipped, and he kissed her mouth hard, fierce yet tender, and, without words, she tried to tell him how she felt. She pressed herself against the cold bite of the mail he wore, uncaring of who might see. In just an instant, their kiss heated to a fire that could fuse metal. He clutched her so tightly, her feet rose off the floor, and she had dif-

Susan Kearney

ficulty drawing air into her lungs. And still, she couldn't get close enough. For a moment she feared they would all die, and she would regret never knowing what it would feel like to have this man love her. She longed to go back to their day at the rock pool, wished things between them could have turned out differently.

Before she was ready, he set her back on her feet and gave her bottom a swat. "Pack your things, Princess."

Through the long hours of the afternoon, Dara remained inside the castle walls with the women, her stomach twisting and turning into a thousand knots. Until his voice went hoarse, Carolan sang songs to entertain the children, leaving their mothers free to cook for the men.

At the first warning, the villagers had butchered a cow, and now the women took turns at the heavy spit, hoping tomorrow they would be alive to partake in a celebration feast. Occasionally men entered the hall, but the news wasn't good.

Advance scouts had spotted the enemy and returned shaking their heads at the overwhelming force they must meet. She'd heard that Strongheart and Gaillard rode in the first line of attack beside her father's finest men-at-arms. Strongheart planned to circumvent the advancing army and attack their flanks from the cover of the woods, where he and Gaillard would pick off men with their longbows.

When she was unable to stand the tension another moment, Dara hurried through the bailey and climbed their tallest watchtower. She found her father standing alone, staring out into the

200

night lit by a full moon. She gasped at the sight of hundreds of campfires dotting the distant fields like so many vermin on a flea-ridden hound.

In silence, she took her da's hand and stared into the stifling heat of the darkness, knowing this could be the last time she and her father stood together on the land she so loved. Tears brimmed in her eyes, and when she refused to give in to them, the drops tickled down the back of her throat. This was where she was born, where she wanted her children to be born, and this was where she wanted to die.

As if reading her thoughts, her father turned to her, his voice swelling with grief. "We may lose the fight before the morrow."

In the distant fields the cattle circled and brayed, as if sensing strangers in their midst and crying out their sorrow. She ached at the regret and defeat in his tone. "Nay, Da. You will find a way to win."

"Mayhap not this time. But you will survive. You must return and reclaim what belongs to us."

Uneasy that he had said "you" and not "we," Dara shook sweaty hair from her eyes. "You sound as if you have already yielded."

Conor spoke with patience as if she were still a babe. "Sometimes the hardest part of valor is to retreat with enough forces to fight another day."

Dara suddenly recalled the Norman's orders for her to pack. Had he and her father made plans about which she knew nothing? Or did her father, knowing the people of Leinster would never accept the return of an O'Dwyre as their king if Conor yielded without a fight, intend to sacrifice the Norman? "Why did you send Strongheart out?"

"I would have gone myself but I thought I could do more here. He's the best man we have." Conor acknowledged the Norman's superior prowess. "I am praying for a miracle."

She sighed at the frustration in his tone. "Surely there is more we can do?"

Moonlight beamed down onto his sad smile, emphasizing the gray of his hair. "Do not fear, colleen. This old man still has a few tricks down his boots."

As if on cue, a brush fire lit the fields near the base of the third ring of stone. Men shouted, and the cattle, always nervous around fire, stampeded away from Ferns toward the armies camping on the hills. Even in the safety of the tower, the ground shook from the thousands of cattle thundering toward the enemy.

Dara heard and sensed, more than saw, the panic and terror of the armies dotting the fields. Dust rose into the air, tingeing the moonlit scene an eerie red.

Grasping Da's arm excitedly, she quivered with hope. "You are clever, father."

" 'Tis an ingenious idea—but not one I take credit for. 'Twas the Norman's plan."

"Will it work?" Was it possible for them to win without the loss of lives? Without wives becoming widows and children growing up without fathers? If they could just hold Ferns, then all the doubts the Norman had put her though would be worth his presence here.

They may have taken their enemies by surprise,

but MacLugh and O'Rourke were not stupid men. Already she spotted a brush fire set in the grass to one side of the cattle, a sign of their attempt to turn the stampede. For a moment, it appeared the crazed cattle would race straight ahead, but then, slowly, they altered course away from the camping armies.

Begorra! As she watched their scheme fail, Dara wrung her hands. "How much damage did we cause?"

"Not enough." Strongheart's voice made her jerk around. He stalked into the tower, helm in hand, his face streaked with soot and his eyes glittering hard.

She was so relieved to see him alive and uninjured, tears came unbidden to her eyes. Glad for the darkness that hid her womanly emotions, she remained silent. While the men talked of battle, she drank in the tall, solid length of Strongheart, the confidence in his tone, the proud tilt of his head.

Her heart twisted with the sudden bitter knowledge that Strongheart had usurped her position as her father's advisor. Part of her couldn't help but fear that the Norman saw Eire's internal strife as an opportunity to grab land, wealth, and power— possibly even Ireland's kingship—from the warring clans. Strongheart could use Leinster as the base of his quest to seize great power. Sadly she foresaw burning fields, looted villages, and many deaths.

She'd lost track of the conversation over battle tactics for a few minutes until her father's mention of her name drew her thoughts back to the present. "Take my daughter to Mata where she will be safe."

"No," she protested, sick fear making her voice shrill. "I will not leave."

Strongheart's eyes glittered in the moonlight. "Where lies safety?"

Her father waved in the general direction of the hills, apparently still unwilling to give the Norman their secrets until absolutely necessary. "To the monks. Take her to Mata. She will guide you to their secret cave in the woods."

Dara glanced back at the fields and the bones in her knees went weak. "We cannot go anywhere. Look."

The invading armies' torches converged, the light of so many beacons clearly showing the inevitable advance on Ferns.

"Take her and go, Norman," the King of Leinster ordered. "If we cannot hold, I will meet you at Dobar's Stone at dawn."

Dara knew better than to argue. The men would fight better without the distraction of worrying over her safety. Still, running from her home in the middle of the night and abandoning her people struck her as wrong, cowardly. It would be better to stay and die. Yet even if they lost, many of her people would survive and they must have a leader. They would need her. Strongheart gave her time only for a quick hug with Conor before he dragged her out of the tower. She grabbed her pack, and Strongheart plucked it from her numb fingers.

A wolfhound howled in the distance, and she, too, wished to howl at the moon, at the imminent loss of her home, at the thought that war could again take from her those she loved. To try to forget the acrid taste of defeat, she concentrated on racing to the stable in record time.

Once inside, she automatically hurried to Fionn, but even his nose thrusting into her hand in welcome did not lighten her heavy heart. In the time she fitted Fionn with a bridle, Strongheart had saddled his warhorse, tied Dara's pack to the saddle atop his, and mounted. He waited for her, and she swiftly followed suit.

"Stay close to me," he commanded in a tone she dared not disobey. "Do not halt for anything or anyone."

"But—"

"If I stop to fight, you ride on. Understood?"

As they rode out of the stable she nodded, her throat tight, tears burning her lids. Would she ever again see her father? Or Sorcha? Would she ever again live at Castle Ferns? This was her home, her people, and without them she felt as adrift as a rudderless ship.

"Understood?" he asked again.

She realized he hadn't seen her nod in the dark. "Yes." She urged Fionn into a gallop to keep up with him.

In an attempt to distract herself from her gloomy thoughts, she lifted her head, seeking what lay ahead. But the grim sight was worse than her most frightening nightmare. Torchlights held by hundreds, maybe thousands of men blocked their path to the west and north. Although Mata was hidden in the woods to the north, they were forced to ride south to avoid the advance and would have to hope they could circle north once again.

Rising out of the darkness, men without torches blocked their path, their silhouettes menacing, their weapons ready for battle. Strongheart slew two men with his sword before their foe realized an enemy rode among them. Dara slid her hand to her waist to rest on one of three dirks hidden there. She wouldn't use the weapons unless necessary. Once thrown, the possibility of retrieving them was unlikely.

It seemed as if they'd rode for hours, but when she looked over her shoulder at Castle Ferns, she saw they were still inside the third ring of stone. If they didn't clear this area soon, MacLugh and O'Rourke would have them trapped. She'd be a married woman by morning. Or dead.

The thought of being forced to marry a man who even now sought to kill her father brought bile spewing up the back of her throat. She'd rather perish with Leinster's men-at-arms, but Strongheart wasn't giving her that option.

The Norman had defeated several soldiers, but more men would soon arrive. She'd just urged Fionn to an even faster pace when, in the bright moonlight about one hundred feet ahead, she spied a kitten huddled in the middle of the field.

Without thought, she slowed and Strongheart's warhorse pounded beside her. "We cannot stop," he shouted.

Behind her, metal clanged on metal, men cursed, and she shivered at a hideous death scream. Shutting out the abhorrent noise, she slowed Fionn some more. It would take just a moment to jump down, scoop the kitten to safety, and be on their way. She slowed to a trot.

As if sensing her refusal to obey his command, Strongheart urged his horse ahead and straight toward the kitten at a full gallop. Did he think to trample the animal in the dust?

"Move, kitty, move." She urged Fionn faster, calling for Strongheart to swerve.

But then the Norman did something totally unexpected—even for a Norman. In the space of a heartbeat, he flung one leg out of the stirrup and over the saddle, slinging his entire body onto one side of his destrier. She held her breath, expecting the saddle to slip as he hung with all his weight to one side.

The kitten froze in terror, and she could only hope it remained still. Riding at full speed, Strongheart meant to scoop the animal to safety. Just then a silhouette emerged out of the moonlit hell of night to confront them. Her heart slammed against her chest.

With his eyes on the kitten, Strongheart could not see his attacker from behind his warhorse. Even if she warned him of the danger, he couldn't fight from his precarious position.

Dara's hand clasped her dirk. Her eyes narrowed in concentration. It was up to her.

She had never tried such a difficult throw while galloping on horseback. Her foe sprinted toward them on foot, spear hefted, a target over fifty paces away. She'd have only one chance to save Strongheart's life.

"Steady, Fionn." Holding her breath, she timed her throw to when Fionn's gait was smoothest.

Flicking her wrist, she hurled her dirk a little ahead of her target, estimating her speed, his momentum, and the need to hit his throat to silence him before he summoned help. The man staggered, dropped his spear, and collapsed to the ground.

Dara's gaze flew to Strongheart, who'd miraculously managed to snatch the kitten from the ground without falling off his warhorse. His mount galloped by without shying at the body on the ground, and the Norman slowly regained his seat in the saddle.

Before she passed on, she had one horrible glimpse of hands clutching a weapon embedded deep in the throat and bulging eyes soon to glaze in death. Once again, she was sick at the necessity of taking a life. Knowing that stopping could cost them both their lives, she battled the need to empty her stomach.

They rode on and on through the night, slowing only to rest the horses. At the first stop, he thanked her for saving his life, but she was in too much shock to acknowledge his gratitude. Dara directed Strongheart through gorse and heather across the rounded uplands, skirting the mountains and hugging the coast. She avoided the thick woods and thickets that would slow their progress. The ride was not a long one and yet tension made each minute stretch to an eternity.

It appeared they'd escaped, sneaking through the net cast by the armies surrounding Ferns. Sickened as she imagined the loss of lives and devastation of property, she wearily wondered if she could ever again go home. Their enemies' occupation of Ferns turned her stomach and, despite the heat, she shivered.

"Are you cold?" Strongheart asked, after they had stopped so the horses could drink at a mountain stream.

"I never thought it possible to sweat on the outside and yet feel so cold within that my teeth chatter."

Concern deepened his tone. "You had a terrible fright. How much farther?"

She tried to answer but her shaking prevented a response. Wrapping her arms around her midriff, she rocked back and forth, trying to work the stiffness out of her cramped muscles.

Strongheart nudged his warhorse next to Fionn, took the reins from her numbed fingers, and wrapped them around his saddle. In one swift movement, he grasped her waist and lifted her off Fionn and crosswise onto his lap.

"What are you doing?" she sputtered, finally forcing words past her shivering lips.

He handed her a flask. "Drink this."

She choked down the fiery liquor and fire flared in her throat. From one of the packs, he removed a cloak and wrapped it over her shoulders.

Leaning her cheek against his chest and closing her eyes, she allowed him to take care of her. He felt so good, so solid, and she drew on his strength. If she had to be on the run, away from home, she couldn't think of anyone she'd rather be with than the Norman. His arms represented a haven of safety in her world suddenly gone mad with war.

Tomorrow she would take stock of her situation and make plans for her future. But tonight, she gave in to the sharp pain stampeding through her head like a herd of cattle. She yearned to collapse into the luxury of sleep.

The Norman kept his horse to a walk. The animal might not have Fionn's speed, but it had the doggedness of a plow horse. Her eyes closed, she knew not how long, before the Norman shook her awake.

"Sorry, Princess, but I do not know the way. We just passed the spot where we had lunch and Mata spoke with you."

She raised her hand to her throbbing temple and blearily opened her eyes. "Head for the base of those mountains. Once we get close, Mata's monks will find us and lead us inside," she told him, before sleep took her once more.

She awakened to the sound of brothers praying in the communal room beside the small alcove where she lay. A low chanting echoed off the smooth rocks of the cave. Torches in wall sconces lit the damp gloom. Nearby, the abbot stirred a heavenly smelling concoction over a small brazier, and beside Mata sat Strongheart, both talking in voices too low for her to hear.

She threw off the blanket, thankful the pounding in her head had ceased, and joined the men by the brazier, grateful for the warmth. Her feet trod over stones smoothed by the centuries of monks' passing footsteps, and her heart ached at the thought of what would become of the monks without her father's protection. Although it was not cold inside the cave, she doubted she'd ever feel warm again.

With his reddened eyes, Strongheart looked as

if he hadn't slept. If possible, his face was even sootier than last night. A small cut at his forehead had bled and scabbed.

She frowned, observing him more closely. He'd removed his mail and his shirt was torn in several places. Brownish stains—blood—spattered his breeches.

"You returned to Ferns last night," she guessed, realizing she must have slept many hours.

Mata handed him a bowl of stew and fresh honey bread with butter. "He just returned."

After selecting a few choice morsels for the kitten, Strongheart set aside his food and took her hands in his. "They took Ferns."

Her throat went dry, and she licked her bottom lip. She had no more tears. Her insides went numb. "My father?"

"He escaped with more than half his men. Sorcha and Gaillard are with him," he told her before she could ask. "We're to meet them at dawn," he reminded her.

Finding herself surprisingly steady after she'd heard the worst, she squeezed his hands, then released them to accept a portion of stew and bread. Da would need her. She must eat to keep up her strength.

"MacLugh and O'Rourke's men are looting Ferns." He sat beside her and took a spoon to his own food.

"The villages?"

"Burned to the ground."

She gasped, well aware of the hardships her people would face this winter without proper shelter. Children would go with empty bellies, some

211

would freeze. Many women who had suffered rape would lose their lives to miscarriage before spring.

Mata excused himself and left her alone with Strongheart in the windowless cave. She longed to cry great tears of sorrow, yet could not. She longed to scream, tear out her hair, and pound her fists on the walls, but did not.

Had the Norman been right? Should she have agreed to let him bring back more warriors like himself to hold their land? She didn't know. The thought that her stubbornness cost the lives of her people and all she held dear ate away at her.

"Why were O'Rourke's men so vicious?" Strongheart asked. "I have seen looting before," he shuddered, "but not like this."

Dara stood and paced the small room. "It's all my mother's fault."

"Your mother? What has she to do with this?"

Dara sighed, realizing how loyal her people remained to her. Not one had gossiped of the shameful story. Somehow now that she'd lost her home, keeping the secrets of the past mattered not. "My mother, Murgain, was very beautiful with long copper hair and the curves of a love goddess. She was known throughout Eire as a woman with unquenchable passions, a woman rich in cattle. Before my mother lived with my father, she was the wife of one-eyed Tiernan O'Rourke. He did not treat her well. Once Murgain set sight on my father, she wanted him. She coaxed him into her bed and became pregnant with me."

Strongheart settled his back to the wall, his long legs spread before him, the kitten on his lap. He didn't comment, but listened with an intensity that made her nervous.

She continued, choosing her words with care. "My father could not stand the thought of O'Rourke beating the lovely Murgain, and he wanted his child, so when Murgain packed up her jewels and herded her cattle over the border, he was full of joy."

Strongheart's brow arched. "What did O'Rourke do?"

"He was enraged. His people laughed at him, saying he was not man enough to satisfy my mother's passions. His fury turned into a vendetta. He raided the border repeatedly. Many lives were lost, including my half sister's."

"Were your parents happy?"

"Aye. For a short time." She raked her hand through her hair and pushed it out of her eyes, the old hurts less painful than the fresh horrors of the night before. "After I was born, the *Ard-ri* visited, claiming he wanted peace among the lesser kings. Once he saw my mother's beauty, the solution to the problem came easily to him. He, the high king, took the lovely Murgain for his wife."

Strongheart's voice rose and the kitten stirred but did not rise. "She was forced to leave her babe?"

Despite her numbed state, the old emotions tasted acrid. "On the contrary, she encouraged the high king to pursue her." She paused, then continued, fighting but failing to keep the bitterness from her tone. "Murgain did not want me. Unfortunately, before she left, she betrothed me to

MacLugh. That mistake and my refusal to marry him is causing more wars."

"But if she loved Conor, why did Murgain leave your father?"

"I doubt she loved anyone but herself. All her life men doted on her beauty, and she enslaved them with . . . her wiles. The power and riches of the *Ard-ri* were more important to her than my father or her child."

" 'Tis unbelievable."

"But true. The high king's pleasure with her did not last long. The *Ard-ri* caught her cavorting with a stableboy and banished her to a monastery to repent her sins."

Despite his exhaustion, his brow arched. "She is still alive?"

Dara tossed her hair over her shoulder and looked him straight in the eye. "I do not know and I do not care. Mata occasionally passes on messages, supposedly from her, but whether 'tis a trick by the *Ard-ri* to keep my da's hopes alive, I cannot say. Do you have any idea of the suffering that woman has caused and is still causing? Because of her long-ago deeds, half a lifetime later there is war across Eire. O'Rourke cannot forgive my father for stealing his wife. My father cannot forget O'Rourke's savagery. Nor can he forgive Murgain's betrayal. And the *Ard-ri*, instead of settling the perpetual dispute, is encouraging my father's enemies. The *Ard-ri* still blames Conor for spoiling Murgain so she would not look upon him with favor."

Strongheart's weary face expressed sympathy,

but his eyes still had a puzzled slant. "Why did you seek to hide the story from me?"

She lifted her chin, knowing all she had left was her pride. "Murgain is a source of shame, and we do not parade shame before strangers."

"Her acts do not reflect on you."

She shrugged. "Some people think they do. Others would see me pay for her mistakes. And lastly I do not like to remember I come from her loins."

She'd told him enough and hoped he'd never guess the rest. Since she'd only hinted at Murgain's vast appetites, it was unlikely he would connect the past to her fears. Besides, she suspected the coming days would be hard ones, and would give none of them time to dwell on the past. They would have to focus all their efforts on surviving the present.

After leaving the kitten with Mata, they rode to Dobar's Stone in silence. Strongheart's gaze darted around in search of a trap, but Dara thought that unlikely. The monks knew these woods and assured her the enemy had remained in Ferns, drinking fine Leinster ale and celebrating their fortune.

When they reached her father's encampment, guards, exhausted resignation on their faces, allowed her to pass through their perimeter. Downcast at their loss, the men-at-arms huddled wearily in small groups around tiny campfires. The smoke, wisps of harsh black in the breezeless air, hugged the ground and made her throat raw.

Many warriors had injuries, and those that could helped men less fortunate. Others cleaned and sharpened their weapons, sewed torn clothing, or dozed. Every one of them worried about loved ones at home, and yet they remained with her father, loyal and determined to retake their homeland.

Gaillard greeted Strongheart with a stern nod. But it wasn't until she spied her father that the true enormity of the disaster sank home.

Chapter Twelve

Conor's sunken eyes peered from his haggard face. Soot deepened the creases on his forehead, and the day-old stubble on his cheeks and jaws only heightened his burning intensity. His unkempt gray hair had been singed, but as Dara neared, she saw the injury had not reached his scalp. With relief, she spied just one cut on his upper arm, a minor one in need of cleaning but not deep enough to require sewing.

Leaping off Fionn, she raced to give her father a hug, but for the first time in her memory, he did not return her embrace. She wound her arms around his chest and hugged him anyway, but at his continued rejection, her throat tightened and a few tears brimmed over her lids and onto her cheeks.

He set her back from him, and she barely had

time to surreptitiously wipe away her stray tears before he spoke gruffly. "Do not make this harder for me, colleen."

Strongheart approached the clearing, but she kept her gaze on her father. "What are you saying?"

Her father avoided her gaze. "The Norman and I have matters to discuss, lass."

Her heart suddenly thumped like a battering ram. "Then perhaps we should—"

"You will remain here."

She couldn't let them shut her out of their plans. Without her there, the Norman might talk her father into escalating the war. Her neck prickled and goose bumps broke out on her back. "No, Da. I have a right to hear—"

The King of Leinster placed his gnarled hands on his hips. "You have only the rights I give you."

He waved to Seumas and the giant man-at-arms led her away and toward a campfire and breakfast. Furious that her father now preferred to discuss their limited options with the Norman, and hurt that he no longer considered her advice worthwhile, she huddled by the fire, unable to choke down a morsel of food.

The Norman and her father, heads bent together and deep in discussion, strolled some distance from the ragtag army. Weary of watching them for clues to their conversation, Dara drew her knees to her chest, crossed her arms, and rested her forehead on her arms.

To retake Leinster her father had two choices: either wait until MacLugh and O'Rourke's army returned to their homes, or seek an ally to lend

Leinster's men additional support. Either way she expected the campaign to be an extended one. She would not go home for some time.

A hand on her shoulder caused her to raise her head. She looked up to see Sorcha's warm brown eyes and a weary smile of greeting. "As long as we have our lives, all is not lost."

Dara embraced the older woman, this time receiving a hug in return. "Och, Sorcha. 'Tis good to see you. Was it very bad?"

Sorcha patted her hand, and they both took seats by the fire. Dara sipped wormwood tea, but the soothing warmth did not dispel her chills. The sun rose above a blood-red horizon, and a wolf howled, flushing a flock of blackbirds from the heather.

Sorcha drained her tea and set the cup by her side. "It could have been worse. We lost Ferns quickly with our men outnumbered twenty to one. The Norman set smoke fires to cover our retreat. Without Strongheart, many more of our people would have died."

"There's more, isn't there?" Dara sensed her friend was holding back. "What are you not telling me?"

Sorcha licked her lips. "Gaillard thought mayhap I should not speak of it. But 'tis better to be forewarned. Borrack MacLugh shouted threats. Many heard his vow."

Dara looked up. Strongheart and her father approached, their expressions grim. "Tell me, Sorcha. Tell me quick."

"MacLugh vowed to make you his wife."

Dara sucked back her gasp, and Morcolle licked

her face, but she barely felt the wetness of his tongue.

"MacLugh searched every corner of the castle for you," Sorcha whispered, her gaze darting from side to side. "Once he realized you'd escaped, he chopped the furniture to bits in a rage so terrible, his face mottled with fury. He will not give up while he still draws breath."

Dara dropped her face into her hands and bit back a sob. Was she destined to repeat her mother's mistakes? Cause misery wherever she went? If she married MacLugh could they all go home? The thought terrified her. She didn't want him, but she had to face the fact that refusing him had cost many lives. It was her fault children would grow up without fathers. Her fault women had been raped. Her fault Leinster lay in enemy hands.

"No one blames you." Sorcha patted her shoulder. "We knew the necessity of your leaving."

Sorcha knew her so well. Although her escape protected her people's interest, Dara detested playing the part of a coward. Flinging her hair out of her eyes, she lifted her chin. "I could marry another to thwart MacLugh."

"And he could make you a widow."

Knowing Sorcha was right, Dara swallowed the lump in her throat. "Marriage to me is his only legal hold to the land."

When one of her father's men rode at a gallop into camp, drawing his horse to a blowing halt and throwing clouds of dust into the air, their conversation ended. The man leapt from his horse, shouted Conor's name, and when men pointed, he sprinted toward her father.

By now Conor and the Norman had joined Dara and Sorcha by the fire. All of them plainly heard the man's message. "MacLugh comes with his army to force Dara to wed."

The Norman and her father exchanged a long glance. Then her father questioned his informant. "How far away is the advance party?"

"Ten minutes, maybe less."

Strongheart vaulted into his saddle. "Come, Dara. 'Tis time to ride."

She looked from one hard face to another in confusion, wishing she could have overheard their discussion. Somehow she knew vital matters had been decided, matters that affected her and her people. Her father was sending her away from all she held dear, sending her away with a stranger, a Norman. "I am not going with him."

Conor pulled her to her horse and practically tossed her onto Fionn's back. "Do as the Norman says. Most likely, MacLugh will believe you are with the main army. 'Twill be safer if you ride off alone." He struck Fionn's flank with his palm. "Ride."

Behind them, her father called the men to arms, and her blood raced at his fiery tone of old. She might not agree with their plans, but the Norman had taken the decision from her hands, and she would not soon forgive him his arrogance.

Who was he to decide her future? And with her father's vacillating memory, Strongheart could speak nonsense and Conor might agree. But in front of Leinster's men, she'd dared not argue.

Even a wrong decision was better than her father losing the confidence of his warriors.

Although she understood her father's reasons for sending her away, pain stabbed her. She'd lost her home, and might never see her people again.

Dejected, she settled onto Fionn's back and the Norman set the fleet pace. She had to admit it, if she had to be protected by a man, she was glad it was the Norman who would defend her to his utmost, and his best was more than any man in Eire. And yet, as they climbed into the hills, she looked back over her shoulder with her heart in her throat. Her father must not sacrifice himself for her.

With relief she realized Leinster's army had fled toward the sea. While her father was outnumbered, he was too savvy to stay and fight. Just as Sorcha's words had eased her conscience and lightened her worries, a weight she hadn't known she'd carried lifted from her back.

Strongheart headed for the cover of the forests in the hills of Leinster, and they left the gorse and bracken behind. Now as Fionn picked his way through the oaks and firs, she concentrated on ducking the low-hanging branches.

While the mountains had a rocky base, on the lower elevations coniferous trees clung to the thin layer of soil. Under the shade of the giant trees, it was dark, and although the day promised to be almost as warm as the previous ones, Dara couldn't shake the ominous chill wrapping around her bones like a blanket of ice. Would she ever be warm again?

Her fingers barely held on to the reins, but

Fionn followed the warhorse of his own accord. After twenty minutes of hard, uphill riding, Strongheart halted by a bed of bog rosemary, his hand going to the jeweled hilt of his sword.

"Listen," he whispered.

A fly buzzed and Fionn's tail swished. In the distance, an animal moved through the brush, its hasty flight marked by the snap of twigs. A raven took flight.

Then an unnatural silence descended.

Strongheart drew his sword. She hefted her dirk, mouth dry and chest tight. No one had followed them, but it was possible MacLugh had anticipated their flight and circled in front to cut off escape. She felt vulnerable in the clearing. But Strongheart must have stopped there to give himself maneuvering room if he needed to fight.

Before she had time to gasp, three men, MacLugh in the middle, rode out of the cover of the trees toward them as if they'd been waiting for her and the Norman. Her blood raced and she fought to remain calm. In the density of the wood, fleeing would be impossible. Standing ground and fighting was the only prudent course. Edging nearer to Strongheart, she took care not to crowd his horse. Fionn, unaccustomed to battle, shied nervously.

"Easy, boy," she soothed.

Without a word, the three men separated to surround them. Dara turned Fionn to guard Strongheart's back. Hoping fear wouldn't mar her aim, she tried to ignore the tension surging through her blood.

"Wait for my signal, Princess," Strongheart whispered.

"So," Borrack edged forward. "You dare to make off with my bride?"

"She will never be yours," the Norman replied, as if bored.

While his tone might have exuded ennui, Dara knew better. The softer his voice, the more dangerous he became. The utter stillness of his body should have screamed a warning to his opponent. But MacLugh had purchased mail and wore a helm. No doubt he thought himself invincible. His cohorts did not wear armor, and as they closed their circle, she took measure of her targets. If MacLugh's men meant to grab her and hold her hostage to force the Norman to lay down his sword, she would fight them to the best of her ability, and her ability was considerable.

But there were two of them. And she had only one dirk in hand. The spare was beneath her skirt, sheathed to her thigh beyond easy reach.

Sword raised, MacLugh lunged at Strongheart.

"Now." Strongheart held up his shield and defended himself from Borrack's attack.

Behind her, horses grunted and metal clanged against shields. Blood roared in her ears. But she had no time to watch the Norman's display of skill.

She'd guessed wrong. Only one man charged her, not two. Spying the opening beneath her opponent's lowered shield, she didn't hesitate. Lowering his shield was the last error he would make. Her dirk took him down.

Without waiting for his collapse, she turned Fionn to aid the Norman. He'd taken on MacLugh and the other man, who was proving, if not skillful, determined enough to keep Strongheart from pursuing MacLugh. Since Strongheart's second opponent did not wear mail, he let MacLugh bear the brunt of the attack, leaping in to distract Strongheart and then retreating out of range.

But when he spied Dara still free, he turned his attention to her. Before she retrieved her spare dirk, he'd grabbed her wrist, yanking her from Fionn's back.

Unwilling to distract Strongheart, she didn't cry out.

Besides, the man didn't intend to hurt her. And that gave her an advantage. Instead of struggling, she went limp in his arms. He staggered under her unexpected weight, but only for a moment before stiffening and dragging her away from the battling warriors.

Stealthily, her hand crept to her skirt, but her captor caught her movement, pinning her wrists behind her in one of his large fists. She attempted to twist away, but his free hand clasped her throat.

On foot, Strongheart backed toward her, MacLugh giving him little time to maneuver. Sweat glistened on MacLugh's brow and dripped onto his nose. "Yield, Norman. Yield or the woman will be hurt."

She prayed the Norman wouldn't heed his lies. MacLugh needed her alive. "Do not—"

The arm about her throat tightened further, cutting off her words and her air. With one last surge of strength, she rammed her head backward, directly into her captor's nose. With a roar of pain, and blood gushing from his broken nose, he shoved her to the ground, no doubt intending to tackle her.

But she rolled toward his dead friend, intending to retrieve her dirk. Before her foe seized her, Strongheart's blade whistled. And her pursuer breathed no more.

"Watch out," she screamed, but the words came out a mere croak in her bruised throat.

The Norman must have heard her warning because he spun and parried MacLugh's deadly thrust at his back. She crawled toward her dirk, and her hands felt the earth tremble. Placing her cheek to the ground, she heard the sound of hoofbeats. MacLugh's men! They would soon be surrounded.

While the two warriors fought, Dara hurriedly retrieved her dirk from the dead man's chest, captured Fionn's reins, and vaulted to his back. "Norman, reinforcements are coming. We must go."

He pressed MacLugh back. "Ride, Princess."

She had no intention of fleeing through these woods alone. "Come with me."

"I . . . am . . . busy." The Norman spoke between sword blows.

"He will die," MacLugh sneered. "And then I will have you."

Not today. Not any day. Could the Norman not see they had no time for swordplay? The thundering sound of horses' hooves were closer now. MacLugh's men would soon be upon them in such numbers they would never escape.

Her dirk wouldn't penetrate mail. Throwing her dirk once more, she caught MacLugh in the thigh. He staggered and shrieked in pain.

She urged Fionn close to the warhorse, captured the animal's reins, and led the steady mount to the Norman, hoping he could slip away from the still-fighting MacLugh.

"Strongheart. We must go. Now."

With a lunge at his opponent's throat, the Norman forced MacLugh back, gaining the needed time to leap into the saddle. As they slipped into the cover of the woods, MacLugh bellowed for help.

Dara took the lead, winding them deeper into the forest in search of a hiding place she remembered from a hunting trip. When she glanced over her shoulder, she saw no signs of pursuit, but knew MacLugh's men followed. Strongheart protected their rear but remained within her sight.

Despite the dangers of low branches and hidden roots that might trip the animals, pushing the horses' pace in the woods was necessary. As they climbed higher, Fionn's breathing became labored, and yet they couldn't rest.

If they didn't find a place to hide soon, MacLugh's men on fresh horses would overtake them. She had not ridden in these hills in many years and, unsure of the exact spot her father's men had camped long ago, she doubted her ability to find it.

She didn't recall the darkness of the forest or the steepness of the ground. Her pleasant memories of men roasting boar around a campfire and rollicking in the stream contrasted sharply with this madcap gallop. The stream. The old camp had been beside a stream.

Listening past the thump of her mount's hooves hitting pine needles, she heard the sound of rushing water. Their long-ago hunt had taken place near the spring, and the mountain snows had created huge falls. But this late in summer, the water would be lower, calmer.

Suddenly she burst through the woods into a stream of clear mountain water. Allowing Fionn to drink just a few mouthfuls, she got her bearings, trying to remember a landmark that might guide her.

Within moments, Strongheart caught up to her, his eyes wary, his mouth set in a grim line. "We cannot stop."

"We must. Fionn and your horse are exhausted. MacLugh's mounts are not. But there is a cave large enough to hide us near this creek."

"Good. Upstream or down?"

She frowned, knowing the information might make the difference in whether or not they survived. Finally she had to admit, "I do not remember."

"Then we go downstream. Our horses are too tired to climb these hills. Keep Fionn's hooves in the water so we do not leave tracks for them to follow."

They walked side by side in the stream, and Dara realized he hadn't rebuked her for her failure to remember. He was risking his life for her and most men would have reminded her of that fact. Not for the first time, she thought Strongheart different from other men. He had not questioned her memories, hadn't demanded if she was sure this was the same stream she recalled from long ago. He had taken her at her word. Instead of crossing and putting more distance between themselves and their pursuers, he'd made the best decision he could with the information at hand, and she admired him for that. Some men would have insisted *she* choose upstream or down so they'd have someone to blame if the choice proved wrong—but he based his decision on consideration for their hard-pressed mounts.

Up ahead the grade steepened and Strongheart led them onto granite rocks along the rapids before reentering the water. Something about the shape of one rock, long enough for a man to lie on and flat as a bed, niggled half-forgotten memories.

She tried to imagine the water higher than her head. The mountain snows would melt and water would rush through this steep area, creating a waterfall and beneath, a pool deep enough for diving. She drew Fionn to a halt. "I remember Da lying on that flat rock and daring me to dive into the pool. We are almost there."

Urging Fionn forward, she rounded another sharp bend and peered at the granite folds to the right. She held her hand to her eyes and squinted. She pointed. "There."

"I do not see anything."

Her voice rose excitedly. "And neither will MacLugh."

They dismounted, and she led him and the horses around the granite wall shielding the cave's entrance. They had to walk single file into the cave, but then the area widened into a huge cavern, its sparkling walls glistening with sunlight from several crevices overhead.

"We need not even venture outside for water." She led the horses to a small pool at the base of one wall and grinned at Strongheart. "What do you think?"

"This cave is perfect." He took a step closer and enfolded her in his arms. "You are perfect—"

"I am far from perfect," she interrupted him, filled with a warm glow from his compliment.

He emitted a contented sigh. "You are perfect . . . for me, Princess. Only one thing could make me happier."

Tilting her head back, she looked into his smoky eyes, and her heart galloped. "And what is that?"

"Making you my wife." His voice sounded in an appealing, husky tone she found impossible to resist.

Strongheart's warhorse insistently nuzzled them apart and saved her from answering. As if unaware of the confusion his words had caused in her, Strongheart chuckled at the animal's antics. "He wants his saddle removed and a good rubdown."

"You have spoiled him," she agreed lightly.

"He serves me well."

Once again she wondered if he were subtly telling her he would treat her with care if she served him well. But after his many flowers, his small kindnesses with the kitten, and the way he always made her feel special, she knew he would treat her well—so well he'd spoiled her for any other man, for in truth she wanted no other.

As he removed their packs and set them down, she left him to care for the horses while she busied herself with their supplies so he wouldn't see the blush on her cheeks. She tried to take an inventory, but she could not concentrate.

This cave had been used for generations, and she'd been told winding dark passages led deep into the mountain. But this open spot, with its flat floor and high morning-gray ceilings was larger than the great hall at Ferns, and would protect them from the weather as well as from discovery.

Strongheart crooned to the animals, and she imagined him speaking to her the same way, gentle and coaxing. She watched his large hands rub down the horses and recalled the pleasure he'd given when he touched her.

The memories alone caused her stomach to flutter and her hands to tremble. She tried hard to clamp down on the emotions she so feared. Was she willing to lose her good sense by permitting passion to overwhelm her? Her people needed her now more than at any time in the past, but that didn't stop her sudden shortness of breath.

She would be spending the night alone with him. That thought should have terrified her, yet it did not. Was it foolish to think she could have the Norman in all ways and still control the passions raging inside her like a wild summer storm? Dare she risk so much for a fleeting pleasure? But then if the pleasure was fleeting, surely she could control it.

As she tossed their blankets aside, her thoughts whirled in endless circles. He'd finished with the horses long before she'd completed the simple task of laying out a meal of bread and cheese and filling their cups with water from the stream trickling inside the cave.

At the pool she took the time to dip her hands into the icy liquid and wash her face. Doing her best to remove the twigs and stray leaves clinging to her hair, she promised to give it a good combing later.

But when she returned to the spot where she'd left their meal, Strongheart had stepped outside the cave. Digging through the pack, she retrieved her comb and began the task of loosening the snarls. Tomorrow before they rode, she'd braid her hair.

"There's no sign of them," Strongheart told her as he returned. Coming beside her, he took the comb from her hand. "Let me do that."

"Are you sure?"

"That they are gone? No. That I want to comb your hair? Oh, yes. Of that I am very sure."

A warm glow filled her. "But our food."

"Can wait."

As if he were a lady's maid and performed such tasks daily, he sat behind her and started at the bottom tangles, working them free. She drew her knees toward her chest and leaned forward, giving him better access to her long tresses.

Inch by inch he worked the comb through the lower tendrils before moving higher. The comb lightly snagged, and with amazing patience, he repeatedly untangled snarls without causing pain.

The soothing motion should have relaxed her, but his task had the opposite effect. Her flesh was especially sensitive where the comb touched her back, shooting sensual spires down her spine, along her hips, and lower. The feminine place between her thighs ached with an odd, prickling sensation.

She shifted to make the odd ache go away.

"Did I hurt you?"

"No." Her stomach tightened. If she couldn't hold still and control her movements when he simply combed her hair, she might lose all control if she succumbed to her yearnings.

He'd worked his way to her scalp, and she tilted her head back and closed her eyes. She could let him run his hands through her hair like this for hours. And yet she wanted to see what he would do next.

"You have beautiful hair, so thick and shiny. I would never tire of combing it for you. Running my fingers through it is like touching the finest silk."

A strange restlessness had her almost squirming. "Have you combed many women's hair?"

If he thought the question odd, he didn't say so. "Only yours."

His answer pleased her. She didn't want to think of him performing such an intimate task for another and realized she would be jealous if he did. She saw little reason to lie to herself. This wasn't just desire coursing through her. Despite fighting it, despite doing her best to think badly of him, despite knowing he was the wrong man for Leinster, she loved the Norman.

But what was she to do about him? Common sense told her she would not be able to resist him for long. She should be worrying about her father making his escape. She should be worrying about her people in Ferns. She should be worrying if their enemies would find them. But instead, it was taking every measure of her considerable control not to turn, throw herself into his arms, and beg him to kiss her.

Not for the first time, she silently cursed the hot blood surging through her. Why must her good sense have to war with the desire in her body and the passion in her heart? She knew the Norman was not for her. An alliance between them would cause strife throughout her land. And yet she wanted him with every fiber in her being.

A shudder racked her.

Strongheart finished his combing but continued to run his fingers through her hair. He found the tense spot at her shoulders and gently rubbed the soreness away.

His searching fingers moved up along her neck, seeking the stiff spots. When he planted a kiss there, another shiver ran through her, and she forced herself to jerk away. Somehow she knew this time, once he started, she would be unable to utter the words to make him stop.

"What is wrong?" he asked, all innocence.

"What is wrong is that I want you," she admitted in a fierce whisper. "I want to tear off our clothes and make love."

He grinned and she wanted to hit him.

" 'Tis natural to want a man. I am just glad 'tis I you want."

She raised her chin with defiance. "How do I know 'tis just you?"

Her question knocked the grin off his face as if he'd been slapped. Before he answered, she continued. "How do I know I would not respond to any man who was good to look upon and who murmured sweet words?"

His grin returned. "Is that all that is worrying you, Princess?"

Frustration sharpened her tongue. "Do not patronize me, Norman."

He rose to his feet and advanced. "Patronizing you is not what I had in mind."

She told her feet to retreat, but they disobeyed, and she leaned toward him. "No good will come of this."

"Children will come of this." He cupped her chin. "Your father has given permission for us to wed."

Chapter Thirteen

"I cannot marry you," Dara whispered, her heart leaping like a jittery Irish hare.

Strongheart drew her chin closer until their lips almost touched. "Why not?"

He stared into her eyes so intently she suspected he might see the real reason for her fear. Yet she could not draw away and instead, leaned closer, surprised to find their whispered argument oddly stimulating—so much so her lips yearned for his kiss, her breasts ached for his touch. "Have you listened to nothing I have said? You are a Norman."

"How can I forget it when you remind me every few minutes?" His brow arched, and he whispered into her mouth, their lips so close she savored the scent of his breath.

She should stop him but was weary of fighting

the yearning of her body, the wild desire of her heart, and him, too. Just this once, she wished to stop her thoughts and shove aside the sharp warnings flaring in the sane part of her mind. "But—"

Sweeping aside her objection, he spoke slowly, his husky voice as mesmerizing as a mystic's. "We are not so different, you and I. We both want this."

His lips finally skimmed hers, creating a whirlwind of torrential sensations, his touch airy as a blanket of dew across the lush grasses on a mist-laden dawn. Her blood coursed irresistibly faster, almost overwhelming her.

"Please," she whispered. "I will never love a man who does not seek peace."

"I would give you peace if I could."

His words were enough. Unable to hold back, she flung herself against him, and the hard muscles of his chest seemed the perfect foil for the softness of her breasts. His hips cradled hers, providing tangible evidence of a need matching her own.

In eager welcome, she wound her hands around his corded neck and into his thick hair, her fingers threading their way to his scalp, her actions an unvoiced craving for him to deepen their kiss. He complied with a soft groan, and shivers of tantalizing delight skittered over her.

Hungrily, she kissed him, giving herself freely to the heady sensation of his taste, his scent, his touch. As she inhaled the intoxicating aroma of his masculine essence mixed with the fragrance of leather, she relished the hot, tangy taste of his mouth. And she was swept away on a tidal wave of delight that was yet to crest when suddenly she was no longer in his embrace.

It was the Norman who had pulled away, his irises so smoky she expected them to burst into flames. "I need to check for signs of pursuit. Then you should eat."

Food would not satisfy the hunger he'd whetted, but she turned away so he wouldn't see the disappointment and confusion in her gaze. How could he kiss her, make every bone in her body ache for more—and then simply stop? Did he have any idea she felt like she'd gone to the edge of a precipice, lost her balance, and only been hauled back at the very last instant?

After he left the safety of the cave, she watched his progress from the entrance. He moved upstream with the supple grace of a wolf, his smooth, lithe movements those of a predator on a hunt.

She lost sight of him for a few minutes, and then he returned to the pool, the same spot her father had dared her to swim in so long ago. Strongheart lay his sword down within reach, yanked off his shirt, and began to remove his breeches. He must have felt as grimy as she did because he intended a quick dip in the mountain stream.

She grinned, thinking if he had time for a bath then so did she. Hurrying back into the cave, she removed soap from her pack. While the water in the pool inside the cave was only up to her knees, it was more than sufficient for a bath.

She bit her tongue to refrain from squealing at the frigid temperature, but the icy water invigorated her. Deciding at the last moment her hair needed a washing, she dunked her head under, the water so cold it stole her breath. She gritted her teeth to endure another good soaking to remove the suds, and when she finally climbed from the pool, her teeth chattered.

Hearing footsteps, she scrambled to dry herself. "Do not enter yet."

"Take your time, Princess," he told her, his voice soft and tender. "I found signs of MacLugh's men passing north of here over an hour ago. Even if they circle back, this cave is too well hidden for them to find us."

Standing naked in the cave while she spoke to him brought a strange tightness to her chest, a pucker to her nipples. She ran the drying cloth over her arms and legs with a vigorous swipe. Although he could not see her, a wantonness heated her and she hurriedly plucked a clean chemise and tunic from the pack.

Slipping the garments over her head, she wondered why he'd pulled away from her when she'd been so close to giving him what he wanted during their kiss. Where she found the courage, she knew not, but the question burned inside her. "When you kissed me before, why did you pull back?"

"Disappointed?"

The tensing of her jaw betrayed her deep frustration. "Tell me why, Norman. 'Tis important to me."

"You were not ready."

She chewed her bottom lip. What did he mean, she was not ready? Did he sense the battle inside her, the war between her convictions and desire? She lost the courage to ask such a question. In-

Susan Kearney

deed she hoped he would not guess why she must reject him. In truth, marriage to any man was risky. Marriage to a man this skilled at seduction was an exceptionally dangerous proposition.

Dara clenched and unclenched her fists and took several calming breaths. She would not be enslaved by her passions.

"You can come in now."

Once more determined to resist him, she thought herself well prepared until he entered the cave with an armload of kindling and a large gutted and cleaned salmon. As he strode under a beam of sunlight, his dark hair, still wet from his bath, glistened. Dark lashes sparkled with water droplets, and she caught herself staring.

He hadn't bothered to replace his shirt, and as he bent to set down his burden, the muscles in his arms bulged, reminding her how vulnerable she was. With strength such as his, he could take by force whatever he wanted. And he'd made no secret he wanted her.

Swallowing hard, she accepted the fish and searched for his skillet to cook the salmon. Concentrating on the task at hand, she sought to keep her mind from wandering into dangerous areas.

As she fumbled through their packs, she asked through stiff lips, "What of the smoke? Do you think 'tis safe to start a fire?"

He didn't look up from his task. "I shall keep the flame small. MacLugh will not find us since the smoke will disperse through the many openings overhead."

While Strongheart knelt and started a fire, she removed a few precious spices from her traveling

240

pouch and sprinkled the fish. Soon the aroma of cooked salmon had her mouth watering.

She sipped some water, then broke her bread into little pieces, topped it with cheese, and chewed nervously. Silence descended between them. She wished she could ask him to don his shirt, but her request would reveal too much. With renewed determination, she kept her eyes averted.

They could have easily been husband and wife, married many years, with little to discuss between them. Only this silence had a honed edge that made nibbling easier than eating.

When their fish was cooked, Strongheart gave her a flaky portion, perfectly done. Was there anything he could not do well? Most of the time he seemed so self-sufficient he appeared complete unto himself. But then his expression heated, his eyes smoked, and his gaze upon her made her tremble.

To break the awkward silence and distract herself from her thoughts, she asked, "When will we leave?"

He gave her a calm, thorough look. "In a day or two."

She bit back a gasp. The thought of spending two days in the cave alone with him seemed so much more dangerous than an open camp where they had to be instantly ready to defend themselves.

She bit into her fish, barely tasting her food, her mind fluttering with anxiety. "What of my father?"

"We will meet him once 'tis clear." He spoke with quiet assurance. "Let MacLugh search the forests and bogs from Dublin to Ferns while we remain hidden and safe."

She didn't feel safe, not when he looked at her like a hungry man intent on devouring his supper. How could she escape her feelings when forced to share such close quarters? Their lives depended on one another. For the next day or so they would eat together, sleep together, and have no one to talk to but each other.

And her father had given his permission for them to wed.

The more frantic the pace of her thoughts, the more at ease Strongheart appeared. In fact he looked contented, almost happy for the first time since they'd met. Did he enjoy having her at his mercy? Was this all a game to him?

When he stood and walked to their blankets, Dara's hands twisted in her tunic. As soon as she realized her actions, she forced her hands to her sides. He flipped open his blanket, laid it beside the fire, and unsheathed his sword. When he turned to spear her with a look, she jerked.

But his voice was tender. "I need sleep and you must be tired, too. Care to join me?"

He *had* been up all night. Maybe he did intend to sleep. So then why was her heart pounding so hard she couldn't draw breath? Wishing she could blame her reaction on her own lack of sleep, she looked down and stared at the cave floor as if she found the dirt utterly fascinating.

He noticed her hesitation and the corner of his mouth turned in a wry grin. "I promise not to attack you."

She wrinkled her nose and shook her head. "Do you always keep your word?"

As if the question was beneath him, he didn't deign to reply. Instead he opened her blanket beside his, kicked off his boots, and lay down, leaving the choice to her. She thought of removing her blanket to the other side of the fire, but then he would think she feared him.

But it was not him she feared. By now she knew he was a man of his word. He would never force himself on her. It was her own banked desires she feared.

Still, she did not want him to think her vulnerable, so she lay casually beside him, careful not to touch him. Once he fell asleep, she would feel safer, and it did not take long before his soft even breathing assured her he slept. The realization he had not made one untoward move relaxed her, and she closed her eyes.

She slept far longer than a short nap. When she awakened on her side, warm and cozy, the sky, seen through the holes in the cave's roof, had blackened, and the flames had burned down to red embers. While she'd slept, Strongheart had fed a few logs to the fire, brought in grass for the horses, and smoked the leftover fish.

At first she thought the warmth was from the fire or the blanket. In her drowsy state she didn't analyze the source of her snug contentment. But then she awakened fully and realized she lay on her side, her head pillowed on the Norman's arm, her hair caught between them, pinning her in place.

If that weren't enough to alarm her, her tunic

had bunched at her waist. Strongheart's chest pressed to her back, his leg flung over her bare thighs, and his hand had slipped under her tunic and intimately cupped her breast. She held still despite the exquisite sensations streaming through her, listening and hearing only his even breathing. She tried to scoot away, but in sleep, his arms tightened, and his arousal pressed gently against the curve of her bottom.

Escaping from his clutches without waking him would probably be impossible. She had two choices: roll away, yank out her hair, and chance waking him; or hold still and hope he released her on his own accord. While she mulled over the decision, his lips nuzzled her ear, and while his hand fondled her breast, his fingers plucked at her nipple as skillfully as the blind bard strummed his harp. Music so sweet she almost cried out with the pleasure of it, sent chords of trilling vibration straight from her breast to her very core.

Surely he could not still be sleeping? And yet he did not move one inch, except his thumb endlessly caressing her nipple. Every sensation in her body kindled into flames from his touch, all of her concentration lingering on the movement of his thumb. When she could no longer bear it, she attempted to yank away, uncaring if she woke him.

She was on the verge of losing control, and if her body didn't find escape from his bittersweet torture, she would give in. Every point of her skin felt invigorated, the potency of his touch pressuring her like pelting rain on a windy day. And yet she ached to revel in the feeling, let desire have its way. Come what may, she wanted to dance in the rain and wash away her past and her fears.

She no longer wanted to think. She only wanted to feel and could no longer suppress the elemental need that compelled her to turn and welcome his kiss. Even finding him awake, his irises reflecting burning embers, could not make her pull back. He had only to dip his other hand beneath her tunic and touch her other breast and nipple, and she was ready to offer herself up to him. Lose herself, become a woman.

He stopped kissing her only long enough to pull her tunic over her head. The cool air whisked her bare skin, and then his warm hands found her breasts, heating her, making her long for more. Her senses came alive as if awakening from a trance. Her sight sharpened, and she'd never seen anything so beautiful as his dark hair and the seductive slant of his smile in the flickering firelight before he kissed her again. She returned his kiss, taking in the scent of the fresh grasses he'd brought in for the horses, the tangy oak burning in the fire, and his musky aroma. Something else, a sweet, flowery smell she couldn't identify, mixed with the others.

The night was as still as a cairn. And she had nothing on. She wriggled closer, longing to memorize the delicious feel of his bare chest, rough and hard, against hers. She couldn't get enough of him. Her hands explored the contours of his back, his warm flesh over sleek muscles, and she pulled him closer, his kiss singing in her veins.

The way he held her made her feel like fragile glass. Like an artist discovering every nuance of shape and shadow, he caressed her skin, delving into the hollows between her breasts. He set her on fire with wanting him. Her pulse raced. The blood heated in her veins.

She knew no shyness, no hesitancy, no awkwardness, as if destiny had saved a perfect moment for them.

"I want you," she gasped, aching deep down in her loins, shifting her hips to tempt him.

"You shall have everything you want—and more," he promised, his voice hoarse with desire, his teasing tone sending a ripple of excitement through her.

Reaching over their heads, he retrieved a branch of honeysuckle that hadn't been there when she fell asleep. He positioned her on her back on the blanket. Immediately she reached for him.

"Not yet," he murmured.

When he tickled her cheekbones with the soft petals, she blew him a playful kiss. But then he skimmed a path down her neck to her breasts, and her pulse raced wildly. The light petals whispered across her breasts like the flutter of butterfly wings, and she inhaled sharply, never having imagined anything could feel so delightful.

Again she reached for him.

"Patience, Princess."

As he traced a trail over her skin, the downy blossom stoked a sensuous fire and her nipples tightened. Her heartbeat skittered like a newborn colt's. Drugged by the scent of the flowers, she quivered under his seductive gaze.

She'd never known her skin to be so responsive, and she marvelled at the sensations the slightest change in pressure caused. But it was the waiting that caused her to grow wild. Not knowing where he would touch her next or for how long kept her strung taut as a bow ready to launch an arrow into an unknown domain.

He swirled the fluffy buds over her belly, then teasingly down her thighs. She parted her legs, closed them, then parted them again when she could no longer resist the heavy ache pooling there. The fever of her responses became disorienting. Her head spun. Her heart went mad. Everything in her world, even her next breath, seemed geared to the ultimate destination of his hand and the silky softness of the honeysuckle petals. Finally he reached her center, but the petals only inflamed the fires he'd kindled, and she ached for something more.

"Please," she whispered.

"Please what? Please stop? Please continue?"

"I want you now."

Finally he tossed the honeysuckle aside, and with his hands began an exploration of her flesh. She sucked in her breath at the exquisite sensations rippling along her like fine silk. When his thumbs flicked the sensitized tips of her nipples, she couldn't suppress a soft moan.

"You like that?"

"I feel so . . ." Words failed her.

A wet tongue replaced his thumb.

She gasped and her hands dug into the muscles of his shoulders. There was no one but the Norman. Nothing but feeling. Sensation. And pleasure.

Gathering her into his arms, he held her snugly.

Susan Kearney

She wanted more. She had to remove his breeches. Her hand reached down the flat length of his stomach, but he stopped her from reaching farther. "No, not yet," he whispered into her hair.

She understood he wished to prolong their desire, but she felt ready to burst. He took her hands and placed them on the blanket pillowed beneath her head.

"Do not let go."

At last he removed his breeches, and she bit her bottom lip at the sight of him—so gorgeously different from her own body. She ached to skim her hands along his flesh, explore the hard muscles of his chest and stomach. She glanced lower and gasped. Could he possibly fit inside her?

Scooting down between her parted thighs, he caressed, aroused, gave pleasure. She gasped again as his lips traced the sensory path he'd traveled with the honeysuckle, from her breasts to her stomach, and lower. Surely he did not intend to kiss her there?

He did.

She squeezed the blanket with her hands. Lust burned in her, branding her with a fiery hunger she hadn't known could be so potent, so powerful. Her feet arched. She never dreamed he could feel this warm, this gentle, this sizzling. Need made her cry out. Her hips gyrated.

Suddenly he kissed her hungrily, and she gave herself freely. He smothered her lips with demanding mastery, and hedonistic wanton that she was, she savored every moment.

When her breath came raw in her mouth and tiny little groans vented from the back of her throat, she released the blanket and dragged him to her with a strength she hadn't known she possessed.

"Now. I want you, now."

He positioned himself between her thighs, and she welcomed the moist tip of his sex. Slowly, he eased into her tightness, hesitated and spoke through gritted teeth. "I do not want to hurt you."

In a frenzy of need, her hands clasped his buttocks. Thrusting her hips upward, she forced his hard shaft deep within her, the ripping of the tiny barrier of no consequence to her pleasure.

She needed flesh into flesh, heat into heat, man into woman.

Her breasts tingled against his hair-roughened chest, her impatience growing to eruptive proportions. She dug her nails into the length of his back, urging him to thrust harder, deeper, but he resisted, easing into her, then withdrawing. Slowly.

Her breath came in long surrendering moans. She wound her legs around his hips, abandoning herself to the whirl of sensation. The hot tide of passion raged through her, drove her into a frenzy. She gasped in sweet agony as she was drawn to a peak of delight she had never known. She screamed, and was dimly aware of his own groan of satisfaction. Every muscle in her body contracted, then released, shooting ribbons of pleasure through her.

When she could again breathe, when a semblance of order returned to her swirling thoughts, she realized he was still inside her and gazing at her with concern. "Are you all right?"

She blushed in remembrance of the noises she

Susan Kearney

had made. Her ears still rang with the sound of her scream. "Why do you ask?"

"You were unusually vocal," he teased. "I am pleased you enjoyed yourself."

She turned her head away from him. She'd enjoyed herself, all right. She'd enjoyed herself so much the passion had overtaken her senses. Despite all her pretense otherwise, she was her mother's child, and the thought made her stomach sicken.

How could she have allowed her feelings to overcome her good reason? And now that she'd experienced the fierce and exquisite pleasure of making love, it would be harder to resist temptation. At the thought of being enslaved by her own passions, bile rose in the back of her throat.

Placing her hand flat on Strongheart's shoulder, she shoved him, and he allowed her to push him away. She ignored the puzzled look on his face and his outstretched hand that would only draw her back into his clutches. Scrambling to her feet, she grabbed her clothes and bolted for the cave's entrance.

"Wait," he called to her. "Dara, what is wrong?"

Strongheart stood slowly. Why had she raced from the cave? By the rood! Would he ever understand her? She'd been so passionate he'd had difficulty holding back. Never had a woman given herself so freely to his touch, and to think she'd done so on her first time had intoxicated him, increasing his pleasure tenfold.

He could no longer think of her as a bonus to making a home for himself in this land. She'd become special. With passion like hers, they would have magnificent sons, spirited daughters. He wanted her with him, always.

But why had she run? He frowned as he quickly donned his breeches and grabbed his sword before following her from the cave. When she'd given herself to him, she'd given herself completely, and she had not held back. She hadn't been afraid when he'd undressed her, caressed her—not even when she forced him past her maiden's barrier. He suspected she'd felt little pain. She'd experienced pleasure—after her ecstatic scream, there could be no doubting that.

His brow furrowed. So where had she gone without shoes and without her dirk, racing away as if the very devil himself had chased her?

From the cave's entrance he could not see her or hear her. Dawn came later in the mountains, and the first early rays of sunshine had risen barely high enough to filter over the peaks and through the trees, not yet hot enough to burn off the early-morning mist.

Hurriedly he skidded down toward the creek, the only route available. In England, an untried maid might have worried about losing her virginity before going to her marriage bed, but he had learned the customs of Eire were different. Here, it was considered a boon if a woman entered the marriage with her belly already swollen with child, for then the woman had proven her ability to conceive.

So why? Why had she run from him? He'd been grateful this time she'd listened to her desire rather than her head, since once he'd taken off her tunic and seen her beauty, he'd wanted all of her.

He reached the stream. In the basin area the mist was a thick fog. Over the sound of water trickling into the pool, he thought he heard a piercing sob. "Dara?"

"Go away," she demanded, her voice hoarse.

"Tell me why," he insisted, hoping to keep her talking and track her by the sound of her voice. When she didn't answer, an eerie sensation prickled the hairs at his nape. Her actions didn't make sense. Why would she make love to him and then run away?

"Dara?" he called again. "Come back to the cave. 'Tis not safe for you to be out here alone."

" 'Tis not safe in the cave," she protested. "You touched me."

Her last words sounded like a wail of accusation—as if she hadn't asked for his touch. She must be close to hysteria.

Quickening his pace, he hurried along the bank and stumbled over her clothes. She'd gone into the water. With the memory of her voice fraught with panic, terror for her safety seized him. Was she trying to drown herself?

He lunged into the water, seeking her through the fog. Suddenly a breeze parted the mist, and he caught sight of her, a sight he'd never forget. With a handful of gravel and sand from the bottom of the pool, she scoured her skin. She stood silent and naked, blood running down her arms and legs.

By the rood! Had he caused her such pain that she would harm herself? That he might have brought her to this madness sickened and saddened him.

His first instinct was to force her to stop hurting herself. But she stood close to a ledge, and he recalled that this pool dropped into another. If she meant to harm herself, he needed to calm her—not send her over the edge.

Clearly she was in deep inner turmoil, the agony inside more unbearable than the mutilation of her flesh. He kept his voice mellow, as if her continual scrubbing didn't pierce him to the core.

He stepped toward her. "Did you not like it when I touched you?"

Her voice turned hard, but he still heard her agony. "Of course I liked making love. How could I help but like it?"

Her answer confused him, but he still took several steps closer. "Then come to me, Princess. I will be gentle."

"No. Do not touch me. If you ever touch me again, I will slice out your heart."

She scooped another handful of gravel and smeared it over her breast. He pounced, grabbing her wrist before she could do herself more harm.

She screamed at him, kicking, biting, and scratching as if crazed, but he did not release her. The noise could alert MacLugh's men to their location if they still searched nearby, and he had to take her to safety quickly. He was about to fling her over his shoulder and carry her back to the cave when she slumped and meekly allowed him to lead her from the water.

Her trembling skin was icy to his touch and her teeth chattered, but she did not seem to notice.

Susan Kearney

After throwing her tunic around her shoulders, he led her back to the cave. They stopped only once, when she bent over to retch.

Could the food have been bad? He thought not, or he, too, would have been sick. Besides, bad food would not account for her scouring her body with gravel.

Once inside the cave, he dried her, taking care to clean her wounds before dressing her, and finally wrapping a blanket around her. Still, she shivered and her lips were blue. Hurriedly, he built up the fire and boiled water for tea.

He looked into her haunted eyes and wondered if she'd lost her sanity. She'd withdrawn into herself and didn't take much notice of him. Instead she sat hugging her knees and rocking. When he handed her tea, she swallowed. When he gave her food, she ate. But she didn't speak or explain.

As much as he wanted answers, he recognized now was not the time to pound her with questions. Suspecting her hold on reality was much too fragile, he straightened her blanket, hoping she'd sleep. She didn't. Perhaps if he spoke of normal things and of the future he could draw her back to him. "We'll leave here in another day. Within a fortnight, we shall meet your father in Wales."

Her eyes widened and her lips thinned. "You need not lie to me, Norman." She spat the words as if he were her vilest enemy and not the man with whom she had just made passionate love. "Da would never go to England."

254

Chapter Fourteen

Strongheart raked a hand through his hair and paced from one side of the cave to the other. "Your father has no choice. Where did you expect him to go?"

Dara spoke in a monotone. "I thought we would remain in Leinster until he recruited more men."

At least Dara was speaking to him, an improvement over her former silence. But like a wolfhound gnawing a bone, she could not let go. Her eyes flashed, and he welcomed the spark, even if she did disagree with him. This feisty woman was the Dara he knew, enjoyed, and respected. The woman by the river, sanding her skin until it bled, had been like an apparition tortured by the demons of hell.

"Where would Conor find additional men?" he asked softly.

Her hands twisted in her tunic. "He could appeal to the *Ard-ri* to pick my husband. I cannot marry both O'Rourke and MacLugh, so the loser of the *Ard-ri's* decision would leave Ferns. Then my father could reclaim Leinster."

How many times must he tell her she would never marry anyone but him? He'd had enough of her nonsense, but one glance in her direction reminded him how vulnerable she was. With a sigh, he calmed his tone. "After what we have shared, you would marry whomever the *Ard-ri* chose?"

She met his gaze without flinching. "I do not have a choice. I have never had a choice."

Since her father had given his permission for a Norman to marry his daughter, she had no choice but to obey the King of Leinster. So then why could she not accept she belonged to him?

Although he knew she had not faked her pleasure, perhaps she had not been as willing to make love to him as he'd first thought. "Did you give yourself to me because your father said we may wed?"

She remained silent so long he thought she might revert to her former withdrawal. But finally, she spoke, her eyes filled with pain. "You got what you wanted. The reason does not matter."

With another long sigh, he took a seat behind her, grabbed her comb from her pouch, and worked on the wet snarls of her hair. It was not unreasonable for her to keep her thoughts to herself when he in turn did not confide in her. Still, she needed to know the plans he and Conor had made. Wrestling with his conscience, he decided how much to tell her.

The truth. He would tell her the truth. Or most of it. "You were right about me—I came to Eire seeking an opportunity to build my home and conquer this land."

She stiffened beneath his fingers. "And now?"

He stopped combing, wishing she faced him to see if she would believe his words. "I cannot deny the opportunity to win a kingdom holds a certain appeal. A thousand Normans could take this island."

"We would fight you."

"And you would lose. Your men are brave, but they lack the armament and skills of modern warfare."

She swung round to face him and snatched the comb from his hand. "Damn you! I have already lost my home. Now you say I may lose my entire land to invaders. Why threaten me?"

Although she hadn't spoken of it until now, he'd known she was homesick and sought to reassure her. "Since I met a beguiling Irish princess with hair the color of fire and eyes more precious than emeralds, I have changed."

She threw down the comb, squared her shoulders, and did not retreat one inch. "You are good with pretty words to flatter a woman. But I have seen you fight, Norman, and know you are a man of war."

"Men change. I have changed," he repeated. "You have made me change. After we regroup in Wales, then return and retake Leinster, I will settle down and raise a few bairns."

Her eyes narrowed and her fists rested on her hips. "You do not seek to be *Ard-ri*?"

"You have made me reassess my goals." He tugged her onto his lap, and she did not object. "I would spend my nights in Castle Ferns with you in my bed rather than fighting and sleeping in cold skins on the ground. While I will not run from a fight, I no longer glory in battle. Perhaps I am getting soft—"

She chuckled and lightly pounded his thigh with her fist. "Aye, your muscles are as soft as a baby's. Why, you have grown so weak, next time your woman will have to make love to you while you lie helpless on your back."

"An idea with merit. But as much as I would enjoy such a pleasure, you may be too sore for—"

She flushed. "Sir, let me be the judge of that."

"I think not." Hardness entered his tone. "Not if you must scrub yourself with sand to feel clean after I make love to you. Did you accept me because your father so ordered? Did you find me so distasteful? Because if so, you need only tell me, and I will not touch you again."

As he spoke, her jaw dropped, the flush receded, and she paled. "Surely you do not think . . . you were responsible?"

"Do you see anyone else here?" He threw his hands wide. "I do not know what to think. I know only that I've never been more scared in all my life, thinking I caused you injury."

Strongheart gathered Dara to him, and she snuggled against his warmth, unsure whether to believe his words. She decided Strongheart had two hearts, one as hard as a diamond, the other as soft and pliant as warm wax. Had he truly changed his plans, or was he lying so she would accept him? Could this warrior give up his dreams and goals to live with her in peace? For a moment she envisioned them together in the rock pool, swimming with their children. And later, when they were alone, making love.

The vision of them together, living happily at Ferns, was so perfect, she doubted the truth of his words. Life never worked out so well. She was a fool to think she could have what she'd always wanted, a home, children, and the peace to watch them grow old.

Had making love to Strongheart already changed her way of thinking? Did she now seek to fulfill her dreams instead of facing facts? The passion they'd shared was so much more compelling than she'd imagined. It was as if he were a wizard, and he'd woven his spell, captivating her by spinning magical dreams and fairy-tale promises. As she leaned against his chest, her head resting beneath his chin, the sensation of being loved and cherished was so delicious, she feared her own feelings had already prejudiced her judgment. She so wanted to believe him, and yet it would be foolish to trust him.

She had to be careful. For now, she would accept his change of heart, but she would watch him, ready to spot deceit.

He waited for an explanation for her former actions, and she could not have him continue to think it was he who had caused her pain. Neither could she speak of the truth, for if what she feared proved true, he would not want her.

Perhaps she could tell him part of her fears

without his guessing the whole. She snuggled against his chest and smoothed her fingers over the skin of his shoulder. "I was afraid to experience passion."

"Because you saw Sorcha's rape?"

"I know men can be cruel. But 'twas not pain I feared but pleasure."

"You make no sense, woman."

She sighed as she summoned the words to explain. "Remember the story I told you about my mother?"

"Aye."

"She could not control her life because her passions controlled her. I was afraid I would be like her. I sought a disciplined life, so I would never forget my duty. I avoided intimacies with men, hoping I would never feel passion."

"You believed if you didn't experience passion, you wouldn't be led into temptation?"

"Aye. And then you came along."

"And?" he prodded.

She flung her hair back and looked at him. "You were different from the others."

She thought he would ask her how he was different from her other suitors. She would tell him of his willingness to listen to her, his small gifts, his tenderness. When he was with her, he never looked at other women. Even when she'd refused to give in to his advances, he'd made his wishes known that he wanted only her. How could she not help but feel cherished?

His hands moved to rest on her shoulders. "Now that you have experienced passion you are afraid 'twill affect your judgment?"

She'd guessed wrong. Apparently he knew he was different from other men and didn't require her to flatter him. Instead, he'd asked a question much harder to answer.

Her heart warred with her mind. "Already I want to believe you. Trust you."

"Why is it so difficult to believe I'll help retake Leinster? I would win back your land for us. I, too, would see our children raised at Castle Ferns, our sons and daughters riding across the lush fields."

"Trust does not come easy to me, Norman."

The question was not *whether* he chose to retake Leinster, but *how* he would do it. Besides, would Leinster be enough for him, or would he use their land as a base to conquer the rest of Eire?

The devastation they'd left behind would take years to rebuild. Her stomach clenched, knowing the castle and its people would never be the same. Not everyone would have survived the battle, and she didn't relish the thought of rebuilding while her husband and father went to war. But her thoughts were jumping way ahead, frightening her more because normally she thought in an orderly and pragmatic manner.

First they had to concentrate on escape without MacLugh and O'Rourke catching them, then meet with her father and form a plan to retake Castle Ferns without involving all of Eire in a war. With a sigh, she climbed from Strongheart's lap and packed her belongings. The sooner they left, the sooner she could return to Ferns.

They rode north toward Dublin, staying within the cover of the forest. Strongheart caught game, and she foraged for berries and herbs for tea.

261

Since leaving the cave, they had seen horse droppings and cold campfires, but their luck held, and they did not come across another hostile force.

They traveled along the side of a lough, the clear waters reflecting the cool green from the mountains and the gray, clouded sky. Avoiding the small herds of cattle had been easy, since in summer, the herds stayed in the rich valleys.

At the peak of a hill, Strongheart held up his horse so Dara could catch up, and they surveyed the city together. She sighed, already imagining the stench of too many people living in too close an area. She never understood the need for people to wall themselves within cities.

She tucked a stray lock behind her ear. "As we near Dublin, hiding will become more difficult."

Strongheart gave her hand a squeeze. "Most likely MacLugh and O'Rourke will have men searching for us at the port since that's where we must attain passage to England."

"We need a disguise."

Strongheart grinned. "I am listening, Princess. What do you have in mind?"

"MacLugh and O'Rourke have their men searching for a Norman and a woman," she spoke slowly, thinking aloud. "If I wore the clothes of a boy and cut my hair—"

"Absolutely not."

She didn't relish the idea of cutting her hair either. "Perhaps I could stuff it beneath a cap. For you, we must find you less distinctive clothes. The breeches must go."

He threw back his head and laughed, his dark

hair ruffling in the breeze. "Determined to make me into an Irishman, are you, woman?"

"You must hide the jewels on your sword hilt along with your armor."

"Soon you will have me walking about naked," he protested with another laugh. "Even if I conceal the jeweled hilt, my sword is still unusual. Yet, we cannot go about without weapons."

"Hide a dirk beneath your clothes. They won't be looking for a man without sword, mail, or horse."

The laughter disappeared from his eyes. "I will not give up my warhorse."

"We'll retrieve our mounts after we return to Eire. I know a nearby farm where we can acquire the things we need, so you need not go home naked," she teased, a saucy smile on her lips. "And since a man of your size—"

"Careful, Princess."

"—might draw unreasonable—"

He cleared his throat. "Unreasonable?"

"—undeserved," she amended airily, "attention, we should find you a tunic that will at least cover your—"

"I am warning you, Princess."

"—your knees," she finished with a not-so-innocent giggle, finding she adored teasing him.

He rarely got angry with her, and despite the urgency of their ride, she'd enjoyed the days spent in verbal sparring, discussions, and gentle teasing. Although they had not made love again since the first time in the cave, it had been Strongheart who said he must stay alert to protect them, claiming she was such a distraction they'd be in danger if he lost himself with her. When he told her he could awaken from a light sleep more easily than he could draw away from her during the heat of passion, she'd grinned and blushed happily, glad she had such powers to divert him.

Knowing he, too, could forget everything except their mutual pleasure made her own failing seem more ordinary. Perhaps if she couldn't control her powerful feelings for Strongheart, it was not such a bad thing—not if their goals were similar. He'd told her he wished to live with her in Leinster, not go on and conquer the rest of Eire. Perhaps he spoke the truth.

As they rode toward Dillon's farm, she wondered if her mother had fooled herself, justifying her actions with this same kind of reasoning. Was she making excuses to rationalize the fact that she desperately wanted to make love again?

Glad for a diversion from her thoughts, she pulled Fionn to a halt beside Strongheart. They stood among tall pines, looking down on Dillon's farm, a conglomeration of wattle and daub huts with thatched roofs. A herd of cattle grazed peacefully on one side of the valley below them, while a raven circled lazily overhead.

"What is it?" she asked.

He dismounted in the cover of the trees and unsaddled his warhorse. " 'Tis possible MacLugh or O'Rourke sent men here to search for us."

She slid off Fionn's back, grateful for a chance to stretch her legs. "Are we waiting until dark to sneak into—"

"Stay here," he ordered, "till I check to see if 'tis safe."

She crossed her arms over her chest and grinned

at his high-handedness. "Just how will you go about that task, Sir Norman?"

"Don't call me that. It sounds ridiculous."

"Well, you"—she pointed her finger at him and prodded his chest with each word—"are ridiculous."

He frowned, and the harsh narrowing of his dark eyes would have quelled her if she hadn't known him well. He opened his mouth to speak, but she beat him to it, speaking as she continued to poke his chest with her finger. "Will you recognize MacLugh or O'Rourke's men? Will you recognize my friends? Can you rid yourself of your fancy accent? And if any stranger is passing through, do you not think they might notice your jeweled sword and a man wearing breeches?"

He folded his arms over his massive chest. " 'Tis too dangerous for you to go in alone."

He didn't fight fairly. He didn't disagree with her wisdom, for he could not find fault with her sense. So instead, he questioned her judgment, which was not the same thing at all.

Even if it made more sense for her to leave him with the animals, the stubborn look on his face warned her he wouldn't alter his decision. "Perhaps a compromise is in order?"

He nodded, without committing to anything, his eyes glinting with wary amusement. She supposed she should be grateful he'd consider her ideas, but instead she resented the leadership role he'd assumed when this was her land, her enemy, and she was the one with a better grasp of the problems they faced.

"We could wait until dark and sneak in together."

His brow arched. "Leave our mounts?"

She appreciated that he didn't just dismiss her idea, but listened to her and respected her opinions. "We'd return for the horses later. We cannot ride in without attracting attention. These villagers are too poor to own horses."

He gave her idea a nod, then raised his brows with a jaunty look in his eyes, a sensual expression on his lips that had her blood suddenly humming. "If our foes are waiting for us on the farm, 'tis doubtful they will search these woods." His tone turned husky. "We have several free hours until dark, Princess."

"How should we spend them?" she asked coyly, trying to keep her trembling heart from inflecting a quiver of anticipation into her tone.

In this glade they were well hidden. Unless someone walked right into the clearing, they'd have the privacy she desired. She wanted him with a ferocity that had been building since they'd made love. Only this time she yearned to revel in the passion, not fight it. For now, she would take him at his word that retrieving the O'Dwyre lands was his ultimate goal. Perhaps, if they defeated her father's enemies, O'Rourke and MacLugh would be forced to accept a Norman king in Leinster.

"Are you tired?" She allowed her tunic to slip off her shoulder and bit back a smile as his gaze was drawn to her exposed flesh.

His eyes gleamed with interest. "I think perhaps I will lie down."

He untied the blankets from the saddle, then spread them across the lush grass. She watched him work, her mouth dry. Last time, they'd made love in the dark, but now the sun was still bright in the sky. This time she would better see all of him.

He lifted his head from his task, and their eyes met. The invitation in his gaze tapped a spring of hope inside her that welled until she overflowed with joy. Somehow, they would overcome the obstacles facing them and make a life together.

Staring directly into her eyes, he raised the hem of his shirt, lifting it an inch at a time, revealing sculpted muscles. It was so crazy, so erotic, him stripping for her, and she was loving every second. She forced herself to breathe. Finally he pulled the garment over his head.

Her gaze took in every magnificent part of him. From his intense black eyes that sent surges of desire straight to her heart to the growing bulge in his breeches, he was a superb, lean warrior—and he was hers. No one else had ever protected and cherished her with such tender courage. The hot look in his eyes left her breathless. With him, she wanted to give and give, knowing the pleasure would come back a hundredfold.

He began to untie his breeches. Suddenly unnerved by her boldness, she looked away and fumbled with the laces at her bodice. Reaching out, he stayed her hand with a touch. "Let me do that for you later, Princess."

She looked at him, standing before her naked. While her cheeks colored under the heat of his gaze, he seemed to have no modesty in cavorting before her bare as a babe on its birthing day. But there was nothing childish about his body.

He was proud male splendor, and she exclaimed in admiration, unable to look away from his broad shoulders, tapering to a flat stomach, and lean hips. He was more stunningly virile than she remembered, his manhood straining upward called to her like a signal torch on a stormy night. She wanted to touch him, taste him, tell him she'd take back every injurious thought she'd ever had about him.

"Tell me what you want, Princess," he murmured, a twinkle of mischief in his eyes.

As much as she was able, she pulled herself together and stilled the roaring in her ears, stiffened against the weakness quivering in her limbs. An opportunity like this one might never come twice, and she would not waste it. "Turn around."

His forehead wrinkled.

"Please," she whispered.

When he did as she asked, she reached out and traced a finger over the cord of muscle in his neck down the proud length of his spine. "I adore the feel of your skin, Norman. The rough, sleek texture against my fingertips is unlike anything I have ever touched before. And you are always warm."

He continued to stand still beneath her caresses. "Just remember, two can play this game," he warned, his voice a caress that did not deter her.

When he quivered beneath the light exploration of her touch, she sensed the effort it cost him to remain still. To think the slight graze of her fingers could cause this man to want her shot a thrill of anticipation through her.

As the pads of her fingers ventured over his lean backside, his voice went hoarse. "Are you having fun?"

"Ummm." From where she found the courage, she knew not. She slipped her hand between his legs.

He sucked in his breath, started to turn, and she withdrew her hand and thought she heard him sigh. A hot ache grew in her throat. Her arms went around his waist, and she caressed the thick muscles of his chest, then dropped her hands to his waist.

He spun then, so fast she had no time to think. Tipping her chin up, he brought his lips hungrily down on hers, demanding, not asking, but taking. She rose onto her toes to give him more. His tongue worked like a drug, lulling her to euphoria while she leaned into him, breathing his musky male essence, her mouth throbbing from his passionate kiss.

"Now, I will undress you."

At his words, her heart took a perilous leap. His thumbs slipped beneath her tunic and pulled it off until she stood before him in her chemise. As his arms slowly went around her and seized the hem, his fingers grazing her thighs, he made no attempt to hide that he was watching her slightest response.

As he reached her chemise, he slowly traversed his fingers over her skin. Blood surged from the spot he touched on her thighs to the top of her head and down to her toes.

"Look at me," he demanded.

Lifting the chemise higher, his fingers grazed

her bottom. The hem tickled the curls between her legs, and her knees trembled. She ached to lean against him, to press her already hardened nipples to his bare chest.

When her hands went to his shoulders to draw him closer, he shook his head. "For now you may keep you hands on my shoulders."

He pulled the chemise off with exquisite slowness, his hands shimmying over her bottom, the hem teasing her thighs, hips, and stomach. When he inched the chemise over her breasts, she squirmed under the sweet, agonizing torture. To bite back a groan, she dug her fingers into his shoulders.

When she finally stood naked before him, all thoughts of modesty had long since disappeared. There was only an all-consuming need to have him. He flung her chemise aside, apparently as impatient as she.

"Turn around, Princess."

She gasped. He apparently was not as impatient as she, for Dara ached to fling him to the ground and make passionate love. But she did as he asked, trembling when his hands came around her waist to cup her breasts. She tipped her head back, arching into his hands. His teeth nipped her throat, and his thumbs flicked her nipples until she panted with pleasure. She thought she might explode standing there as he caressed her.

As if sensing her desire and prolonging the torment, he lowered one hand to her stomach, dipped lower to the center of her need. As the sun warmed her breasts, his magical fingers parted

Conquer the Mist

her and slowly found the bud of delight at her core.

As if on their own accord, her hips tilted back and forth, rubbing herself against his finger, faster. Her muscles tightened and she expected pure pleasure to take her over the edge.

But he withdrew his hand, scooped her into his arms, and set her down on the blanket. She parted her legs to welcome him. When he did not accept her invitation, she groaned in frustration and opened her eyes to find him sitting on his heels between her legs, staring at her.

She huffed an affronted sigh and instinctively tried to close her legs, but he would not let her. "You are beautiful, Dara. I love every part of you, sweetheart."

"Then love me," she held out her hands to him.

But he shook his head with a little smile, indicating he wasn't done with her. "Soon," he crooned.

He slipped his finger inside her, and she forgot everything but the sensations he created. She closed her eyes, shuddering. Droplets of perspiration broke out on her skin. There wasn't a place on her body not slickened by heated, yearning moisture, including the fire licking between her legs.

She'd go mad if she didn't have him. With a strength she didn't know she had, she clutched his shoulders and rolled him under her, capturing his length between her legs, riding him and demanding her pleasure. She rocked her hips frantically and he helped her find a rhythm. Reaching for her breasts, he played with her nipples until she gasped, so close to attaining elusive pleasure.

"Hold on, Princess."

He rolled them once more until she rested on her back. He was thrusting into her.

"More," she demanded.

"Greedy wench."

"Faster," she pleaded.

He took her over the top, and she soared free, the pleasure stealing her breath. Dizzily she came back to earth, her gaze focusing on his face. "Och, Norman," she whispered, her hands tangling in his hair, her heard pounding against his. "I love you."

Chapter Fifteen

Strongheart held Dara tight in his arms. "Does that mean you don't intend to scrub yourself with sand and gravel?"

At his dry tone, she giggled. "It does."

"You agree to our marriage?"

"I must speak with Da first," she hedged, fully aware the Norman had not returned her words of love.

Yet warm feelings of contentment washed over her. Strongheart and her father might never retake Leinster, but the Norman wanted her for his wife, proof she meant much to him even if he did not say the words. While no other good could come of losing her home, at least she could revel in the fact that without her land, title, or wealth, Strongheart wanted *her*.

Hugging the delicious thought to herself, she

barely noticed the misty rain washing her clean. The sky darkened with billowing gray clouds, and she shivered. Even the Norman's heat could not warm her, and she rolled away, donning soaked clothes that left her just as cold as before but grateful they would soon be inside a dry house.

Leaving their horses, they crept down the hillside, using trees and brush for cover whenever possible. Although the chilling rain numbed her hands and feet, the precipitation had driven everyone inside but a barking hound, who had picked up their scent. No one checked the hound's baying, so they continued toward Dillon's farm as quickly and silently as possible.

Dara, her teeth chattering, knocked on the door of a medium-sized hut, hoping she remembered the location of the correct house because everything looked different in the dark. Strongheart had ducked around the corner out of sight, waiting for her signal.

"Come in." A man with a hoarse voice shouted an invitation, and she pushed the door open tentatively.

The scent of a spicy stew invaded her nostrils, making her mouth water. Before her blazed a fire much too large for a crisp summer night, but to Dara's eyes it was more than a friendly welcome. She stepped near, her gaze seeking the old man, bald, with a white beard down to his waist.

Dara approached the old man with a grin. "Is that you, Donal?"

"Who else might I be?"

Watery blue eyes peered out from a wrinkled face through the smoke. "Come in, Dara, you little devil. Shut the door, and make yourself at home."

Dara scooted back to the door, waved to Strongheart to enter with their packs, and shut the door behind him. "I brought company, Donal."

The old man's knees creaked as he stood. "Holy God! Ye brought the Norman?" He shook his head. "Well, at least ye had the sense not to flee Leinster alone. O'Rourke's looking for the two of you. There's a hefty price on your heads."

Dara warmed her hands by the fire. "I thought MacLugh wanted me alive."

The men shook hands, and Donal reseated himself by the fire. Strongheart set their packs by the wall, and then joined her, putting his arm over her shoulders. He gave her arm a squeeze. " 'Tis no matter. You are mine and neither O'Rourke nor MacLugh shall have you."

Donal laughed and then the laughter turned into a hacking cough. "Ah, the passions of youth. What I would give to be young again."

Dara spotted a pitcher and poured the old man a goblet of ale. She held it to his lips until he swallowed.

"Your hands are like ice, child. Help yourself to a blanket and take off those wet clothes."

"If men are looking for us here," Strongheart asked, "are we putting you in danger?"

"O'Rourke's men crossed the border yesterday," Donal said. "They may return but probably not until after the rain stops." While Dara and Strongheart shared a silent glance, the old man stirred the stew, ladled it onto a trencher, and handed them each a piece of thick wheat bread laden with butter. "Eat. As for the danger, at my age I have not much to lose."

"Donal, are you ill?" Dara took his gnarled hand, knowing her father would not wish his old friend to suffer. But in truth, where once she could have sent a servant to help, after losing Ferns, she could do little for him.

" 'Tis just the ague, acting up in the rain."

That explained his need for the oversized fire. As she retreated to a dark corner, removed her wet clothes, and wrapped a blanket about her, Strongheart added more wood to the fire before eating his meal. "I will cut more logs before we leave."

"No need. My grandson looks after me," Donal told them, his voice softening with affection. "He's hoping I will give him Morallach, Great Fury." He gestured to a gleaming sword with pride. "My father's father fought the Vikings with it."

Dara scooped the delicious stew onto her bread and washed it down with ale, noticing while Strongheart had cleared his side of the trencher, Donal hadn't eaten much. She gave the Norman half of her huge portion, knowing his belly would not yet be full.

She feared his prodigious appetitive was easier to appease than his need for Irish clothing. Not many of their men were of his size.

"We hoped to find clothes to disguise us," Dara mentioned. "A lad's clothes for me. Anything that will make the Norman look like one of us."

Donal's eyes narrowed. "Where are you headed, girl? I hear your Da crossed the Irish Sea and fled to Britain."

When she would have answered, Strongheart elbowed her to be quiet. "For your own safety, sir, 'twould be best if you knew naught of our plans."

Donal sighed, combed his fingers through his beard, then jerked his thumb toward clothes tossed into a corner. "Och! 'Tis a sad time when the only way a man can help his friends is by his silence. My grandson's clothes and a hat to cover her hair will serve Dara well. But as for you, I have to think on it."

Dara tried on the tunic and cap, pleased the loose garment did much to hide her curves. She yanked on the cap and shoved her hair inside. "Will this do?"

"You are much too pretty for a boy." Strongheart cupped her chin, his fingers gentle. "Remind me to spread some mud across your face."

She stuck out her tongue at him. His eyes glittered, and if they'd been alone, he would have kissed her. Instead, he swatted her backside.

A moment later, Donal snapped his fingers and pointed. "Look in the bottom of that chest. When my grandfather defeated a Viking warrior, he kept the man's tunic."

Putting aside their playfulness, she and Strongheart lifted the lid of the chest and dug past blankets and tunics. Despite the musty-smelling contents, she searched and sneezed her way to the bottom. Strongheart held the lid while she pulled out a neatly folded black woolen tunic. "Is this it?"

"Aye," Donal said. "There's an amber brooch to hold the shoulder pieces together."

Unfolding the garment, Dara held it to Strongheart's shoulders. " 'Twill do."

"Only if you sew up the rent in the back," Donal

murmured. "My da said grandfather could not take pride in the Viking's death but he knew not why. I always suspected the man was taken from behind."

Dara flipped the tunic over. Long-faded blood-stains had stiffened the material. A straight gash rent the wool from neck to waist but it would take no time for her to repair the damage. Retrieving needle and thread from her pack, she set to mending, pleased to have such a soothing, ordinary task to perform.

While Donal asked no more questions, it didn't take an educated monk to figure out they intended to meet with her father in Britain. As she sewed, her father's old friend filled them in on the border patrols and the latest conditions in Dublin.

Eyes nearly closed, his hand combing his beard, Donal settled back in his chair. "I suppose you can hide the hilt of his fancy sword, and the clothes may fool O'Rourke's men—until the Norman speaks. What will you do about his accent?"

Dara finished her sewing, knotted the thread, and bit the end free. "I will do the talking."

"No, Princess."

She wagged her finger in his face. "You must stop calling me that."

" 'Twill seem odd if a big man remains silent while the younger boy talks," Donal said.

"Not if I explain pirates cut out his tongue."

"But I have a tongue," Strongheart protested.

How could she forget his tongue? As her thoughts turned to what they'd shared earlier on the hillside, she reddened, unlikely to forget just where his tongue had been and how she'd writhed in pleasure. To think of such a thing at a time like this made her snap out her words. "If you keep your mouth closed, no one need know I lie."

As if Strongheart had read her thoughts, he winked at her, and she flushed from her cheeks to her toes. She stammered, "I—I will say I saved his life, and he is now my faithful servant," she improvised, turning to Strongheart and hoping he would see the sound reason in her argument. "That way you can protect me and no one will think anything of it."

Donal started coughing. "Aye, but pirates?"

"I have heard they ply the sea between here and Rome," she told him.

Strongheart shook his head. "No one will believe you."

"I do not care whether they believe me or not," she raised her voice in exasperation. "What does it matter—as long as they don't guess the truth? As long as they stay out of our way, we shall make good our escape."

Strongheart raked his hand through his hair. "Letting you do the talking could get us into trouble."

"You will have to trust me, Norman." She tossed the finished tunic at him. "Try that on. And unless you can learn to speak our tongue without sounding like a barbarian or have a better idea, do not mock mine."

"Ah, she always was a feisty little devil. I do believe she gets her passion from her mother."

Both men shared a long look and chuckled. Dara glared and they ignored her. Finally Strongheart contained his mirth and shrugged into the tunic. Although it was a bit tight across the chest and a little short in length, just shy of his knees, a pair of brogues could solve that problem. She adjusted the amber brooch at his shoulder and stepped back to admire her handiwork.

Just at that instant, three men barged into the hut, the pinging of the rain having masked their approach. Strongheart reached for his sword. Dara moved in front of him and knocked it down, hoping they wouldn't notice the gems on his sword hilt glinting in the fire's light.

"Come in and shut the door before my bones freeze," Donal complained in a much weaker voice than before.

"We heard you had visitors," said the largest of the three intruders.

Although her hands itched for her dirk and her heart raced, Dara fought to keep her face serene. There could be no mistaking O'Rourke's right-hand man, Ewen, with his cheek scarred from a long-ago border raid against her Da. Although she knew of him by reputation, the man had never seen her, and she hoped to talk her way out of a fight. Who knew how many men waited outside? If only she could outwit them and prevent the Norman from using his warrior skills. Beside her, she felt him tensing for a fight.

The wily Donal coughed twice. "My sister's grandson, Pol, and his friend have come to visit."

Thankful for Donal's reminder to play the part of a boy, she hoped Strongheart had also picked up the message. His overprotectiveness could get them all killed.

"Friend?" Ewen, clearly suspicious, leaned so

close, his sour breath left a bad taste in her mouth. "Can he not speak for himself?"

She dared not move away and expose Strongheart's sword. "He lost his tongue to pirates," Dara said, her lie sounding ridiculous to her own ears.

"Why, he's a giant. Ain't he a wee bit large to be playing with the likes of you?" Ewen's beady eyes turned on Dara, the Norman's size apparently more suspicious to him than her wild story.

"You leave him alone," she demanded. "He went simple after he lost his tongue. He's harmless unless anyone tries to hurt me. Ma nursed him back to health and thankful he is."

"Where did you come from?" Ewen muttered, losing interest in the simple giant who kept his eyes downcast and shuffled close to Dara.

It was a good thing Ewen and his men couldn't see the fire she knew blazed in Strongheart's eyes. She needed the men to move on before she or the Norman made a fatal mistake.

Quickly she made up another story. "From the North. We fled the fever in the city."

As if on cue, Donal coughed. The men backed away, eyes suddenly wide. Unaware Donal's cough was due to age, they feared the malady that often led to fevers, then death. Taking advantage of their ignorance, Dara stepped forward and coughed, too. She raised a trembling hand to her mouth. "We are not sick. Would you care to share our meal?"

The men practically fell over one another backing out the door. She slammed it behind them with a satisfied grin, dusting her hands as if she'd rid the place of vermin.

Strongheart grabbed their packs. "We must leave before someone informs them Donal does not have a grandson named Pol."

Donal grinned. "But I do. Stay a dry night under my roof and leave at dawn. You will be just as safe here as fleeing through the hills in the dark."

"He is right," Dara agreed, eager to spend the night by the fire and out of the rain. "Besides, in our disguises as an Irish lad and his simple mate, we cannot do anything to create doubt. Traveling before the rains stop would be suspicious."

Strongheart, eyes gleaming with light reflected from the fire, dropped the packs and advanced on her. "So I am simple now, am I?"

She stepped back, her mouth going dry at his hungry expression. "I did not want them to realize how dangerous you are."

His hand snaked out so fast to seize her, she gasped. Before she could think to struggle, he'd drawn her against his chest. Her cap tumbled to the floor, spilling her hair down her back. Ignoring Donal's chuckle, the Norman's hand wound into her hair, tipped her head up, and he kissed her with a pent-up passion that left her breathless. All thoughts of the lies she'd told flew from her mind. There was only Strongheart's warm heart beating against hers, his lips sending new quivers surging through her, and the intoxicating musk of his essence overwhelming her.

Although the Norman couldn't love her the way she knew he wanted with Donal across the room, he held her close through the night. Never had she felt so cherished.

After they bade Donal farewell, and through the next weeks of their journey to Wales, the Norman allowed her to take charge during the days, but at night, as he took her to his bed and his powerful arms curved around her, he left no doubt who was truly in command.

Long after leaving Fionn and the destrier to Donal's care, they reached the shores of Wales. Dara looked at the foreboding mountains and endless succession of shale slopes and ached for the rounded green hills of home. Although they travelled upon horseback, she kept sliding in the English saddle and missed Fionn's broad, familiar back.

As they passed through towns, tall, dark-haired, and longheaded villagers looked at them with suspicion, their strong, ridged brows frowning in swarthy scowls, and she longed for the open warmth of Irish hospitality. Although it was no colder than Leinster, the only time Dara felt warm was at night when the Norman held her in his arms.

Her heart grew heavier with every mile of boulder clay they trod. Although she tried to be brave, she missed her land, her people, her home. The rough bands of old rock from numerous headlands appeared like gnarled fingers reaching around her throat to choke the breath from her. The dark, harsh countryside held a mysterious aura that left her with chills of dark foreboding she couldn't put aside no matter how hard she tried.

They broke through a windswept forest and reached Cardiff Castle, a stone edifice with distinctive round towers, in the dwindling light of a dusk rain. Her father's men camped around the hill, and Seumas told her she'd find her father inside with Warren DeLacy, Strongheart's friend.

The round keep, four stories high with very thick walls, had its entrance on the second story. To reach it, they entered a forebuilding which led to a drawbridge. In the castle courtyard grooms mucked out the stables and fed the horses. A smith worked at his forge on horseshoes, nails, and wagon fittings. Domestic servants emptied chamber pots. Laundresses soaked sheets, tablecloths, and towels in a wooden trough that smelled of wood ashes and caustic soda.

They entered the drafty and gloomy hall of the inner bailey. Dara hid her distress at finding herself dependent on strangers for food and even the roof above her head. Surveying the dirty hall, with its spiral staircase leading to the basement and upper floors and battlements, she doubted DeLacy had a wife, for cobwebs, thick as birds' nests, occupied several niches. The floors, though strewn with rushes, lacked herbs such as lavender or hyssop to sweetly scent the air. Indeed, she had to raise the sleeve of her tunic and breathe through it to avoid the fetid odors of rotten food soiling the floor. Wax candles impaled on vertical spikes supported by wall brackets lit the murky room. The trails of spiraling stale smoke left a musty taste in her mouth. The central hearth was bordered by stone, and at the high table and dais she found

Warren DeLacy, a tall, square-faced man, with her father.

Conor gestured wide with his arms. "I will not wait until spring to retake my home. We must act quickly."

"Da!" Dara raced from Strongheart's side to her father and threw her arms around his chest. "Are you well?"

The King of Leinster wrapped his daughter in an embrace. "As well as a man without a home can expect. But we will soon remedy that." He steered her away from the man down a narrow, drafty hallway. "Now that Strongheart has brought you safely to me, we can begin a campaign to retake our home."

As soon as she knew the others couldn't hear her words, she stopped and faced him. "Did you promise the Norman I would marry him?"

Her father gave her a sheepish grin. "We need his support, and I could not help but notice the way he looks at you. The man knows how to take care of a woman."

Her father cupped her chin and smoothed the hair back from her face. Her cheeks heated, and she remembered how Strongheart had cared for her, slowly taking off her clothes, her linen tunic between his teeth. Begorra, how she wanted him beside her for the rest of her days. "Will our people accept a Norman laird?"

"Our people are loyal," her father assured her. "Besides, once you are wed, there is not much even the *Ard-ri* can do."

But without the *Ard-ri's* approval, there could not be peace. A prickle of fear crawled down her spine. "There will be war. 'Twould be better if the high king legitimized our marriage."

"There has already been war and we lost our lands," Conor reminded her, as if she were a forgetful child. "Resign yourself. We must fight to regain what is ours."

Dara shivered. "With O'Rourke and MacLugh united against us, we do not have enough men to defeat our enemies."

"You let me worry about the battle plans. You warm yourself before you catch a chill." He opened a door and led her into a small room that had not been aired.

Refusing to be put to bed, Dara protested. "What of your new ally, DeLacy? What does he want in return for his help?"

Strongheart entered the dark room and the space seemed to shrink with his size. "You leave DeLacy to me. My friend will jump at the opportunity once I explain the way of things."

Anger and fear twisted around her heart and squeezed. "What are you saying? Surely DeLacy will not return to Leinster with us?"

"He can raise an army of trained knights," Strongheart told her gently.

Her voice rose to almost a shriek. "Norman knights?"

Conor frowned. "You did not tell her?"

"Tell me what?" she demanded, her fist raising to her mouth at their betrayal. The Normans would bring war. Her half sister's screams echoed in her mind. Visions of Sorcha's bloody thighs after the rape sent her senses reeling.

"We need men to retake Leinster," Strongheart

told her, his eyes not quite meeting hers.

"Strongheart can pay the Normans with gold," her father added.

Blood drained from her face. "Are you daft? Every king in Eire will raise an army to fight us."

Strongheart's fist slapped his open palm. "But we will win. Do you not want to go home to Ferns? How many times have you told me you wished to raise our children there?"

"But we will never have peace," she whispered, sheer black fright sweeping through her. They planned madness. All of Eire would fight over Leinster. Her knees buckled, and she sank onto the straw mattress in misery.

Damn him! He'd lied to her. Strongheart and her father had made this arrangement behind her back.

Knowing how she would fight this scheme, the Norman had made love to her, never once telling her his plan. If he thought to use her heart, to wait until she fell in love with him before telling her the truth, he would find out he'd misjudged her. As she looked at him, standing before her, his handsome face carved into a mask of concern, his dark eyes pleading with her to understand, she felt as if her heart were being ripped into pieces and devoured by vultures. Dropping her face into her hands, she shook with rage. "Get out. Both of you leave me."

Her father patted her back awkwardly. "Dara, 'tis the only way. Surely you see we need the Normans?"

Raising her head, she ignored the tears spilling down her cheeks. "Will they leave us when you ask it? Or will they use Leinster as a base to subdue the rest of Eire?"

"Leinster is enough for one man, Princess," Strongheart spoke softly. With hand outstretched he offered her a bouquet of white campions with yellow eyes amid their petals. She pictured the flowers growing in a field above a thousand graves, and recoiled.

Fear and anger stabbed like a dirk in her gut. "How can I believe you? You know how I feel about inviting Norman armies into Leinster, so you did not mention your plan. What else have you not told me?"

Strongheart shook his head sadly. "Once we defeat O'Rourke and MacLugh, no king, not even the *Ard-ri*, will challenge my right to hold you or Leinster."

Her hands bunched into fists. "If you defeat the kings of both Munster and Meath, what will prevent you from conquering their lands and then Connaught, Ulster, and the Pale?"

"My self-restraint."

"Och, we already know you have none. You go after what you want and take it—that is your way."

At her insult, Strongheart tossed his rejected blossoms onto the mattress, his face tight and pinched, his eyes hard. "I am a man of my word."

Pain rose up to choke her, and she responded through broken gasps. "You lied by omission. If I had known your intentions, do you think I would have welcomed you to my bed?"

Her father shook his head, looked from one of them to the other and left the room. The door shut with a click as hollow as her heart, leaving her alone with the Norman. She didn't want to face him, didn't know pain could be so sharp. She'd fallen in love with him and now she would have to give him up or risk plunging her country into civil war.

Lord, help her. Where would she find the strength to leave him?

Chapter Sixteen

Dara sat on the bed hugging herself, refusing to look at Strongheart. A sharp rap on the door followed by Gaillard's murmured voice barely registered in Dara's thoughts.

"What is it?" Strongheart called.

Gaillard spoke from the hallway. "DeLacy and Conor require your presence."

To make their war plans, Dara thought miserably. How many more people must she lose to war and greed?

"Can they not wait?" Strongheart measured her for a moment, then held out his hand. She ignored him, and his eyes darkened with her reflected pain.

He would leave her to hire his army, plan his battles, and create a war the likes of which her countrymen had never seen. As much as she longed to return home to Castle Ferns, she couldn't face years of border raids, starvation, and death. With superior Norman weapons and mail, Strongheart could conquer her country, but outnumbered, the Normans would have difficulty holding the land. There would never be peace. Once again Eva's innocent face rose to haunt her. Dara would not be like her mother and yield to a passion she couldn't control.

Gaillard's voice grew urgent. "A messenger leaves within the hour to raise mercenaries."

The Norman reached to cup her chin. "I will be but a moment."

She jerked away, her throat aching, her voice bitter with defeat. "Go. Go do what you do best, Norman."

An uncertainty crept into his expression. His hand dropped to his side. "We will talk later."

Her hands twisted in her tunic, and with her head dropped, she hid her face behind a veil of hair. "Your words will change nothing," she said brokenly, "not when your actions speak so loudly."

"Strongheart," Gaillard insisted, "you must come, now."

"I will send Sorcha to you." The Norman left her, and for once her eyes didn't follow him out of the room. Perhaps she no longer loved him?

Not so, her heart whispered back.

When Sorcha entered the room, Dara sat in the same position, her knees drawn to her chest, rocking. Her eyes remained dry. Tears would come later when she recovered from the shock.

Warm brown eyes full of concern, Sorcha sat on the bed and took her into her arms, rocked her as if she were still a child. "There, now. Everything will be fine."

"I fell in love with the Norman," Dara blurted the words, taking little comfort in Sorcha's hug.

Sorcha smoothed the hair back from Dara's face. "Och, it had to happen sooner or later for 'tis the way of the world. Did Strongheart bring you these lovely white campions? Why, the man must be in love with you."

As she tried to maintain her fragile control, Dara's stomach clenched tight. "Strongheart intends to lead a Norman army into Leinster."

Sorcha's full lips thinned. "There's naught wrong with recapturing your birthright. Do you not want to go home?"

"More than anything." In her heart she'd always been afraid, but now panic rooted within her. Without the familiar solid walls of Leinster around her, waves of dread swept through her. She faced a lightless future, her throat raw with unuttered screams of protest. "Strongheart will not stop with regaining Leinster. Why should he? With the army he will raise, he'll have all of Eire at his feet."

Sorcha frowned. "The *Ard-ri* will not yield without a fight."

"Aye." With a moan of distress, she wrenched away from Sorcha's arms and paced the room before she yielded to compulsive sobs. "For that reason, I must give the Norman up."

Sorcha's forehead creased. "I do not see why you must sacrifice—"

"Without me, Strongheart has no legitimate ownership to the land. Whether I marry him or not, his claim cannot be legal except by the sanction of the *Ard-ri*."

"My poor colleen." Sorcha collected the strewn flowers with a sigh. "All this is not your fault. Your father has commanded you to marry the Norman. There is naught you can do."

Dara closed her eyes, the pain inside a sick and fiery gnawing. The weak, the old, and women and children suffered the most when men went to war. Despite his age, Donal would feel compelled to defend his home. And what would happen to the blind bard, Carolan, and the monks in the hills? She could not bear the thought of another child needlessly dying like Eva, or another woman raped like Sorcha. She would do anything to prevent civil war from breaking out in Eire. "I can run away. Return to Ireland."

"What good could come of such a rash action?"

Through the grief and despair, a small hope wormed its way through her misery. Perhaps she could have Leinster and the Norman, too. "If the *Ard-ri* sanctions my marriage, then with his help, we can regain Leinster without the use of Norman knights. We might have peace."

Sorcha clucked her tongue. "Love has blinded you to the truth. After backing O'Rourke's and MacLugh's bid to take Leinster, why would the *Ard-ri* switch sides?"

"The *Ard-ri* once held tender feelings for my mother. Perhaps he will grant my request."

"Surely you have not forgotten the high king has no liking for your father. He will hold you hostage," Sorcha countered.

"The *Ard-ri* will not want a Norman army to invade Eire. Perhaps he will agree to a marriage between the Norman and me if Strongheart agrees to occupy only Leinster."

Sorcha set the nosegay on the pillow, turned, and wagged a finger in her face. "You always were too brash for a woman. You cannot ride across Eire by yourself, looking for the *Ard-ri*. Tell your father or Strongheart your plan and send a message to the *Ard-ri*."

"No." Dara's voice grew stronger with conviction. "They are men of war, set on fighting and revenge. While they dream of carving a kingdom for themselves, they will not negotiate."

Sorcha sighed with exasperation. "But even if you are successful with the *Ard-ri*, how will you convince your father and the Norman to settle for Leinster, when they can take all five counties by force?"

Dara straightened and lifted her chin. "Let us hope the Norman loves me as much as I love him. I may be forced to marry him and bear his children, but as long as war is more important to him than my wish for peace, he will lose my heart."

"That is it?" Sorcha rubbed her forehead. "That's your plan? Go to Strongheart, now, and tell him he will break your heart if he conquers our country."

"How can I ask anything of him when I don't know where the *Ard-ri* stands? As long as Strongheart thinks it necessary to defeat O'Rourke, MacLugh, and the *Ard-ri* to retake Leinster, he will not listen to talk of peace. The high king has sent me several messages through Mata, indicating his willingness to compromise. If I persuade the high king to negotiate, Strongheart will see things differently."

Sorcha placed her hands on her hips. "You realize most likely your plan will fail?"

With renewed courage and determination, Dara faced Sorcha. " 'Tis a risk but one I am willing to take. This is my only chance to get what I want—Castle Ferns, Strongheart, and peace. If I do not try, I will spend the rest of my life knowing I had an opportunity and failed to take it. You must say nothing until after I leave."

"I will go with you."

Dara opened her mouth to protest.

Sorcha prattled on without giving her a chance to disagree. "Do not argue or I will tell your father."

At her loyalty, warmth spread through Dara. Although guilt stabbed her for putting Sorcha in jeopardy, she would be glad to have company on the journey to Dublin.

"Thank you." She hugged Sorcha tight, thinking this woman had done much to make up for the loss of her own mother. "Be ready to leave at midnight."

"I will see to the horses and provisions," Sorcha promised.

After Sorcha's departure, Dara's thoughts focused on Strongheart. When he returned, she would have to use all her wiles to make him believe she'd accepted the use of Norman knights. Although she didn't relish the thought of lying to him, perhaps they need not discuss anything at all. With a smile of satisfaction, she called servants and had them fetch a bath. She put all thoughts

of leaving him out of her mind. There would be
plenty of time later for regrets. This would be their
last night together for a while. This might be their
last night together, ever. She intended to make it
special.

After serving a meal of stewed mutton, peas, and
beans, servants removed the leftover food and
brought in a large tub. Soon a brigade of boys
filled the tub with buckets of hot water. Dara
plucked white petals and tossed them into the water, scenting the room.

She disrobed, and eased into the hot water with
a contented sigh, hoping the heat would soothe
stiff muscles and infuse renewed strength for the
journey ahead. She washed quickly but then must
have dozed for just a minute or two, because when
she awoke, the bath water remained warm.

At the creaking of the door's hinge, she recognized Strongheart in the dim room. Without looking at her, he lit every candle in an extravagant
gesture that left her heart fluttering.

Rising to her feet, she stood before him, fully
naked, offering herself to his attentive gaze. His
bold stare assessed her frankly, and she almost
grabbed the drying cloth to hide. But when he
broke into a wide-open smile of approval that sent
her pulse racing, she was glad she'd dared this seduction. Holding out his hand as if she were
dressed to meet the Queen of England, he helped
her step from her bath onto a thick carpet.

A spark of fire smoldered in his eyes. "Let me
dry you, Princess."

She quivered at the memory of the last time he'd
dried her and almost lost sight of her task. This

night was to be for him. Grabbing up two drying cloths, she wrapped one about her hair, the other around her back and under her arms, tucking the excess cloth between her breasts.

"I would bathe you, my lord," she said shyly, using the Norman term of address, "while the bathwater is still warm."

He glanced at the petals floating across the surface and chuckled. "Do you wish me to smell as sweet as a woman?"

Her hands raised the hem of his shirt, her eyes downcast to the bulge in his breeches. "No one would ever mistake you for a woman."

She removed his shirt, and as the drying cloth tucked between her breasts loosened, he stayed her hand from retying it. In a silent whisper, the cloth pooled at her feet, once more leaving her bared to his gaze. Clearly he wanted her naked. The thought of teasing him with her nudity while she bathed him tightened the invisible web of passion Dara felt spinning between them.

A brief shiver rippled through her at the pleasure of touching his chest, skimming her palms over his firm muscles, lingering at the sensitive place where his shoulder bones reached the hollow of his neck. As she dipped her hands to his flat stomach and lower to remove his breeches, she tilted her head to look into his eyes, to drink in his expression and hold it within her heart for all time.

His dark brows arched at her brazen behavior, the light of desire illuminating his smoky eyes, his smile as intimate as a kiss. Nervously, she moistened dry lips.

With her palms tingling against his hair-roughened thighs, she slid his breeches over molded muscles. Kneeling to remove them, she let out a gasp of dismay at her mistake. She'd neglected to remove his boots. So much for her well-planned seduction. Allowances for her relative inexperience at disrobing a man would have to be made.

His lips twitched, but he offered not one word of advice to help her out of her dilemma. As she stood and searched for a chair, she thought she heard him swallow a chuckle.

A giggle escaped her lips. "I take it you would prefer to bathe without your boots?"

"Aye."

She set the chair beside her and returned to her place before him. With his breeches pushed down to his knees, she had him at her mercy. With a saucy grin, she took advantage, brushing along the inside of his knees, tracing a sensuous path of tiny circles, each caress a bit higher than the last. She teased, she taunted, but she ignored his jutting man part until his breath grew ragged.

Finally hooking her ankle around a chair leg, she shoved the seat behind him. He sat so quickly she bit back a grin of satisfaction, hoping his knees were as weak as hers.

Facing him, she grabbed the heel of his boot with the palm of one hand and the back of his calf with the other and tugged. It wouldn't budge. She wanted to stamp her foot in defeat. The boot would not come off.

Slowly and seductively, his gaze slid over her breasts. His brow rose at her frustration, his silky tone rife with challenge. "Perhaps if you turned around?"

She stiffened, momentarily abashed. Although he had already seen and touched every part of her, an unwelcome blush burned her cheeks. He wanted her to face the other way and straddle his outstretched legs, a perfectly acceptable act—if she'd been wearing clothes.

But she wasn't.

Refusing to allow a small difficulty to interfere with her plans, she flicked her hair over her shoulder and did as he'd suggested. If he wanted to look at her wiggling bottom, she would give him an eyeful he wouldn't forget.

She captured his knees between hers, bent to remove his boot, arching her back a bit more than necessary to taunt him. When his palms lightly squeezed her bottom, she squealed in surprise.

He laughed aloud, his merriment buoyant. She suspected her body had gone crimson, for a heated flush engulfed her. His legs might be joined together by his breeches, but how could she have forgotten his hands were free? She should have remembered he never missed an opportunity for a caress.

As he continued to stroke her, she grew fiery hot. A warm wetness pooled between her legs, and she lost the strength to remove his boots. The tingle along her bottom emphasized the ache between her thighs. She no longer wanted to give him a bath. She didn't want to wait another moment to have him inside her.

Finally she forced her fingers to remove one boot, throwing it across the room in frustration.

She tried not to think about what his hands were doing while she worked on the other boot. "Are you deliberately cocking your ankle to make this harder?"

"Ummm." His husky voice swished across her like a whisper of silk. " 'Tis a beautiful view. One that deserves my full attention."

He fondled her in much the same manner as she'd done to him. Except every so often, his fingertips delved between her thighs to play in her curls, distracting her from her task. But no matter how she wriggled, he refused to give her the satisfaction her body demanded.

She took a deep breath to steady her racing heart, gripped his boot firmly, and prepared to pull with all her might. When he pinched her bottom, she yelped and the boot finally came off.

Dropping his boot, she attempted to rub the sore spot. His hands grabbed her waist, blocking her arms from reaching back, and his tongue licked the pain away. He hadn't pinched her after all. "You bit me!"

" 'Twas just a little nibble. I could not resist."

Her breasts quivered, and she trembled then, knowing he would nip her again. The delicious anticipation of his caresses combined with her vulnerability held an undeniable excitement. Secure in the knowledge he would never truly hurt her, she waited, breathless, on the edge.

His tongue tickled her bottom, and at the base of her neck, a pulse beat and swelled as though her heart had risen to her throat. Occasionally his hand delved between her thighs, but never for more than a moment. Never enough to satisfy the frenzied need mounting inside her.

When she feared her knees would collapse beneath her, he bit her other cheek, and turned her around before him. The slight sting combined with his caresses had her biting her lip to contain a moan. He held out his legs, and as she finally removed his breeches, his hands fondled her breasts. Her breath came in gasps. She ached to drag him onto the bed.

A glance showed her he was ready, too. When he held out his hand she took it, surprised to find he'd placed a small object in her palm. "Come, Princess. I believe I shall enjoy my bath with scented flowers after all."

She opened her hand and gasped at the exquisite emerald necklace he'd placed there. "This is lovely."

He spun her around to look into a small circular mirror, mounted in a metal case and made of polished glass. " 'Twas my mother's jewelry. I thought 'twould complement the shamrock that reminds you of home. Wear it for me during our bath?"

She lifted her hair, expecting him to place the necklace around her neck. But first he nibbled and kissed the sensitive valley of her neck, his warm breath making the small hairs there prickle.

In the mirror she caught sight of her face, flushed, dreamy-eyed, wanting. Just as his hardness complemented her softness, his swarthy skin next to her fair flesh seemed a perfect contrast.

Finally he placed the emeralds around her neck, centering the shamrock necklace in the middle, and tears brimmed in her eyes at the thought of leaving him. When the clasp clicked, she brushed the thought away with a determined sigh. Memories of tonight would have to last, and she was determined to savor every delicious moment.

She started to release her hair from where she held it on her head when he murmured in her ear, "Hold still."

Feeling wicked and wanton and wonderful, like the most desirable woman in the world, she posed for his pleasure. He raised his hands from beneath her arms and cupped her breasts, his thumbs flicking the nipples while his lips continued their exploration behind her ears.

She licked her dry lips, determined to end this wonderful torment so she could catch her breath. "Perhaps you do not need a bath."

He tweaked her nipples, shooting a flame straight to her belly. She gasped, the tension inside her so taut she was ready to explode. As if sensing she couldn't take much more of his teasing attention, he again took her hand and led her to the tub. From the sweat trickling on his brow as he stepped in she guessed prolonging their union was as difficult for him as it was for her.

"Close your eyes," she ordered, her voice shaky. With his hands and lips no longer upon her, she regained enough composure to lift a bucket of water over his head and douse his hair.

Strongheart closed his eyes, reluctant to lose sight of her. As her hands scrubbed his head, he realized how much she meant to him. He adored her wild beauty, but he'd met many beautiful women in his travels. It was her courage and passion he admired, the way she threw her whole heart into everything she did, giving of every part of herself. When he demanded more, she gave him that, too.

She rinsed his hair, and as her hands boldly played across his chest, he realized what a treasure he had found. He would have wanted her without her dowry, without her title. She explored further, and he opened his eyes to catch the mischievous grin on her face. He sucked in his breath when her hands closed around his erection. As her soft hands soaped him, his thoughts skittered, and he emitted a soft groan of approval.

She leaned forward to kiss him, her hands continuing to caress him. While he ached to pull her into the tub, he couldn't wait another moment to have her. But when he raised his hands to scoop her into his arms, she playfully nipped his shoulder.

"That hurt," he complained, more wounded that she'd stopped him than from any lingering pain.

" 'Tis your turn to hold still," she demanded, her lips coming down on his, preventing any further discussion.

She tasted of wine and the flavor intoxicated him. Her tongue moving in conjunction with her hands was almost more than he could bear.

Standing in the tub, despite her protesting gasp, he lifted her into his arms. Without bothering to dry himself, he carried the giggling woman to the bed.

"Did you not like my caresses?" she teased with an impudent grin.

For an answer, he swatted her bottom lightly after placing her on the bed. She rolled to her back and reached for him, her gaze hungry. "I want you."

He stood over her, admiring the firelight dancing on her fair skin, the lovely curve of her rosy-tipped breasts, the delicious roundness of her bottom. "Do I not always give you what you want?"

"Eventually." Her lips rose in a pout. "You make me wait."

" 'Tis proper for a woman to wait on a man," he teased, running a finger from her chin, between her breasts, and through her curls until he found the raised nubbin of her desire.

She was more than ready for him, her hips lifting to urge him on. He almost gave in to the need to have her now. Only the utmost control allowed him self-restraint.

"Hold still," he ordered once more.

Dara gasped at the golden glow of passion flickering in his gaze. As his fingers, light and painfully teasing, worked their magic, she tried to remain still. But it was impossible. A tiny whimper came from the back of her throat.

Lunging to pull him down with her, she seized him, frantic to have him inside her. When he entered her, she felt as if she'd been hit by lightning, and her heart pounded with thunder. She clutched the hard muscles of his back. His chest against her breasts spread fire, searing her with unimaginable bliss. She arched her back and exploded, sounding an outcry of delight as pleasure radiated outward.

With head thrown back and muscles clenched, Strongheart followed her with a roar of pleasure.

"I love you." She pulled him closer, reveling in the feel of his pounding heart against hers. As her breathing returned to normal, she hoped he would remember her words. Hoped he would one day forgive her for what she was about to do.

He smoothed her hair off her forehead. "When do you wish to marry?"

Her glowing happiness faded. The thought of setting a date for the wedding, knowing she would not be there, brought a throbbing tightness to her throat. "Tomorrow. We can discuss our wedding tomorrow."

Snuggling against him, she breathed in his luscious male scent, trying to memorize him for the time they would be apart. He pulled a blanket atop them and one by one the candles flickered out.

Soon he breathed deeply in sleep, and still she stayed by his side, a heaviness in her chest. The minutes to her departure flew by all too quickly. Finally, her face tight with emotion, she swallowed the lump lodged in her throat, forced herself out of bed. Shivering, she dressed, longing for one last kiss, but not daring to take it for fear of waking him.

He would have to guess at the reason for her disappearance and that pained her more. If she knew how to write, she would leave him a note. But such written knowledge was for monks, and she'd never learned beyond her artistic drawings. She dared not trust anyone with her secret for fear they would wake her father or the Norman. She could not risk anyone stopping her. Perhaps she could send a message before they crossed the Irish Sea.

Susan Kearney

Her gaze clouded with unshed tears as she looked back at him one last time, biting her lip to control her sobs, touching the necklace to give her strength. Would she ever see him again? If she did, would he still want her?

Now that she'd found her love, walking away was much harder than she'd ever thought. A deep, biting loss beyond tears gripped her. Careful to open the door slowly so it wouldn't creak, she slipped out of the room.

"Good-bye, my love."

Chapter Seventeen

Strongheart slept deeply and awakened refreshed. He reached across the mattress for Dara and discovered she wasn't there, and he assumed she was visiting her father.

Using a basin of cold water, he washed, then dressed in a long-sleeved overtunic and mantle to chase away the morning chill, and entered the main hall, his stomach rumbling. The scent of a rasher of bacon and fresh breads led him to the trestle table where he ate quickly, washing down his meal with ale.

One by one, Gaillard, DeLacy, and Conor joined him, but Strongheart saw no sign of Dara. With a frown, he turned to Gaillard. "Have you seen Sorcha this morn?"

His squire shook his head.

DeLacy set down his ale and tilted back his chair

Susan Kearney

with a satisfied belch. "The ladies prefer the gardens to my company. No doubt you will find them there. But first, we must make arrangements. I have sent messages to a few friends and word will spread that we are hiring mercenaries."

Strongheart frowned. "You did not tell them of the mission?"

"I saw no need," DeLacy replied.

Conor thrummed his fingers on the table. "How long will it take for these men to gather?"

"A few weeks for an advance party," DeLacy told him. "Maybe months to assemble a sizable army."

When the knights finally arrived with warhorses, armor, and equipment, Strongheart needed to be prepared to transport them. A few hundred knights would be a considerable force in Eire, especially against men without armor.

"We must retake Leinster before winter," Conor said.

Strongheart more than understood the king's impatience to return to Eire. But haste would not serve them well. As the men planned the details of their campaign, a scribe wrote their final decisions in a ledger. "Each knight will arrive with several mounts and limited supplies. We will need food for men and their horses, arrows, extra swords, and shields."

"Since there are to be no ransoms, no booty to be won, money payments must be prepared," DeLacy reminded Strongheart.

Wishing the planning and preparations over so they could be on their way, Strongheart reined in his impatience. Many a campaign had failed due to lack of forethought. "Each knight will fix his own rate of pay."

Although anxious to find Dara, for Strongheart thought it odd she still hadn't appeared, he remained with the men, determined to settle the details. "Our most vulnerable point will be when the ships land."

"Not necessarily," Conor contradicted him. "There are many desolate bays along the coast. If luck is with us, we could arrive unnoticed."

They spoke through midday, and finally Strongheart could not sit for another moment. "I suggest we adjourn for the day. I still must arrange for payment to be brought here."

The journey to his buried gold and silver was a two-day ride, one he intended to make with Gaillard, but first he would seek out Dara. Rising to his feet, he stretched the kinks from his back, eager to stretch his legs.

"If I had such a comely maid interested in me," DeLacy teased, "I would hurry off, too."

Conor ran his hands through his gray beard. " 'Tis not like Dara to disappear while a battle is being planned."

"Your daughter listens when you talk of war?" DeLacy asked, his voice rising in obvious amazement.

"She usually insists on riding with us," Conor added.

DeLacy's jaw dropped. Never before had Strongheart seen his friend speechless. But Strongheart was too concerned by Dara's absence to enjoy his friend's astonishment. He and Conor exchanged worried glances.

Strongheart headed toward the drawbridge. "Check the keep. I will search outside."

His first stop was the stable. No one had seen her this morning. About to search elsewhere, he slowed when he overheard stableboys talking about two missing horses.

"Were saddles missing?" Strongheart asked.

"No, sire. Strange, is it not?"

Who else would take a horse without a saddle? No one. Damn her! She should know better than to ride off in a strange land with probably only Sorcha for company. While she could protect herself with her dirk, she was no match for a contingent of men.

"When did the horses disappear?" he asked, reining in his temper so not to frighten the lads.

The shorter lad piped up, "Near as I can guess, 'twas the middle of the night, my lord."

Damn it to hell! Had Dara made love to him then crept from his bed? Thinking back to last night, he realized how odd it was that she hadn't questioned him about using Norman knights in Eire. Instead, she'd seduced him. The subject that had so upset her earlier had not come up.

With a sinking sensation in the pit of his stomach, he continued his search. No one had seen her. She had not broken the morning fast.

He searched the elaborate garden, calling her name, but the sound echoed as hollow as his heart. She'd made love to him with frenzied abandon. Told him she'd loved him. Left him. Had her act of love been a ruse to allay his suspicions?

Suspicion of what? What could she be planning that she needed to steal? Obviously she was up to something of which he would not approve. Heaviness settled in his chest, and he broke into a run along the garden pathways. If she and Sorcha had left last night, even if he could guess where they were headed, he might not catch them.

Dara knew no one in Wales, so where could she have gone? His heart slammed into his chest, and he skidded to a sudden halt. With his gut churning, he clenched his fists, unable to draw in air. His thoughts raced, suddenly certain she could have gone to only one place.

Eire.

His anger layered with fear for her safety as he spun and headed back the way he'd come. She was gone. And she'd taken everything he'd pinned his hopes and dreams on. What was worse, if he could only have her back safe with him, he'd capitulate and agree to train the Irish men into knights—even if it took years. But it was too late. She had left him.

He questioned everything he most valued. What good were his warrior skills without her to come home to? What pleasure would winning Leinster hold without his feisty woman? Without her by his side, his life appeared bleak, his hopes for a home in shambles.

He gave up the useless search in the garden and met Conor by the stable. One look at the dejected king's face told Strongheart, somehow, that her father knew she was gone.

"Did you argue?" Conor demanded.

Strongheart steeled his face not to show the emotion roiling in him. "The lass would not run due to a simple argument. From the beginning, she refused to accept we needed Norman knights to hold Leinster. When she learned our plans, she ran."

"To Eire?" Conor guessed. "To avoid your marriage?"

The air around them was foul with odors, but then so was Strongheart's mood. As one thought after another hammered him, he called himself ten kinds of a fool. Was she running from him? Possibly. "Or is she running to Eire to marry another?"

Putting aside his sorrow, fresh anger at her betrayal surged through Strongheart. She should never have put herself in danger. It was bad enough she travelled with only her maid for protection. But must she go riding straight to the enemy, too? "Where would she go? Surely, she wouldn't return to MacLugh?"

"She despises MacLugh, but she might marry him to avoid war," Conor admitted, a harried look on his face.

Strongheart wasted no more time. He sent riders to the port in case Dara hadn't already sailed. But she'd had more than enough time to escape.

They finally decided that Conor would take his men back to Eire and look for Dara while Strongheart raised the Norman knights. With Dara gone, Strongheart intended only to wait for an advance party before setting off behind them. Meanwhile, he would wait for a message from Conor and try not to think of her. But she invaded his every waking thought, and when sleep finally claimed him at night, she haunted his dreams, memories of the short time they'd had together tearing at him.

Recollections of her long red hair cascading across the sheets taunted him. He ate what was put in front of him, but it was Dara's sweet lips he tasted. It tore at him that he might never again have her in his bed, her beautiful legs around his waist, his hands tangled in her silky hair.

A wave of longing hit him, surging with the breath he needed to take. Sweet Jesu! There were so many things he wanted to do with Dara. He wanted to have children together, a red-haired daughter like her mother, a son that had a childhood before he became a man. But there was only one thing that really mattered. He wanted all of Dara's heart before she gave it to another.

The journey to Eire had been tiring, but Dara, traveling in boy's attire and as Sorcha's son, welcomed her weariness. Instead of thinking about the man she'd left behind, she concentrated on their next move.

They'd debarked with their mounts from the long clinker-built ship when it was drawn up onshore above the waterline and into a ditch behind the security of an earthen bank beyond. Small encampments dotted the landscape before them.

Dublin was the largest of the settlements and where she hoped to find the *Ard-ri*. The Norsemen had long ago established bases on Eire's coasts for their incursions into the interior. After they'd built and fortified the town of Dublin, named for the dark waters of the Liffey which passed north of the original settlement, the Vikings had stayed. Just as the Normans would stay if they gained a foothold.

Once Dara and Sorcha rode inside the city, there were no large open spaces, reminding her more of the towns she'd seen in Britain than the fresh, clean air of Leinster. Though most of the houses were built of clay and wattles, some were stone, and it was to one of these that they headed.

Many years before, her father had built the city house for her mother, who'd enjoyed the bustling markets. After her mother left Conor for the *Ard-ri*, her father had seldom returned, finding the reminders of his first wife too painful. But Dara had visited several times and knew her way through the twisting streets.

As they rode through the city, Dara wriggled her nose at the foul odors. Horse manure dropped to the narrow dirt roads, mixing with rotten food, and the stench made her glad they had not eaten yet today. Children played tag, ignoring a fly-covered dead swine in their way. She tried not to cringe at the many little children with festering sores, the eye disease in another, or the boils on still another, and wondered if the lack of cleanliness had something to do with the rampant diseases.

The city possessed many noxious odors and a hurry-scurry atmosphere. Everywhere they went, craftsmen worked, building houses and ships. She watched millwrights, chariot makers, leather workers, fishermen, smiths, and metal workers—all landless men and unfree tenants. Her father had never kept slaves, saying he preferred other forms of wealth. Their domestic servants performed household tasks for coins, and they had good service from them.

Indeed, as they rode into the courtyard, a stableboy greeted them, a wide grin on his face. Clearly he recognized her, even disguised as a boy.

"We were not expecting you." His grin faded and his eyes widened. "Did you come alone?"

"Aye." Dara tossed the lad a coin. "Feed the horses well. They've had a long journey and are probably more tired than we are."

After pocketing the silver, the boy whistled. At his signal, two servants hurried from the house.

"The lady is tired," he told them, puffing out his chest with importance. "See to her needs."

One servant rolled her eyes at the youngster's antics. The young woman and boy shared a similar coloring, and Dara recalled they were sister and brother.

She yearned to ask if the *Ard-ri* was currently residing in Dublin, but bit her tongue. Although she did not doubt her people's loyalty, an innocent slip could lead to disaster. She dared not allow MacLugh to find her before she spoke with the *Ard-ri*.

Dismounting, she shifted her pack from her aching shoulders to her hand. "Please, tell no one I am here. 'Tis very important to keep my presence secret."

The boy nodded. "MacLugh is searching for you still."

So even the servants knew her plight. MacLugh's men could be anywhere.

The boy spoke solemnly. "We will say nothing."

His sister shoved him toward the stable with a good-natured push. "Be gone with you. Get about yer work now."

Susan Kearney

The second maid held out her hand to relieve
Dara of the burden of her pack. She shook her
head. "Help Sorcha instead. I fear she is even more
tired than I."

The long night on horseback followed by the sea
crossing had been hard on both of them. In the
past weeks, Sorcha had lost weight, her tunic
hanging loosely about her normally full hips. Sorcha had not said a word about Gaillard, but Dara
knew she missed the squire. Her brown eyes were
as warm as ever—although a few more lines
creased the corners.

The passing days had not lessened Dara's longing for Strongheart, either. While she ate a simple
repast of nettle potage, she remembered the meals
they'd shared, the flowers he'd scattered in unusual places that had almost always brought a smile
to her face. Her hand raised to her neck. She still
wore the necklace he'd given her beneath her tunic, hadn't taken it off since he'd placed it round
her neck.

Sorcha, sitting across from her in the house's
main room, cleared her throat to gain her attention. "Now what? 'Tis dangerous for you here.
That disguise only works with people who do not
know you."

"We need rest and we need to learn if the *Ard-ri*
is here in Dublin without raising suspicion."

"I could go to the market, buy a few supplies,
and listen for gossip," Sorcha offered.

"Thank you." Dara squeezed Sorcha's hand.
"Please do not take any unnecessary risks. You are
a good friend, and I think of you as my mother. I
could not bear to lose you."

"A woman could not have a more courageous daughter." Sorcha bit her bottom lip and cleared the trenchers from the trestle. "I just hope this works out the way you planned."

"It has to." Dara took the thought with her to her bed. As she lay tossing and twisting on the skins, unable to sleep despite her exhaustion, her musings returned repeatedly to the Norman she'd left behind. Would he ever forgive her for leaving him? Would he change and become bitter at what he considered her betrayal? She shivered. Would he come seeking revenge?

It took Sorcha just one day to learn the *Ard-ri* was not in Dublin, and another three days, precious time wasted, to discover that if Dara wanted to meet with the high king, she'd have to travel to Waterford. They packed supplies and planned to leave the next morning.

Dara awakened in the dark to Sorcha shaking her shoulder, a candle in her hand. "Your father just arrived."

Her heart pounded and her fingers trembled as she dressed. Could they already have gathered an army of knights? Was it too late to stop them? "How did he get here so fast? Is Strongheart with him?"

"I know not. Come."

The two women hurried into the hall. Dara spotted her father among a small group of men, none tall enough to be Strongheart. She didn't know whether to feel relief at not having to face him or disappointment that he hadn't come, too.

Her father sipped ale with several of his men, including a stranger, obviously Norman, tall, dark, and broad-chested. The sight of the man made her longing for Strongheart all the keener. "Dara, meet Sir William Fitzralph, Baron of Kidwelly. Treat him well, for he has sent for Norman knights to help us."

Had her father forgotten his agreement with Strongheart? Or merely put his pact with him conveniently aside? Stunned by her father's announcement, Dara nodded at Sir William. "What of Strongheart?"

"Bah!" Her father gestured wildly. "Strongheart may not arrive in time. William can have his knights in Eire within a fortnight."

She strode closer to William, wanting to look the man in the eye. "What will you gain from helping our cause?"

William's eyes widened at her boldness but she read no treachery there. "Your father has promised me a choice of Meath or Munster for my efforts."

She tapped her foot and folded her hands beneath her breasts to cover her agitation. "Meath and Munster are not my father's to give. Even if they were, the *Ard-ri* would never—"

William spoke softly but with steely determination. "What I win, I hold. The *Ard-ri* will not have a choice." His tone gentled then, and he held out his arm in a gallant gesture. "But you are too pretty to worry over politics. Perhaps you would care to walk in the courtyard and watch the sun rise?"

Her gaze flew to her father, who sipped his ale, his innocent gaze meeting hers above the rim of his goblet. What mischief had he concocted? Had he neglected to mention to William her betrothal to Strongheart?

Deciding it would be easier to worm the information out of William than her father, she placed her arm through William's, vowing to find out what had been said. She led him through the back of the house to a walled courtyard where her mother had planted a garden. During the intervening years a gardener had maintained it. But when she breathed in the scent of cornflowers it was not her mother she thought about, but a dark-eyed Norman. Where was he? How soon before he would arrive? What would he think of William Fitzralph, Baron of Kidwelly?

"I watch the sun come up every morn," William told her, his hand too proprietary on hers for comfort.

She drew away and faced him. "Why?"

He seemed taken aback by her question. Then he chuckled and in the first rays of dawn she noted he was a handsome man—not as swarthy as Strongheart, nor as tall, but he shared a certain confidence of manner with Strongheart that she'd always found appealing.

He raised his hands to her shoulders and from the glint in his blue eyes she thought he might kiss her. " 'Tis the promise of a new day when all things are possible—a new land, a new woman."

"Have there been many women in your life?" she asked, steering the subject toward his discussion with her father.

"Not like you."

Begorra! She'd been right. The man was flirting with her.

She placed her hands on her hips. "Just how would you be knowing such after our short acquaintance?"

He chuckled again. "Never has a woman challenged me. Although 'tis most unusual, I rather like it."

" 'Tis doubtful you'll like it when I have Da send you packing."

William shook his head. "Your father needs my men too much to do anything so foolish. Did something I say offend you?"

Offend her? When she wanted Strongheart so much she ached, this man's mere presence offended her. For the first time in her life she wished she could be more like her mother. She missed Strongheart so badly she wished another man could make the pain in her heart recede. But perhaps this once she could test herself to find out the depth of her love for Strongheart. Before her stood another handsome Norman, eager to please her. If she encouraged him, no doubt he'd kiss her, and she would finally know if her love was true.

Taking a deep breath, she coyly peeked at him and uttered the flirtation. "I think you are most comely."

He leaned closer, their lips less than a breath apart.

She could not appear too eager. She placed her hand on his chest to keep him back. "I am betrothed."

"Betrothals can be broken." He captured her hand and lowered his lips to hers.

She allowed the kiss, testing her response to an attractive man. Her elation soared when she felt absolutely nothing—not even a tiny flicker of excitement in her breast. William's kiss could have been the kiss of a brother, a father, a friend.

The discovery that she was not interested in her new suitor lightened her heart like the joy of a new day. As the first rays of sunrise spread lovely pink tentacles across the sky, a weight lifted from Dara's shoulders. She wanted to sing aloud that she was different from her mother. Not any rich handsome man could win her. The last of her doubts about her love for Strongheart melted away with the dark.

It was only Strongheart she wanted, and one man was enough for her. Hugging the delicious knowledge to her, she knew she owed William much for banishing her last doubts, leaving her free to fight for Strongheart and their future together.

But she didn't explain, instead she watched the sun rise and faked a yawn. "I fear 'tis much too early for me to be up."

"I look forward to our next meeting," he told her formally, and she briefly wondered if he was as untouched by their kiss as she.

She recalled her first kiss with Strongheart when he'd tumbled her to the ground. The sparks between them could have set the dry grasses aflame. She'd wanted him then, only she'd been too frightened by her awakening desire. Now, she would settle for nothing less.

Leaving William in the garden, she returned to her bed. She needed her sleep for her ride to Waterford this night. This time, a smile on her lips, she fell asleep almost immediately.

She stood on a rocky spit of land, the wind whipping tendrils of hair back from her face, her hand to her eyes to shade them from the light of a rising sun. She wanted to run toward the sea and Strongheart, but her skirt swirled around her feet, tripping her.

Strongheart came to her, his strong, bronzed body rising from the sea, spindrift spewing in his eyes, his dark hair slicked with water droplets and spiking his long lashes. His lip curled with a lazy smile, and his hard thighs churned toward her, creating ripples of ever-broadening splashes.

When she realized he wore no clothes, her eyes widened with surprise, then pleasure. She would let nothing stand between them, and she threw off her clothes, strewing them across the shoreline as she ran toward him. "I love you. Only you," she cried out, flinging herself against his chest.

He gathered her into his strong arms, and she lifted her face to kiss him. They had so much to discuss, but more importantly she needed him to tell her he loved her, that he would always love her.

His familiar lips formed the words, "I love you."

Then his face changed. He was no longer her Strongheart but the other Norman, William Fitzralph.

She screamed in protest. Her fists pounded his shoulders. Her bare feet uselessly kicked his shins. William laughed and slung her over his shoulder, carrying her back toward the sea.

A wave slammed into her face, and she gulped and sputtered. Struggling wildly, her back arched in an attempt to lift herself higher, out of the water. Too late she realized William would drown her. "Let me go! I cannot breathe."

She thrashed and awakened for the second time that morning to Sorcha's shaking. " 'Tis a bad dream, lass. Och, I fear what I have to tell you is not any better."

Blearily, Dara rubbed the sleep from her eyes, a dark foreboding slithering down her spine. "What is it?"

Sorcha's warm brown eyes teared with worry. "Your da has betrothed you to Sir William."

"But I am already betrothed to Strongheart." Dara threw her blankets aside, thinking her father had lost his reason. "I will go remind him."

Sorcha grabbed her hand. "He has a priest waiting to marry you in the other room. If you go in there, you will not escape this marriage."

Chapter Eighteen

Without Sorcha's quick thinking, Dara would
never have escaped the city. Luckily her provisions had already been packed and it was a simple
matter for Sorcha to have a horse waiting in the
gardens.

Dara had climbed through a window, left Sorcha behind, and escaped Dublin. She knew her father's desperation to regain Leinster did not
excuse his outrageous behavior in marrying her to
the first mercenary who promised to lend them
men. But she suppressed her anger at her father,
for truly his memory was worsening. Her escape
from an immediate marriage to William Fitzralph
would at worst delay her father's latest scheme. At
best, her flight might win the right to marry the
man she loved.

Hoping her disappearance would deter William

from bringing the knights to Eire, she rode hard. Heading south, she estimated, if all went well, she'd reach Waterford in less than half a fortnight. She passed through the wild and mountainous hills of Glendalough, picking her way around impassable bogs. She skirted Wicklow, Ferns, and Wexford, arriving in Waterford on her fifth exhausting day of travel.

As much as she hated arriving at the *Ard-ri*'s residence in her grimy traveling clothes, she did not have the luxury of time. She rode in, listening to Waterford's residents buzz with the news of many ships spotted on the horizon. *Strongheart and his men!* With the knowledge of a coming attack, the residents had thrown up a temporary fort around the stone structures in the middle of the city. No one paid attention to the slight lad riding amongst them.

Dara left her horse in the stable and requested an immediate audience with the *Ard-ri*. She'd met the high king only once before when she'd been but a lass of ten. Even then, he'd seemed enamored of her red hair, which was just like her mother's.

Hoping her name and his curiosity to see how she'd turned out would gain her an audience, she smoothed the wrinkles of her tunic as best she could and combed her fingers through her hair. Fretting at the time wasted, she paced the small alcove. How long until Strongheart arrived?

As much as she longed to see him again and explain the reasons for her flight, his sudden arrival would put a dent in her plans and worse, bring the war she dreaded. She'd hoped to slowly sway the *Ard-ri* to her way of thinking, but now she must use more direct methods.

Finally a maid returned to fetch her into the hall. "The high king will see you now."

Dara followed the girl into a great hall where men dressed for battle in leather jerkins huddled round their leader. The *Ard-ri* was short of stature, but the commanding breadth of his shoulders under the rich silk tunic trimmed with fur left no doubt to his station.

When the *Ard-ri* lifted his shaggy, gray-haired head and pierced her with a cold-eyed stare, a shiver of apprehension walked across her shoulders. Suddenly her plan to convince him to see her way of things seemed foolish.

Drawing a deep breath for courage, she curtsied, hoping she wouldn't have to present her plea in front of his men-at-arms. The room grew so quiet she could hear her own heartbeat. Why didn't he say something? Anything would be better than this nerve-wracking silence.

She licked her dry lips and realized that being the image of her mother could work against her with this man. She could only hope he still harbored some small feeling for the woman who'd betrayed him with a stableboy. Or maybe he wouldn't hold the sins of the mother against her child. She forced herself not to shudder at the memory that this same man had locked her mother behind the walls of a monastery where she remained until this day.

"Has Murgain's ghost come back to haunt us a full year after her passing?" asked one of the *Ard-ri*'s advisors.

So her mother was dead. The answer did not unduly disturb her. How could it, when she couldn't even remember her mother's face? Still, a fleeting sadness washed over her. Now she and her mother would never speak.

More important, the messages from her mother through Mata had been a trick. The *Ard-ri* had wanted her da to suffer and think the woman he loved remained locked behind monastery walls.

The *Ard-ri* pushed his way through his men. "Rise, Dara O'Dwyre, and tell us what brings you here."

The crowd murmured. A hushed voice rose above the others. "She's not a hostage?"

"I come of my free will in the hopes of preventing war," she began.

Hoots of derision and laughter followed her pronouncement and a sick knot of fear settled in the pit of her stomach. Despite their reaction, she continued. "As we speak, Strongheart draws closer. You cannot defeat an army of Normans using longbows, wearing mail, and fighting upon horseback."

"Do you think so little of our abilities, lady?" sneered one of the men.

"O'Rourke will stop the Norman's army before he leaves the coast," stated another.

"What do you think we should do, colleen? Surrender?" the *Ard-ri* asked to much chuckling among his men.

"I would have you sanction my marriage to Strongheart the Norman."

The *Ard-ri* banged his spear into the ground with anger. "You are betrothed to MacLugh!

Would you go from husband to husband as did your mother?"

"No, sire. I do not wish to cause a war. Having men fight over me and never knowing if my children will grow up in peace is distasteful to me. But the contract between O'Dwyre and MacLugh was made by our mothers and is not valid."

The *Ard-ri* turned away as if the discussion was closed. "A new contract will be drawn."

Dara refused to let him turn his back on her dreams so easily. "Wait! If I marry MacLugh, two counties will be united under one king. The other kings will be jealous. A marriage between myself and MacLugh could cause civil war, even jeopardizing the power of the *Ard-ri*."

The face of one of the men-at-arms turned red with fury. "She speaks treason."

"Nay," the high king countered. "Like her mother, she is shrewd in her assessment of the political situation."

"Then you will agree to my marriage to the Norman?" Dara asked, her heart tripping with rising hope.

The *Ard-ri* raised his voice. "Give a Norman Eire's richest county as a deterrent to invading our land? Let him infest Eire with his army of knights? I would rather die with honor upon the field of battle than allow such a thing to come to pass."

Dara's hopes plummeted. She had her answer. Her analysis of the political situation might be correct, but men would prefer to battle than concede to their enemies.

"Take her to the tower. Dara O'Dwyre of Leinster, you are now my prisoner."

"I came to you in good faith," she protested, her chin high. Inside, she trembled, knowing she had lost this last desperate gamble. She'd lost her home. And she'd lost the Norman's trust. She'd come all the way here for nothing. War was inevitable.

The *Ard-ri* flicked his hand. "Take her away. She might be useful later. Someone send a message to MacLugh. Tell him we have his bride waiting."

Laughter filled the hall and two retainers led Dara away. In their male arrogance, their hands loose upon her arms, they had no idea of the dirk she possessed. No one had searched her person, and she still carried weapons beneath her clothing. Should an opportunity to escape arise, she meant to take it, but she was not so foolish as to take on two burly men at one time.

From her locked cell in the tower, she had a view of the countryside. She watched as Strongheart's ships sailed onto the beaches under the attack of O'Rourke's men. Despite the disadvantage of their position, the Normans soon drove O'Rourke's men back from the sea and toward the city.

Dara lost sight of the battlefield under the canopy of leafy trees surrounding the city. But it did not take great imagination to picture the arrows, shot by longbows, picking off Eire's men.

Unable to root for either side since either Eire's men would defeat the man she loved or the Norman would win by defeating her countrymen, she paced, her hands twisting in her tunic. Why did men have to be so stubborn? Why had she fallen in love with the most stubborn man of all?

She hated the thought of Strongheart finding her here, trapped inside the tower, completely at his mercy. Worse. Suppose MacLugh or O'Rourke reached her first? Her heart sank like a wounded bird. She must flee to meet with Strongheart on more equal territory.

A creak in the lock warned her the door was about to open. Heart pounding, she pulled her dirk from her sheath and stood to one side of the doorway, ready to attack.

Sorcha told Strongheart Dara's destination, but she did not tell him of Dara's near-marriage to William Fitzralph. She feared that doing so would deter Strongheart from getting Dara safely away from the *Ard-ri* as soon as possible. It was the right decision, for Strongheart sent Fitzralph back to Britain without a second thought.

Sailing with three thousand knights, he headed for Waterford on the next tide with a veritable army set on winning this land. Two days later, they fought their way ashore, cutting through the enemy standing between him and Dara. He let O'Rourke's men retreat without pursuit, anxious to rescue her before she suffered harm.

Although Strongheart had enough knights to retake Leinster, without Dara by his side, any victory would be empty. She meant more to him than all the land that comprised Leinster's riches. Despite her betrayal, despite her lack of trust in his ability to do what was right for both of them, he wanted her. Without her, his heart was like creeping ivy, which would wither unless it had Dara to entwine around. Strongheart awakened each day with thoughts of her. He recalled her sleepy-sweet smiles in the morning, her sparkling laughter during an afternoon ride, her long legs wrapped around him at night. She had brought a warmth to his days, a luster to his nights. Strongheart had no intention of reverting to the man he'd been before meeting Dara—and ending up a cold, bitter warrior like his father, who used his children as pawns to gain wealth and more wealth.

Through men racing away on foot, between the ruins of smoking buildings, O'Rourke, with a patch over one eye, rode out to meet Strongheart. Although he rode straight in the saddle, his bearing didn't conceal his gray hair and weathered skin, tough from years of hard campaigns. Clearly, his glory days were over.

Strongheart raised his sword, hesitant to fight an older, weaker man. "I have no quarrel with you, O'Rourke. Go home."

O'Rourke drew his horse to a halt. "Conor stole my wife. Now I shall have his daughter to replace the woman he took."

Dara had been right. Half a lifetime later, men still fought over the perfidy of her mother. Nevertheless, Strongheart would never give Dara up. "Dara is mine."

O'Rourke dug his heels into his horse's flanks. The valiant animal charged forward. Strongheart held his ground, hefting his sword and waiting to defend against the attack.

The animals brushed so close, Strongheart smelled the other horse's sweat, saw its eyes widen and its nostrils flare. The sound of hoofbeats thundered in his ears.

O'Rourke lunged to the right. Strongheart raised his shield arm, protecting his body from a mortal blow. At the same time, he thrust under his opponent's shield, finding his mark.

Mortally injured, O'Rourke slid from his horse, hate in his eyes. "My son will avenge my honor," he vowed, before his eyes glazed in death. Before he sank to the ground, another man took his place. Strongheart smote him down, and then another. The Irish fought the Normans, until the streets ran crimson with the blood of the injured and dying. The wounded screamed in agony and around them buildings burned, red sparks curling amidst black smoke and searing the throats of the living.

His knights fought their way through the city to the fort surrounding a few stone houses. They laid siege to the city defended by the high king's men, hoping no one would realize the value of the hostage within the fort.

Strongheart would give up his dream to own Leinster if he thought the gesture could save Dara from harm. Where was she now? His gaze scanned the stone buildings, searching for a sign of her. Damn it! Where was she?

He took in the fortification, estimating the number of men he would lose if they rushed the barriers. The *Ard-ri*'s men held the advantage and could pick off his knights with their spears. He would risk it, if he thought they stood a chance of success.

Gaillard rode up, interrupting his thoughts. "One of our men noticed a house projecting over the walls and supported by props from outside. If we cut the timbers and the house falls, we might breach through and rush the fort."

"Let it be done," he ordered, stilling his racing heart, unable to put away the hope of seeing Dara soon. "The first man through shall earn ten pieces of gold."

Inside the fort, the *Ard-ri* pointed to a tunnel that led out of the city. "Go to MacLugh," the high king ordered Dara. "Marry him before all is lost."

Dara would not permit the high king to maneuver her life like a playing piece in a game of chess. When she'd been brought from the tower, she thought Strongheart might have arranged her release. Instead, she'd learned the *Ard-ri* wanted her to escape to marry MacLugh.

"No, sire." She trembled, her whole body shaking at defying her king. She deeply regretted fleeing Britain. She'd stupidly sacrificed her love for naught, naively thought the *Ard-ri* would prefer peace to war. How many men had died because she had come to Waterford?

How many more men would die before they could have peace? They'd heard O'Rourke, her mother's first husband and her father's old enemy, was dead. The *Ard-ri* and his men could not withstand an assault from the skilled Normans. Did Strongheart realize that, with his army, he could push North to Dublin and capture the heart of Eire? After that, it would be a simple operation to conquer the rest of the country.

Before the *Ard-ri* shoved her through an escape tunnel against her will, she heard an enormous popping sound. The earth trembled beneath her feet. Dropping to the ground, she coughed on dust rising into the air. The *Ard-ri* retreated at a run.

Men panicked, shouting of a breach in their defenses. Knights poured into the streets. She spotted Strongheart among the first men through the opening, his tall frame and warhorse easy to pick out among the throng of knights.

She would have gone to him, except her knees felt as if they were made of water. Dara called out and waved from the ground. Somehow, through the noise and confusion, he heard her, and within moments, he'd scooped her onto his warhorse.

Squeezing her eyes tight, she hugged his mail, welcoming the bite of metal rings against her hands. She'd never been more relieved to see anyone in her entire life. She'd been wrong to run from him, wrong to place herself in danger, and she intended to tell him.

The fighting around them died within minutes. The *Ard-ri*, knowing he was outnumbered and losing, sounded a retreat. His soldiers, carrying their wounded, withdrew to the forests.

"After them," Strongheart shouted, the words she'd feared most.

Dara opened her eyes. "No! Let them go."

"I will have the *Ard-ri*," he said grimly, his voice granite-hard.

As the Norman urged his destrier into the woods after the *Ard-ri* and his men, Dara slumped in the saddle, too weary to cry. Strongheart had lied to her. She'd been right not to trust him. Just like every man, he craved power. Why else would he go after the *Ard-ri*?

Perhaps she should follow in her mother's footsteps after all. She could enter a monastery to find the peace she sought. For how could she bear to watch Strongheart spend years fighting her people to conquer and hold this land? Her people would rebel, and she would be torn. And as the man she loved inevitably aged and weakened, it would be up to their sons to spend their lives fighting to rule.

As shouts went up in the woods to find the *Ardri*, her father's men emerged from the forest, cutting off the high king's retreat. Drawing his destrier to a halt in a clearing, Strongheart waited, his arms tight around her. For several long moments, he said nothing and the tension between them grew.

"You will never run from me again." His voice harsh, bitter, grated on her nerves.

Though she'd meant to apologize, the words stuck in her throat. In their time apart, Strongheart had grown more forbidding. Perhaps it was the helm covering most of his face, perhaps it was the dark eyes burning through the holes, or maybe it was the stiff way he held her, but a knot of fear swelled and grew tight inside her.

Had she killed all his tender feelings for her? Would he treat her with this stiff coldness for the rest of their lives?

Swallowing the tight lump, she decided not to allow that. And then, with a sharp pain in her heart, she realized he could treat her any way he chose. No one could stop him. He would take her land. He would take her people. He could take her every night if he so desired and no one would dare gainsay him.

Susan Kearney

She slumped in hopelessness, bitter gall rising in the back of her throat. Nothing she could do would alter her fate. Strongheart would conquer as he willed, and all her protests would come to nothing more than a mosquito irritating a bear. If she bit him, he would swat her down. He wouldn't physically hurt her—she knew him better than that. But watching him subjugate her people would cause her more pain than any beating.

Gaillard rode into the clearing and halted beside Strongheart. "We have the *Ard-ri*."

Strongheart wheeled his warhorse around. "Bring him with us into Waterford. I shall speak with him there."

Stunned that the *Ard-ri* was alive, Dara wondered what Strongheart wanted of the high king. Did he intend a public execution? She shuddered and fought the queasiness in her stomach, wishing for a quiet moment to lie down and settle her thoughts.

But that was not to be. The ride through the flaming streets, with the bodies of the dead and dying strewn around, agitated her upset stomach into a roiling nausea. Dara had witnessed many border raids, but this destruction by the Normans seemed far worse.

At the fetid stench of burnt flesh, she covered her nose with her sleeve, but the odors seeped through the cloth. Giving up the battle to keep down her last meal, she leaned over the side of the horse and heaved.

Strongheart brought his horse to an immediate halt, his forehead creased in a frown. "Are you ill, Princess?"

She dismounted, glad for a moment to be on solid ground. "What your people have done to mine makes me sick."

His swarthy skin paled at her remark. His lips tightened, but he didn't reply. Instead he handed her a flask of water, and watched her intently.

She washed the sour taste from her mouth and handed back the flask, uncomfortably aware that his dark gaze had never left her face. She frowned. "What are you staring at? Are you afraid I will drop dead before you can force me to wed?"

"Does your sickness mean you carry my child?" he asked stiffly, dismounting when he finally realized her reluctance to remount.

Damn him! How could he have guessed before she had? With all he had put her through, it was no wonder she'd lost count of the days. Still, that did not necessarily mean she carried his child. But it did, her heart argued back. The moment he'd said the words, she'd recognized the truth.

Apparently reading the answer in her eyes, he reached out to steady her, a pleased expression on his lips.

She dropped her hand to curl protectively over her flat stomach. A bairn! The next generation. She had to be strong, not only for herself and her people but for the new life she carried in her womb. Lifting her chin, she peered square into his eyes without flinching. "Loving you is not enough compensation for the years of war I anticipate."

His tone softened. "What would you have me do?"

"Send the Norman army back to Britain."

He shook his head, taking her elbow. Together

they walked toward the cathedral, one of the few remaining buildings untouched by fire and, from the horses tied outside, his temporary headquarters. "We need those men to retake Leinster and to make a home for our children."

She tried not to think how pleasant it would be to make more children with this man. Her heart warmed a little that he wanted her still. "Do you wish our child to be born in a country torn apart by war?"

His voice hardened, but he spoke gently. "The best way to protect you and our child is to retake Leinster with Norman knights."

Perhaps she should allow him to make the military decisions. "I dream of living with you in Leinster, raising our children there." Her hand gripped his, tightly. "But I would rather give up the land than lose my children to raiders in the same way I lost my half sister, Eva. The thought of losing you, of losing a child, terrifies me."

"I will keep you and our children safe," he promised.

Vultures circled overhead. A pack of wild dogs raced through the streets, while slowly villagers returned to recover what they could.

"Empty are your promises, Norman. With your ambition, I could be a widow before our child is born." She stopped then, released his hand, and raised her chin, ignoring the pain that flickered in his gaze. "You can force me to be your wife. You can force me to bear your children."

"I have never forced you to my bed."

"Though I cannot control my body's reactions to you," she admitted, "you will find my heart as elusive as Ireland's mist unless you give up your ambition to rule all of Eire."

He raked his hand through his hair and emitted a sigh. "I told you before that I had changed, that I no longer want to conquer all of Eire."

She'd been a fool to believe him. "You gave me sweet words to allay my suspicions. What I have seen this day are powerful warriors killing my people."

His lips tightened in anger. "Should I have allowed the *Ard-ri* to marry you to MacLugh?"

She slung her hair off her face and straightened her spine in challenge. "So, Norman, do you intend to conquer Ireland or my heart?"

Gaillard rode up and the question she'd thrown down like a gauntlet between them remained unanswered. "The archbishop is waiting in the church with Conor."

"And the *Ard-ri*?" Strongheart asked.

Gaillard frowned. "Is proving stubborn."

"I shall see to him myself." Strongheart strode off without a backward glance, leaving Dara with Gaillard.

Sorcha came running into the street with a wide smile on her face. She hugged Dara, answering her question before she could ask. "I sailed with the men from Dublin. And I brought you a wedding dress. Come. We must hurry. Your Norman has given me only thirty minutes to prepare you for the ceremony."

Dazed at the pace her life was racing forward, Dara sat numbly in a small room off the cathedral, letting Sorcha brush her hair, wondering if the

Norman groom was killing the Irish high king while the bride readied herself to wed.

She fingered the emerald necklace Strongheart had given her, her hand catching on the shamrock that reminded her of home. "Should I again try to run from the Norman?"

Sorcha warm brown eyes narrowed. "Och! Where could you go? Your father is here. The *Ardri* is here. And your child needs a father, aye?"

"What will I do if he marries me and then goes off to make war?" Dara asked.

Sorcha clucked her tongue. "You will do what women always do—wait for their men to come home, raise their bairns, and pray."

With all the running Dara had done, she hadn't escaped her fate. Perhaps it was best she meet it head-on. Then why didn't she feel joyful? Why didn't she feel at peace with her decision to yield to the Norman?

Perhaps because Strongheart respected her wishes in only small matters. Or perhaps because the Norman had never told her he loved her. Deep down she thought a wedding should be joyful, not an arrangement of land ownership, and then scolded herself for wishing for a romantic marriage. Romance was a silly child's dream, and she must put childish dreams behind her.

Sorcha finished with her hair, leaving it combed to a radiant shine and loose over her shoulders. She helped her into a fine silk undertunic and a cream overtunic trimmed with gold embroidery. Her friend had even brought matching slippers.

She hugged Sorcha. "Thank you. Thank you for everything."

"Och! I almost forgot." Sorcha hurried to her traveling pouch and pulled out an exquisite gold girdle. "This is from Strongheart."

Dara sucked in her breath at the delicate workmanship, tiny golden flowers woven together in a daisy chain. Would he be so thoughtful if he didn't care for her? She thought not, and where there was feeling, there was a chance to sway him from his relentless course. For the first time that day, a smile formed on her lips.

"You are still too pale." Sorcha reached out and pinched her cheeks. "There. Go to him and be happy."

"I will try."

The wedding passed in a blur. The smoke outside cast a pall over the ceremony as did the *Ard-ri* glowering from his pew. Dara did her best to ignore everything but the man kneeling by her side. His implacable heat radiated through the black linen of his fine tunic to the tips of his polished leather boots. He'd washed his hair, and, still damp at the nape, his locks gleamed, their fresh scent wafting to her, and she recalled the enjoyment of running her fingers through his thick hair.

Shouts from outside suddenly interrupted the ceremony, and her heart pounded. Something was wrong! Gaillard went to the massive double doors at the entrance and returned down the center isle at a run. "MacLugh and O'Rourke's son have set our ships afire!"

They had begun the ceremony amid burning buildings and death, ended it with fresh assaults.

Susan Kearney

Dara felt doomed to a life of war. A great, heavy sadness welled within her chest.

"Finish," Strongheart ordered the archbishop.

The archbishop nodded. "I now pronounce you man and wife."

Strongheart turned to Conor. "Take care of her."

Her husband of two minutes did not even kiss her before he sprinted out the door and left her kneeling at the altar. Instead of wedding chimes and laughter, she heard the battle cries of war.

Chapter Nineteen

Strongheart frowned at MacLugh's tactics. The coward had not stayed to fight. The King of Meath had set their ships on fire to force the Norman army to march to Ferns. Instead of fighting, MacLugh had retreated.

After deploying his men, Strongheart returned to the small room in the church he'd set aside for his and Dara's use. He knocked and entered to find his bride changed out of her finery and back into boy's clothes, her long hair braided and neatly pinned to her head.

She stood beside a table sorting through small packets of herbs. Relief that he had her where he could protect her washed through him. Putting up her hair and wearing boy's clothing could not hide the aristocratic beauty of her high cheekbones or the proud tilt to her head. He deeply regretted the necessity of spending their wedding night on a forced march to Ferns instead of in a soft bed aboard ship.

She didn't look up from her task and spoke softly, but he heard the bitterness in her words. "So, MacLugh is now fighting O'Rourke's son for control of Castle Ferns."

" 'Tis good our enemies fight among themselves."

"Is it good the war has escalated? That more crops will be ruined? More men will die? And how long before the clans of Ulster and Connaught learn you hold the *Ard-ri* hostage?"

"I let the *Ard-ri* go."

She spun around to face him, eyes wide, her long lashes emphasizing her surprise. "Why?"

He shrugged, barely containing his smile of satisfaction at keeping his word. "I do not need another enemy."

"And?" she prodded, her arms folded under her breasts as if unwilling to believe he'd followed her wishes.

"The *Ard-ri* and I have come to an understanding."

Her eyebrow arched with skepticism. "Truly?"

"When I retake Leinster, he will legitimize our marriage."

Since he'd accomplished what she had set out to do, he thought she would break into a wide smile and embrace him with joy. Instead she bit her lower lip. "Did you draw this agreement in a written pact?"

How many times must he tell her the same thing? "My word is ironclad."

"But the *Ard-ri's* is not." She lifted her chin and despite her words, hope shone in the green mists of her eyes. "The high king is capable of selectively forgetting his agreements."

A hardness crept into Strongheart's voice. "He will not have the luxury of forgetting this one. Once I retake Leinster, the *Ard-ri* will not have a choice. He will either stick to his bargain or face my knights."

Dara exhaled a long sigh. "More battles of glory for you to fight, my lord?"

He'd taken enough of her sarcasm. Striding two steps forward, he gathered her into his arms. He'd spent too many nights longing for the sight of her smile to deny himself the taste of her lips and the feel of her breasts crushed against his chest.

As his lips covered hers, she gasped. His arms went around her shoulders, and he tenderly drew her closer, losing himself in the sweet scent of her hair, the soft feel of her lips, the exciting taste of her mouth. She was everything he wanted in a woman, and he was through denying to himself how much he wanted her for his wife.

Putting the feelings he couldn't speak into his kiss, he showed her what she meant to him. He gathered her closer and his heart lurched madly. He would use his warrior strength to protect her. In the days spent apart, he'd discovered that real wealth was the freedom to be the kind of man Dara loved.

She wound her fingers around his neck and into his hair, her eagerness exciting him more than winning any battle. He would never regret his decision to conquer this woman instead of Eire.

Those many years ago, his father had led him down the wrong path, an endless cycle of carnage, war, and revenge. He saw Dara's love, not Eire, as his last chance to lead a worthy life. As he kissed his wife, he imagined his mother smiling down at him, and for the first time in many years he felt at peace.

He drew back from their kiss, but kept his arms around her, enjoying her snuggling against him. "If we ever wish to live in peace, we must defeat Leinster's enemies."

"Yes."

"Is that my wife I hear agreeing with me?" he teased. "Mayhap I have a fairy sprite in my arms instead."

She stiffened, but a smile twitched across her lips. "Norman, I warn you fair, I will not share my husband with a fairy."

"Ah, now that sounds more like the wench I married and have come to love."

"Love? Did you say you loved me?"

He chuckled and the warm sound enfolded her like a velvet wrap. "Must have been a slip of the tongue."

She drew her fingers into a fist and punched his shoulder. He didn't flinch but looked at her with a fiery hunger that stole her breath away.

"Tell me," she demanded. "I need to hear you say it again."

"I love you, Princess."

He loved her. At Strongheart's words, Dara felt a bottomless satisfaction and joy. Blissfully happy and fully alive, she tugged his head down and rewarded him with another searing kiss. Could she truly have everything she wanted? A husband that loved her, a baby, and peace?

Through kiss-swollen lips she whispered, "Once we retake Leinster, can we live without war?"

His tone turned serious. "We must hurt Mac-Lugh and O'Rourke's son so they will think twice about attacking again, but not defeat them so badly their wounded pride cries out for revenge."

She grinned, her eyes shining with relief and the pleasure of going home. "You know us so well."

Although she now agreed with Strongheart to retake her home with the Norman knights, a niggling doubt remained. Would her husband be satisfied with just Leinster? Or would he grow bored and seek Eire's high kingship?

His hands wandered inside her tunic and cupped her breasts, his thumbs flicking over her nipples. She moaned softly, shards of heat shooting to her belly. Squirming, she tried to set aside her doubts, allowing his husky voice to convince her he'd meant what he'd said—Leinster would be enough for him.

He nibbled her ear. "I aim to know you better. I do not think I will be bored watching your belly fill with my child, your breasts plump with milk."

She frowned. "I will grow fat and you will not be able to make love with me."

He laughed. "There are many ways to please you." He whispered in her ear, telling her exactly how he planned to take her, until her cheeks heated, and her face burned crimson at his intriguing suggestions.

Unfortunately he only spoke words of love and had not the time to act upon them. Events did not permit them even an hour of privacy before they mounted and rode north toward Ferns.

"I wish you would stay and let me send for you later," Strongheart muttered.

"The safest place for me is behind your sword," she countered.

Her da agreed, his face excited at the prospect of going home. " 'Tis better to allow Dara to ride with us than to have her follow on her own."

Sorcha chose to ride with them as well, and Dara didn't miss the frequent looks her friend shared with Gaillard. She expected theirs might be the first wedding after they retook Castle Ferns.

The ride north was a slow one. Advance parties scouted far ahead searching for ambush or trickery, but oddly the trip remained peaceful. Following the Okinselagh trail, they passed Wexford, through great herds of grazing cattle. Leinster's country folk urged on the Norman calvary armed with long lances and clad in mail armor, along with English archers, whose bows so accurately carried death at a distance. Along the way, minor lairds paid homage to her father and Strongheart, repledging oaths of fealty, agreeing to pay tribute to help support their army with food.

They covered the distance from Waterford to Ferns in a hard two-day ride, in ever-falling rain, skirting the mountains and bog land. Dara looked proudly on her father and husband, riding side by side, the two men of great size who were popular with her people.

The Norman gave her people hope. Brave and fierce in war, he was a tremendous fighter, possessing inexhaustible energy. He constantly rode to the front line and back, checking the state of the army's readiness and gauging their fatigue. An hour's ride from Ferns he called a halt and ordered them to set up camp for the night.

Tomorrow they would retake Ferns.

The rain softened to a drizzle, and Dara looked up from stirring stew at her fire to spy a rider coming their way from the direction of Ferns. An odd premonition chilled her.

Strongheart noted her shiver and placed a warm arm over her shoulder. "One more day and you shall be home," he promised.

The Normans stopped the rider at their perimeter and searched him for weapons before escorting him to Strongheart. The rider's dirty hair was matted in clumps over his ears, but it was his haughty eyes, cold and chill, that made Dara inch closer to her husband.

"I have a message for ye from King MacLugh."

Strongheart stepped between Dara and the other man. "Does MacLugh wish to surrender?"

"On the contrary. He wishes to fight you at dawn. Winner take all."

Strongheart didn't hesitate. "I accept."

"No!" Dara tugged on his arm, attempting to pull him away. Though chilled, her body broke into an icy sweat. " 'Tis a trick."

Strongheart led her into their tent. "Do not ever gainsay me again, woman. I know what I am about. Do you think I fear MacLugh? Do you think I cannot defeat him?"

The blood drained from her face, and she forced words past a mouth gone dry with fear. "We have the upper hand. There is no need for you to risk your life. With your army of knights, we cannot lose."

He crossed his arms over his broad chest, adamant in his decision. "I am not a coward."

His words were flat and abrupt. Resolute.

She twisted her hands in her tunic and spoke with care not to insult his honor. "I saw you fight with swords once before. Remember? You and MacLugh appeared evenly matched."

He shot her a cocky grin, his midnight eyes sparkling with excitement. "That is exactly what I wished him to think. This challenge will save lives—and that is what *you* wanted. We can retake Leinster with the loss of only one life—the King of Meath's."

Damn him! While she felt sick with worry, he would enjoy the battle. How could he risk his life so carelessly? She dropped to her knees and grabbed his hand, pleading with him past the lump in her throat. "I beg of you, do not do this. I would rather lose half an army than you."

He kneeled with her. "I will not lose, Princess."

"You are doing what he wants." A sob escaped her. "This fight between you is the only way MacLugh can win."

Strongheart framed her face with his hands, his voice firm. "I have already accepted the challenge. I will not go back on my word—not even for you."

Tears washed down her face, and she let him see her pain. "Do I mean nothing to you? Do you not wish to see your child born? Do you not wish to grow old in my bed?"

He tried to silence her with a kiss, but she would have none of his caresses. Turning away, she rolled onto her side on the blanket, knees drawn to her chest in dread. Something awful would happen tomorrow.

He held her through the night, and she awakened exhausted. The rain slicing from the cloudy sky in the grayish dawn mirrored her fears. Trying not to distract him from his preparations, she remained silent by their small fire.

He came up behind her and wrapped his arms around her. "I will be back soon, Princess."

"I am coming with you." His mouth opened to object, but she spoke quickly before he could get a word in. "I will remain quiet. I will not distract you. Please, do not make me wait here." Her voice broke. "Waiting is worse than fighting. Watching you risk your life is hard enough but not knowing is even worse. I could not endure remaining here and wondering what was happening."

"You shall come with me."

When they arrived in the appointed field, Gaillard had the Norman knights placed around half of the perimeter of the circle cleared for the challenge. MacLugh's men lined the other side, clapping one another on the back, drinking ale, and betting, giving the scene an oddly festive atmosphere.

Between Norman knight and MacLugh warrior stood the *Ard-ri* with his men-at-arms, his harpist playing a rowdy ballad. At least the high king could be forced to legitimize their marriage if Strongheart won—*when* he won, Dara thought, in an attempt to push her doubts aside.

It was not so much that she doubted her husband's ability that made her tremble but that she distrusted MacLugh. The man was without honor. The way he looked at her made her skin crawl as if it were infested with bedbugs. She did not deign to look his way, but she could feel his sordid gaze upon her as she took a place beside Gaillard.

She fastened her gaze upon her husband as he unhurriedly removed his mantle and drew his sword. He moved with the dangerous grace of a mountain lion, his lithe movements economical and unhurried. His swarthy, handsome face looked particularly arresting, his eyes alert, his lips determined and clearly eager to face his opponent.

Their fight would be on foot. Both men wore helms, clasped shields in their left hands, and held swords with the right.

MacLugh might not be as tall or as broad as the Norman, but he had the lean, wiry strength of a predator. The look in his eyes was hungry, cruel, and the hair on her arms prickled in response.

The combatants, looking into each other's eyes for weakness, circled each other warily, testing. Strongheart smiled then, a slow, cynical smile that left an obviously maddening impression on his opponent's self-control. MacLugh thrust wildly but skillfully, and Strongheart parried without losing his mocking grin.

Was MacLugh's loss of temper a good sign? Dara closed her fingers into fists and reminded herself to breathe. The trampled grass soon became muddy. Several minutes passed without either man drawing blood.

Onlookers on both sides of the circle shouted encouragement. Dara realized her home was at stake, but all she could think about was the Norman. Any man could slip or make a mistake. She wanted this to be over, and yet as long as they both took the other's measure, Strongheart could not be hurt.

MacLugh suddenly lunged forward, his blade bouncing off Strongheart's shield and slipping around to nip his arm. As blood welled, Dara bit her lip to keep from crying out.

Again MacLugh advanced, his sword nicking Strongheart's thigh, enough to draw blood but not enough to lame him. MacLugh's breath became ragged and sweat beaded on his head, mixed with the heavy mist, and trickled into his eyes. Since Strongheart appeared as composed as ever, clearly the two minor injuries were nothing she should worry about.

But she did worry. If Strongheart had deliberately allowed the other man a small victory to make him overconfident, her husband played a dangerous game.

Gaillard squeezed her arm and whispered in her ear. "Have courage. Strongheart's just warming up and already MacLugh tires."

Just then Strongheart attacked, his broad blade flashing up, down, back, and across so quickly her eyes barely followed his lightning movement. He ended with a blow so powerful, he split MacLugh's shield with a cracking sound.

Dara jumped, her chest tightened.

With a chivalrous gesture, Strongheart discarded his own perfectly good shield. Dara let out a small moan, then clamped her hand over her mouth, determined not to utter another sound.

"He knows what he is about," Gaillard told her calmly. "He's toying with MacLugh."

"Then why is he bleeding?" Dara whispered.

"Both men are bleeding."

Both men wielded their weapons with care, slicing and parrying. While a strong blow might disarm an opponent, the same powerful strike might cause one's sword to snap.

Strongheart attacked, giving his opponent not a moment to recover from one strike before beginning the next. MacLugh slipped in the mud, rolled, and scrambled to recover. Damn Strongheart for letting him regain his feet. Why did he have to be such a gentleman? This wasn't a tournament, but a fight for life.

MacLugh retreated toward Dara. Strongheart pressed his advantage. With a backhanded move almost too quick for her eyes to follow, he sent the Irish king's sword flying from his hand and out of reach.

"Yield!" Strongheart demanded.

"Never!" cried MacLugh, leaping backward, pulling a dirk from a sheath at his back.

Within the space of a heartbeat, MacLugh grabbed Dara, spun her into the circle out of Gaillard's reach, and held the knife to her throat. The sharp edge of the blade pricked her flesh and hot liquid trickled down her neck.

Dara didn't dare reach for the knife at her waist. She held perfectly still, but the tiny movement of each breath caused more blood to seep from her neck.

MacLugh sneered. "Lay down your sword."

Strongheart's face paled, fear for her glimmering in the depths of his eyes. "Do not hurt her."

"Lay down your weapon," MacLugh repeated, battle madness dancing in his eyes.

It was his fault she was in danger. He never should have permitted her to watch this spectacle. As he'd always known, there was no room in this life for weakness. Once again, Dara had used the gentler side of his nature to sway him into letting her go where she did not belong.

Lust dazed a man. Love killed him. This time his lack of judgment might kill his wife and unborn child.

He could face the possibility of his own death without flinching. But the thought of losing Dara caused a vigorous surge of fury to flood him.

Strongheart bent slowly, placing the sword in the mud without taking his gaze off MacLugh. Every muscle in his body quivered taut.

The man was simply too far away for him to grab. His heart leapt in his chest. If he dived, MacLugh would slice Dara's throat. If he remained still, MacLugh would slice Dara's throat.

Dara's forefinger flickered, pointing to the dirk at her waist. She was waiting for him to make a move.

Obviously she thought he could do the impossible. While her faith in him amazed him, he would not fail her by refusing to make an attempt.

From a crouched position, Strongheart lunged, thrusting with his powerful thighs, a bloodcurdling scream on his lips. As if on his signal, Dara's hands snapped upward around MacLugh's wrist, gaining an instant of time.

Love and fear gave Strongheart's legs the extra

strength, catapulting him into MacLugh, knocking Dara free, but not before Strongheart seized her dirk for his own. Without hesitation, he plunged it into MacLugh's black heart.

He expected Dara to fling herself into his arms, but once again she surprised him. With her boot on MacLugh's shoulder, she retrieved her dirk, calmly cleaned the weapon of blood and thrust it back into the sheath at her waist. She held out her hand to him, and when he took it, she raised it over her head.

The Norman knights cheered and banged their shields with their fists as she led him toward the *Ard-ri*. The cheers died as she spoke to the high king in a voice that carried to most of the audience. "I would have you hold to your promise and legitimize our marriage."

When she forced the high king to acknowledge his promise, Strongheart had never been prouder. Dara motioned a scribe forward to set the pact in writing.

The *Ard-ri*'s gaze flickered to the army of Norman knights and nodded agreement. "The bards will sing of Strongheart's bravery for years to come."

"You, sire," Dara said, "will be remembered as the *Ard-ri* that united the Princess of Leinster with her Norman love."

The high king signed his name to the document. "Your Norman has won a fine kingdom."

"And conquered my heart," Dara added softly, her face glowing with happiness.

Once the paper dried, Strongheart presented

the document to her with a flourish. " 'Tis time to go home, Princess."

Home. The word sounded good to him. He hadn't had a real home since his brother died. But home wasn't a place, home was beside his fiery Irish princess.

"Aye. Let's go home, my love."

Epilogue

Five years later

Dara sat curled in a chair by the fire and stared past the newly installed panes of glass, through the mist to the bailey below. The rain around Castle Ferns had let up this noon, and as if marking the momentous occasion and reflecting her happiness, the sun splintered through the clouds.

After securing Leinster and training Irish replacements, today her husband was sending the last of the Norman knights back to Britain. Waving good-bye to the knights, Gavin, her eldest son by two minutes, rode with Conor, while his four-and-a-half-year-old twin, Geoffrey, clung to Gaillard, the only other Norman besides Strongheart to take a bride and remain in Leinster.

Despite the persistent ache in her back, Dara

shook her head with a grin as Strongheart handed their toddlers, Daniel and Duncan, to Sorcha. Her husband had carried all their children in slings before they could sit, one fastened to his chest, the other to his back. She had to admit her babes seemed to enjoy the rocking motion of a warhorse, and the time spent with their father gave her a dearly needed respite from her energetic brood.

The patter of little feet preceded Gavin's headlong rush into her room, a posy of daisies in hand. "Beat you," her eldest teased Geoffrey, and climbed onto her lap.

"Did not," Geoffrey muttered, then his face brightened when she made room for him, too. He handed her one large daisy. Her second child preferred quality to quantity, and while Gavin would race to gather handfuls of flowers, she imagined Geoffrey had spent hours choosing the perfect bloom.

"Thank you for the flowers," she praised them equally.

Geoffrey rested his head against her breast, his cuddly warmth pressed to her side. "Papa said he would find me a pony."

Gavin, never one to sit long, kissed her cheek and bounded onto the bed with a leap. "Me, too. A fast pony. The fastest pony in Eire."

Before Dara could respond to this newest announcement, her husband entered the room with Daniel and Duncan. Fascinated by their elder brother's antics on the bed, as soon as Strongheart put them down, they toddled to their brother, arms outstretched.

"Up. Up."

Gavin, intent on his own fun, ignored them. It was Geoffrey who scooted off his mother's lap and lifted the younger twins onto the mattress. Soon all four boys were jumping in unison and giggling madly.

Strongheart bent and gave her a kiss, then scooped her into his arms and deposited her on the bed in the middle of their rambunctious and squirming children.

The cat that had been napping by her pillow attempted to slink off, but Gavin grabbed its tail. "Stay, kitty. Stay and jump."

"Gavin, do not torment that cat," Strongheart said sternly.

Her eldest turned hurt eyes on his father. "I didn't hurt it. See?"

Gavin had a way with animals. Indeed, the tabby was curling up in his lap.

"No more jumping," Dara scolded. The back pains she felt earlier had returned, and she rubbed her side discreetly, pretending to smooth down her gown.

"Cease," Geoffrey ordered the others with a perceptive frown. "Mother's too fat to bounce. 'Tis bad for the baby."

Dara ruffled Geoffrey's hair. "I will be fine, but 'tis good of you to look after me like your father."

Gavin poked her belly with his finger. "Her stomach wiggles like custard."

"She's sweet as custard," their father agreed, his dark eyes twinkling with hunger as he stared at her mouth. "Now out, all of you. I'm suddenly in the mood for a sweet."

As if knowing how quickly Dara's children tired

her out so close to the end of her pregnancy, Sorcha entered and carried the babies downstairs while Gavin and Geoffrey scampered off, claiming they were too old to take naps. Dara relaxed, knowing Sorcha would tell them stories and feed them tarts by the hearth until they fell asleep.

When the door closed behind them, her husband pressed a kiss to her palm. "I brought you a present."

"You spoil me," she protested, enjoying every minute.

He still gave her gifts every day, and he was teaching her children to do the same. She had a wonderful collection of feathers, bird nests, and rocks. In spring and summer, Ferns always carried the pleasant scent of fresh flowers, and in winter, she placed small flagons of dried flowers in every room to brighten their life.

Not that her life needed brightening. Her marriage to Strongheart had brought her what she most desired—protected by a powerful husband who worked to keep peace, Leinster was free of war, and their children were surrounded by love.

Reaching into his pocket, he pulled out a velvet cloth with a gold drawstring. With shaking fingers she opened the delicate pouch and shook a necklace into her hand. Etched into gold was a scene of four boys holding hands around Castle Ferns. She laughed. "No wonder you sent the Normans back to Britain."

At his puzzled frown, she placed the ornament around her neck and explained. "You are growing your own Norman army."

He did not appreciate her attempt at humor. "After this child, you need a rest."

"Ummm," she agreed, remembering he'd said that after the last two pregnancies and how easily she'd changed his mind.

"I mean it," he insisted.

"Yes, dear."

With a sigh he raked a hand through his hair. "I do not want to lose you."

Knowing it was impossible to reassure him, she changed the subject. " 'Tis a beautiful gift."

"Do I get a kiss?"

A pain seared down her back. She gripped his hand tight. " 'Tis time."

He knew that look. Without leaving her side, he bellowed for Sorcha to bring the midwife.

The birthing pain eased, and her hand on his relaxed. "You will not regret it if this time I give you a girl?"

His mouth twitched into an adoring grin. "I would adore a little girl with red hair and green eyes like her mother. I will even teach her to ride like a hoyden," he promised.

She gasped as the pain lanced through her once more. "And throw a dirk?"

"Aye."

Two hours later, she delivered red-haired Eva, named after the half sister she'd lost so long ago. As the baby suckled her breast, her husband gazed down at her proudly.

"How did you know 'twould be a girl?"

"Woman's intuition," she said with a wide grin.

He leaned down to kiss her with a sweet tenderness that her tired soul wanted to melt into.

She deepened the kiss, savoring the moment. "I love you, Norman."

He smoothed back her hair. "I love you, too."

Later they lay snug and warm in bed, as a light rain fell outside. By morning the air would gleam misty across the Wicklow hills. Dara cuddled happily against her husband's broad chest. Just as he'd conquered county Leinster, he'd conquered her heart.

MADELINE BAKER

Beneath Midnight Moon

Winner Of The *Romantic Times* Reviewers Choice Award!

He comes to her in visions—the hard-muscled stranger who promises to save her from certain death. She never dares hope that her fantasy love will hold her in his arms until the virile and magnificent dream appears in the flesh.

A warrior valiant and true, he can overcome any obstacle, yet his yearning for the virginal beauty he's rescued overwhelms him. But no matter how his fevered body aches for her, he is betrothed to another.

Bound together by destiny, yet kept apart by circumstances, they brave untold perils and ruthless enemies—and find a passion that can never be rent asunder.

_3649-5 $4.99 US/$5.99 CAN

PATRICIA GAFFNEY Fortune's Lady

**"Like moonspun magic...one of the best historical
romances I have read in a decade!"
—Cassie Edwards**

They are natural enemies—traitor's daughter and zealous
patriot—yet the moment he sees Cassandra Merlin at her
father's graveside, Riordan knows he will never be free of
her. She is the key to stopping a heinous plot against the
king's life, yet he senses she has her own secret reasons for
aiding his cause. Her reputation is in shreds, yet he finds
himself believing she is a woman wronged. Her mission is
to seduce another man, yet he burns to take her luscious body
for himself. She is a ravishing temptress, a woman of
mystery, yet he has no choice but to gamble his heart on
fortune's lady.

_4153-7 $5.99 US/$6.99 CAN

Heart's Magic

Flora Speer

Bestselling author of *ROSE RED*

In the year 1122, Mirielle senses change is coming to Wroxley Castle. Then, from out of the fog, two strangers ride into Lincolnshire. Mirielle believes the first man to be honest. But the second, Giles, is hiding something–even as he stirs her heart and awakens her deepest desires. And as Mirielle seeks the truth about her mysterious guest, she uncovers the castle's secrets and learns she must stop a treachery which threatens all she holds dear. Only then can she be in the arms of her only love, the man who has awakened her own heart's magic.

___52204-7 $5.99 US/$6.99 CAN

Catherine Archibald — HAWK'S LADY

Haughty young Lady Kayln D'Arcy only wants what is best for her little sister, Celia, when she travels to the imposing fortress of Hawkhurst. For the brother of Hawkhurst's dark lord has wooed Celia, and Kayln is determined to make him do the honorable thing. Tall, arrogant and imperious, Hawk has the burning eyes of a bird of prey and a gentle touch that can make Kayln nearly forget why she is there. As for Hawk, never before has he encountered a woman like the proud, fiery Kayln. But can Hawk catch his prey? Can he make her...Hawk's lady?

___4312-2 $4.99 US/$5.99 CAN

Dorchester Publishing Co., Inc.
P.O. Box 6640
Wayne, PA 19087-8640

THE HIDDEN JEWEL

VIOLET IVANESCU

Dominique Chantal is already in mortal danger. She has been entrusted with the delivery of a precious medallion to a group planning to overthrow Napoleon. But her plight only increases when her carriage is ambushed, the medallion taken, and the lonely beauty captured by the emperor's henchmen. To her dismay, she soon discovers that her sentence is a sham marriage to Andre Montville, Napoleon's best spy.

They make a deal—no questions and no touching—but it isn't an easy pact to uphold. And as Andre saves Dominique time and again from danger, she yearns to know more about his past and his true loyalties—and aches to know the pleasure of his forbidden caress. But she soon finds that she will have to sacrifice more than her body and her innocence in order to lure from Andre...the hidden jewel.

___4291-6 $4.99 US/$5.99 CAN

Dorchester Publishing Co., Inc.
P.O. Box 6640
Wayne, PA 19087-8640

Please add $1.75 for shipping and handling for the first book and $.50 for each book thereafter. NY, NYC, and PA residents, please add appropriate sales tax. No cash, stamps, or C.O.D.s. All orders shipped within 6 weeks via postal service book rate. Canadian orders require $2.00 extra postage and must be paid in U.S. dollars through a U.S. banking facility.

Name_____

Address_____

City_____State_____Zip_____

I have enclosed $_____ in payment for the checked book(s).

Payment <u>must</u> accompany all orders. ❑ Please send a free catalog.

"Catherine Lanigan is in a class by herself: unequaled and simply fabulous!"

—Affaire de Coeur

Even amid the spectacle and splendor of the carnival in Venice, the masked rogue is brazen, reckless, and dangerously risque. As he steals Valentine St. James away from the costume ball at which her betrothal to a complete stranger is to be announced, the exquisite beauty revels in the illicit thrill of his touch, the tender passion in his kiss. But Valentine learns that illusion rules the festival when, at the stroke of midnight, her mysterious suitor reveals he is Lord Hawkeston, the very man she is to wed. Convinced her intended is an unrepentant scoundrel, Valentine wants to deny her maddening attraction for him, only to keep finding herself in his heated embrace. Yet is she truly losing her heart to the dashing peer—or is she being ruthlessly seduced?

_3942-7 $5.50 US/$7.50 CAN